The Sword and Scabbard

Thieves and Thugs and the Bloody Massacre in Boston

ALLEN WOODS

Boston Heritage Publishing,
Greenfield, MA

Author Photos: Abagayle Andrews Photography and Design
Cover Design: Peter Chilton, Peter Chilton Design, peterchilton.com
Cover sword image courtesy of www.sabresempire.com
Map reproduction courtesy of the Norman B. Leventhal
Map Center at the Boston Public Library

This is a work of fiction. All of the characters, organizations, and events portrayed in this novel are either products of the authors' imagination or are used fictitiously.

ISBN: 978-0-9908841-0-1 (sc)
ISBN: 978-0-9908841-1-8 (e)

Rev. date: 12/31/2014

TO IRENE

My one and only

Boston 1769

Section I

One

My PROBLEMS with Ezekiel Tobin began in 1766, during the time the British still thought they might collect money from the tax stamps they ordered Americans to buy before they could legally sell everything from paper to glass. It was just a few months after I first took a room above the Sword and Scabbard tavern, so that I could serve the drinks and tend the crowd for the Widow Maggie Magowan. But I was already familiar with Tobin and his visits to collect from Maggie to insure her license. This time, when he came through the door and began brushing dust from the sleeves of his coat, I found my teeth clamped tight so no words could escape and betray my wish to strike him before he could sit down or open his mouth.

He tugged at his green satin waistcoat before he sat, though it would never stay over his round belly. I guessed him at nearly forty years and his face was pinched, as if someone had drawn his mouth up tight like the strings on a purse. He was middle-sized with a body shaped like a pear, and his wig bobbed up and down with his head when he talked. But it was his air which angered me, every move smug and sure, as if he knew he held the winning ticket in a lottery before it was drawn.

Maggie had to pay Tobin a consideration every month to be sure she received a tavern license each year and that no one lodged a complaint against her. The arrangement wasn't legal, but it was like many back in

England for those who were no better than footpads but had the power of the law behind them. He waved me away after I swallowed hard and politely brought him a cup of ale. "Send the Widow out, it's her license." When I went to Maggie in the kitchen, her face turned dark, like a rain squall across a sunny deck, and I could see her lips move in a silent curse.

She sat opposite him at the table near to the kitchen door and close enough to the bar at the back so I could hear while I rearranged the pottery mugs for ale on its top. "You're not due here till the middle of the month," she began before he had a chance.

His face showed what passed for a smile. "That's why I'm here. There'll be a change starting now." He stared at her hard and continued in a patient voice. "You've gotten by easy since your husband died. You've got more in the door than ever and most others are scraping the bottom." He took a long drink from his cup and wiped his mouth with his sleeve. "The fee will be the same, but I'll visit you in your quarters when I come to collect every month."

He held up a hand to her before she could speak. "It's a small price, since you know I've got the sheriff's ear. Just a few words to him or one of the pious selectmen that decides on your license and you'd be shut down for being disorderly." His head stopped bobbing for a moment and he licked ale from his lips. "I could even arrange for your lease to be cancelled. Mr. Brown follows my direction like I stood in the pulpit. Your rent is no more than a trifle to him, and if I encouraged it, he might just want to start up a new tavern here himself." His lips curled in a tight smile and his head continued to nod slowly.

I started towards the table, eager to flavor his ale with his own blood, but Maggie looked hard at me and I ground my teeth together and went back behind the bar where I worked at tapping a new cask of rum beneath it.

Maggie said nothing at first, but her eyes glowed with fire and I could see the blood color her oval face, making the scar trailing down her cheek show white against it. I knew then that Tobin should fear for his health, but he seemed all the more excited by the look she gave him, his mouth open like a great hound ready to mount a tiny bitch.

She looked down for a moment and composed herself before answering him with a terrible calm. "Come back two nights from now like usual," she said, "just after supper. We'll discuss it then." Tobin probably missed it, but there was iron in her voice, and her look was as sharp as a butcher's blade.

We talked little the rest of the day, even when the tables were empty between dinner and when the first of the mechanics came after a day's work. Maggie finally slammed the front door at about 10 p.m., narrowly missing the backsides of the last two tars who'd spent most of the last hour with a single cup of rum, boasting of their bravery in standing up to captains and mates.

"I'll not have it," she said to me and to herself at the same time, her voice mixed with anger and fear. "I can't go back to the other life and the thought of that bastard lifting my skirts makes me retch." She lifted an eye my way as I brought down the portcullis on the bar for the night and started to snuff the few candles still lit. I'd filled us both a cup of the good rum from the barrel in the kitchen and set them before us on the table.

"And I won't leave either," she said now as the natural warmth in her voice turned icy. "I've started over enough times already, and I've spent enough of myself keeping this fine parlor open." She scanned the room with its six rough tables and benches, three in a row on each side of the fireplace which took up the back wall and stood next to the door to the kitchen and the stairs to the second floor. They were scarred from seamen's knives, and the single picture over the fireplace was so darkened from the smoke that it was hard to tell that it represented a sunrise over the harbor at Kingston. It looked more like a sunset on a cloudy day.

I guessed that she was imagining some of the rooms she'd told me about in her months as a high-class moll in London. But she'd finally fled with Capt. McGowan, afraid of the French pox and the trade that turned most girls into hollow chaff blown by the wind.

I shifted on the bench to stretch my leg to the side and her eyes lit brightly again as she raised a finger toward me. "And don't you start in on marrying again either, there's no help there."

"I was drunk, Maggie. I only said it because of the license." It might have been true, but not for the full weight.

"The selectmen would never give you the license they give me, they think it's the only way to help a poor widow survive. They'd turn you out, unless you slipped a purse of sterling in their pockets, or one of their mates, and you won't have that much before the moon turns blue." She was in a righteous anger now but it faded quickly because she didn't know what to do, only what not to do. "You've never heard me say I wanted another husband." She searched my eyes for a moment to see my reaction, but I turned to look at the ends of the fire instead.

She took a long sip of rum and I did the same, feeling the pleasant warmth down my throat, nothing like the fire that came from the barrel under the bar we used for flip. Maggie got two or three cheap barrels at a time from a warehouse by Scarlett's Wharf and didn't have to pay the excise. Without the sugar and the hot iron to foam up the flip, the cheap, straight rum would make a man cry like a baby if he wasn't used to it. For a moment, I wondered if Maggie was going to cry, but I should have known better. When she turned back to me, her eyes had changed from the easy blue of an October sky to the flashing blue steel of a new bayonet.

"I'll just have to find some way to fix him," she said quietly.

When I'd taken the room upstairs, Maggie had run the Sword by herself for nearly a year. She'd been given the license for the Sword and Scabbard as a widow after Capt. McGowan's body had been taken from the rocky beach towards Salem. Apparently, he'd fallen from his own rowboat as he fished, although it's doubtful he ever hooked a cod, staying too busy scouting the coast for landing spots out of the view of customs. The bruises about his face probably came from banging against the rocks at high tide.

But the stories said that Maggie had made it happen herself. Some said she got one of McGowan's smuggling crew to kill him, paying him with the entire proceeds from their last shipment to do the deed and disappear, probably to New York. That stood up, since she'd never shown a fat purse later, but no one knew for certain.

Others said that she went with him herself and beat him senseless, using a small bag of lead weights she'd gathered from fishing nets and lines which were always about the docks, before dumping him into the dark waters. After they'd opened the tavern, McGowan had been a brute when he was drunk, knocking her down if she spilled a bit of his rum on the way to his table or rummaging under her skirts to show her fine legs to a crew just in from London and willing to pay a few shillings from their cache. She'd struck him back once, with a loggerhead standing by the fire, but not hard enough. That's when the scar at her eye had appeared, changing in their two years of marriage from an angry red welt to the narrow white line that contrasted with her skin (which echoed the color of honey), and hair that changed from brown to red and back with the light. McGowan had carried a blade as keen as a surgeon's.

I'd never asked her about it and didn't intend to. I'd always shied away from planning murder, but I'd never been at the mercy of someone like McGowan, either. To my mind, a cold killing is different than what might happen in a fight. I'd known some who would drain your blood for a price, but I never wanted to join them. It seemed a stain that could never be washed.

Maggie must have seen the thoughts cross my face because she started in again before I had a chance to say anything. "Don't think the worst. Drink your rum and finish up. I need some time to think about it. You might put your brain at it, too, if you care."

"Why would you ask that, Maggie? You're . . . " I stopped because the right words wouldn't come, a common feeling when I talked with Maggie, and I didn't want them tangling my feet like an uncoiled bowline. "Maybe the Lord will strike him dead in the street as a punishment for wicked thoughts," I offered and Maggie's face softened for a moment. "But if he did, God would have to empty every pew in North Church before he was done."

When I'd slept that night, hanging my hammock on the hooks near the back door I'd put in especially for nights like this, the air was soft and the smell of the ocean and the docks was pleasant and mild, but my dreams were filled with the smell of blood and powder and shackles.

When Ezekiel Tobin, Esq., came back, we were ready. I expected that he might wear a shirt with ruffles or show some extra powder on his wig, but I was wrong. He looked just as rude as he did in his offices, scribing contracts for Tobias Brown and staying as near his arse as he could without wearing his clothes. He'd started as no more than a scrivener but now he called himself Esquire like the rest of the lawyers and Brown relied on him to make contracts as tight as a bung in a barrel. The only way out was with more money than you owed already.

One of the tables was full with the usual mechanics complaining about their wages while another held just Mouse, squinting slightly at the newspaper I would hang by the door the next day. As Tobin swaggered up to the bar, I managed to say quietly, "Widow McGowan says to proceed directly to her room, up the stairs in the back, and I'll have the coins when you come back down."

A few moments later, I stood at the foot of the stairs and heard Maggie call to him and the door open and close, I nodded to Mouse, who would watch the tavern room, and climbed the stairs silently. With my ear cocked outside the door, I could hear Tobin shuffling about and imagined his fevered breathing as he saw Maggie beneath the blanket in her bed.

"You'll take off your shoes and your breeches, Master Tobin, my bed isn't a barnyard. Put your stockings and breeches on the chest."

Again, I heard the shuffling of clothes and Tobin shifting his weight back and forth, struggling to undress while standing up. Then there was a pause and I heard Maggie say in a loud voice, "Now's the time."

I was through the door in a flash, knife in hand, as Tobin turned at the sound, awkward in surprise and with his member pointing out beneath his shirt tails. I grabbed the front of his shirt and my knife came up from below, menacing his lower parts. His face was close enough to mine that I felt the spittle that sprayed from his lips on my cheek.

Maggie was out of the bed quickly, still fully dressed, and her eyes blazed with contempt and fury. "And what would Mrs. Tobin think now, Master, you in your tails ready to fuck a fine widow? Or Reverend Harper? Or even Mr. Brown who gives you so much money for your scratchings?"

Tobin continued to sputter, turning slightly to see her over his shoulder and his legs began to quiver. "Stand still, Tobin," I whispered, "or you'll lose more than you bargained for." His eyes went wide and he shifted his weight slightly, trying to keep the cold steel at a distance.

"You'll sign this paper and we'll take your shiny buttons for a keepsake. You'll miss your payment this month, but next you can come back and we'll all act like this never happened," said Maggie, taking the paper we'd prepared the night before from the small desk she kept in the corner. She shoved his breeches on the floor and took the ink and quill from the desk top. "I'll put it here and you can read it. It won't take long." She lit a second candle and placed it next to the supplies on the chest.

Tobin wanted to look behind him but didn't dare move. "I'll move the knife now," I said pleasantly, "but I'll have no trouble finding the same spot if there's any problems." When he turned to see the paper on the chest, I offered, "You'll probably need to kneel down to see it, like you were in church. I'll just take your buttons while I'm waiting."

Tobin looked at me, mystified, while I took his waistcoat and cut away three brass buttons, each decorated with the outline of a flower, one from the bottom and top, and one from the middle, rattling them in my hand like dice.

The note was simple.

April 5, 1766

I came for the Widow McGowan and they took my buttons.

"Make sure you sign it in your usual hand," said Maggie. "We've got it on our lease right here to compare." She took a folded document from another pigeonhole in the desk and waved it in the air.

I saw a drop of sweat fall from Tobin's chin as he looked at the document. The vein in his neck throbbed next to the flat of the knife blade where I'd laid it gently on his shoulder. He started to talk, "It won't work, I'll . . ." until I tapped the blade gently near his neck and he picked up the quill.

The bigger problem came when I followed Tobin out the back door. He was shaking when he'd come down the stairs and I couldn't help myself. His was just the type of business that made my blood boil up. He would take from us, Maggie more than anyone, simply because he could, and then go to church and act like he would never understand the sinful ways of those beneath him. His power came from money and nothing else, and he would be blessed in church simply because he could buy a pew. Now that we had turned the tables against him, I wanted to make his fear last, make him tremble in his sleep, even though his sheets smelled of powder and his mattress was made from down. I followed him out so he could feel me close and remember the blade against his skin.

But I misjudged him. He walked a few paces from the back door in the dark and turned to me, where he could see me outlined against the candle light. He spoke in a low voice, his teeth close together like he had a bit of gristle between them, and his head stayed stock still now. "It won't work, Gray, sooner or later I'll figure it out and she'll be a whore on the street. She'll be lucky if they take her in the workhouse without branding her first or taking her skin with the whip. You . . . you'll wish you could swim with the shit in the gutter. You're not smart enough to end anywhere but the gaol or the gallows."

I was only a few steps away and I closed them before he could get his body turned. I caught him on the side of the neck with the edge of my hand and he dropped like a sack of cornmeal. I kicked him once in his belly, full I'm sure from the partridge or salmon they served at the Coffee House.

Two

It was a long and twisting path that had brought me from Oxford to London, then Jamaica, and finally to Boston in 1765 where I later teamed with Maggie at the Sword and Scabbard. It was nothing like a pleasant stroll down a winding English lane, but more a forced march through hedgerows and thickets and thorns. I'd never been able to see an end, and each time I thought I'd come to a clear patch, I found it a dead end instead. Some of the lords in England had garden mazes built for pleasure, but one would only vex me with its confusing turns and false promises.

I was left an orphan at eleven after my mother wasted away with consumption and my father fell dead on the steps after his day of cleaning Duke Humfrey's library in Oxford. I ran away to London a year later from a man and wife who used me badly as a servant and I eventually found shelter there by running errands and cleaning rooms at a bawd's house. I found that surviving in the city streets demanded a mixture of hard blows and quick wits, but I learned quickly until the Royal Navy took me at sixteen when I was drunk in a tavern. Up until then, it was a story that many of the boys in the Navy or those beginning to rot in Newgate prison could tell just as well.

But the Navy didn't suit my nature, and I felt as near to a black slave as to a free white man. We made it through the battle in Quiberon Bay against the French on the *Dover*, but the deck slick with blood, the air choked with the smoke from cannon blasts, and the fear of standing at the unlucky spot where a cannonball might tear my head from my body and send pieces flying in all directions kept living in my mind. That was when the worst of the dreams started, and it seemed that something broke loose inside me soon afterwards. Before we reached Jamaica to patrol the Sugar Islands, one set of scars from the nine tails had just begun to heal, and yet I still couldn't hold my tongue at orders I didn't like. I found myself in chains below deck in Kingston Harbor and as soon as they let me out to work in the rigging again, I watched until I found a way to escape. Later, I fought too hard when a lieutenant and two others thought they would take me back, and soon the word went out that I'd be hanged for murder if they found me. I stayed hidden until after the *Dover* sailed back towards England, and a few weeks later entered Boston in the dead of night from among the barrels in the dark hold of a molasses ship.

Within a few weeks, I heard that the *Dover* had gone down in a typhoon and all on board had been lost. The news meant that most who knew me from the Navy could no longer point me out, but I was still a deserter and possibly wanted for murder. My trip to the gallows at Tyburn or here at Boston Neck would be short and sure if anyone found me out. It was a story I told no one, not even Maggie in the warmth of her arms.

I took the name Gray since it was close enough to Graves and there seemed to be someone named Gray at every street corner. My only thought during my early time in Boston was to make sure no one marked me as different from the other tars and mechanics crowding the docks. Plenty of them were deserters as well, but the force of the Royal Navy stood thousands of miles away, and any of the Tories who lived here were too busy lining their pockets from government posts, or Customs work, or trade to care. They had no time for deserters and there was no reward for pursuing them.

I found a steady place within a month. Since I was handy enough with a saw and hammer, I agreed to help Benjamin Downing put in glass windows (before they could be taxed by the Stamps) in the Stag's Head tavern he owned on Orange St. in the South End in exchange for room and board. Later, I stayed on with him and helped with the tavern while he was busy buying a second building. He was an upstanding man who'd no sooner think of stealing pennies from the change of a gentleman drinking his twentieth toast than of walking naked down the Mall on the Common. No one gave me a second look and I had time to get to know the wharfs and the smugglers and the other business that went on.

But the Good Lord had other plans for Downing although I couldn't find what he'd done wrong. The next year, his wife caught her skirts on fire when she went to stir the stew pot and by the time Benjamin beat the flames down and threw water on her from a bucket, most of her skin had been burned away and she died screaming within the day. After she was buried, good Benjamin became melancholy. His daughter had already married and moved out to Needham and his other children had died before they were ten. He paid a girl to cook and clean but he showed no interest in any of the younger girls that hopeful fathers brought to him so they could marry him and keep his home.

I wasn't surprised a few months later when he broke his neck in a fall from a ladder as he helped the fire companies fight a blaze a few buildings down from the Stag. Downing was getting old for climbing ladders and it seemed some times that he'd just as soon break his neck as go about his business the next day.

I'd come to know most of the taverns and their owners in town, except for the high Tory dens that would throw me out before my second foot hit the floor. The Sword and Scabbard stood in the North End near the corner of Fleet St. and Ship St. It was one in a row of brick buildings, formerly wood but rebuilt with some of Thomas Hancock's' money after the fire of 1760. It stood between a rooming house and Robert Pearson's cooperage, just a hundred yards from the water and Scarlett's Wharf. When Maggie offered a room there above the tavern and a job behind the bar, I took it with my heart in my mouth. Not only would I have a new bed and meals each day, but Maggie stirred me like few others. We'd had few private words, but I felt there was mystery in her, and the strong steel of a dagger, and the beauty of a rose among weeds, even with the scar down her cheek.

I'd been bold enough one night to start in with her about the sign. "I don't know how they let you keep it hanging. I'd think they'd at least make you take it down on the Sabbath. The gentleman with the sword seems right ready to run it into the lady's scabbard."

Maggie gave me her smile and brought another pint. "They've been hanging there three years now, and if they're havin' at it in the middle of the night when no one's looking, well, it's none of my business. He must be mindin' his pullbacks though, since we've got no little ones running about." She reached for my empty mug and stared me straight down. "And I'd say she's enjoyin' it, too. She doesn't look a day older." She swirled away as I nearly choked on my ale.

She'd left the sign up and always joked with the sailors about getting a girl until it came time for money to change hands. They tended to drink regular and quick until Maggie sent them off to the house they called Whitehall or one of the others. After I'd been there awhile, I'd suggested we make a deal with one of the mothers and get something back for every jack we sent, but Maggie wanted no part.

As the time stretched out and no one asked or cared about the Royal Navy or the Sugar Islands, I began to act as if I belonged in Boston as much any other man in the muddy streets. I took what I'd learned in London and gathered a small crew that sometimes made hard money (not paper debts, like so much business on the docks) by helping unload the hold of a ship before Customs could search it for tax. Other times, we took small goods from a store or warehouse and sent them down the Coast to sell before anyone realized they were gone. There was no pay for me at the Sword, and Julius worked for a pallet in the kitchen and meals as well. Gillam Powell lived by gambling at dice and cards, and Mouse kept himself so far in the shadows that I never knew exactly where I might find him. We each had a part and we planned our work carefully so we could enjoy a few silver coins rather than suffer the shackles or a noose.

But if I was stone silent about my past and careful in our travels at night, my tongue still got loose when my blood boiled up. I made an enemy in Tobin who wouldn't forget my words or my spite at his fine clothes and dirty hands. He wasn't like some tar I put out the door of the Sword who might threaten murder or take a drunken swing, and then forget it the next morning. He was a man filled with pride who had a long memory and enough money and connections to dog my steps at every turn if he chose. Soon, he showed that a man with a quill can be just as dangerous as one with a club or a sword.

Three

LATER THAT NIGHT, after we'd sent Tobin away out the back, Maggie announced, "I think it'll work out just as we planned." But I knew she was trying to convince herself, too. "We've got his paper and his buttons."

Our idea was that losing just three buttons—top, bottom, and middle—would be hard to explain to his wife or servants. We gauged Tobin not quite rich enough to throw away a waistcoat without someone in the household noticing, and the buttons were unlikely to come off in those places if he made up a story of a robbery or a brawl. They weren't worth enough for anyone to steal them, not like his shoe buckles, and it would be too hard for him to replace them with matching ones, since near every waistcoat in Boston had a set that looked differently. He would have to invent a tale about the waistcoat in the next few days, one his wife or a servant would remember if we chose to deliver the signed note and buttons to his house. He might bluff out a story by inventing more lies, but we hoped it would be just enough trouble that he'd choose to avoid it. He couldn't be sure we wouldn't talk about the extra he collected to insure the license, either. We weren't the only ones he visited to keep his purse full.

Maggie paused before blowing out the last candle. "No, I think Ezekiel Tobin, Esquire, will limp home, wash himself up and be at Brown's tomorrow at the appointed time, just like the months before."

I never prayed, but I spent a moment that night with my eyes closed in the dark, hoping she was right.

Our plan worked even better than we'd planned as far as the bribes and the license and Tobin's hopes for Maggie, since he never came back for his monthly fee. But a few weeks later, I looked up to see the sheriff and his deputy and some other squat toad file through the front door of the Sword one after the other. We'd just finished serving dinners to the coasting captains who came regularly on Wednesdays when they weren't out on a run. The eight of them had tucked away plenty of the pork pies Julius made and three bowls of punch before leaving and we cleaned the tables.

They stood in a row across the door with Sheriff Greenleaf out front. He acted as if he knew me and seemed eager to speak. "Nicholas Gray," he announced in a formal voice when I stopped cleaning up, "we've come to satisfy your debt to the heirs of the estate of Benjamin Downing."

Maggie came from the kitchen as well, uneasy with the sheriff standing in the room. She'd always said that letting the law inside could only lead to trouble. I could just see Julius over her shoulder, out of the sheriff's view. I kept a sharp eye on them but my mind started picking at a snarl of memories. Downing always kept scrupulous records of everyone who stayed and what they ate and drank and of course kept mine as a guest as well. He kept a separate account book while I was there, which detailed the work I'd done for him and the time I'd run the tavern while he was out on other business. He'd listed it all as a reckoning to see how our bargain played in the year I was there and was satisfied each time he'd added his figures. He said that more food and ale was bought when I was there as well, since my eye and my tongue were a bit more lively than his.

After he died and I moved on to the room at the Sword, his daughter and her husband hired a country lawyer, some string bean from Needham called Briggs, to settle things and he'd arrived soon after that to ask me about the accounts. I'd informed him of our arrangement, one that many knew about who came to the tavern. I'd taken a private room from the beginning, since I'd spent enough time sharing the air below decks and in irons, and my debt for more than a year's room and board was a bit over £28. But I'd done plenty to offset it which Downing had showed in the book for my account. When Briggs left, he seemed well satisfied.

But when the rest of the estate became too complicated for him to sort out, the heirs gave his estate over to the Boston sharks that worked for Tobias Brown. I'd seen a notice in the *Gazette* some weeks back, one in a whole column of others, but I thought nothing of it. Anyone who owed Downing money should pay up so the good Mr. Brown could settle his affairs,

I looked at Greenleaf, who may have had suspicions about my night work, since there is always some talk on the docks, and seemed anxious to take me now. "I've got no debt to that estate," I laughed, but it was more scorn than mirth. "I explained that to their country lawyer."

Greenleaf shook his head. "We've got a signed warrant here from Tobias Brown that says you're listed at a debt of twenty-eight pounds, ten shillings, and six pence for private room and board at the Stag's Head from November 1765 until . . ."

"Of course I stayed there, everyone knew that, I helped him with the windows and . . ."

"There are no records extant," croaked the round little man just behind them.

"Extant!" My voice had risen and I could almost feel the net being drawn about me. "Who are you?"

"Josiah Williams, representing Mr. Tobias Brown."

I glared at him over the sheriff's shoulder, "What do you mean, extant?"

The sheriff moved between us a bit more but turned to him as well.

"There aren't any." He blanched as he spoke. "There are no records which show any debt of Mr. Downing to yourself."

"I saw it myself, a small ledger book, smaller than the one for the tavern or for his other property, bound up in thick paper, not leather like the others. He kept it in with the others behind the counter . . ."

"All of Mr. Downing's records are now in our possession since Mr. Briggs of Needham turned them over to us in January. Mr. Tobin made a list of them and . . ."

The knot came undone in a flash. Tobin wanted me locked in the gaol to pay for the sharp edge of my knife on his skin, and didn't have the decency to wait till the town finished building the new one. I was backed in a corner and it was just someone like Tobin who could manage it.

"Tobin!" I exploded, "he's behind it, isn't he? He's got a reason to come after me but he's a coward, so he uses you and the sheriff and the law. He's got his hand behind your backs like Punch and Judy." Greenleaf looked puzzled. "Puppets, he's working you like puppets."

The sheriff started forward at that and Maggie quickly appeared between us, glancing back at me with a warning. "Nicholas doesn't owe any money, he's been with me for a good time now . . ." her voice was her most soothing, no affront to the sheriff.

"We're here to satisfy a legal debt and no more," he said, although again I thought his manner too eager. "Will you pay it now, Gray, or do we take you?"

"I can't pay that amount in sterling, you knew that before you came, but I wouldn't pay it if I had it because I don't owe it. And I won't be going along with you, I'll stay here and help the widow and you can send Brown or Tobin or someone else to clear it up. Stand off now, I won't have your hands on me . . ."

The sheriff had brushed Maggie to the side with an arm and moved to take mine. I backed up and shrugged him off. Williams hopped backwards toward the front door like a frog and turned even whiter as

I growled at the sheriff and moved to pick up the poker standing by the hearth but as I did, I realized that the deputy wasn't in front of me. An explosion like a powder ship going up, complete with arching streamers in the sky, went off at the back of my skull.

MY MIND finally shook loose the dreams and came swimming up for air. I struggled to open my eyes and my head throbbed like someone was firing a 16-pounder beside my ear as fast as they could load. But when I managed to pry one eye open, it seemed darker than when it was closed. It could have been too much rum. It wouldn't be the first time I'd opened an eye hoping to see a face or a room I recognized so I might account for my whereabouts. I took a long breath through my nose and my stomach clenched like a fist, bending me double so my face scraped my knees.

It wasn't the effects of too much drink that set me gagging like I'd bitten into maggots in the ship's hard tack, but rather the smell. It was one I knew too well—the stench of human waste and human fear, soup made from rotting vegetables, untended boils and fevered breath, sweating walls and bone cold earth. It was the smell of prison.

Before I could open my eyes again, the odor mixed with those which poison my dreams and come unbidden at chance moments—I could smell the blood on the nine tails, the blood where shackles tore at my wrist and ankles, the acrid odor of gunmetal and powder so strong I could taste it in the back of my throat. My gorge began to rise and I sat bolt upright in the dark.

But just before I added the stink in my stomach to the foul air around me, I worked to close my eyes and fill my mind with pictures that could blot out the smell. First came Oxford as a child with the Isis River flowing silently between green hills, and then the moment on deck when a fresh wind caught the sails and pushed us from the harbor. I took air slowly through my mouth, and the promise of open air came to me like a woman's at hand at the back of my neck, like the scent of orchid trees near the sugar cane fields, like drops of rain on the crusted salt of my unwashed forehead.

My heart slowed and stomach calmed, and I kept my eyes closed for a moment. My memory began to come back and I realized I'd gotten too soft, acting like I was safe because the room wasn't dark and I wasn't on a silent wharf or a street filled with thieves and pickpockets. I'd let the sheriff's man get behind me.

LATER, I tried to think of a way out. I had a few coins hidden away but not near enough for the debt. Maggie might come up with some as well, but it seemed we'd just begun and I had no right to ask her. She'd probably have to risk money she needed to pay the rent at the Sword, and Tobin was already threatening her lease. I could ask her to use Tobin's note and waistcoat to bargain with him, but they were meant for protection for the license more than anything else. Tobin wouldn't give all that I needed, and he was the one that was behind my arrest from the start. It took hard cash to get a debt off the books once it was legally entered, nothing short of silver coins.

I couldn't ask Mouse or Julius or even Gillam Powell to arrange a job to get money for my debt since I was the one who always made the plans. Even if they tried, there just weren't many pounds sterling to be had. Almost everything in Boston was on credit now except for the fees that customs charged for every scrap of paper they demanded for legal trade and every signature from their fine quills. Everyone said the chests at the Custom House could barely hold it all, but they were too well-protected for anyone to get at.

The food was nearly as bad as I got in Navy irons and since Downing's estate (in the person of Tobin) was responsible for my care, I got nothing but the worst—pale soup, stale or moldy bread that the bakers couldn't sell, and water that I knew better than to touch. Maggie paid for two pints of beer a day so that I wouldn't get the bloody flux or some other bowel disease that would keep me within a yard of the privy bench even as I choked on the smell. Several had died in the gaol and some others looked like a heap of rags on the ground. Town meeting always listened when the keeper complained about his income—they paid him fees for each time he turned a key in a lock and let him sell beer and food to the inmates who could pay—but no one seemed to care when unworthy dogs like me died in the dark of the town gaol.

I knew I could break out if I chose—it had been done plenty of times before—with a little help from the few inside who weren't raving mad or sick or kept in the safe room before trial. Poor John Stinson offered to help even though he was a hollow man now, in gaol through the winter after he'd tried to take firewood for himself and his family from the town supply on the Common after the water barrel in his kitchen froze. He showed me how the last two had gotten out and suggested I might try digging beneath the far wall, too.

But escaping wouldn't get me what I wanted—I didn't want to run off the Boston Neck to the country or start out again below decks without knowing where I might end up or if I might get sold out along the way. I wanted to go back to the Sword and Scabbard and serve rum from a barrel and listen to the loud voices as they argued politics and boasted of the sights they'd seen in Portugal or Barbary or Jamestown. I wanted to settle up with Tobin somehow and feel the excitement of moving goods through the dark while a customs collector or a fat merchant slept behind glass windows with the shutters closed for protection. I wanted to see Maggie with a smile and a spark in her eye and the slight cock of her head toward the stairs when she invited me to lie with her. I wanted to breathe the open air here in Boston, suck in the smells of salt and fish and tar and mountains of oyster shells. Because of the Navy, I would always have to keep watch over my shoulder, but this seemed the best spot to do it.

The next week was miserable, though I soon got numb with the pattern—nothing to do for the day except stand and move about to keep the blood flowing, the nights filled with the choked breath and nightmares of people in a cage while I sat up and brooded and schemed escape and revenge. But on May 19, 1766, a date I remember, the world outside came in.

The noise and excitement were tremendous, people and carriages continually up and down Queen St., people calling out to one another with shouts and congratulations, different bells in town ringing over the afternoon and seemingly all at once as it began to get dark. Some shot their muskets into the air and we heard that there would be fireworks after sunset. It was enough to put me in mind of breaking out somehow and worrying about what might happen later.

The British Parliament, it seems, had given up, and repealed the Stamp Act. Boston and some of the other colonies had acted as if it each stamp on a contract or newspaper or deck of cards would choke a noble man to death or poison him and his family because it took a bite from his freedom to haul in money.

The newspapers and pamphlets and broadsides used up barrels of ink trying to explain the cocked-up difference in one tax and another—internal and external they called them—and of course the stamps were the wrong kind. Mouse told of town meetings filled with hours of speeches about freedom and natural rights and stamps. In my mind, there's nothing wrong with simply wanting to keep a few more shillings out of the hands of the hungry taxmen from London. But no one in Boston would say it was that simple.

Instead, they'd sweated as much as any dock hand to explain why they refused to buy the stamps. They had pushed the crowd to tear down the new stamp office and force the new collector to resign as he stared at a tar barrel and a hanging noose. It was same men who shouted and danced around the fire kindled on the lawn of Lt. Governor

Hutchinson that night. They had worked till dawn at his mansion after he fled, burning his furniture and books and legal papers; breaking his china; drinking the wine in his cellar; and stealing his silver plate and hidden money. For most of them, it was just a night of great sport, a rare chance to destroy what they wished for but couldn't have. That night, they enjoyed the freedom to steal from a Tory house and smash whatever they couldn't carry.

The news that the lords in London had finally given in came just as I began to rot in gaol. John Hancock and the others decided they'd set off a celebration like none before. We heard that he was going to open one of his small purses and have lights all over town and fireworks and free food and drink at several places, depending on where you belonged–the upper crust would come to the door of his mansion off the Common and be invited in, the talkers who drove the mobs and kept them like dogs on a leash could go to the Bunch of Grapes or the workhouse for some food and drink. The mechanics and sailors and dockmen who'd actually swung the cudgels and thrown the stones and heated the tar could gather outside Hancock's house and get treated from a cask.

We knew quickly enough when the news came in, with the bells ringing and muskets going off and people shouting in from the streets. But now, as the town prepared for a great celebration, listening from the inside was enough to make me grind my teeth like millstones. All I could do was look out the barred windows and through a missing slat in the fence, my head just scraping the ceiling, and think about the free wine I might be having in the soft spring night and the gruel and stench I got instead. I saw Tobin's face when I shut my eyes and vowed to make him pay with blood or money or both.

The day had turned to night and the noise had gotten even louder when Prentice, the turnkey, started calling off names, including mine, almost twenty of us. When we gathered at the front gate with the others at our back, he announced with a grimace, "You're all free to go and you've got John Hancock and the Sons of Liberty to thank. He's paid all your debts."

I could barely talk, and got through the door before any more could be said, although I heard someone call out to the disappointed Prentice, "You don't have to worry about your business, gaoler. There's plenty more where we came from."

I'd never met Hancock or spoken to him, although he was hard to miss. Some said he was the richest man in town. Years before, his uncle had made enough for several fortunes by smuggling goods and selling them in Boston and friendly ports in Europe with the help of the friendly customs collector Benjamin Barons. After that, Thomas Hancock had multiplied his money again by getting the contracts to supply British troops in the war with the French and Indians. I was told it was mostly his money which rebuilt Boston after the fire in 1760, with a good return then as well. When he died, he left his nephew the business and the fortune and John quickly built a mansion which stood like a royal palace above the Common. He paraded through the streets in a canary-colored coach with his coat of arms on the side and wore silk suits colored more brightly than the fish in the Sugar Islands.

As much as I wanted to be out, I didn't want to owe him either, since I've always felt bound to pay an honest debt. It was a debt for certain, hard cash paid out to clear the account book, but I'd never asked for it. We were told it was a gift, but I'd never seen one without a hook in the middle. I quickly tried to judge what he or the Sons could demand of me later without tipping the balance too far.

I lurched into Queen St. with the others, blinking as if I'd come into a bright sunlight even though the sun had gone down an hour before. Candles burned in all the windows and when I turned down towards the Common, the fireworks began, throwing fiery light into the sky and making faces in the crowd glow orange and red as they gaped at the streaks above.

I'd only been in a few days, but it seemed forever. All of the colors about me seemed brighter—the red brick walls of the houses and shops, the garish gold and green on painted carriages, the yellow and pink in ribbons floating at the brim of the ladies' straw hats. The air smelled as clean as miles out to sea even when I walked past the garbage piles set out for the scavengers.

Mouse appeared at my elbow just as I approached the Common, a smile splitting his narrow, pox-marked face. He took my elbow, but as always, he struggled to speak the words he wanted, his lip quavering as he tried to begin. "W . . . w . . . we're glad to see you." Another explosion came from behind him and he winced terribly, placing his hands over his ears. His delicate hearing was able to detect whispers at yards away and it seemed his eyes could see through the dark, so fireworks or cannon blasts or gunshots were painful. "I . . . I'm going back now, but we can start in again tomorrow."

I started to ask what we might be starting in on, but another blast went off and Maggie's face was lit up behind him. Her smile was wide and her arms held me a little too long because I started to get weak in the knees. "Stand up now," she warned me with a smile, "or they'll arrest you for being drunk in the street." She backed away and held my shoulders. "Of course, you look about as steady as most of the others tonight. You should see the macaronis standing at Hancock's door."

She turned to look toward his great house and the tall column made with lamps burning brightly on a frame. "I closed the Sword tonight—I'd probably have to serve for free if I didn't—and everyone's out patting each other on the back anyway. I've got some food put aside or you might be able to poach some at the Grapes." Her smile was guarded when she looked back. "If you can wash some of the bugs and the stench off you, we might even visit the same mattress."

Four

I'D ESCAPED what Tobin had planned as a way to pay me back only because of Hancock's help, although he wouldn't know me from a door post. But I had no doubt that someone for the Liberty side was keeping names and accounts carefully. It wouldn't be money they expected to pay the debt–Hancock had enough already to buy up the town–but they sometimes needed a bit of secret work to gain some prize or put fear in a Tory' heart. I kept a sharp eye on the door at the Sword through the fall and winter, expecting someone to walk in and announce my debt almost like Greenleaf had, but no one came, and soon I'd nearly forgotten the tangle I'd help make with my angry attack on Tobin. I'd escaped one enemy, but it wasn't a year until I started down a path to make another.

The colors of spring in Boston are a gift after the cold iron of winter, and when the green showed on trees on the Common in 1767 and the ground turned soft underfoot, people walked down the promenade there and idled past the docks as if they had no cares in the world. Even the summer was quiet, with the Tories and Customs unwilling to tip the boat and stop the money that flowed into their pockets through trade and government pay. The riots that persuaded Parliament to take back the Stamp Act faded into a memory. Except for the true British and the hardest Tories, nearly everyone in Boston seemed so happy that the rulers in London had lifted Stamp taxes that they forgot everything else.

As people went about their normal business, so did our crew. We still helped move some barrels and crates so that when the Customs searchers arrived they found an empty ship or warehouse or one that held only legal goods. When Gillam Powell had used his picklocks at one of John Rowe's stores, we came away with some shoe buckles and a pair of snuff boxes that fetched a good price in Newport when Gillam sold them. But mostly I acted the honest barkeep while Maggie played the saucy maid. But one night I got an offer that seemed too good to turn down.

Jeremiah Brand managed the business of the merchant Marcus Draper along the docks, whether it was a full ship of goods to stock his store through the winter or a smaller order mixed with other goods. Brand was in his late thirties and looked like he'd been put together from squared-off blocks of wood. He had a broad face and flattened ears, a body that appeared as wide as he was tall with thick shoulders and tree-stump legs, and arms too long for a short man. I'd seen him manage a crew of mechanics as they carried Draper's goods off the ship and load them onto his wagon, his thick forearms and hands folded across his chest. But he unfolded them in a flash when a careless shoreman almost let a case of china drop off the back. Brand had been quick to the wagon to save it and even quicker with a blow that sent the shoreman staggering once the china was safe.

After drinking a pint at a table by himself, Brand stood before me, his forearm like an oak yardarm on the bar. "You seem to do well here," nodding around the room to the tables and benches which were nearly filled that night.

"It comes and goes. These days most of the tars are asking for credit because they don't get out to London enough, and then there's the new taxes coming . . ."

"That's sure, but there's plenty that come and go that Customs doesn't know about."

I just nodded my head, since it was easy to agree to something that everyone knew.

"Do you know of Marcus Draper?" asked Brand.

"I know his store but I've never been in it. They say he wants to be the next Hancock."

Brand let go with a slight grin. "He's the one I answer to, and I think they're right. But I'm not sure he's got enough time, what with his wife and his mistress and some agents from London coming around for pay."

Again, I simply nodded, letting him play out what he wanted to say.

"But he's willing to pay for a job well done, especially when it's night work."

"I wouldn't know much about that. I'm here working most nights."

Brand looked at me for a moment before he gave a slight grin. "That's a good answer, Mr. Gray, one for the law and the town criers, but you've done some work after midnight and that's what Draper is interested in." He took a pull at his ale while I widened my eyes and stood up straighter at such a bold accusation. "And don't look so shocked now, like I might injure your reputation. I've been around the docks since before you arrived, and to your credit, you've been very careful. I'm good myself, but I'm getting a little old. Now everyone knows my connection with Draper's Dry Goods so I can't take too many chances," he said before turning toward me directly. "Mr. Draper thinks you might be a great help in the future."

I stared at Brand, at first with some feigned anger, then to see if his eyes would shift too quickly. He stared back, comfortable, with a bit of a smile. We talked a bit more and I felt like I could trust Brand, since we were in the same business and he had a careful air about him, both in his movements and his words. But when he took me to meet Marcus Draper the next day, I didn't feel the same.

Brand led me to the rear of Draper's store on Cross St. at dusk. It was about a quarter mile from the docks in the North End, about a half mile south of the Sword, and the smell of the ocean came with every breath. The store was a brick building which had two floors and proved larger than it looked from the street, extending back almost a hundred feet while the front measured only about thirty across with large windows on each side of the door. There was an alley running northeast up the right side, just wide enough for a horse and cart, so goods could be delivered to the back.

Brand led me down the alley and rapped smartly on the back door three times. Marcus Draper opened it and got us in quickly, even though there wasn't enough light outside for anyone to see much. We followed him into an open warehouse of two stories with a gallery and stairs built along the outside walls and goods stacked everywhere. Small casks of nails stood against a wall with boxes of pins on a shelf above them. Cloth bolts extended down the middle with barrels of bohea tea mixed in. I guessed a small locked chest in a corner held garter buckles or necklaces, canes were in another corner, lamps for whale oil and cases of candles sat cheek by jowl with writing quills, fine parchment, and baskets of lemons.

Draper led us down the dark center aisle towards a desk and lamp near the front. I'd seen him from a distance before, but when he turned I saw that he had the face and bearing of a gentleman, unmarked by everyday troubles. I judged him about my age, not yet thirty, and he was dressed well even here in his storeroom–his wig well-fitted with some powder; a bit of ruffle at his neck and wrist; his waistcoat a shiny, wine-colored satin; his shoes with a square, silver buckle.

I studied him as we neared the front and he turned towards us. He was average height, but didn't carry the weight of most merchants, and there was a quickness about him–quick feet and hands, but mostly quick eyes which never seemed to settle for long on anyone or anything. His face was smooth, his nose narrow and regular, and his smile was like a fox in a henhouse. When we were near the desk, he turned and took another minute to wander back among the goods, placing his hand so gently on a bolt of silk I might have thought it was a woman's breast he caressed. Each bit that caught his fancy got a touch, even a lemon which he lifted to his nose before turning back to us.

He started in as if I was a customer he knew well. "Do you need lemons at the Sword and Scabbard? These make a punch that the gentlemen who've been to Spain or the Sugar Islands favor especially." He looked at me expectantly, then went on without waiting. "No, I guess those gentlemen don't come to your tavern, do they? A pity, the prices they're willing to pay."

"It's not mine, it's the Widow McGowan's. I just work there. But Julius makes a punch second to none."

"I'm sure, I'm sure, and you must serve the Widow well, night and day, or she'd have you out in a flash. At least that's the stories that are told." He tried his smile again but got nothing back from me.

He turned and walked back through the goods again, this time lighting at an unopened tea barrel. "I've got plenty here to sell, but you can never have enough, can you? When I walk about town or visit another shop owner, I see things I could use, things I could sell through the front door or the back. I won't beat about the bush, Gray, Mr. Brand has told me all about you. If I tell you what I want, can you get it?"

I took a moment to look at him, his eyes restless now, moving about the cases and barrels and boxes, all so familiar, but never enough. "Sure I can," I said quietly, "if the price is right."

"I've always been generous, ask Mr. Brand. I may bargain a little but that's part of the game, isn't it?"

Brand nodded. "Mr. Draper knows the risks and he's willing to pay a fair price."

"Is it hard money we're talking then?" I asked.

"I pay in sterling when I can, but you know how much of that's about. But there's plenty here to choose from if the coins aren't handy.

We'll set the price ahead of time and you'll get that in trade if there's no specie."

"At front room prices?"

Draper laughed. "You should go on exchange yourself, Gray, you could drive down the Jews in London. No, you can get your goods at merchant prices."

When I nodded acceptance, Draper quickly turned his back on me and began to walk away. "Mr. Brand will make all the arrangements. It wouldn't pay for me to be seen talking to you." He stopped, his hand fingering the tail of a scarlet ribbon on a roll, then turned back quickly and walked toward me. "Should we shake hands on it then, or drink a toast?"

I stared into his restless eyes. I felt a bit uneasy, but I wasn't willing to leave what seemed a bird in the hand. I shook my head slowly. "No, Mr. Draper, I'll skip your little show, because I've seen a toast to good business turn bad, quicker than the wind dies in the harbor. It's not a handshake I need or a bit of brandy. It's your money and your lips sealed tight. I don't relish the feel of shackles on my hands and I'm sure you wouldn't either."

Draper was silent for a moment too long, shocked that I spoke so directly to him, since I was just a step off the docks. He acted the gentlemen, but, in truth, his store barely put him at the feet of the great merchants like John Hancock and John Rowe. He withdrew his hand and said nothing, staring for a moment before waving us away as if to a servant clearing a table.

Five

WORKING FOR DRAPER was good business for a few months. I'd see Brand on the docks or he'd come to the Sword and tell me what Draper wanted and what he was willing to pay. Gillam Powell and Mouse and I would go to get it at night and we'd deliver it a few nights later to Brand at the back door of Draper's store. We didn't have to worry on finding the right person to buy or haggling about a price which was too low for stolen goods. I was surprised that Draper, through Brand, often paid in cash, and if he didn't, Maggie and I would go in the front and choose what we wanted. Draper would act like we were regular customers and put it on an account, talking loudly to be sure that the indentured boy who swept and his clerk thought that everything was above deck.

It wasn't a chest of gold but it kept us without worries for a time. I gave Maggie a small share since there was some risk she'd lose her license if we were caught. It fattened the purse she kept tight behind a beam in her room and it gave me a chance to act like a fine gentleman once in a while, bringing her a hat or a fan, even a stomacher to cover the laces of her leather bodice, but she usually laughed at me since she said she had nowhere to wear a lady's clothes.

I couldn't help but marvel at Draper as well. I'd see him about town, dressed in bright colors, a macaroni to rival Hancock, with his wife on his arm. She always looked like she'd drunk sour milk and they said it was because it was her dowry he'd lost in London gambling on horse races. Sometimes he'd pass in a carriage with one of the other shop owners he'd told us to rob, smiling as if he was a bosom friend. It must have been the same at dinner when he'd sit at one of their homes, making gentle conversation with the upper merchants while his hand, through mine, was under the table stealing what he could from them. He was rising up, no doubt, and no one seemed to think there was a reason to be suspicious.

But in the fall, we nearly fell off the dock. He'd sent us to one of John Rowe's stores a second time, the one at Rowe's Wharf by Fort Hill. I made the same plan as before, relying on Gillam Powell to get us in the front. He was a thin man with a narrow, hawk's face, long dark hair and dark eyes over a drooping mustache. But I always noticed his hands, as delicate as any lady's with long graceful fingers. They were one of the reasons he could deal any card from a deck without suspicion and why locks were useless against his picklocks. He kept his tools in a pouch under his shirt day and night, with a bit of cloth packed in so they wouldn't rattle. We planned to get away with the cloth bolts and finery that Draper wanted and then close up shop behind us, leaving the shopkeeper to explain what was lost.

Like before, we kept Mouse near the door so his sensitive ears could hear anyone stirring in the dead of the night. When he heard someone a few streets up, it was probably just some drunken hands getting back to their ship, but we didn't want to take the risk. We left in more of a hurry than we wanted, and this time, the keeper would know that someone had lifted some goods as soon as he opened the store next morning.

We'd come away with the goods—two dozen pair of silk stockings, some taffetys from England and India, a bolt of Spanish silk, a couple of boxes of ribbons—and kept them in our usual place in the warehouse by Halsey's Wharf, just below Hancock's. The minder there let us use a corner in exchange for ale at the Sword and an occasional roll with a doxy who was soft for Mouse. She thought it was like giving Mouse a gift

I smiled when I thought of how she favored him—a small man, thin and marked by the pox, eyes as light as if they'd been washed with water, dressed in clothes just better than rags and unable to speak a sentence without repeating the first word a few times. He might have been called Mouse for his looks as much as his silent feet. But they were a good match—she was shaped more like a barrel than a reed—and to my mind, she appeared most favorable when the candle was out.

We heard the next forenoon that Rowe didn't take his new loss as kindly as before. He was a rich man, but he was still looking to climb, and this time he acted like our work was a personal insult. According to a tar who came in early, Rowe was out with Sheriff Greenleaf early that morning, red in the face, asking all around the stores and wharfs. The deck hand mocked him with his loud voice that demanded justice for "some rogues who make our fair town seem a den of thieves."

I wanted no part of Greenleaf and any suspicions he might have about me, so I decided to arrange delivery direct to Draper's warehouse that very night. You could never be sure who might have seen me or Mouse or Gillam around our own warehouse and who might be willing to point us out to the sheriff in exchange for ten shillings from Rowe's pocket.

I walked with Maggie up to Draper's store after we'd finished serving dinner at three. We left Mouse watching the bar, Julius in the kitchen, and Gillam getting up a game of dice with three sailors just in from Halifax who would soon be very unlucky

I always stopped to admire the clean and tidy windows on each side of the shop's door. They might show new hats on one side with china plates on the other, but Draper kept up a good game of switching things about in the windows and on the shelves. The casual butterflies would think that his sales were so brisk and his merchandise so choice that they'd want to come in and join the fun. But the other reason was that it was a good way to mix in bits of what he might acquire at night with what arrived during the day, without getting anyone's nose up.

While Maggie looked at some trenchers that we might use at the Sword, she slipped Draper the note which simply said "Midnight Tonight." After he glanced at it, he sent his boy to sweep in the warehouse and glanced about to be sure his clerk was still in the back office. He turned to me and hissed beneath his breath, "Not tonight, Brand is away. I'll tell you when, like always."

I tried to make my voice pleasant, as if we were bargaining on the trenchers. "We'll be here tonight and if you're not, we'll leave the goods by your back door."

Draper was hot, trembling almost, but didn't dare raise his voice. He glared at me as if I might be cowed with a look, then turned away smartly.

"I think what we have is good enough for now," said Maggie, finishing up our entertainment as Draper's clerk appeared in the doorway, "but if these are still here next month and you come down just a bit, you might sell them all to us."

Draper turned to us with his smile back in place. "Widow McGowan is shrewd enough, isn't she, Mr. Gray? It's a wonder she needs your help at all." He'd said it as a joke, laughing afterwards, but his eyes showed sparks hot enough to set the room on fire.

THIS LOT of Draper's goods was a bit too bulky to be carried by hand from the warehouse off Fish St. It wasn't a long haul, not more than about three hundred yards if you went direct down Fish and then up Cross to the alley. But the watch had a box hard by the corner of Fish and Gallop, so we always had to take the long way around, up toward Prince, then down Middle Street past the New North Meeting House. They'd started paving some of the streets in the South End a few years back but they quit before they got to the North when the taxes didn't pay enough–they said the port trade was too slow–so we followed the ruts through the dirt in the middle, near the sewer. Boston had none of the streetlights of London either, so it was a dark journey, much the better for us.

I had Mouse and Julius with me–Gillam thought himself a bit special because of his way with locks and claimed he might bungle his precious hands if he was required to lift anything heavy. When we guessed the time at about three quarters past eleven, we loaded the hand cart from the warehouse, locked up, and took off down the streets as quiet as we could be. The cart was old but we kept the axle and its two wheels quiet with plenty of ship grease.

Mouse and I went with the cart, keeping as close to the middle as we could, although the shutters were closed on all the buildings we passed. Even when the heat of summer made the rooms like a baking oven, there were few who dared to keep their shutters open, afraid to know the mischief that might be happening in the dark street. Julius watched behind, invisible in the shadows, partly because of his dark skin and partly because he'd spent more than a year hiding in the bush of Jamaica. It was there he'd learned to be silent as death, since if they'd found him, he would have been butchered or burned or starved like the other slaves who'd followed Tacky and fought against their owners.

Things went well until we got past the meeting house. We knew the watchman down the block and he slept most nights for his thirty shillings a month. But an earwig must have interrupted him or some dream of the constable knocking the side of the box, because he was up and walking when we didn't expect it. His voice came down the street. "Hallo, hallo. Stop for the watch. Who's about there?"

Mouse and I froze. We might have left the cart with the goods, but it was precious money sitting there, and someone might have connected the cart to the warehouse, and who knew what would happen then. If we turned it around, we'd be too slow to escape. I motioned to Mouse and we stepped backwards towards the buildings.

"Who's there? Answer smartly now." He was a large man but his belly walked before him since he started on the watch, sleeping every night after a late meal. He was coming with the lantern in front of him and he was almost within sight of the cart when Julius appeared behind him. He carried a short stick which bent like a willow on a leather loop about his left wrist, fixed with a lump of lead at its head, and swung it before the watchman could turn. He rescued the lantern from the watchman's hand before he collapsed and quickly nodded to us before blowing out the light. He was a fearsome apparition, long and lean and deadly, draped in a dark cloak, as he stood by the watchman's head, a shoe on his cheek to discourage him from looking up or considering a fight.

Mouse and I grabbed the cart and continued on as fast as we could without waking the dead. Julius would hold the watchman for a bit, a half hour or so, before giving him another light blow and disappearing into the dark.

When we got to Draper's back door we were sweating and out of breath. Draper opened after a light tap and started to upbraid us. "You're late. This won't happen again, it's Brand you'll deal with . . ." but stopped when he saw our faces

"Shut the door and stuff your mouth." I pushed by him after we got the cart in and walked toward the front where a heavy curtain separated the front of the store from the warehouse. "Put out that lamp. Can they see a light from the front?"

Draper's face lost color before putting out the lamp, worried in a way that must have been rare for him and more common for us: someone was out and looking and might do him harm. The warehouse was as dark as the hold of a ship at night. "He'll probably get the constable and be out again in about an hour," I explained. "They'll search about, looking for break-ins and they'll hold anyone who's out without a reason. We'll have to stay here till dawn."

"Is it that savage from your kitchen? What if he harmed him or killed him outright?" Brand once told me that Draper had picked out Julius in a crowd at the market one day, struck by his height, gaunt face, and hooded eyes.

I said nothing until a bit later. "We'll have Mouse listen out front and wait for the sun. With luck, there's nothing for them to find. The cart isn't heavy enough to make deep tracks and there's no reason to pick out your store more than the millinery shop or the hardware store or the coffee house. They're all locked down secure."

I could hear Draper's breathing, quick and panicked now, nothing like the cocksure merchant sniffing at the Tory coattails and parading before the British and American ladies like a peacock. Maybe he saw himself dancing at the end of a rope like the wretches on the gallows, the crowds crowing and calling out as a thief or a murderer strangled slowly for their enjoyment. Maybe he feared getting stripes on the Common or a notch in his ear.

But if he was afraid, he shouldn't have been. It would be me and Mouse and Julius who got the sharp end. The judges and governors and the sort that owned country houses and pews in church were afraid for their china and their silk stockings, their quail and Madera, so we would pay with the only thing we had—our blood or our lives. The uppers like Draper who stole from greed and gained more in a month than we did in a year would never suffer like that. He might pay a fine or lose his business, but his life wouldn't turn on the whim of an officer who might whip him for sport or a judge who might send him to choke in the bowels of a gaol.

He started to talk but I cut him short. "No words now—none. We need to let Mouse listen."

I was right—the watch came back with the constable and two others, making a racket in the street, knocking on shutters and rattling doors to be sure they were secure. They came right to Draper's front door and shined their lanterns through the windows, and later to the back, pounding and shouting for anyone to come answer to the watch if they were inside, as if a thief would walk out and greet them if he wasn't caught red-handed. I was bit afraid since I was stuck with nothing to do but imagine the worst, but I was more afraid that Draper might panic and cry out—we sat a few yards apart in the back of the warehouse and I could hear his breathing get ragged and uneven. But finally they moved from the back to the next door down and later all was silent.

We left just before dawn, Mouse and I going separate ways and armed with stories about the night we'd spent with a friendly bawd who'd back our story any time. Draper looked a wraith after his long night and his sweat had dripped the powder from his wig down his temple. He would stay and distribute the goods throughout the warehouse, mixing things in so all seemed regular, and he'd send his boy later with the cart to the warehouse like a regular errand.

Maggie was into the hall as soon as she heard my foot on the stairs and I raised a finger to her lips before she began. "We've got Julius to thank, he's the best watch there is. Maybe I'll recommend him to the constable next time I see him."

"So it's done?" she asked, "Rowe's goods are with Draper?"

I nodded. "There's no worry for us now. Even if Draper were to get caught, it wouldn't help him to have us in court—we didn't force him to buy stolen goods and he wouldn't want us to tell how he ordered up his goods from other shops, just like he would from London. But this will be our last business with him—when they came sniffing around, it seemed as if he glowed in the dark, like Elmo's fire."

She looked thoughtful, blue eyes pale in the half light of dawn, the long scar down her cheek barely visible. "Steer clear of him then. There's plenty more who need a steady hand." A smile lit her eyes then and just tugged at the corners of her mouth. She turned and gave that little cock of her head towards her door. "I might use a steady hand right now, Mr. Gray, if you can find the right place to put it."

Six

I turned Brand away the next time he came. "Draper's not solid enough," I told him. "If the wind blows wrong, he'd let me swing without a thought. And I suspect he'd do the same for you."

Brand accepted it without a question, since I hadn't promised to do Draper's work forever. After that, I only saw Brand in passing on the docks through the winter and exchanged some harmless words. But he came back one night in early spring, tight-lipped and wary, his broad face a mask. I filled a pint and gave him a smile, but got none in return. He emptied it in just a couple of draughts standing at the bar. He spoke quietly enough so the four on their benches in the corner didn't hear. "Draper needs you."

I thought for a moment and started to dodge, "It's the same as before, Jeremiah. I'm not sure that he'll stand up if it gets hot. He'd be better to take on something less risky. . ."

Brand cut me off, his lips still tight and his jaw working hard. "It's not like before. He's in some trouble and needs your help and he's ready to pay for it." He looked down at the wide, rough planks on the floor, then back up at me. "You'd be helping me as well."

It couldn't have been an easy thing for Brand to admit he needed help, no more than it would have been for me, so I knew they weren't empty words. He'd stood on his own for a long time and was proud of it. When I nodded to him, the hand holding his empty mug seemed to relax a little, even if his jaw didn't.

"Come tonight after you close, 'round to the back like before. He'll be there to explain." He placed the pint back on the bar and left without another word and not a glance toward Maggie who was straightening the benches by the wall.

Mouse appeared at the side of the bar. He must have been in the kitchen, although I didn't know he was within shouting distance of the Sword, let alone whispering distance. I was always startled and a bit angry when he appeared like that, like he'd caught me out with my hand on someone's purse strings. Mouse could hear a feather fall to the floor or a baby breathing across the room.

He faltered, like always when he started, "Wh . . . What . . . What do you think it'll be?"

"What?" I answered a little coarsely, "the next ship Brand will be out on?"

Mouse looked a little embarrassed, and he shuffled his feet a bit, but didn't back away. "What he needs help with. Do you think he has an eye for some goods from Dorr this time?"

"I don't know, Mouse, but I'm sure you'll find out as soon as I talk to him, whether I tell you or not."

BRAND LET ME IN the back door while Draper sat at his desk in the front corner of the warehouse, two lamps burning but trimmed down to show the papers on his desk while his face was just in the shadows. When he looked at me now, there were dark circles under his eyes and his waistcoat was unbuttoned, not the dandy who slipped a smile and a squeeze to all the servant girls and who, they said, danced lightly in the candlelight of a Tory ball. He looked ragged, desperate, like a worm was eating at his gut.

I didn't feel kindly toward him or truly sure of what he might do in a pinch, but since it was Brand who asked, I was willing to listen although I couldn't limit my tongue at first. I waited while he arranged his papers, moving them about on the desk without any purpose I could see. "Doesn't your wife worry about you being out at night, with all the footpads and thieves about?"

But he wasn't cowed, smiling and answering back boldly. "She knows I've got business all about and if I'm gone, she believes I'm at contracts in Deadham or with a captain in Salem. And sometimes I am."

"Let's get to business," said Brand, his voice tight and his arms across his chest. "We need a plan for tomorrow night and if we don't step lively, we could lose it all."

A look passed between them. "Explain everything," I said. "I might help and I might not. But I won't if I'm left in the dark."

Draper looked at Brand who nodded back at him. Draper began quietly enough. "I found a chance to double or triple what I might make on a full shipment of goods. Someone came to Mr. Brand and made an offer good enough to make some of these"—he held up a sheaf of bills—"disappear and the London agents go back home with their pockets full. Not to mention helping with the rent and servants and the endless millinery bills for Miss Clark." He paused for a moment, and his tone shifted to that of a moonstruck boy. "Have you seen her, Gray? I met her at the Widow Griffiths' shop on Hancock's Wharf and before I knew it, I was there most every day. I was happy to find her a place on Orange St., but she doesn't seem to understand that I've got any expenses other than her hats and gloves and scarves."

Draper saw I was listening but with no tears for his burden, so he put the bills back on his desk and continued. "They offered a full ship of goods and sundries—even some gunpowder and pistols mixed in—for one third price as long as I took the schooner as well." He stopped for a minute to see how satisfied I might be with this bit, but went on when my eyes asked for more. "I could buy the schooner and all its goods as long as I made them disappear."

I sat back on the tea barrel I was perched on. I was never surprised at the smuggling the Boston merchants did every day to avoid Customs. Starting back with the molasses years before, everyone knew the traders had to get some in without paying duty so they could make a good profit from distilling it into rum. Keeping a bit out of Custom's greedy fingers was just a normal part of business. But making a schooner full of goods disappear might stir up a hornet's nest in London.

"They insured it at full value at Lloyd's Coffee House," continued Draper, "and my captain found a small crew he trusted to disappear once they got across. Everything went perfectly–Capt. Graham made it in less than eight weeks and put in where we planned, on the south corner of Nahant Bay where the river comes in, a spot we've used before."

My eyes must have shown some surprise, because Draper continued with a hint of pride. "What's wrong, Gray? Did you think that all I wanted was the few pounds of cream we skimmed from the other stores? That didn't add up to the interest the loaner charged, the one from London with a front by the races, let alone the five hundred pounds I borrowed to begin with." When he began again, his voice scorned me. "Your work bought some hats for my lovely Miss Clark and a feather duster for the store. But my breeches and snuffbox are worth more than you could steal in a year."

I could feel my blood begin to rush warm through my arms and shoulders, as I stood up from the barrel. "It was you that came to me, Mr. Draper, not the other way around. If you wanted to risk your neck and your name for some nun's hats, it's none of my concern. And as for your snuffbox, if I wanted it, I'd have it." I didn't care what he thought of me or my work, but I wouldn't let him have it on both sides, needing my help and spitting on my shoes at the same time. At least not face-to-face.

Draper colored as well and his eyes narrowed. Speaking of his mistress as a whore might cause a duel after a dinner party, or a brawl in a tavern, but Draper wouldn't think of challenging me here. Brand stood up and moved between us, thick fingers on my chest and a heavy arm pushing me gently back towards my seat on the barrel while he looked at Draper. "There's no cause for anger here. We've got a proposition for Mr. Gray that we hope he'll accept and if you still have differences after that, you can look to satisfy them then. We'll talk of business beginning now and nothing else." He held Draper's eyes for a minute in the dim light, then turned to me. I started to begin again, but his fingers in my chest pressed hard enough to stop me. "Sit down, Mr. Gray, and I'll continue our story."

I looked away from Draper and breathed deeply, trying to clear the anger from my eyes so I could see what lay ahead.

Brand continued. "Like Mr. Draper said, the schooner put in at Nahant Bay, and I paid the captain for his work and he went his way—up to Halifax I think to try to ship out as a seaman before we declared the schooner lost. We'd used the spot before, so we were prepared to unload with some lighters and then the goods would get here later, a wagon at a time around some paths through Cambridge. I was ready to sail the schooner in ballast to St. Lucia or somewhere in the Sugar Islands to sell it."

He paused and his jaw tightened again and his words became short. "But someone sold us, Ebenezer Richardson or one of the informers like him, and five or six Customs men came rowing from the beach before we knew it. We couldn't fight them, they showed muskets over their shoulders and the flag at the bow. When they got close, we got off the far side before they could get a good sight of us, and I took all the papers with me. Thank God we changed the name on the stern the very first thing, I've got a man who took off the old and mounted a new one in just a few hours."

I continued to look at Brand so that Draper didn't enter my vision. "Where does it stand now?"

"Customs has it and they marked the mast with the King's arrow, but it will take some time for them to figure out its real name and where it came from and why it was abandoned like that. We need to rescue it and sail it away before they can guess our plans."

It wouldn't be odd if Customs lost a ship they'd taken, since they had no troops to support them and only a few men and weapons of their own. A crowd with painted faces had taken a ship back from the Customs men watching it at Newburyport just a few months before. The Indians had carried off the cargo while the tidewaiters and searchers were surrounded and held with threats. Afterwards, the owner swore in court he knew nothing of the crowd or the cargo, and Customs had no proof that he had received any goods at all. Even when they offered a full pound for a reward, they couldn't find anyone willing to point a finger. The owner got his ship and cargo back while the commissioners lost the hundreds of pounds they would have gained from seizing the ship. They were furious that they couldn't lay more silver plate on their tables or plant an orchard at a country seat.

But a crowd wouldn't work for Draper, even if he could find the men and get them to the isolated spot in time. The news about a seized ship would probably get back to Lloyd's in London before they decided to pay the insurance. And if they paid before they learned the ship had arrived safely, they would make more trouble than Draper could handle. The money men at Lloyd's had very long memories when they paid out full value instead of putting ten or twenty percent in their pockets.

"How much is it worth?" I asked Brand.

"It was insured at nine hundred pounds, although I won't get that much when I sell it without papers."

"And me?"

Draper broke in before Brand could answer. "You're the strongarm, Gray, what else? You and that savage and any helpers you need can muffle whoever's left at the schooner, until Capt. Brand here can sail it away."

"Without unloading it?"

"Unloading would take too long and involve too many people here," put in Brand. "The schooner still has to disappear for the insurance to pay and if we used a crew to unload, word would get back to London sooner or later."

I took a moment to think, gazing about at the goods piled high in the warehouse. For no reason, I noticed the small square chests of spices on a shelf nearby and hoped that I never needed Maggie to apply the cloves for a toothache again. The last one had nearly split my head before I'd gotten drunk enough to let Gillam pull out the tooth by its stump.

"How much?" I asked Brand, although I knew it was Draper who would answer.

Draper answered readily. "Fifty pounds for the lot of you. That's better than you can get in months of stealing buttons and pins, and it'll keep you in ale for a long time."

I shook my head. "Not enough. If I'm going to get tangled with Customs straight out, it'll have to be more than that." Draper looked skeptical but I went on. "If they get any of us in their Admiralty Court across the water, we're hanged for sure. The judge is the jury, and the lords in London would love Jack Ketch to have a Boston man dancing at the end of his rope. No, not enough by a long shot."

"What do you want, Gray? I'll give you the fifty pounds now so you won't have to worry."

"You can't do it without us, and we're taking more risk than any. I'll take the fifty now and then a share just like a Customs commissioner—one third—once the schooner and goods are sold. I'm sure Capt. Brand can bargain for six hundred pounds, so we'll take two hundred when it's done, with fifty of it right now."

Draper rose from his desk and paced towards the back, fuming and sputtering. I guessed he'd been in the same position many times—too desperate by half, with no choice but to knuckle under—and he didn't like it any better this time, especially at the hands of someone he saw equal to a servant. "It's one fifty, Gray, and no more, after Brand returns. It shouldn't be more than a month or two."

When I nodded, he went on, "Wait in the back while I get the fifty." Brand and I went towards the back door in the dark, but I could hear Draper haul a strong box across the floor to his desk and then open its heavy lock with a key from his pocket.

Brand put his hand on my arm. "I'll get it. I don't think he wants to see more of you."

"That's just as good for me, it's only his money I want to see, not his face. And if I don't, he'll answer one night when he's dreaming of Miss Clark."

Seven

I BOLTED THE FRONT DOOR at the Sword after Brand arrived the next morning. It was just ten in the morning, too early for dinner, but we sometimes got a man or two wandering up from the docks or in need of a swallow right away after a hard night in a bawd's house.

Brand sat at one end of a bench with Gillam next to him. Julius sat beside me across from them and Mouse pulled a bench from the next table, far enough away that he could bob up and down from his seat without bothering us. Maggie was in the kitchen, but near enough to hear.

I'd filled a round of pints for us and began without introductions, addressing Brand. "Do we have to do this tonight? I'm one that likes to plan the best way, not rush through a door and find it's the dragon's mouth." Gillam nodded silently as did Julius. We'd been at it enough together to think the same way.

"If we hadn't been sold, you wouldn't need to do anything. And if I find who it was, they'll breathe seawater." Brand's eyes were dangerous now and he seemed a man not likely to forget or make a threat without weight.

"It was none of us here, I can swear to that, but Mouse will listen to what's talked around. You may get your chance. But it's tonight that worries me now." I turned to Mouse, "Did you hear anything at Customs this morning?"

I looked at Brand and put up my hand to him so he wouldn't interrupt Mouse as he stumbled on his first words. Once he got started, Mouse could say what he needed.

"I . . . I didn't hear everything myself, but I know the server there, too. They talked about it, how there were no papers and no crew. They asked the searchers if they'd ever heard of it before, but no one seemed to know."

Brand showed a small smile at my look. "I named it the *Grace*, after a maid I knew when I was younger. I'd never heard of a ship named for her before."

I motioned for Mouse to go on.

"They . . . they'll keep at least three men since it's so far away and some will have muskets. One of the Commissioners, Robinson I think, has a nephew who will stay on board, they're giving him a chance to prove himself. Paxton is excited and wants to keep this one for certain until he sorts things out. He thinks they'll get all the goods and sell the ship, too."

"Anything else?"

"The Navy doesn't know about it." This bit made it safer for us, but no one was surprised. Customs and the Navy worked against each other in seizing ships, even though they were supposed to be on the same side. A Commissioner of Customs legally put away a third of the profit for himself from seizing an illegal ship and its cargo, and each level below him got a bonus as well. Navy captains and their men worked under a similar agreement. There was no profit in one helping the other. It made our work easier since Customs had no cutters to chase down a ship at sea, and the Navy had few of the informants that Customs relied on to point them at a likely ship. While Customs and the Navy watched each other, they missed most of what we unloaded.

"It won't be easy with Commissioner Robinson's nephew there, Hardy I think it is–I'm told he's got an eye for rising," I added. "We'll have to get close enough to them so their muskets won't help. If we knew where they were on the ship, we could plan our steps." I didn't like the idea yet, hoping we could come up with a plan that didn't involve battling armed Customs men. I thought we could win, but the trouble after would be too great.

"I know the area," said Brand, "and where the *Grace* sits. She's at anchor just off the river mouth. We'll need to use boats to get to her, but we've got some there now, ready for when we were going to unload." He again looked about, staring at Julius a long time before continuing.

Julius spoke very carefully among white people, not because he faltered like Mouse, but more that he feared his words might strike from the wrong direction, even if he'd aimed them right. He spoke like a British lord, since he'd spent years serving the master of a great pen in Jamaica, cooking fish and turtles from the lakes and slaughtering a beef cow on holidays. He wore a broad-brimmed hat outside, and his arms were bare when he cooked so the sleeves wouldn't catch fire, showing muscles like braided tackle rope. In most cases, his look prevented any unwanted questions–a gaunt face with the color of dark coffee and the substance of granite, a flared nose, and coal black eyes set back in his head. It was easy to miss his eyes because of his size and presence, but when you looked at him directly, his stare fixed you like a cricket in a corner, easy to squash with a quick step.

I'd approached him first after he left a pair of brawlers on their knees in Fleet Street when they insisted he was still a slave, no matter what the medal on the leather around his neck said. After we'd worked a few night jobs together, we sat on a dark wharf one night and he'd told me stories from his time in Jamaica. I knew the story of the uprising from my time in Kingston, how Tacky and the slaves who'd followed had gotten arms from a magazine at Port Maria on the north coast and torched houses and cane fields as they went, except for the few whose masters were thought fair and kind. In the end, the British had needed the help of the Maroons and some other slaves to hunt them down.

The masters had freed some of the slaves that helped them hunt the rebels, and gave them medals to prove it, though most ended up working like slaves anyway. I showed surprise when Julius first showed me the free medal he wore, trying to imagine him tracking down slaves in the bush. But he trusted me by then, and after a few more questions, he admitted he'd actually fought with Tacky. He'd taken the medal later from the body of one of the freedmen who'd ventured too far from Kingston, and it was good enough to keep him free in Boston. Now he cooked at the Sword, serving up stews and meat pies that showed some of the fine tastes he learned in Jamaica before the rebellion.

"We need to come from behind, I think," he said carefully, "and the best way for that is if they're looking ahead."

THAT EVENING, Brand took us out of the harbor and up to Mystick River between Charlestown and Noddles Island with Brand and Julius doing most of the rowing. We kept north and east past Hogg Island until we came to a spot on the north bank where two farm wagons and horses and Brand's schooner crew of five waited for us. They took us on a narrow path for a half hour until Brand stopped at a spot on the south side of Nahant Bay where we could just make out the outline of the *Grace* by the quarter-moon. There was no way to tell how many were on board or where they might be, but we were depending on their zeal.

Brand stayed with his crew, ready to board once we had control of the ship. Mouse took one of the carts away from the beach so he could circle back and come at it straight on from the north. Gillam and Julius and I waited with two more boats, staying silent and ready to slip into the water when Mouse drew them on.

While we waited, I prayed the commissioner's nephew and the others would be as anxious as we thought to make a name by arresting a smuggler. I wondered about the rest of our plan as well, banking on a frail man who faltered in his speech playing the part of a loud and bungling driver. But we needed the rest of us for strong arms and Mouse's small, pointed face lit up when we suggested his part in the ruse.

He'd lit a lantern and drove straight up to the beach swinging it back and forth, then covering it two times quickly then swinging it again. He rattled about in the wagon as much as possible, banging the sides of the cart as if rearranging things, then repeating the jig with the lantern which might have been used as a signal to unload.

We were lucky that someone on board was awake. We could hear him moving about on deck, then showing a lantern himself. In a few minutes, Mouse began "halloing" in a voice he must have hidden for years. He sounded like a speaker off the gallery at the Town House, wishing he could be heard in London. I thought later that we should always let Mouse speak in the dark if we wanted to hear him more easily.

Straining to see, we made out two from the schooner who climbed down the rope ladder on the starboard side away from our view to row the hundred yards to shore. Mouse bellowed even louder, now. "Bring me what you've got," he shouted, "I can't wait here all night."

Julius and I put in silently, the frigid water biting our legs, and I began pulling the muffled oars as rapidly as I could to approach the Customs boat from behind. If we didn't get there quickly enough, they'd make it to the beach and we'd lose our advantage, especially if they were carrying muskets. My lungs burned and my arms were beginning to feel heavy when we closed on it. I could hear Mouse continuing to shout into the dark, drawing their attention as we approached.

Julius slipped into the water and covered the last ten yards in an instant. The man rowing flinched and shouted as Julius appeared suddenly over the side, a dreaded sea creature in the night. The forward man turned toward the noise and struggled to raise his musket while holding the lantern in one hand. His friend cursed and fought to stay dry, but Julius got a strong enough hold on his coat to drag him over the side. The forward man put the lantern on the seat of the boat, and then got a grip on his musket to steady it and fire over the side just a few feet away.

I took the oar out of its lock and made a wild swing toward his back, and I nearly tumbled into the water with Julius, but I caught just enough of him to tip his balance and send him over the side in a confusion of arms, legs, lantern, and musket. His finger must have been caught in the trigger because a shot exploded into the night before he surfaced, thrashing like a shark on a pike.

Julius let the first one go and climbed shivering over the side to join me as I got the oar back in the lock and tied their boat's leader to ours. Mouse turned the wagon around and went back the way he'd come while the Customs men shouted and floundered in water deep enough they couldn't stand. Julius kept shivering, near frozen, his cloak around him now with the hood pulled down. I pulled as fast as I could to get us to the *Grace*, all the while hoping that Gillam had been able to do his work and that we wouldn't take a musket ball in the chest as we tied both boats to the schooner.

The plan was for Gillam to climb the ladder to the deck on the side away from the shore and creep across it as the man on deck peered out to the confusion of Mouse shouting and our attack on the rowboat. Gillam would give his head a solid knock and quickly put the flour sack and rope over his head and shoulders. If he needed to, he would deliver another blow to calm him, and be sure that the rope kept his arms tight at his sides.

Gillam and Brand stood on the deck when I got up, the Customs man on his knees a few paces away. Gillam gave him a last light blow to the head to convince him that he'd be better served by staying still on his knees, while his musket leaned against the rail where he'd left it. Julius stayed in the tied-off boat below. "What'll we do with him?" asked Brand, quietly.

"Gillam can take him for a swim near the other two. They'll get ashore but they're too far from help to cause us any further trouble tonight."

I stood with Brand on deck as his crew prepared to sail and Gillam took the Customs man down the rope with the bag still about his head but his arms free.

"When will you be back?" I asked, knowing the time of a voyage was never a sure bet.

Brand looked away, south down the coast where he'd sell it all. "I don't know."

His shifting stance made it clear to me. "You're not coming back, are you?"

Brand backed away a step and made sure that one of his crew was on deck behind him. "It wouldn't have happened if we hadn't been sold out, I'd be sailing an empty ship that wasn't worth enough for my comfort. But you know that Draper would cast me off just as quick if he had a chance." He took a slight step forward and lowered his voice. "Come with me, Gray, we've got a sound ship filled with goods and a decent wind down the coast. You'd be worth a third to me."

I saw it just for a moment, putting in at a cove near St. Lucia, getting the doubloons or guilders in hand, the rains moving in each afternoon while the fruits danced on the trees, waiting for word to load or unload a cargo or sail a brig round to another island where business was better. There'd be no more ice in the water buckets in January, rum as dark as coffee and cheaper than beer, and ports where the only law was the money in your pocket and the speed of your blade.

But it would mean leaving Maggie behind. I saw her face in the dark and it made me ache to think of leaving her. I couldn't cast her off like an empty oyster shell, she'd given me too much already, even if the money and the prospects looked good if I sailed off with Brand. I would have to short Julius and Mouse and Gillam as well, something they wouldn't understand and wouldn't forget.

"No, Brand, I won't be going and I'll miss the pay we worked for tonight." Fighting with Brand and his men by myself wouldn't help and the boat that held Julius could be easily cast off if they needed.

Brand stared at me a moment before he began. "I'd rather you weren't at my back. Draper's arms don't reach far enough—all he offers is money—but I'm not sure about yours." He turned back to his man bringing up supplies and retrieved a sack from a pile on the deck and dug a purse from it. "Here's another fifty from what Draper gave us for provisions. It makes a hundred pounds for a night. If you keep up at this rate, you'll buy Draper's shop from under him."

I hefted it a minute before accepting it, knowing it was the best we'd get. "It's still lighter than we were promised. I'll take it, but the slate's not clean. If I see you again, I'll expect you to square the accounts."

"We'll see what happens if it comes to that," he replied, but there was no menace in his words, or in mine. "But you didn't trust it, anyway, did you? Too easy for the wind to change?"

"I was never sure you'd be back. I wouldn't in your shoes. Draper keeps busy but I don't see the end to it. He'll need another hat to keep Miss Clark in his bed and when he makes a mistake, it's one of us will pay for it."

I started towards the rail and Brand called out to me. "Good luck, Gray, but you'd better step a little lighter. They'll have a new Customs board soon and the merchants will be watching their goods closer than ever. You'd make a good prize for any of them."

We said little on the trip back, except for Gillam who described the oaths the commissioner's nephew, Frances Hardy, swore before he'd gone swimming in the surf. In the dark, I could just see Gillam's eyes glittering like a hawk in his narrow face, and I knew his hands were as quick as a serpent strike. "I think he covered us all and all our families back to Adam and Eve. He swore he'd find us out and when he did, we wouldn't see the sun before London." He shifted in his seat. "I don't think he saw anything that would help, but he did sound determined. I doubt his uncle will give him another plum if he doesn't get us back."

We came onto the Neck through the watch after first light. Brand had arranged a ride in a farm wagon heading for market and we were two extra buyers with a slave in back. "Come tonight at closing and we'll settle," I said as we stretched our legs near the market. We were all exhausted and looked towards a bunk before anything. Julius had laid down in back beneath some hay, but he it wasn't enough to take the chill from his bones.

I'm not sure how Mouse got back, but he was at the Sword before I was. He looked excited, ready to find out all that happened, but I waved him away till night. I hadn't told any of them that we'd been shorted, but it would hold no surprise. I just hoped they didn't swear vengeance on Brand. It would be just another score to settle and not one I meant to follow. Brand had done what I would and given us a portion when he didn't have to.

Maggie listened intently as I undressed to get some sleep before we served dinners. "I'll take what's given every time, rather than gamble on what's not," said Maggie when I'd finished. "He may have done you a service. You can be shut of Draper and still fatten your purse." She watched as I counted out our shares from the hundred pounds, twenty for the others and double that for me–I got a captain's rate. As always, when she had no direct hand in, I gave her a tenth of mine. It seemed a reasonable bargain for the risk she suffered at having us so close.

Eight

I KNEW it would be a month or more before Draper was on alarm, so I tried to put him and his business out of my mind. I found it easy for the first weeks, and then far beyond, since I didn't see Draper regularly. He would never venture through the door of the Sword—it was well beneath any place he'd step in his fancy shoes and shiny buckles, and I certainly had no cause to enter his store or the new house he was building in the South End. Since he could only guess at what happened, I didn't fear he would send someone to waylay me from an alley.

But what truly stole my thoughts was the trouble that was boiling up in every street and on every dock. Now, it was the new Customs taxes passed on by Townshend that split the people in town as clean as a block of oak beneath a maul and wedge. But it was hard to keep track of the sides, since we all lived together in a tangle.

I thought it was just the same as the Stamps, except we were all a year older. The Sons of Liberty howled about "freedom" and "the rights of man," but at the center were two circles of rich people fighting over the money in the middle. They fought about the size of the fortune the merchants could build for themselves and how much of it the Customs men and the King could take for their chests. I tried to stay clear and let them fight over the pounds and shillings I'd never see, but the troubles were like an English bog—one tiny step and you were in to your knees.

If the players weren't always shouting in our ears, it would have been near a comedy to watch. The new taxes weren't much different than the Stamps, which started Boston on "nonimportation" all over again. The Sons told the crowds that they could punish the English by refusing to import goods. The great merchants—Hancock, Rowe, Dorr, and a few others—were all for it, since it would line their pockets and drive out the smaller ones who challenged them. Those with large stores or more than one would sell goods they had stored in their warehouses without having to import anything new—and get high prices because goods would be scarce. The small merchants didn't have goods in storage and would soon go out of business because they couldn't import new goods to sell.

It meant little to me, or most of those that drank at the Sword, except that the ship trade would slow down again, and keep more angry sailors in Boston and London than out to sea. But I did worry that Parliament tried to give the dogs at Customs more teeth. They'd decided there should be a new Board in the Custom House in Boston to collect silver from every colony in America. To help them along, Parliament gave Customs their own Vice Admiralty Courts so they could seize a man like me in Boston or Newport or New York and take him to London for trial. That way they could be sure he'd pay or end in prison without risking that a jury in the colonies would free him. When the new Commissioners had arrived with royal papers in hand in the fall of 1767, they were sure they were the cocks in the yard.

But the Boston merchants were determined not to let Customs get both hands in their pockets. Although they had power in the courts, Customs still didn't have enough men or arms to face down an angry Boston crowd. Capt. Malcolm had set the example by standing before his locked cellar door with a brace of pistols in his belt and a crowd at his back. He swore loudly that no one would enter to search for undeclared goods, and the unarmed Customs men melted away. Later, he may as well have knocked their wigs off and used them to dust the council table. He marched in to the new Customs office and requested the "customary indulgences" for his ship loaded with sixty pipes of Madeira wine, meaning he was willing to pay tax on twenty.

When Commissioner Paxton and the new ones informed him that there were no indulgences like in years past, the story tellers said Malcolm smiled at them and thanked them for their time, and then smiled again when he came back three days later with legal papers that said the same ship had arrived in ballast.

It was easy for the Customs searchers to see that the ship was empty since he'd unloaded everything a few miles to the south before returning to the harbor. As obvious as he was, there was nothing they could do—they had no proof, no willing witnesses, and they couldn't search his house or warehouse without men and muskets to back them up. They knew that wagons of smuggled goods passed them on the streets every day and there was little they could do about it. For these proud Tory masters, dressed in snow-white wigs and daunting black robes, it must have been like eating gruel.

Soon, Hancock decided to join the parade and put a foot to their breeches. He' become a great hero on the docks since he'd paid off my debt and the others as well. Most thought it was his money that bought what Adams and the Sons of Liberty needed, and the pair now seemed joined like matched horses that never strayed too far from the other. King Hancock, as some in the streets called him, announced that no Customs men would search his ships, as if he could make his own laws. The Tories held a special hatred for Hancock because he acted like a lord when he had nothing but money to raise his rank.

When Customs had the grit to board Hancock's ship *Lydia* in April, the searchers gave up their attempt to inspect the hold when they stared down the muskets of the crew. In the following days, the Commissioners and Hancock's lawyers had wrangled about in the Customs office, with the Board eager to bring Hancock into their new Admiralty Court, either here or in London. They tried every legal trick they could think of, but Hancock seemed to be winning, just like Malcolm had before. They'd raised plenty of toasts to him at the Sword for the next week. It seemed that smuggling goods for sale in the colonies at a high price made him a pure hero to the Sons of Liberty and a pure enemy to Customs.

A few weeks later I was walking the docks in the morning when I passed by the warehouse at Hancock's Wharf, just a few hundred yards from the Sword. Hancock kept stores of rope and rigging and canvas there, and all else to keep his ships supplied and sailing, although Hancock himself never came near it. It was a spring morning and the air was light with the promise of a warm sun later.

I had just taken off my dark green woolen cloak and slung it over my shoulder when John Carleton came blinking from the door and hailed me. "You're lucky to be out walking, Mr. Gray, it's dark as a dungeon in there and you'd think it was December for the cold." He rubbed his hands together and blew on them, then hitched at his breeches. "My knockers feel like they're made of brass."

"I'm glad to be out, Carleton, but I thought you had a moll on Back Street to keep them warm."

"Never mind that, Gray, that's for a morning when I'm busy at night." Carleton was known to run a crew for loading and unloading for other merchants while Customs slept, as well as managing Hancock's warehouse. He turned serious now. "Could you use a bit extra?"

I moved a step towards the warehouse door and spoke a little more softly. "There's always room in my purse, but it depends on the job."

"We're going to need another strong arm when the *Liberty* comes in. The waiters aren't as easy as before, now that Customs offers them a few shillings if they find more for duty. It used to be as simple as a bottle of rum and a good laugh while they watched us unload."

After a bit more conversation, I agreed to help. I'd gathered some crews myself, just like Carleton, but decided there were other ways to make money at night without straining at hogsheads in the hold. But I'd felt a new and uncomfortable debt when I stepped out of gaol using Hancock's silver, and I thought helping Carleton might even that debt a little and put coins in my hand at the same time.

As soon as the *Liberty* came to dock in early May, Customs put two tidewaiters on deck. Carleton was determined to get the goods off the first night, before the Customs men could get up to more mischief.

I was the first one on, just an hour past midnight when the dark was its deepest, climbing silently over the rail where the cargo net hung. And they were right about the waiters on board. The first was ready to shout for help when I offered him a sum to stand in the stern.

"Let's see your face," he demanded, but I took him down from one side before he could swing his whale-oil lantern around to look at me. We found the other one drunk and dead to the world so we left him lying there while I stuffed the first one in the carpenter's closet on the second deck and nailed a board across the door.

It took most of the night to get ninety-six pipes of Madera, more than a hundred gallons each, up and out of the hold. Two men rolled one up the ramp then used the winch to drop it in one of the six wagons we filled. I didn't know where they went, but I didn't care to know either. We left twenty-five of the great barrels so Hancock could appear a legal merchant and pay full duty on them. After we'd finished and pulled the nails from the door, Carleton left the waiter with a threat in his ear and coin in his hand.

The next morning, Hancock's captain took the papers into the Customs office, a legal manifest that showed twenty-five pipes of Madera, only about a hundred short of the real load. Mindful of Carleton's threats and fingering their gelt, the two tidesmen signed the declaration and there was no one willing to say different. That night, there were more toasts to brave Hancock in the taverns because he'd fleeced Customs again, right to their face. Everyone imagined Paxton and the rest spitting mad, but there was nothing to be done. What would they do, try to arrest Hancock when they had no proof? Face a crowd of a thousand and risk their windows and houses and a club to the ear?

But just like a fight between young boys, one weak blow brought another in return. Outraged Tories and the frightened Governor Bernard and the Customs commissioners had all sent desperate pleas to Captain Corner in Halifax. He took their cause and sailed the warship *Romney* to anchor just outside the harbor at the end of May. He was intent on teaching the town a lesson, and started by turning the *Romney's* fifty guns broadside to the docks.

On Lord's Day in June, Maggie and I had kept the Sword closed and took a stroll with the holiday crowd out to breathe the air on a fine sunny day near the docks. We were just two streets up when we heard the shouts from Long Wharf and followed the rest out to the end to see what had stirred a quiet crowd.

Across the water, we could see a press boat from the *Romney* approaching the two merchant ships at anchor in the harbor, and everyone knew their business—they would take whatever men they could find. The merchant ships had seen the same thing and each threw a boat in as fast as they could. We watched and cheered for the sailors as they pulled their oars like madmen to beat the press boat to dock. When they won the race, the crowd began raining stones big enough to crack a skull down on the press gang so they couldn't land. A few thought there might be more sport in welcoming them on shore. "Let them come," they offered, "they can float back, belly up."

If there were any from the Sons of Liberty in the crowd, they would have pushed the crowd to throw the stones, but there were enough sailors about that didn't need any words. They cursed a press boat on sight and many had battled to escape press gangs before in London or New York or Boston. Getting taken into the Navy could be the difference in life and death, and many thought it was no better than gaol even if you lived through it.

Maggie and I decided to open that night, and the crowd was happy and drank their fill at the Sword and the other dock taverns. They celebrated again a few nights later because they surrounded the *Romney's* press gang on shore and rescued the one tar they'd taken. It was illegal to take him, since he was a merchant seaman for an outgoing ship, but if the crowd hadn't freed him, he would have been hauling anchor for the Navy with no way out. I doubt he would have liked his choices any more than I did a few years before.

But unlike the quiet summer after the Stamps, Customs and the Navy kept poking at the Boston crowd until they exploded like one of Hancock's fireworks. Everyone was shocked when they towed Hancock's *Liberty* out near the *Romney* and its guns. Our night work had been turned upside down when the tidewaiter I'd handled changed his story once he got to the safety of the Navy ship. He claimed he was threatened and nailed shut in the hold while he heard men unload a hundred pipes of wine. Customs now hoped to take the ship and sell it, along with its remaining cargo.

Because the news about the *Liberty* spread along the docks like water on a pitched deck, there was an angry crowd waiting when Customs Inspector Harrison and the son of Commissioner Hallowell rowed back to the dock, and the mob set on them like locusts. Mouse said that few of the bricks and stones found their targets, and the crowd seemed to cuff them about more for entertainment than for breaking bones—but they were beaten down several times and dragged through the garbage and shit in the gutter in the middle of the street.

Later that night, after celebrating and drinking a few more pints along the way, the crowd found Harrison's pleasure boat and paraded it about town before lighting a fire with it near the Liberty Tree in the South End. They howled like a pack of dogs and ventured on to the houses of Harrison and Hallowell to break out the glass with their stones and sticks, stopping to smash a few other Tory windows along the way.

The screaming crowds and heavy rocks unnerved the Customs families. A gaggle of them, upwards of sixty, were first taken to the *Romney* and then to Castle William in the harbor. During the next weeks, they acted as if they were off on holiday there, inviting people for tea and dining. They were convinced that troops would come to rescue them this time, since Gov. Bernard said he couldn't guarantee their safety in town.

In the harbor, a string of ships waited to get out to London to bring back goods before nonimportation would begin, but they couldn't get papers because all the Customs idlers were hiding in the castle. When I walked through the town in the mornings, and listened to the sailors and mechanics and tradesmen in the Sword, there was sand in every stew, bugs in every bed, nettles in every garden.

It had all been like bearbaiting up to then. The dogs in the colonies entertained the crowd by racing about here and there, taking flesh and fur from a hind leg or ripping at a shoulder while the English bear strained on its chain and swatted at the pests. The royal governors and Customs were chained tight, with no troops nearby and no courts to back them. If they could get a man in irons and back to England, they would happily kill him, gutted like a terrier that gets too close, but in the colonies, their chain was too short.

But at the end of the summer, we learned that the English would take the bear off its chain, and the town went silent. London had grown tired of fighting for each shilling in Customs, tired of resistance to the taxes to pay for the last war, tired of impudent insults and threatening crowds. The fearsome British army would come with their cannons and muskets and bayonets. They would take over the town and force us to our knees.

Section II

Nine

IT SEEMED no one could talk of anything but the troops, with the men in the tavern making idle threats and the Tories celebrating and dreaming of watching the loud colonials cower and quake at the sight of redcoats and flashing steel. That's why I was surprised when Draper's boy came asking for me, months after I thought he might. I considered brushing off the invitation and letting Draper chase me, but decided instead that it would be easier to set it straight and look ahead. In the end, it was no help.

Draper had lost all the way around–he'd paid a cut rate for the schooner and its goods, paid me fifty pounds to help with the rescue, given Brand several hundred pounds for provisions and payment, and hadn't gotten a penny back. I tried to prepare myself to act angry at Brand, since I would have been owed a hundred and fifty pounds when he came back, but I wasn't the actor Maggie was, or Gillam for that matter. We'd put away a large sum for our work, and I'd have to walk in Shakespeare's shoes to show anger I didn't feel.

I started out facing Draper again in his back room, a tea barrel for a seat and the lamps burning low at dusk as he sat at his desk amid the stacked goods. None of the piles seemed much smaller to me and I noticed that they still were getting switched about, with most of the tea barrels against a wall now, and ladies gowns hanging on a bar close to the curtain for the front. Draper had his coat off and his waistcoat was thick velvet of a rich brown color.

After letting me in at the alley, Draper returned to his desk and had no time for greetings. "He should have been back long ago."

"Maybe the weather was bad or he had to put in for some reason."

"I think he's gone," said Draper, waving his hand toward the ocean, "I think he stole it from me."

I waited a moment before answering. "That's a serious thing to say about a man. If he shows up tomorrow, I'll be sure tell him how far you trusted him."

"I'm not worried about what you say to Brand, and my trust is the least he'll have to worry about if he's not back with my money."

Again I waited, trying to separate what I should say from what I wanted to say, but I didn't wait long enough. "What'll you do, Master Draper, report him to the sheriff? Or send your 'dentured boy to find him and pester him with a broom?"

I was surprised to see Draper smile back at me. "You're too sure of yourself, Gray. You're not the only strongarm on the docks, you and your savage, and I've found plenty who'll do as I ask for less than you. You're a good thief, but not much more. I could probably get the Sons to stick you in a tar barrel if I told them you were an informer. Mackintosh is always ready for some fun and mostly in debt now besides." His smile disappeared and he gripped the edge of his desk with his left hand. "But it's not just Brand I suspect. I think you were in it from the beginning, picking my pocket first, and then his to keep quiet."

I should have been angry at his accusation if it wasn't true, lashing back with my words or a hand, but it was all I could do to keep from smiling. He'd been taken by his own designs, made a plan that didn't work, and lost enough to buy the Sword twice over. I thought he was in over his head, his eyes in the sky with his feet stuck in the mud. I sat quietly for a moment, then rose to leave.

"So that's how it is then, Gray? You'll steal from me, just like Brand, and still come close enough to spit on?"

I took a step toward him and my hands quickly made fists, but I kept my arms anchored at my sides. Striking him would do no good, but my hands shook with the effort. "Think what you want, Draper. You'll know where I am, and if you don't, it's not because I'm hiding from you. But I'll wager I'll never see you again, because you don't have the spine."

I turned and walked directly toward the back, but Draper called out. "I'll get what's mine, Gray, one way or the other, what I paid you and what Brand paid you as well. You think you're a lord on the docks, but you'll be a beggar soon enough."

Draper's threats didn't worry me much, although I should have realized he was an enemy just as dangerous and determined as Tobin had been in getting me in debtor's prison. The days and evenings that followed were busy at the Sword and the streets were alive with all types of business that people wanted to finish before the troops stormed in. But at night, I sometimes found myself awake and in a sweat. Some of the dreams had come back, where the dark was like a gaol with no escape and I was held fast at the ankles and wrists. No candles could burn in the foul air, and the smells of blood and gunpowder and scurvy choked my throat and left me gasping.

If I opened my eyes and stayed still long enough, I could find the outline of the window in my room on the back wall of the Sword and the small chest which held my second shirt and breeches and a pair of knives. But the dreams gradually went away and I thought of Draper as only another gentleman without the spine to back up his words.

ONE REASON the Sword stayed so busy was that we had started to draw more from the middling men after the rough crowd frightened the Tories and got rid of the Stamps. Some smaller merchants, shopkeepers, smiths, and builders began to come in and they mixed a bit with the mechanics and tars. The law-abiding Whigs and the men who made their speeches needed the hard edge from the docks to back them up, while the brawlers needed someone to choose the right targets for them.

William Molineux was a hardware merchant, but a rough man that ruled the gang in the North End streets near the Sword. He always looked like the blood was up in his face and his fists were clenched, searching about for a likely villain. One night he sat at a table with a friend and started in on the leeches in the new Customs board. He rattled off the offices and their salaries like a schoolboy with the alphabet—five commissioners at five hundred pounds each, clerks at one hundred pounds, a solicitor for two hundred, a cashier got another hundred, the same as the comptroller, not to mention inspectors, tidewaiters, and searchers.

When he finally got to the end, he blessed them all with a string of oaths. "They do no more service than a rat in the hold, eating our food, and stealing our money," he announced to the heads that turned his way, but I found myself mumbling under my breath. Of course they were stealing, but I didn't see that what they took belonged to me or any of the crowd that was listening, since Molineux was the only one in the importing trade.

Whenever Molineux or one of the others started in on the Tories and the King, which was most nights by this time, they usually ended up on the informers like Ebenezer Richardson who'd made his way for several years by naming the smugglers and getting a good percentage in return. Even the treasurer of Massachusetts, a full-blood Tory, had complained when he found that Paxton paid his informers out of the one-third share that was supposed to go to the province, while the other thirds went to himself and the governor. It was no wonder Richardson never set foot outside without a hatchet beneath his coat.

Ebenezer Mackintosh from the South End came sometimes as well, something he wouldn't have done before Hancock and Adams persuaded the gangs from the South End and North End to stop their regular brawl on Pope's Day and march down the street together like a rough and ragged militia. Mackintosh still took care to venture into the North End with at least a pair of fighters with him. He was as thick as the soles of the shoes he made, but cocksure ever since the Sons got him off for the wreckage of Hutchinson's house. His face was flat, his nostrils flared, and his arms were thick with muscle. He wasn't one to try using words when a club would do as well. The Sons of Liberty kept him like a guard dog, and he was proud to sit up when they offered a bloody bone. It was Mackintosh that Draper felt could be easily persuaded to do me harm for the cause of liberty, since it was clear a few shillings and a well-told lie was enough to set him loose.

But I paid special attention when Samuel Adams began stopping in every few weeks. I guessed that he and the few that came with him must have tired of talking to the same crowd at the Bunch of Grapes and the Salutation Inn, places where they planned their mischief and could curse the King without a care. Some said Adams worked like a coaster, stopping at each port in a loop, visiting every tavern on the waterfront and most that were set back in the streets, leaving out only the high Tory fronts.

Everyone knew the story of how the Tories had hounded his family near to the alms house. His father had the sand to begin a bank for Americans to get around the need for British coins, but the Tories wouldn't share a penny and eventually charged him with debts even a rich man couldn't pay. Now, Adams worked as hard as any beaver in the forest to punish them for their deeds.

I'd heard about Samuel Adams long before I'd seen him, since I had no place as a freeholder at the Town Meetings and even less interest. But Mouse went often to sit in the gallery or lean in a corner, and gave a fair report of all Adams said. "It's . . . it's . . . his words, Nicholas. You wouldn't give a farthing for his clothes, and you'd wonder if he could carry a bucket of his own beer."

"That's no worry," I replied, "since they say he hasn't brewed enough to wash his feet in the last few years, and not much more before that."

"But . . . it's hardly a proper meeting if he isn't there."

Adams looked no better when he sat at the table to the left of the fire in the Sword with a pottery pint in his hand. He wore a tired red coat of plain broadcloth and he looked like he might use all of his strength to lift a quill pen, and even then he couldn't stop his hand from shaking with palsy. For a brewer who'd never sold enough to support his family, he had little interest in the beer in his cup, about the same interest he showed in collecting the taxes about town. Each year in his time as a collector, he ended with overdue bills three or four times more than the other collectors. It seemed he always forgot those for the likes of Mackintosh and Molineux and any others who led the gangs in the street. Until he opened his mouth, he might have been a small man of no account, mildly watching the world go by.

According to Mouse, he didn't give the longest speeches at Town Meeting, and he let James Otis or some of the others spin a web for a few hours for the people willing to sit. In the Sword and the other taverns, Adams would mostly listen while the angry men spilled out their complaints. He'd smile and nod, watching with knowing eyes and shabby clothes, and most believed he cared about their stories and understood how they'd been wronged.

But with ten or fifteen standing about the Sword, it was easy to bring him out. He was careful with his words, since the wrong ones could get him hanged for treason. But a few sentences would burn like lightning in a summer sky, flashing down to a point with a terrible growl and rumble in the background. He'd have the idlers cheering at his talk that the British had no right to tax us without our consent. It made no difference that not more than one or two in the room were freeholders and had property that would risk a penny of tax in their lives.

His words stirred the fighters in the crowd, and they would start to shout and pound the tables and get ready to rush out to gather stones for some Tory windows and possibly a tar barrel in case they met some Customs dog on the way. But just as he'd set the spurs to them, he brought the bit up in their teeth just as quick, warning them that violence without cause or for private gain made the true patriots look rough and crude and unworthy of consideration. "We should show them our resolve and save our bullets for when they are truly needed," he ended.

Someone usually bought a full round of drinks after he'd finished—it always seemed there was a proper purse for the talkers, even though they were being taxed to the bone—and Maggie would serve them around with a twirl and gleam. Adams himself took no more beer and no notice of Maggie, and sat with a small smile on his face, as if his mind was beyond the walls. I thought that if Adams had taken to the pulpit, he could have written a sermon that made the congregation burn as they left, ashamed of their own actions and eager to correct any others who strayed.

By September, everyone in town knew the troops were coming, although the frightened Gov. Bernard wouldn't admit it. But the news took the cork from the bottle and Adams was heedless of what poured out. It was a dark time, like the hours at sea waiting for the storm that was thrashing on the horizon, except the people of Boston stood watching for weeks.

The rumors were as thick as London fog on the docks— they'd arrest everyone in Town Meeting, close down the port, pull down the Town House, stand guard at every corner. It seemed Adams couldn't help himself. He stood near the fireplace in the Sword one day, his eyes hot as the coals beside him, his shaking hand kept firmly in his coat pocket, and spoke like he'd practiced every word.

"The bloodybacks are coming to take our town and the Tories say we'll faint away when we smell the gunpowder. But we'll fight them instead. There's not a soldier alive that's a match for the brave men of Boston and Massachusetts fighting for their freedom. If we let them land here, there will be nothing to stop their designs. Governor Bernard and his council will take the bread from our mouths and the roof above us. You've seen what they intend—they'll keep adding placemen in Customs, they'll take away our government and strangle the voices of free men." He paused and his voice got softer. "Soon, they'll have men paying taxes on their own land! If we don't stop them, they'll force us straight down the road to Rome. We'll answer to the Pope and be beggared if we don't kneel down!"

Some of the tars at the tables stood up now, and their low voices combined to make a growl like a cur with its lips pulled back.

"They've let slip the dogs of war," Adams said darkly, his voice almost a whisper now, "and there's no turning back. We'll meet them at the docks, our muskets loaded and primed. They'll find us ready to protect what's most sacred—our rights as free men."

After a bit, Adams left with two he'd come with, but Peter Burns remained behind, sitting by himself at a table while the benches were filled with drones showering oaths on the soldiers they'd soon greet. Maggie and I had just refilled their cups and I sat down across from Burns as he counted out two shillings and six pence for the twelve gills of rum we'd just served out—a fair price at two and a half pence each.

Burns would have been another of the firebrands to graduate from Harvard, like Samuel Adams, but he'd had to give up the school and go home after Nathan Wheelright went bankrupt. When the French gave up fighting in the last war, there was no more money to be made by selling supplies at high prices to the British troops and Wheelright was just one that turned belly up after borrowing heavily to buy military goods he hoped sell quickly. He took Burns' father and several others down with him. Burns found an easy enemy in the Tories—like Adams and Otis, the money men had given him a lasting target by mistreating his father. Young Peter began working in Matthew Hovey's law office after leaving Harvard. He had the tongue of a lawyer already, although he mostly wrote contracts and prepared suits and read whatever law books he could borrow, though he said there were few to be had.

When the mood struck him, his blue eyes danced beneath a three-corner hat and his hair was the color of corn, tied at the back. His nose was straight, never broken, and he was one of the few who had escaped pox marks. With a London suit on his slim body, he would have matched any of the young dandies, but his plain blue coat was already worn at the sleeves where he leaned at a desktop and his waistcoat missed a button at the bottom. When he picked up a cup, his right hand usually showed ink from blotting a spill. He was dark now, with the thoughts of ball and powder still hanging in the air.

"Have you come up that far now you can stand drinks for the crowd?" I asked.

He shrugged. "I'm just carrying the purse today."

I wondered if it came direct from Hancock or if some other merchant gave it so that the Sons of Liberty would smile on him. "Has Adams made the same speech before?"

Burns looked puzzled. "Not the same words, but the point's the same."

"I just wondered," I offered, "since a Tory might take those words and call them treason. If any would risk swearing they heard them, Adams could hang in London."

Burns' eyes flashed anger now. "But we're not in London, and the dog that took his words to the Council wouldn't last out the day." He glared now, as if I'd given him an insult. "But what else is there to say, Nicholas Gray? We'll have redcoats in our soup if we don't stop them."

"That may be, but why mention land tax and kneeling to the pope? Anyone that thinks can see that's all smoke up the chimney."

"Did you see anyone here question it? A man who burns hot enough will load a musket without thinking."

I shook my head at him as I got up to take the coins to the box under the bar. "He'll probably be the first to catch a ball in his ear as well."

I continued thinking about Adams as I squatted down to get a tray for empty cups from beneath the bar. Hearing him call for blood had unsettled me some, but it wasn't until months later that I wished with all my heart that I'd never heard his words.

Ten

I LIKED TO WALK THE DOCKS in the morning, even during winter as long as I could find a path through the snow. I'd leave the Sword just after sunrise and make a circle, first north a quarter mile to Capt. Greenough's Shipyard, then back south near the docks, passing Hancock's Wharf and the others on Fish St., past Long Wharf near Faneuil Hall market and Town Hall and the Custom House, and keep going all the way past Fort Hill and the British long guns at South Battery, into the South End where Samuel Adams lived with his frugal wife and big black dog and Negro servant who was a slave before he freed her. I could stretch my legs with space ahead, no scarlet ship's walls or barred prison doors to turn me back, no shackles to make me shuffle and fall.

But as we waited for the troops that would come to punish us, the fear and anger seemed as dense as any thicket. I usually stopped to talk along the way—a foreman at the shipyard, dockmen ready to load for London, line and net menders, mechanics hoping for work at the ropewalks, the haunted man they called the Crab because one arm stayed curved like a claw after he'd gotten it crushed in an anchor chain. He should have been in the almshouse but chose to sleep in a door or a pile of nets as long as he didn't freeze. They would all trade a bit of gossip or news for a few stories from the Sword or one of the other taverns, whether they were true or not. Now, I felt like we were weaving a bit of thin, bright cloth to hold for a moment, as if it would protect us from the hard wind that would follow the troops down our streets.

For most of my time in Boston, I'd found more peace on the docks than anywhere else. When the weather was fair and the air didn't feel like an icy hand at my neck, I would often walk the length of Long Wharf, near a half mile out into the harbor, and stop for a few moments. It was the heart of Boston, the center of the tangle of ships and docks that brought in most of the traffic and the money, legal and illegal. I would find myself staring out, past Castle Island to the emptiness beyond, where a storm could take the strongest ship to the bottom like it was no more than a splinter. In my mind, each ship that docked had won a victory, each that sailed placed a wager on fair weather and likely winds, a process repeated hundreds of times every year. My heart often swelled and quaked at the sight of a ship heading out, even if it was no more than a brig loaded with salt cod.

But on the last day of September 1768, I walked between the shops of Long Wharf on one side and the moorings on the other with a deep sense of dread. At the end, I looked out and finally saw what I expected: royal troop ships gathering to the north, six in sight and more in the distance, a ship of the line at the head bristling with three ranks of guns. Here was the grand British Army ready to invade Boston, as if we were a French garrison or a Spanish fort.

The Tories in town would say we'd brought it on ourselves. I thought that story was like locking some poor wretch in the pillory after she'd been caught lying with a married man. She had a willing partner but it was her alone that took the blame and suffered the stones and filth on her face. I'm sure the rich Tories were nearly breathless with excitement, preparing to celebrate, and I'd bet the same for the Customs commissioners and their families. They had been hiding at Castle William since June and couldn't wait to set their dainty feet back in Boston—as long as the soldiers went ahead to protect them.

IT WAS EARLY MORNING when they started and dark before they finished, rank after rank of soldiers parading down the shops on Long Wharf straight up King Street to the Town House, Negroes drumming, flags flying, bayonets fixed and glinting in the sun, swarming out of the transports like fire ants in Guadeloupe. They were here to teach us a lesson, like a master who caned his apprentice or the captain who flogged a yardsman for being the last one to reach deck. Each carried sixteen musket balls in his case, and the grenadiers in their pointed bearskin hats reached near seven feet tall. The officers fancied up ahead and behind, looking down from their mounts at the crowds they would soon be bullying about. The lines seemed like they'd never end as one ship after another crowded the harbor to unload. The cannons dug trenches in the streets direct to the spot where they fixed them to point at the Town House door. If the *Romney* or one of the ships of the line fired broadside, they could put the town to flame in an hour.

I watched more than a thousand march in the first day and by the time they'd all arrived in November there were four regiments, nearly three thousand men, the 14th and 29th followed by the dregs of Ireland in fancy red coats from the 64th and 65th. They could set a man to watch every house in town and have enough left over to roam the streets searching for trouble. If they didn't find it, they could make it themselves.

The mood was grim at the Sword for a long time. Before the troops came, the tars swore vengeance on any that would try to rule them with arms and steel. But most knew underneath that it was easy to say the words, and harder to do the deeds. None were afraid to mix in a brawl with their clubs and staffs, but there weren't many who wanted to keep walking down a musket bore when a British regular had it full cocked. They'd seen enough at sea and in the ports and they knew the redcoats were the best soldiers in the world—they'd even turned out the French a few years back. The Boston dock crowd hated the British regulars but it didn't mean they were ready to take a shot at close range.

Adams had persuaded everyone bring their muskets to a town meeting two weeks before the troops came–they informed Governor Bernard they were worried about a French invasion–and the number was enough to think of firing when the ships landed. Just the noise of stacking them gave Gov. Bernard the faints, but by the time the first Army boots hit King St., there weren't enough Americans who were ready to draw blood and give their own.

The soldiers were everywhere in their bloody red coats. While the talkers in meetings argued every point till it collapsed dead on the ground, it was the men in the street that got most of the trouble. The patrols and the watch at the Neck and off-duty regulars made free with their gun butts and bayonets. Plenty of them were just one step out of Irish prison or Newgate or a noose. Now, a uniform gave them license to have their own way. When the mechanics took the liberty of walking at the side of the street where the wagons wouldn't hit them, bloodyback regulars would shove them about, claiming their right.

When they were off duty, they searched about for a place to drink up their scant pay and a whore willing to lift her skirts. The money went so fast that the army took to paying in bread and meat rather than letting the troops put every penny into the hands of a Boston tavernman. Of course the army had to pay military prices for the food as well, only about twice regular.

There was money to be made, with almost three thousand men ready to eat, drink, gamble, and whore. As soon as the officers walked on the wharf, they began scouting for rooms while the regulars froze in tents on the Common. Most landlords held out at first, knowing they might lose their windows if they rented to the Army, but it didn't take long to change. Molineux, once the leader of the liberty men in the North End, rented out a warehouse for a barracks and got more each month than he usually did in several. Wealthy John Rowe had always been a trimmer, though he claimed to be a Whig at heart. He rented places all about town to the officers at twenty pounds or more a year, rates no one else would dream of paying. His name got on the provisions contracts, too, and if he didn't clear enough from that, it seemed the Tories and officers invited him to dinner every night. Even our liberty lawyer James Otis seemed ready to topple over, but he'd been on the short list with Adams and Hancock for hanging at Tyburn if the Londoners could prove sedition, so the British officers shunned him.

Most of Boston fell in line, and the Customs sharks came back, too, after setting off fireworks at the Castle when the troop ships came. They couldn't wait to pay back some who'd ruffled their wigs now that they had soldiers to protect them. They immediately began a round of high entertainments and dinners, with Major General Gage and his officers wearing their gorgets and polished swords and toasting King George and every lord and Tory from Boston to London.

Samuel Adams had to be content with putting thorns in the beds of the soldiers and the Tories instead of facing them behind a row of muskets. There were plenty who took their time to plan ways to vex them, but it was usually Adams who got the blame and the credit. They started out by hoisting a tar barrel on a mast on Beacon Hill. People made sure the Army and the Tories heard the plans to light it when all was ready. Everyone in the country around Boston would see it and rush to town at once—ten thousand muskets killing redcoats and Tories with every shot. After the upper families and the Governor's Council worried at it for a few days, Bernard finally ordered the sheriff to take it down. The crowds had a good laugh when it was found empty.

London thought they'd punished Adams and his followers some months back by shutting down the General Court. They were banned from meeting until they took back the letter sent to the other colonies suggesting they work together to resist the Townshend duties. Instead, the Sons called a new meeting just before the troops came and named it a convention so it wouldn't be illegal. Nothing came of it right off, but now they took advantage of their punishment. Since there was no General Court, there was no one to pay salaries to Bernard and Hutchinson and the rest of the provincial government. There couldn't be a commissioner for the troops, either, since he had to be named by the Court, so there was no one to officially provide quarters or provisions.

The town meeting stoutly declared the redcoats should stay in the Castle in the harbor and the town wasn't required to provide quarters till it was full. That would work well for the Sons, since Castle William was too far away for soldiers to help if a crowd took to chasing a Customs man. So Colonel Dalyrimple took the job of seizing buildings wherever he could, including Faneuil Hall and the Town House, but he was still forced to argue with Adams and the like about quarters. Most of the Army regulars were left in cold tents on the Common, where the officers helped them raise the devil with drills and drums, horse races and floggings.

It was already freezing at night and no one had thought the royal army would be forced to sleep outside. One regiment tried to get in to the old, empty Manufactory House in the North End, but the Sons helped the squatters there and they boarded themselves in and the lobsters out. They took pains to sneak in food past the watch at night until they finally made a mistake. An Irishman somehow got in through a side door and the soldiers took the building and ran the squatters out.

Maggie and I figured we could keep the Sword filled with soldiers if we wanted and we might even raise our prices, like the merchants and landlords who gladly took the King's money. The coins we took in would look and spend just the same as those paid by the Sons. But we couldn't stomach the thought of being on the same side as Paxton and the Governor and the high and mighty who thought they owned the streets and the air we breathed. A few redbirds came in during the first month and we told them straight out to go further on. Some of the dock crowd stood behind me and Julius when we refused them and they decided moving on was best as well, though they stopped to spit just outside the door.

We hated the sight of the redcoats, but I knew I might have been wearing one if I was a bit younger. It was easy enough to get on the wrong side of a constable in London or drunk enough so you wouldn't know the shilling thrust in your hand was the King's and legal reason you could be taken. It wasn't like being pressed into the Navy, but there were plenty taken off the streets who would do almost anything to get out. The soldiers got fed, but that was the best they could say, and some of the food would turn a dog away.

Some deserted almost as soon as they set foot on land. There were plenty in the first weeks who hoped for a new start in the colonies if they could only find a place to hide. But the ones who couldn't met their end quickly.

Early on, the army made a show of bringing back a deserter in irons and parading him out to shoot him. Maggie and I joined the crowd that walked to the Common on a cold day, our cloaks pulled tight. The spectators were an odd lot, a mix of boys and mechanics and fishwives alongside curious merchants. The Sons of Liberty were there as well, like they always were if more than two people stood together. I spotted some of what they called the Loyal Nine, Avery and Chase and Field, who met in the South End to find ways to poke at the royal government. But there were Tories, too, some that would have given up dinner for a chance to hear the drums beat and watch the red uniforms march about.

"Where did they catch him?" asked Maggie as we approached the Common up Queen Street.

"I'm told he traded off his coat in a bawd's house on Salem St. and tried to get out by the Neck on a farm wagon after a couple of days. It was against his luck that someone from the 29th who knew him was at the check there."

We kept walking and the crowd got thicker. You could feel the excitement in some as they got nearer while others fell more silent. "What's the good in killing him here for everyone to see?" asked Maggie.

I was puzzled for a moment, and turned to look at her, since it seemed plain as the King's nose. Her cheeks were colored red from the wind. "It's the same as the pillory and the gallows. They think it might make some a little less likely to try sneaking off." We lined up in the crowd, and the drummers began and the bugles started in, too. I looked about and saw some eager faces and felt a wave of anger flush through me. "Look at them—there are Tories here who own shops or have a sum from Britain that love to see good discipline, the kind that ends with someone else's life. Everyone stays in their place, and there's no question where it is."

"There wasn't much for this boy," muttered Maggie, "just the army or the graveyard."

They were beginning to bring him out from a little stockade they'd built, and the crowd buzzed like a honey bee. I had to move closer to speak in Maggie's ear. "It's a cruel thing to kill a boy for trying to get away. The officers will stand and give the orders like they're ordering a plate of stew and act just as high, if not higher, after the drummers scrape him off the ground."

The little squad marched out now and their officer checked their weapons. They put a blindfold on the boy and you could see his pink cheeks flushed, like he wouldn't need to shave for a year yet, and he sagged down with his hands behind, back against a wide beech tree. He started to whimper and cry and the orders seemed to move as slow as a scull on the swells as the officer went down the list that got them ready to fire. It wouldn't test their marks much, standing less than twenty feet shy.

Maggie's hand clutched my arm now and clamped hard when the order came to cock and present. The report echoed off Beacon Hill and the buildings behind us and the smoke lifted quickly in the chill air. The boy's body went down and pooled blood out his chest and the smooth gray tree bark was tattered and bloody behind him. The officer continued his orders for cleaning and shouldering before the doctor went to him and pronounced him dead. They had the Negroes pick him up and take him off in a wagon.

Maggie still clutched my arm and I looked aside at her. I could see the muscle in her jaw flexed tight. She continued to stare toward the wagon as it went back down the hill. Others in the crowd turned to go. One shouted out, "Well, there's one less to come at us now" and got some hearty shouts in response.

She spoke without looking at me. "It's all a part of the same, isn't it Nicholas? I understand hanging murderers for what they've done to others, but this is all for naught. They wouldn't even be here if it weren't for the quarrel over a few shillings of duty one way or the other."

I was surprised because I wouldn't have guessed her mind would travel that road, and I thought a bit before answering. "It's not pretty, but it's not much different here than somewhere else. If they weren't here in America, they'd still be hanging and shooting some for deserting."

"But this is going to turn Nicholas, I can feel it. Between Adams and the Sons and the thick heads in London, there'll be shooting soon enough." She turned and pointed me back down toward the Sword after the others. "Will you fight, Nicholas, once they start?"

I shook my head, tempted to tell her about my time in the Navy, but I drove those thoughts away, sure there was no good to come of it. "That's too far to say, Maggie. It won't happen right now and I'd do everything not to. But when it does, there won't be room in the middle to think about it. That's the easy way to get shot—if one side misses there's always the other to take a turn."

Eleven

I'LL NEVER FORGET when Grendel first stepped into our lives a few months later, tearing at the night like a bear that's caught one of the hounds, leaving bones and skin and flesh scattered about. It wasn't the first time I'd had to face down a dangerous man or wished for another set of eyes so I could watch in front and behind at the same time. But this time, it wasn't just my own neck I worried about. His threats extended beyond, to a woman I thought that I loved–though I still stumble at the meaning of the word–and a man or two that I'd begun to think of like brothers.

It started as an ordinary evening in Boston in early 1769. We'd made it through our first winter with the troops clogging every street and corner. I was in the middle of another argument with Peter Burns on the truth and lies printed by the Liberty crowd in the *Journal of Occurrences* when Grendel filled the tavern door with his great body.

Outside, spring was still too far away to see but the ground was gradually thawing, releasing the smell of damp earth mixed with the garbage that had been frozen beneath the snow banks. I had brought a candle from near the bar and begun to read, leaning close to see the words, when I heard the creak of the front door and Burns strode in and sat opposite me.

"I'll just have some cider, Nicholas, my throat is dry." His three-cornered hat was set precisely on his head and though his coat was a dull green and ink stained his fingers, his eyes were dancing. No one would guess him a tradesman, like Paul Revere with his scarred hands and bare wrists, but he had no gentlemen's airs about him either.

"No doubt from talking too much." I said as I went to the bar. "You don't want spices do you?"

"No, just the hard cider."

"That's good since we don't have any and you'd have to go back to your friends at the Bunch of Grapes or visit some Tory house to get them." After I brought him his mug, I sat down to look at the paper again.

We'd become friends of a sort. Even before the troops came, he would enter the Sword with a flourish, have a mug of ale or a gill of rum and wait for someone to sit with him so he could begin arguing. He wasn't particular about the subject, although he always managed a speech about the virtues of the Sons of Liberty and the sins of the Tories.

On a slow night, I'd sit with him and we both came to enjoy it, though the words we exchanged weren't all friendly. We'd argued about nearly everything, beginning with the British taxes and the mob wrecking Governor Hutchinson's house. Later, we moved on to Samuel Adams counting votes at town meeting from anyone who could stand on two feet instead of just freeholders and how refusing to import goods favored the rich merchants–both Tories and Whigs–over the small ones. I hated the lords and the Tories in England and in Boston as much as anyone, but I always played the devil with Burns because he was so sure of himself, just so he'd be forced to explain.

"You're a serious reader, aren't you, Gray."

I nodded but didn't see a need to answer.

"They say you'll stand over the hardest men at the end of a scuffle, but there's more than once I've found you reading like a scholar. It's not a common mix."

I quickly saw one of the pictures my mind turns to when I can't bear to keep looking at what is around me. My father took my hand as we climbed the steps to Duke Humfrey's library at Oxford on a warm fall day, afternoon sun streaming in from the tall windows trying to warm the cold stone floors. We got a nod from the keeper near the door since my father cleaned the rooms and precious books, the smell of rosemary bright from my father's hands and the stone floors where he rubbed it in. We walked down the center aisle, dust floating silently in the shafts of light, readers standing before the desks, the books spread flat and trailing their chains to the shelves behind. The scholars were so intent on the words they didn't look up as we passed, as if the ink and flat paper might yield gold and silver if they searched hard enough.

"It's the reading came first, but it didn't help when there was a hand squeezing my neck." We were quiet a minute before I spoke again. "I see that they sent our famous painter Copley to fix the Governor's portrait at Harvard. It must have been a sad sight with the heart cut out."

"A sad sight but a true likeness. It would have been a better picture if they could have taken out his spine as well."

I laughed and shook my head. "Who is this Amicus who signs the *Journal*? It would take more than one man to make up all these stories."

"Make up stories? You must have missed some of the words right at the head. There it is," he pointed, "*A True Account*."

I laughed again. "Amicus may be a friend to some, but I wouldn't want him telling tales on me. I'd guess about one in ten is true." I gestured down at the paper on the table. "Is it Samuel Adams who writes all of this?"

Burns took a moment to think, and looked about quickly before he decided he could speak a bit more freely. "There's a group that works together."

"And you?"

He shrugged. "I've had a hand in when they need help."

"Why have it printed in New York? There are plenty of printers here."

"So we're sure all the colonies know what's happening. It's easy for them to forget since they don't see redcoats on every corner and a harbor filled with warships. This way it's printed and sent out without fail. Here, we'd have to get the copies on a coaster or put them on a wagon to pass the redcoat guards at the Neck and who knows what could happen then?"

I nodded because I could see the need, but I still felt a burr in my boot. "There's hardly enough soldiers to commit all these robberies and insults and rough handling of our dear women." I pointed to the paper. "Here's a mild merchant pierced with a bayonet for no reason, there's a child beaten with a gun butt in the streets. And don't forget the grandfather who finds a bloodyback lying with his virtuous girl and nearly dies from shock and the scuffle when he made to complain."

Burns shrugged again, like what I'd said was of no moment. "You know what happens on the streets with the soldiers, and there's nothing we could say about Customs that would make their crimes worse than they are."

"So printing up lies is all right, as long as it's the right people doing it?"

Burns flared up a bit now, his eyes hot. "That's the way it's done, Gray. We're under siege, there's a soldier around every corner ready to take your money and your liberty. Adams calls it 'working the machine' and we'll keep at it until the fire burns too hot for them. If everything's not true, there's enough that is." He stopped for a moment and gathered himself. "People get used to things and before you know it, some would be saying we're better off this way, with the soldiers spending their money and the Army buying our goods and paying rent." He stopped to shake his head. "No, people need to remember what's at stake and they might not if we didn't paint a bright picture."

When I studied Burns then, the dim light reflecting off his fair cheeks, he looked a boy to me, though he was only about three years shy of my twenty-eight years. He was tall, bright, and handsome, unmarked by pox, fair hair tied in a neat tail on his neck. He was a candle burning at both ends, but with plenty left in between.

My years in the London streets and the Royal Navy and living as a wanted man had made me older. If his eyes saw a fine castle on a hill, mine saw the poor wretches carrying the stones and giving their blood and sweat to build it and who were lucky to get a crust in return. Or I would imagine the dungeon beneath it, built to cage anyone who tried to get back some riches.

I was ready to go on, to poke at the Sons and their fine words, but the door opened before I could get started. I'd seen Grendel many times before, since he was so hard to miss, but I'd tried hard to stay clear of him.

He'd given me pause since he'd first set foot on the docks more than a year before. He'd come across on the same ship as Customs Commissioner Paxton and the new commissioners, Hulton and Burch, and had been given a few shillings to protect them and their families until they had they walked safely down the gangway and Long Wharf to the waiting carriage. By chance, they landed on Pope's Day, when the brawlers ruled the streets and knocked heads for fun after the parade mocked the Papists. Crowds of them took the airs of gentlemen when they knocked on doors and demanded money with a monkey's rhyme. Paxton knew Boston and the danger that day, so he sought out a man whose name on the passenger list was Greendale. Everyone, including himself, called him Grendel.

He was easy enough to find, taller than anyone on board and broad-shouldered as well, so big he would have been forced to stoop low in the rooms beneath the deck and turn sideways to fit through cabin doors. I am taller than most in America, a full six feet, but Grendel looked down on me by three inches again. The surprising part was that when he stood by himself at a distance, he didn't seem large, his arms and legs thick but natural in size, like smaller men who lifted crates on the docks. The single exception was his head which was too large for someone even his size, broad across the cheekbones, his nose flattened and turned to one side. Curling brown hair hung to his shoulders beneath a dark flop hat. He breathed loudly through his mouth and his lips were pulled back just enough to show crooked teeth.

The Sons of Liberty claimed that they had only planned to show the new Customs officials their contempt that day and do them no harm, instructing the crowds to be satisfied with printed signs and catcalls and empty threats. But I thought it was the look of Grendel as he walked beside the officials, wives, and servants that kept the stones in their pockets and the tar in the barrel. When someone appeared a true menace, he made his way into the crowd and stared until they backed up. It would take a determined man to face him, not someone out for a bit of sport with a soft gentleman and his following.

But he showed he was new in America in the few weeks after by visiting the taverns near the docks and expecting to trade stories and drinks with the tars and shoremen. He'd get his pint but return to find his table empty. When he sat on a bench where others were jawing and spinning lies, the table soon became quiet and he found his new mates drinking up and leaving, only to reenter a bit later to sit across the room. He got the same treatment as the new Customs men and their families—they were shunned by everyone except the other Tories drawing the

King's shilling. Commissioner Hulton's sister told a shopkeeper that the ladies of Boston would treat a maid with smallpox better than they did her.

But Grendel wasn't so mild in his comments. According to Mouse, who was invisible in every crowd and seemed to see and hear everything from one end of the docks to the other, Grendel eventually stood up at the Red Cross and challenged a mechanic who'd moved from his bench, wanting to know if he wasn't good enough to share a pint at his table. The man was shaky at the sight of him. But with the crowd at his back, he managed to tell him clear, "You're free to drink a pint where you like, just like you're free to take coins from Paxton and his lot, but you won't find friends here while they're robbing us and getting richer."

Grendel had glared hard at him and seemed ready to take them all on but decided against it. "You're right. I'll drink where I want and you can wager I'll find friends as well. I don't care where the money comes from, it spends just the same." He drained his cup and stared at each man in turn, breathing heavily with his teeth showing, and most turned away.

I had no interest in crossing him and had been careful to step around him if the path was narrow, but it was a small world on the docks. Now it turned out that he was interested in stepping on me, rather than around.

He took the table near the door, across the room from two dice players nursing a pitcher of flip and one table removed from where I sat with Burns. His size took up most of the bench. Maggie McGowan looked in from the kitchen and our eyes met so that she knew I wanted her to serve him. She brought him grog, the watered rum some Navy sailors favored, and after he took a long drink, he motioned me over.

"What might I do for a man your size?" I asked mildly.

He nodded at the seat across the table. "You're Gray, aren't you? You're the man I've come to see."

I sat and admitted what I couldn't deny. "I am Nicholas Gray, humble barkeep for the Widow Maggie McGowan and a friend to those who come to drink and talk. And you?" I looked him in the face and realized that he was breathing through his mouth because his nose had been mashed up once too often and gave him too little air.

"Friend, eh? Suppose I were to break your door off the hinges or smash all those mugs and the barrels behind the bar. Would I be a friend then?"

I took a minute before answering. "No, you wouldn't, and it might cost you a few more lumps than you think. We take care that the Widow's property stays safe. But why would you think about some mischief like that when no one here has done you any wrong?"

"I'm not in the business of making friends, Gray, especially not clumsy thieves. I'm friendly with those that pay me and sometimes a few I pay. I'm sure it's the same for you. Your little night crew would desert you in a minute if they got a better offer."

There was no point in going round the bush with him. "That may be, but it's no concern of yours."

"What about Mr. Draper, would you welcome him in as well?

I didn't know what this rasping giant knew or didn't know, and there was no need for me to help him along. "Draper? You mean the merchant with the store on Cross St.? He'd be welcome if he wanted, but from what I hear I don't think he'd find the Sword and Scabbard up to his standards."

Grendel stared at me for a minute before his face changed to what might be considered a smile, although it would have served better to frighten a dog. "You're a liar like he said, but I'm not surprised. I collected debts in London and heard stories that would make a statue weep, if they weren't bald lies. It's amazing what a man will say when he's scared." He stared at me hard, hoping I'd show fear right then and make his job easier. His presence had already frightened the dice players and they'd drained their pitcher and left, but Burns stayed, sitting forward now to watch closely, his eyes bright. "My name's Grendel, if you haven't heard it already, and I know you won't forget it."

I've got plenty of fear, but it usually comes with dreams at night. During the day it stays locked far away, and I feel it more after I've had a chance to think about some danger rather than when it springs up in my face. I felt wide awake, my eyes alert and my muscles alive. If I had to fight, I was ready, even anxious to get started. I'd either stand over him or he'd stand over me and the pains I'd get would probably be less than I'd felt on my back from two dozen stripes with the Navy's nine tails.

"Say what you want and get out. I'll be glad to throw the bolt behind you." The back door swings quiet but I'd heard it twice and knew that Maggie had probably gone just down near Hutchinson's Wharf where Julius sat sometimes when it was warm enough. She had a nose for trouble and you couldn't miss the menace that Grendel wore like a cloak. I kept my eyes on Grendel, and both Burns and Grendel turned to Julius as he entered behind me. But even gazing on Julius didn't cause him to flinch. Julius is taller than I am, with coffee-colored skin, arms roped with muscle, and hooded eyes in a gaunt face. When he's intent on harm, Julius looks as cold as stone, a dark vision of menace.

Grendel turned back to me. "I took a job from Mr. Draper. He'll give me a piece of the two hundred pounds you owe him once I collect it. You can pay it all at once and never see me again or I can come to collect every month. Which one will it be?"

I stood up and pushed my bench back from the table before I started talking. "I suppose it's best for you if you don't know anything. That way you won't get a headache trying to work the cow's brain you've got under your hat. I don't owe Draper a penny and you'll kiss the Queen before you get anything from me."

He stood up, too, his breathing a bit faster but excited as well, quickly checking the room behind me and fixing Julius who was moving towards us from the kitchen door. Grendel's head nearly scraped the ceiling.

My voice stayed low though it felt like I was shouting. "Get out, Grendel, and don't come back. You're big enough, but I've chopped down trees before. If you knew Draper and his ways, you'd lift what you could from him rather than worrying us for money we don't owe and don't have."

Without looking away from me, he scooped up the bench with his left hand and stood it on end. He grabbed the nearest leg with his right and began to push down until it cracked and split off into his hand. He held the thick leg out to his side like a quail bone. "You're lucky this isn't your arm, Gray, because I might pull it out of your shoulder when I get a hold. There's more than one cripple in London who didn't take my warnings."

He swept his mug off the table in front of us with his club, the redware pottery smashing at our feet, then swung it easily down against the table top, not quite hard enough to split the pine boards, and looked to see if we'd come for him then. Julius and I flanked him but I shook my head and backed away slightly. I had nothing in my hand and whatever happened, the room would look like a hurricane had hit. Grendel was wary enough to back out, kicking the cat out of the way when it brushed his foot and throwing the bench leg on the floor before turning to the street.

I picked it up and my shoulder ached as I thought of Grendel with his great hands pulling at it. I turned to Maggie, her eyes wide with a mixture of fear and anger. I spoke to break the silence more than anything. "I can get Dartmouth the joiner to fix this up tomorrow morning. He'll be glad enough for the work." Julius and Maggie still said nothing and I bent to pick up the pieces of the broken mug from the floor. "And we'll figure a way to fix up Grendel as well." My head felt as hollow as a dried gourd and just as light and brittle.

I'd almost forgotten Burns, who looked a bit disappointed rather than scared. "That was a long tale he told, Mr. Gray, but he left out the beginning."

I turned on him then, some anger left over. "It's a riddle to me, Burns, but it's nothing to you, nothing at all." Of course I was lying, and by the end, Burns was in it deep enough to swim.

Twelve

WE'D MADE IT THROUGH our first winter with the troops and nearly to spring when Grendel first darkened our door. His threats nagged at me during the day and stabbed me at night. Too much worry brought back some of my dreams, and I often woke with shackles bloodying my wrists, choking on the foul air below decks or in a prison cage. Sometimes, I saw Maggie there, too, though she always stayed clean and dressed as a tavern maid. Soon, a full night without stirring was as rare as a guinea in a bag of pennies, and just as valuable. Waking at night made me cross in the morning, as if something had been stolen from me that I couldn't get back.

Julius was always up early to stoke the fires, folding his bed up on its hinges so it stood against the wall and there was room in the kitchen to move about. Maggie came down about the same time as well, and we often ate our bread and bit of cheese with cider or small beer together at a table in the tavern room once it had warmed up.

I'd gotten the bench leg fixed after Grendel's visit, but we hadn't talked much beyond that until Maggie asked a few days later. "So what will we do about, Grendel? I can't have him in here regular to smash things up."

I had no true answer, but I wanted to say something to give us some peace, whether I believed it or not. "I don't think we'll see him again.

He's the kind that gets people to do what he wants because they're afraid. I think he saw we'd be a barrel of trouble, so he'll probably keep on with the lambs and leave us to our business."

I saw Julius turn his head to look at me. His frown was clear and he shook his head a bit from side to side. Maggie turned to him first, then back to me. "I agree with Julius, Grendel's not the kind to let go of trouble once he has it in hand." Our cat jumped up beside Maggie on the bench, then moved into her lap, finding a spot among the folds of her skirt. Julius had begun feeding her scraps and bits from plates and in return she killed some of the rats which ate about half the flour on the docks. She had one ear with a piece out of it, like a thief who'd been marked, but was otherwise whole. Now that she spent some time inside and was pampered with a bit of milk or rind of cheese or scrap of meat when it was around, her black stripes were brighter against her gray fur. I began calling her Jezebel, since she seemed a woman who did as she pleased, and Maggie called her 'Bel.

"Do you think we should pay him something just to avoid the trouble?" she asked. "It wouldn't be much different than when we paid off Tobin for the license each month."

I'd considered paying Grendel as well, but shook my head against it now. "No, I've known some like him. He'd want too much and if we show we're afraid by paying, he might just as easily come back for more any time it struck his fancy. It's the fear he likes as much as the money." I took a bite of my bread and chewed hard.

"The only answer for a man like that is to kill him," said Julius quietly.

My gut felt hollow, like a keg with no bottom, knowing he might be right. "That's down the road, Julius, it hasn't come to that yet."

Maggie moved Bel from her lap and stood up quickly, taking her wooden trencher with her. I heard her place it near the bucket we used for washing, then come back to the door. When her mind was at ease, her blue eyes drew me in and held me there with warmth and laughter. But now her oval face was troubled, a wrinkle showing on her forehead, and her eyes were guarded as her mind turned things over. "If we were to do something different, Nicholas, what would it be?"

I was surprised at the question and too tired and vexed to make up a dream on the spot. I shifted on the bench to stretch a leg. "I haven't thought of it, Maggie. This is what I know."

She stared at me for a moment, then turned to go back upstairs where she often counted the purse and figured accounts at her desk before we opened for dinner at noon.

I looked at Julius in puzzlement but his face was quiet, his eyes blank, giving no hints. Later, he finished in the kitchen and I walked with him to the market near Faneuil Hall. It was spring and the muddy ground smelled warm and rich, an odor finally strong enough to drive out the cold, wet smell of coarse snow and grey ice that lingers in Boston for weeks after it's gone.

In the summer, a jumble of farm carts crowded the area with everything from salted beef and pork to red and black berries gathered in the woods. But it was too early for the new year's vegetables, so it was mostly cured meat, some turkeys and pigeons shot now the snow had cleared between the trees, huge lobsters and oysters brought up from the docks, and hard vegetables that farmers had stored away in a cellar.

We had to pick our way through the wagons, jostling with the other cooks and maids, until Julius offered a shilling each for a basket of turnips and one of onions to keep the stews filled. A grim farmer, whose head looked as much like a turnip as what was in the basket, took the coins and turned to his wagon to fill the coarse bags we brought. Mostly it was pleasant enough, like a tiny piece of London, with sellers trading a few oaths as they crowded in for a prime spot. We laughed a bit when we watched a hard-faced cook plant an elbow in the stomach of a smaller maid to insure she got the best chop from the side of pork.

When we stepped away down Ann Street, each with a canvas bag, I was enjoying the early sun of spring and trying to forget Grendel, and Maggie's questions on top. When I looked up, I found Hardy the tidewaiter in our path. Since we'd spilled him into Nahant Bay when Brand made off with the *Grace*, he'd kept up as searcher but hadn't risen up to surveyor or inspector and still suffered along on his sixty pounds a year. Mouse was told he offered too little money to get good informers, but took every chance to complain to his uncle and vowed he'd get those who dumped him over.

He wasn't a big man, but had the raw hands and easy gait of a mechanic even though he wore a London suit and wig to the Custom House. In the jam around the market there wasn't enough room for all to walk between the horse posts and buildings, and stepping into the street meant dancing with the horses and carts and could easily mean a broken toe or worse. It was easy enough to step aside, but it was easy to play at privilege as well.

Hardy was with two others and after he said something over his shoulder, the three spread across the walk. Julius and I stopped and waited, Julius just behind me.

"Why, Mr. Gray!" started Hardy as if welcoming a cousin just stepping down the gangway from London, "you're out in the daylight! I'd heard you only came alive after dark."

There was little to do other than speak with him, though there was nothing for us to gain. "I'm sorry sir, I don't know your name."

"Oh you must," he continued, staring hot at us, then looking around to be sure his friends would hear. "They say you know everything about the docks and more about thieving."

I could have knocked him down right there and gotten a pat on the back from a Boston jury, but I clutched the onions tight with one hand and kept the other in my cloak. "We haven't been introduced, but I'm guessing your name's Hardy, some relation to a Commissioner? Are you on record or just another Tory bastard?" His face changed and he began to move toward us, clutching his walking stick at the end. "And you're the one that's fond of swimming in the ocean at night, aren't you, even if some thought you might be better off guarding the King's new ship?"

"I'll see you on your knees . . ." he spit out as he raised his stick, but I'd seen it coming from before I said my first words. I dropped my bag and moved to his right, catching the stick before he could begin a good swing. I wrenched it from his hand and tripped him forward at the same time, bringing the stick around with a hand at each end like a staff to give him a good shove across the shoulders. He landed on his knees and elbows in the soft earth, his wig jostled to a side, wet mud staining his breeches and the forearms of his light blue broadcloth coat. Julius had moved up at my back silently, staring threats at Hardy's companions.

I held the stick by an end now, down at my side. "Come ahead if you like, but you might find blood on your clothes instead of mud." We stood for a moment there, waiting, but neither came forward, and Hardy rolled about, ready to get up. A small group had gathered behind us and a farmer's delivery cart stopped in the street. I scanned the crowd. Hardy hadn't planned well because there wasn't a sympathetic face to be seen. The only redcoats were at the corner of the market, too far to be of help.

"We'll leave you your stick, Mr. Hardy, but you should be more careful so you don't stumble again."

I'D CLENCHED MY TEETH as we walked back to the Sword, grinding away at what I wanted to do to Hardy right there and the same time regretting it had ever happened. I had enough trouble with Grendel and I didn't need another dog waiting around the corner. I suspected that Draper must have told a tale that put suspicion on me with Customs, without a shadow on himself.

I was muttering to myself as we brought our bags into the kitchen where Julius could take what he needed and put the rest in the cold closet on the back wall. Maggie came in, ready with a word but stopped herself before she started.

"What have you done now, Nicholas? I can tell it's no good from looking at your face." Her tone was like a mother to a small child.

"That Customs waiter, Hardy, picked me out and stood across the walk, called me a thief in front of a crowd."

"You couldn't get around him?"

I looked to Julius, who answered for me. "Hardy brought it on, and it wouldn't have helped to stand quiet. We weren't going to fool him."

Maggie swung around to glare at him. "You're just as bad as he. You'll scuffle about till the Sheriff takes you."

"There was nothing for it, Maggie," I tried, "there's only so much room to walk."

"Have you never tried turning around the other way? How bad did you hurt him?"

"Not at all, Maggie, he just fell in the mud."

"Fell? I'm sure you knocked him about, didn't you? That's worse than an oath on his mother to most Tories, especially from a footman like you." Her color was up and her eyes sparked hot. "Now he'll pay any price for a charge against you, even if he has to get a loan and pay an arm's interest." She went to the fire and busied herself there. "They'll come for you one day, and I'll be lucky they don't take me, too, or at least shut the doors with some excuse or other."

It wasn't bad enough that it was Grendel at me, and then Hardy, but now Maggie was looking at me crossways.

I threw up my hands. "Maybe I should leave then, Maggie, if all I do is make a trap for you. You could find some gentleman to carry your onions from market and scuttle about like a crab."

She straightened herself up then and turned slowly before she spoke. I expected an angry tone, but got cool weather instead. "Do as you please, Nicholas. I won't tell you which road to go. Not that it would do any good." She turned to the fire again and scraped about at it, though I could see that Julius would rather stir it himself. She spoke low then, almost to herself, but loud enough to hear. "It's hot enough now, we've got redcoats and Grendel and the Sheriff who'd love to take you down, and instead of cooling things, you take a bellows to the fire." She stopped and then spoke so low I had to strain to hear. "I'd rather you leave a free man than stay and get taken." She said no more and when she turned, her eyes were hard. I wanted to speak back, but I was out of words and instead, I went out to pull up the portcullis and fiddle behind the bar.

We served our dinners like usual, about ten men eating from the three stew bowls on the tables. Maggie and I didn't speak, though between talking and scooping their mouths full, I'm sure the customers didn't notice. One tar I didn't know tried to make off with a spoon but I counted before he got to the door and he gave it up at the same time I warned him against coming back.

I helped Julius clean the tables after and we stood for a moment before he went to the kitchen to wipe off the dirty bowls and cups with a rag. "Maybe Maggie's right, maybe now's a time to move where no one knows my face or my business," I offered. Julius said nothing, just cocked his head a little to the side. "It would be easy enough, just the same as when I came here. There's New York and Philadelphia and Charleston, but I don't fancy the heat and the swamps there. At least I'd be able to walk about without a damned placeman threatening me."

There was silence for a beat before Julius answered. "For how long?"

"How long? Long enough to find a crew I could trust and some jobs that wouldn't send the dogs sniffing my heels. You could come and I'd vouch for your medal or pretend to own you, whichever was best." I realized that Julius had been at my back for some years now and the thought of going without him made me feel like I'd stepped outside without my clothes.

Julius stared back at me for a moment before he decided a full conversation was worthwhile. "What about Maggie? You've had some words, but those can be forgotten. You know she's a special prize. Why would you think of leaving?"

"I don't know, Julius, I don't know what I think. She doesn't seem to care one way or the other."

"Do you think that's what she just said?" asked Julius, cocking his head again, making sure he'd heard right. He might have been one of the parrots in the islands.

Trying to explain Maggie's thoughts made me itch for some other talk. I gave a small wave with my hand to say I didn't know. "But what about you, Julius? Would you come with me?"

Julius stared again, judging what he might tell and what he might not. "I don't fancy leaving right now."

"Why not? It can't be sweating in the kitchen here that would keep you and we're certainly not getting rich by lifting trinkets."

Julius took a long breath before he began. "You've seen the slave hunters here, but there's only a few, and I know to stay a mile away from the traders when they stand at the wharf and buy and sell for a day. But they don't have nearly the chance of getting chains on me here as they do farther south. These docks are mostly too rough for them and there are too many dark faces who walk free. There's more fear I'll be pressed by the Navy than of a slaver taking me, especially when I work here." He gave a slight smile, then stopped to make sure I was listening. "But that's not all of it, at least right now."

I looked a question at him, before he answered. "There's a girl I've come to know, a free girl, she serves in the house for the wife of Charles Steuart."

"The new Customs cashier?"

"The same. She worked for them when he handled accounts in Jamaica and they brought her to help with the house." His voice softened and he looked past me to the picture hanging above the fireplace showing Kingston Harbor. "She knows about the Blue Mountains and how to cook cassava bread . . . I've seen her some nights after her kitchen is clean and the mistress in bed. She has to be careful though, she's afraid her mistress might turn her out if she thought Eve was lowering herself to see a slave or anyone too rough."

"Eve?" He simply nodded, but he had a soft look on his face. "You mean you'd stay for her, even if it turns risky?"

"I imagine I would, Nicholas, but I don't know where I'd be going to anyway. What's down the road that's better?"

I didn't have an answer and he turned toward the kitchen and his washing bucket and I began moving the chairs and benches about for no purpose. After a moment, I went out the front door and down the street to the docks. I sat where I could hear the ocean slapping the pilings and feel the sun, warmer than it had been in months. But I couldn't get my mind loose. I was like a dog worrying the end of a rope, chewing till it fell in shreds.

Thirteen

WE SERVED those who came that night, though I'm not sure I spoke a single word with any of them, and I don't think Maggie said much more. After she threw the bolt, she went straight away to her room.

After our words that morning, I couldn't help but think back on all we'd done together—how we'd come together warily as she worked to make the Sword her own with her own license, how we figured a way to put Ezekiel Tobin in a box so he couldn't collect a visit to Maggie's bed along with a pound every month, the way she tried to step in front when the Sheriff took me for a false debt, the way she welcomed me when Hancock paid it off.

But most of all, I remembered how she came to me at night when a dream made me sweat and shake. Early on, Maggie seemed to know every time I sat up in the dark, either because I cried out or from some extra sense. She would come without a candle, I knew the rustle of her shift, and simply sit on the edge of the bed holding my hand until my breathing slowed and my eyes showed less white. Once I'd started to talk but she held a finger to my mouth and we sat in silence after that.

Sometimes she led me to her room down the hall in the dark and we lost ourselves in a fever, one move answered with another, her hands urgent at my back, her cries and moans mixed with mine until the dam burst and we finally lay spent and slack. Later, when the sky lightened, I would creep softly back to my bed. She'd never mention it the next day and sometimes I wondered if I'd dreamed her visit just as I'd dreamed shackles on my wrists.

After a few minutes cleaning cups and replacing them on the shelf behind the bar, I couldn't help myself. I let down the grate and went up the stairs to Maggie's door, passing my small room in the hall leading to the bigger front room overlooking the street.

She answered my knock by calling out for me to come in. She sat at her desk in the corner, with the money purse out from behind the beam and the coins all sorted into piles, a cup of cider beside it.

I was surprised and asked, "You'd invite anyone in to spy all your treasure?"

She shook her head. "I'd have heard one of the doors if someone came, and I knew it was you from your stride, Nicholas, you have a certain way of climbing the stairs, like there's a prize at the top and no time to waste." She looked away again toward the desk. "And I knew you'd have more words."

"How much is there, Maggie?"

"Fifty three pounds, seven shillings." A small part had come from the thin slice we gave for our night work, but most was from getting more customers at the Sword over the months. She put it back in the purse and held it for a moment, but I could see its weight didn't make her happy. She turned to me, her hands unsettled, her mouth a straight line with no hint of a smile.

"It's more than I've ever had," she said with a look that told me she was remembering her younger days as a high-class moll in London, where the money came fast and went just as quickly. She had no more than her clothes when she'd finally fled with Capt. McGowan.

I grinned. "And it's probably more than you'll ever have again, so let's drink a toast."

I'd meant it as a joke, but her color turned, she dropped the purse on the desk, and her gaze turned hard at me. "But it's no help, not if I stay a tavern maid and you a thief."

I stared at her in the flickering light of the single candle and she back, until her eyes glistened. She looked away toward the pitcher and bowl which stood on her chest, the only fine thing in her room, blue scrolls on white china, chosen from Draper's stock when he owed for a turn at a store in the South End. She might have cried a tear, but I saw her back stiffen and her shoulders rise and fall with a deep breath. I knew the muscles there, shoulders and arms that could roll a cask of ale from a cart and lift the full kettle from the hearth, and I knew their perfect color as well, golden skin spread from waist to neck, chestnut hair trailing in curls down her back when her cap came off.

"You're not a maid, Maggie, it's your license, your tavern. I'm just here to help." The town fathers hoped that running a tavern would keep a widow out of the poor house where they would have to feed her thin soup.

She turned back to me and her knuckles showed white when she gripped her cup. "I'll always be a maid because I've got nothing of my own. Tobias Brown might take the air one day and decide he'd rather open a shop here than rent to a widow. Or, he could sell to any one of the crows from London who'd just as soon pick our bones as collect a fair rent. Especially since I'm sure Tobin still dreams of getting us back."

I wanted to wave my hand to brush off her words or answer back smartly, since I thought the business done, and I'd only been trying to help her. But I knew it was my anger that made Tobin remember us in his darkest thoughts.

She stopped just a moment to gather her breath. "Brown or the others can't order me around like the slaves in their kitchens or make free with their hands when I bring the pitcher, but I'll never sleep like the ladies either. They're put out when the tea's not right or there's a spot on the cup, but they're not worried about the workhouse."

I looked at her hard and for the first time since I'd known her, I saw a tiny shadow of fear, like a candle guttering before it dies. "There's more there on the desk than most on the wharf right now," I answered back, "more than you would have guessed a few months back, and now you're worried? When you weren't before?"

Maggie turned away from me and shook her head like she was trying to wake from a dream.

"What do you want, Maggie? You want to become a lady so you can twist your hair into a castle and have a maid to keep your stays so tight you can't bend? You want to stay abed in the morning and sip tea in the afternoon?" She still said nothing and I could feel blood roaring up toward my head. "If you think that's going to happen, you've been listening to the talkers too much. It's a pretty dream they have, what with 'honest' Americans deciding who'll have to pay and how much, but it's not going to put you in a pew at Christ Church or me walking the gallery at exchange, trying to decide what to do with my money. We'll still be at the bottom, even if we do manage to stay out of the gaol."

When Maggie looked back, her blood was up, too. "Oh, I'm not the colt you think, I know my standing better than you. But I've nothing of my own and I can't put out to sea or hire out to hammer nails and boards like you. I'm a maid, Nicholas, nothing more, as long as I've got no holdings."

I studied her for a moment then shook my head. "I didn't know you were a climber, Maggie, I'd never have guessed when I saw you twisting through the tables with your pitchers and mugs."

"And what's wrong with wanting a bit of ease then, wanting to own a building or land, something that won't break or run away, something that can't be stolen, at least not by a thief like you."

"You might scramble up a step, Maggie, if you stay a widow and keep the license. But they can steal anything you've got, one way or the other, it's easy enough in court if your friends are lawyer and judge."

"Well, I'd rather take my chances there than with the likes of you and Gillam."

I could feel myself getting hotter yet. "Are you too good for us now that we've filled the purse? Will you pray for our souls when you see us hanged or just cheer like the rest?"

We stared at each other for a long time. It was the first time we'd had cross words, other than the bit of grousing we'd have around the kitchen and bar. I had no taste to be like the innkeeper and wife whose first words of welcome are a list of the other's sins. I finally shuffled my feet, ready to walk down the stairs and out the door, hoping to see someone to knock out of my way.

"Stay, Nicholas, don't go. Please." Her eyes were softer now. "Get us some rum if you like and we'll sit at a table. It won't do for you to run off with the blood in your ears, you're liable to do something that will make you sorry."

I went down the stairs and wanted to walk through the door but my feet led me to the bar instead. My thoughts were racing about and my fingers felt thick and clumsy. I filled our own pottery cups with some Barbadoes rum and took them to the table nearest the fire where Maggie now sat, her face solemn. Bel had climbed into her lap and Maggie was stroking her without thought.

"I'm sorry, Nicholas, I have no right to judge you. I've been with it every step and I've done enough in my time that could bring a rope round my throat as well." She sipped her rum, then scratched Bel between the ears. "Do you look beyond tomorrow, Nicholas? Where will you be when the winter wind blows next year or the year after?"

I stared at her in puzzlement, wondering what she might be driving at. "I'm no gypsy teller, Maggie. You'd do better to go back to London and find a witch with tea leaves than ask me."

"Is it just one day after the next then, just like playing in Gillam's card games, where you don't know what card will show up, but it's someone else holding the pack?"

I shrugged, not sure how my future had suddenly become a card game. I had no words, at least none that would fit. Sometimes I wished Maggie and I never had to talk.

"Aren't you afraid they'll be dealing from the bottom some day, and take what you have?" she asked.

"They've been dealing from the bottom ever since my father dropped dead at the Oxford gates, ever since I was pressed out of the Black Ram in London, so drunk I couldn't run. They can't take what I have, because I don't have anything. But they'll take me instead." I thought of the purse in her room. "I take back what I can, and give back a bit, but you say it's not enough."

She looked away as she felt the weight of my words. I charged on. "But they've never dealt you the straight cards either, Maggie, at least not what you've told me. What do you think, that if you change costumes like a player on stage, they'll forget who you were before?"

She leaned forward and spoke in a rush. "We could get away, Nicholas, we could go to a town starting up in New Hampshire or north on the coast or even in towards Springfield or one of those towns the drivers talk of. If we saved a bit more we could buy a tavern there or build one. We wouldn't have to worry about a lease and we wouldn't have to pay off for a license or watch for the Sheriff. You could tend the business or . . . or build houses . . . or become a schoolmaster, you know as many words as anyone . . ."

"And what, Maggie? Serve farmers their bit of beer and listen to their tales about the rocks they've dug up? Or settle in to thrashing the children when they forget what comes after 'e.'? Maybe you could start quilting with the ladies and tell them stories about the fine company you kept in Boston and London. No, Maggie, I'd whittle down a King's pine before I'd move from the docks. I'd get out there and start screaming just to hear some noise."

Maggie stared at me in silence then, her eyes steady, and her gaze cooled me like I'd turned a corner into the wind. Even so, the words kept coming. "I don't know what to think, Maggie. I've no interest in marching out to the frontier so we could scramble up to a middling class and sit by the hearth like a pair of firedogs. You and I together don't have enough, even half enough, to think of buying this place from Brown and I'd have to steal every snuff box in the council room to come near. I don't know what's coming any more than you do, but we can go about our business, we can eat and drink and burrow in the blankets at night, summer and winter, here at the Sword." I tried a grin to melt some of the ice I saw coming into her eyes. "It's more than we've ever had."

She stood up then and picked up her cup and moved toward the kitchen. But she stopped and turned before she got there. "But it's not enough, Nicholas. And you'll never understand why."

Fourteen

THAT NIGHT I SLEPT POORLY and woke up thrashing from a dream. I gave the ropes beneath the straw mattress another turn, but it didn't help. I felt sour the next day, like someone had forced spoiled milk down me, and when I looked at Maggie she looked away or stared at me like a stranger. I knew Julius must have heard us from his bed in the kitchen, but he kept his peace and so did I. There were times I believed I loved Maggie, although I had no pictures of a happy couple to compare. But if this was part of what the poets sang about, I thought I would choose a different road. When I filled the cups at the bar that evening, I said little and kept far enough from the tables that I wasn't invited to sit.

When Peter Burns strode through the door, he gave me a big grin and began to head straight for me. I gave him a look meant to keep him away, and he stopped at the table near the fireplace where four that loaded and hauled for Greenwood at his shipyard sat with cups and dice. Burns had been in enough by now that most of our crowd knew him by sight and even though he was two steps above them, he was welcome for his words and the purse he sometimes used for drinks.

He slapped his palm down on the table so they looked up from the dice and he spoke out like he was in a courtroom. "Here, here, let's drink a toast to your barman, Nicholas Gray, victim of an unwarranted attack by a vicious Customs man near the market last morning. But Gray gave him what he deserved and left him in the mud. A toast to his health."

They turned and raised their cups. "Would you like me to take up your case with the Sheriff and have Hardy before a judge? I'm sure his uncle wouldn't object," crowed Burns towards me. His amusement made his young face shine and it was all he could do to keep from dancing a little jig. His clothes weren't much better than a workman's, but his eyes sparkled and glinted so much that he appeared well-dressed.

I had too much in my mind as it was and I was determined not to let my little reel with Hardy get puffed up into some act of politics and principle. I shook my head at him before speaking. "I'll be glad to serve you what you'd like, Peter, but I won't be writing a speech for you or Samuel Adams or anyone else."

"What's wrong? You dropped a Customs man in the street and you're not proud of it? What better service could you do our town and province?"

"It was defense, not service. Hardy made a mistake, and I doubt he'll make it again."

"But he abused you, threatened you, acted like you had no right to walk on the same ground as he did because he's a high Tory."

"What do you know of it? I didn't see your face when I looked around."

He grinned broadly. "You know better than that, Nicholas. If something happens, we know it, because the friends of Liberty are everywhere." He continued looking at me and smiling, hoping I'd join his good humor. "Why don't you serve me up some rum and I'll sit quietly by the fire until you want to talk a bit more."

He was as good as his word, and after seeing to the other tables and standing silent for a bit to keep my dignity, I sat at the table across from him, bringing a cup for myself as well.

Burns started right in. "Hardy's not really a brawler and he's not been one to stand on privilege, since he's just a step off the floor at Customs. Why did he single you out?"

I liked the fire in Burns, coals ready to flame up at any time, but I wouldn't trust him with more than what others knew. "He bears me a grudge because he thinks I had something to do with him losing that ship in Nahant Bay."

"Is he right?"

I paused for moment, looking straight at him. "That's neither here nor there, is it Peter, since you and the Sons and all the rest will believe what you want anyway."

He grinned again. It seemed things were a genuine circus show for him at the moment. "Why do you have such a poor opinion of us? We've done little to you other than drink up your pints at night and help the poor sods in the room understand the danger they're in from vermin like Hardy and the rest." I waited him out as it seemed more was coming. "Rather than cross me each time I come in, I'd think you'd be thankful for all we've done."

At heart, I'd like to turn the Tories upside down as much as anyone, but sometimes I have trouble swallowing the words of the Sons as well. Most days I would have let his suggestions go by, but it wasn't a day for that, and I could feel the pressure building in my chest. "All you've done? Let me count it up now. There's a new Customs court here, determined to strangle the trade. There's soldiers having cockfights on the Common and flashing steel in the streets. I hear you'll have a committee now to look behind every merchant's door to be sure they're not importing goods."

Samuel Adams had packed the merchant's committee with all the rabble that could fit in the Town House and they'd voted to start nonimportation again. It was no wonder Hancock stepped from his new golden coach long enough to write letters for it. He and Rowe and some of the others would be able to sell off all their stored goods at high prices, and they could watch the small shops sink at the same time.

Burns was grim then. "It has to be done, Gray, we've got to make a stand."

But I'd started now and couldn't stop. "And I'm sure the committees will be fair about it, too, just like last year when everyone celebrated about Hancock smuggling Madeira. Then a month later, a crowd rescues a poor Irishman's ship full of molasses so Customs can't sell it. The crowd thinks it's all the same, good fun and twisting the Board's nose and helping a friend of liberty, but the selectmen tell them to give it back to Customs so Boston doesn't look like it's a constant riot. I guess his barrels of molasses weren't as important as King John's wine."

Burns considered me seriously for another minute but again turned to a smile like one he'd give a dumb animal. "You don't think we can just pull everything down at once, do you? There are some times when it's better to give a little back. We need to make a point, but we can't be lawless either. Our friends in Parliament would turn against us."

I laughed. "It's easy enough to give back when it's just an Irishman's molasses and choose to make a point when it's Hancock's precious Madeira." I sat back a minute then, tired already from two days when it seemed I was talking at odds with everyone, even myself. Burns would see what he wanted and anything that helped the Sons was fair, even if some of the poor men got hurt.

But Burns wouldn't let it rest either, I'd said too much, chopping at his roots with a broadax. "You don't appreciate principle, do you Mr. Gray? We've stood for what's right and we'll keep it up until we have our freedom."

"I can take your principle and two pennies and buy a pint of beer. It puts no money in my purse and comes closer to putting me in gaol than it does keeping me out."

He was still serious but I saw his face relax a bit. "That's funny, Gray, I'd heard it was the other way around. I'm told you might still be in gaol for debt if the Sons didn't pay off for you."

It had been three years since John Hancock had opened the door to debtor's prison in the celebration for the end of the Stamp Act. It was the first time anyone connected to the Sons had brought it up, but I had expected I'd hear about it sometime. It was money that Hancock would never miss, but someone had kept track. "I didn't complain, but it was nothing I asked for either. Are you here to collect a debt now? I'm not sure this one is any more real than the one that got me in gaol at first."

He turned his mug about, first one way, then the other, then again before he answered. I noticed his fingers were long and fine, perfect for holding a quill or plucking a violin but too weak to haul a rope on deck. I was told he formed a fine figure for some of the young Whig ladies after dinner, even if his prospects were small. "You've never even joined in when we needed a crowd about, though you seem to enjoy a scrap more than the next man. You'd be a great help when there's work to be done."

I laughed out loud, but more from surprise than humor. "You don't need me. You've already got more than a hundred who'll come with a club and some Indian paint if you ask, and if you add on the others out for a lark, you can get a thousand. You give direction to the street scrappers like Molineoux and Macintosh and the others stand at half cock waiting for orders. One more won't turn Parliament's head."

"But you could lead, Nicholas, other men look to you even if you've just met. You're like Revere—you can speak when you choose to, but you'd fight three or four at a time if they came at you and they'd be sorry they started. One like you is worth ten or twenty or a hundred more."

I was surprised at his words, but determined to turn him away. "He's a silversmith, not a barman, and they'd do better following him than me. It's more than once I've been headed toward the gaol when I thought I was going to church."

Burns gave a short laugh and studied me more closely than ever. "What is it then, Nicholas? You're no Tory–that's plain enough from looking about–and I've heard you tear Customs and Parliament apart limb by limb when you thought I wasn't listening, but you won't help throw them over either. Are you like our great merchant John Rowe, who'll study the flags every minute to make sure he's always walking with the wind?"

I took a short drink then, returning the cup to the table before answering. "If I didn't know you, I might throw you out the door for comparing me to Rowe. He counts his pounds and shillings, that's why he tiptoes about like a rabbit. Do you think I've got enough coin to worry about losing it? Do you think if I angered every Tory in Boston that it would change the weight of my purse?"

He turned square on me then, looking deep, with no hint of humor. "Why then, Nicholas? If you keep by yourself in a corner for too long, you might not get out."

There must have been too many bugs nibbling at me, because when I answered my voice grew loud and angry. "I believe you're right in most things, Mr. Burns, that we're not treated fairly here and that Parliament takes our money and gives little back. The Tories have no right to rule us and I'd spit on their shoes every time they take a step. They'll press honest men into the Royal Navy and treat them like slaves. I could make some of your speeches myself, and then double them up."

The table of mechanics looked over and Maggie stared. I took a sip of rum and found enough control to speak softer so that none but Burns could hear. "But I don't trust the Whigs or even the Sons much more than that. I've been on the wrong side of some of them and they wouldn't show an ounce more mercy toward me than the Tories. If I'm in the way, I'll get knocked in the gutter just the same, whether it's a Whig or a Tory leading the parade."

Burns wouldn't let it go. "Why don't you join the march then, instead of risking standing in the way?"

"Because I can't stand to listen to them lie with a straight face. I watched when they cheered the crowd at night when they tore down the Governor's house and scared the Tories into the Castle, and then heard them tell everyone the next day how horrified they were by the mob." I found my hands gripping the table instead of lying quiet. "And there's some you count on who talk about principle, but the only principle they know jingles in their purse. They're the same as the Tories—they'll say anything to get what they want, and if they get it, they'll be no different. They'll gobble up the property and the money and eat off china plates while the crowds who took the risks for your 'principle' go back to scrambling for crumbs."

Burns considered this for a minute, his eyes filled with fire now, no time for play. "So you'd throw it all out because we don't meet your measure for honesty?"

I thought for a minute before I answered. "You'd have me believe that things would be different if the Whigs could control the town and the port and God knows what else. Well, things might change for you and the lawyers and merchants, but I don't see things changing that much for me or most in this room. I'll still have to keep an eye out that I'm not arrested or hanged, and I don't think a Whig rope will help me breathe any more than a Tory rope."

I could sit no more, my feet were ready to stride away. I'd said more than I'd wanted, and too much of what I really thought. I got up, ready to walk for the door. "I'm sure Maggie will serve you what you want. I'm off for a walk about. There's not enough air in here tonight."

Fifteen

THE SPRING SUN got warmer every day, but it was dead winter for Maggie and me, though I doubt any of the customers knew. Maggie still smiled like a whore to sell a table of ale to the young ones, joked with the captains and the speechmakers and merchants, and even looked warm to those like Mouse who looked like they'd crawled from a hole with their last penny in hand. I ran the bar like always, ready to sit with a table when there was a chance, laugh on the rare chance someone said something funny, and question the regulars while they read the news from the frames hung on the wall or when I read it to them.

But we rarely talked when we closed up at night and she never invited me to share her bed. She even stopped touching me in that casual way she had, her hand on my forearm when she came to ask for drinks or a soft touch on the back to warn me she was behind. Now it was just her voice and never in the tone which invited a wink or saucy look.

And she stopped coming to me when I awoke in fear in the dark, whether she knew my terror or not, and I began to imagine her awake but hard at heart. Before I slept again, I'd feel a bit of anger that she held herself apart now, that she'd given me her warm hands and soft breasts and open thighs, but now kept them locked away like the Queen's jewels. It seemed as if we lived on either side of an ocean, and what we'd had was washed away like sand at high tide.

I felt restless and vexed when I walked about in the mornings, like there was a bit of grit in my eye that wouldn't come out. First I'd think of Maggie, and as soon as I'd get clear of her, Grendel and Hardy would take her place, and I had no answers and no plans for any of it.

It was only about a week or two later when I spotted a comely girl at the shop on Wentworth's Wharf—or it might have been that she spotted me. When I walked, she always seemed to be at the door of Widow Marden's dress shop, where a gentleman could find a skirt for his lady and a girl for his company. She would be carrying out a package or sweeping the boards in front though they looked to have been swept before. I guessed her at twenty if she was a day, with raven hair and white powdered skin that made her face look like a china doll. She was small and delicate, but she moved as quick as a cat after a bird. Her skirt was gray and plain but she wore a scarlet ribbon on her cap which drew my eye and I saw that her lips were painted, even in the morning, and her eyebrows done with blacking.

As was my habit, I was always courteous and friendly to young ladies, at least ones I didn't know yet, so each time I caught her glance, or her mine, I'd give her a smile and dip my head a bit, and I saw the gleam in her eye. But there wasn't much else that passed between us until one morning when I slowed a bit as I passed the shop and she came out in a hurry, head down, a package in hand and headed straight for me so quickly I had to catch her by the shoulders to keep from being run down.

"Pardon me, Ma'am. I thought I might I might use this bit of walk as well." She just looked at me, not much surprised, with just enough wanton glitter that I felt a quiver between my legs. "So much in a hurry that you've no time to look?"

"Well, I'm on a delivery, Mr. Gray, but I've enough time to look at what interests me." Her eyes challenged me, waiting to see if I'd join her in a bit of flirting to see where it led.

"If you know my name, I should know yours."

"There's not many about the docks who don't know your name, Mr. Gray, you seem to be about at all hours." She smiled a bit and looked sly. "Even Sundays, when the better sort are in church, you seem to have time on your hands, just as I do." She stopped and waited a moment to see if I'd make a suggestion. When I just smiled back, she went on. "I could let you guess at my name but I think that would take too long, with all the girls' names you've known before."

"There's no crime in being friendly, is there? If there was, you'd be watching over your shoulder for the sheriff as well."

She considered me a moment before answering. "I'm free to pass a word with you, but they say in years past you shared more than that with the maids about town."

"And if I did, it's something I kept between us. It sounds to me like you're gathering news for a broadside."

She colored a bit, but then stepped forward instead of back, reached inside my cloak and laid a hand on my arm. I felt it like an iron bar just cooled by a smith, still hot enough to burn if I touched it too long. "Why don't you come around some night? I stay in the back and if you let me know, I'd burn a candle, although I'd wager you could find your way without it–that is as long as Widow McGowan doesn't keep you."

My words stumbled when she used Maggie's name, and she didn't wait for me to sort it out before squeezing my arm and stepping quickly around me down the walk. But she stopped short and threw a last word over her shoulder. "And my name's Lilly, so you won't make a mistake in the dark."

We went on like regular at the Sword the next few days, Julius cooking and tending the fires, Maggie serving and keeping accounts, while I stood ready to pour and mix up the drinks the crowd was so thirsty for. It grew tiresome listening to so much talk–it seemed every tar and mechanic had a speech to make, even if he didn't understand all the words—but there was no shortage of things to talk about, and I heard every bit.

John Adams, a cousin of Samuel, found enough words in the laws to free a sailor in court who'd killed a press officer with a harpoon. Everyone had expected him to dance at the end of a rope, but instead, it was the lieutenant's death that was erased like an ink spill blotted with sand. The Army officers had their black drummers whip a grenadier to death on the Common, tying him up so he could stand for the last fifty stripes because the first two hundred weren't enough. The Sons' committee of seven claimed to inspect all the ships coming in to see if they had goods prohibited by the nonimport agreement. If they found fine satin instead of the sailcloth on the manifest, or port wine tucked in with the molasses barrels, the small and middle merchants had to claim it as a mistake and store their goods instead of selling them, while the dock loaders whispered that Hancock and Rowe and a few others were getting the same but their goods were offered for sale without a word.

But whatever went on in the streets, my mind was mostly on Maggie and how I'd drifted away from her, like a dory from a dock in the fog at night. When I thought of her and what I'd felt just a few weeks before, it all grew dimmer and farther away, until she was no more than a shape in the dark.

In the few moments when thoughts of Maggie weren't at the front, those of Grendel marched ahead and grew more fearsome. Although we'd turned him out, he'd put a seed of fear in my chest, since I couldn't predict what he might do. I found myself taking up old habits, ones I'd learned in London and Jamaica, steering away from buildings and alley corners where someone might hide, checking around the door before stepping out, fingering the hilt of the knife I'd taken from my chest and now wore in a sheath I'd sewed into my breeches, solid against my hip and hidden by my shirt on the left side.

After a few more days with my thoughts itching like lice, I called to Maggie as she got ready to go up to her room after we'd closed. She stopped at the foot of the stairs and her eyes were flat when she looked at me, like I was another tar off the street. "What is it, Nicholas?"

I found that I didn't know exactly what I wanted to say. I stared a moment. "That's my question, Maggie. What is it?"

"You mean with us?"

I simply nodded.

"I don't know, Nicholas. What is it you want?"

I could feel an edge now. "Do you mean to act like nothing's different?"

She stood in the same spot, although I'd walked two steps across the room. "It seems we've talked enough to make it clear." I shook my head, since it was all mud to me. "I've got to look to my future, and you won't give it a thought."

My chest was tight now, like a cooper had bound it with an iron hoop. "What do you think, Maggie, that I can make coins appear like magic? That I can turn this room into a country house?"

She took her turn shaking her head. "There's no need to keep after it, Nicholas. I can see where it lies."

"Are you turning me out, then?"

"Listen, Nicholas, if you've got ears. We've got no terms, we never have, and we're not married and never will be. I've never told you what to do and I don't plan to now. If you leave, it will be your own doing."

"And us . . . ?"

"What do you want, Nicholas?"

"I've kept company with you, Maggie, and no one else . . ."

"That was your choice, Nicholas, you've never heard me make demands . . ."

"You may not say it, Maggie, but you make it plain what you want."

She stopped then, thinking, her hand tight on the coin purse from the day. Her face changed and it seemed the scar on her cheek glowed as she turned her face just an inch. "Is there another fish on your line, Nicholas, is that what this is about?"

I felt my face flush then, and my hands close to fists. I saw Lilly's teasing face and felt the blood stirring between my legs. "Make yourself clear, Maggie, I've got enough puzzles as it is."

She took one long look at me before turning to the stairs. "Do as you like, Nicholas. It's not my place to stop you."

The next morning was bright enough and, without much thought, my feet took me to the Widow Marden's as I walked about after breakfast. I stood in sight of the front windows, staring at a coaster which was quartering to dock at the end of Long Wharf. Before long, I heard the shop door and turned to see Lilly walking toward Ann Street, a basket on her arm. After she'd gotten out of sight of the front windows, she turned my way.

"You'll come then, won't you?" is all she said when I got near enough. My stomach danced as I drew near but all I could do was nod. "Tonight?" I gave another nod. She smiled then, and her dark eyes flashed. "I'll wait then, but try to remember your tongue. You might find a need for it." She turned quickly and was off while I stood silent, no words forming.

We closed up the Sword like usual that night and Maggie went straight away upstairs like she'd been doing for the last weeks. My talk with Lilly had been in the back of my mind all day, and whenever it came to the front, I could feel my blood stir and the itch in my breeches. But each time I looked about the Sword, the fire died again, thoughts of Maggie crowding out the memory of Lilly's hand on my arm and the spark in her eye.

I poured a cup of good rum while I sat in the quiet and the room started to get cool with only the banked fire for warmth. I listened to the silence, and felt as if I was back on board the *Dover*. There, the night air was always filled with the sounds of the rolling sea, creaking timbers and rigging, wind sighing as it found the cracks and slipped through them. But even with the heavy noise of men breathing and groaning as they turned about in hammocks, the world always felt empty, like I had no connections and lay in a coffin with no lid, cut adrift where I might never hear a human voice again.

I filled my cup again and didn't bother to sit. I emptied it quickly and shut the back door silently as I left, just like I would on any other night I had need to be out.

Lilly was as good as her word, a candle at the window in the back on the first floor so that a quiet tap brought her quickly. She blew out the candle and opened the back door near her room. She put a hand to my mouth so I didn't speak and led me the few feet to her room in the dark. She moved close to my chest and spoke in a whisper. "Next time you might bring a bit of the rum for me as well. The Widow won't let us keep it here."

I started to answer but she put her hand to my mouth again, then helped me off with my cloak and sat me down on the bed to tug off my shoes without a word. I could see and feel just enough to know that she wore only her shift while she unbuttoned my shirt and pushed me gently on my back to get at my breeches. By the time she was done, I was hard as a rock in her hand and my breath was uneven.

I'd known since I saw her on the walk that she was a lady of pleasure. The Widow Marden was well-known for offering bright-eyed molls to some of the middling and richer men for a dear price. I'd paid whores back in London and even gave a bit more if they'd worked extra hard or brought me a laugh. But there wasn't a whisper from Lilly about coins and as I lay silent on my back, she climbed astride quickly and began riding me like a post horse, first a slow trot, then a rolling canter. In the end, I held tight to her hips and when she threw her head back I saw her white throat stretched taut. I was lost then, and gave a low growl before I made a final thrust and she seemed to suck all the juice from me.

Later, we lay for a bit without words, the heat beneath the blanket as good as sitting before a roaring fire. Just as my mind came back and I thought of Maggie alone in her bed, Lilly whispered a few words. "You will come back, won't you? I've got some questions for you . . ." She must have felt me tense a bit because she quickly moved her hand down my stomach and added, " . . . and if your mast stands straight again, I'll hang a flag on it." She moved her hand a bit and I nodded silently as I nuzzled in her hair like a colt.

Sixteen

THINGS WERE DIFFERENT FOR ME at the Sword after that, though the tavern kept up as usual. It was spring and when I walked, the sun made me forget what was behind and see bright things ahead, at least for a few hours at a time. I tended my business as bar man and visited Lilly some nights, and when I looked across to see Maggie, I buried the ache I felt by remembering a cold look she once gave me or some words of hers which cut like a knife.

In Lilly's bed, there was no room for worry. We were alive with heat and sweat and demanding rhythms, our bodies hungry and seldom filled. But when I lay by myself some nights near to dreams, I saw myself drifting in a long boat after a ship went down. I couldn't make headway without an oar and couldn't even tell if I changed position, riding the swells up and down, no landmarks to tell me if I moved east or west, or first one way and then the other, or stayed still as death.

Gillam and I found some silver jewelry in a merchant's chest in the back room of a shop one night, the same night he and his round belly were out dancing a minuet with his lady and Commissioner Robinson and the rest of the Tories and uppers from Customs. We were careful not to take too much–enough to make it worth our while, but little enough it might not be discovered right away or might be thought lost or misplaced. It wouldn't pay to have the whole Tory crowd up in arms searching for thieves and watching their treasure. But it wasn't enough to send Gillam to New York to sell, either, so he hid it back in our warehouse corner till we had more. We had a small pile of buckles for garters and shoes, snuff boxes and gold points for tailoring, goods small enough to carry beneath a cloak, but there was no one to buy them in Boston without raising too much alarm.

Mouse had decided that he should learn to read. He'd stand in a corner in the gallery of the Town House and listen to hours of talk and speeches there, but there were newspapers and broadsides everywhere as well and he felt it was important that he kept up. I was sitting with him one afternoon, the paper spread between us, his thin finger following the words in the *Journal* and a frown twisting his narrow face which was marked on both cheeks by the pox. He knew his letters and I helped him along in making them work into words. I looked up when the door opened to see Burns walking in.

He hadn't been in for a few weeks, not since we had our last words over my loyalty to the cause of liberty and I'd walked away into the night. I didn't know his intent now, but he sat down with us and his look was friendly enough.

"Shall I get you a drink, Mr. Burns?"

"When you have time, Nicholas. I've just come to rest my legs a bit."

Mouse continued on with the words in the news, but now whispered his tries at making them out rather than speaking them out loud.

Both Burns and I were silent for a bit after I brought him back a mug of hard cider. "A lot of work is it? Stoking the fire and stirring the pot?" I asked.

He gave a slight grin. "You don't know, Nicholas—and I doubt you want to know—but there's constant work to do if we want to get free of the King's soldiers and his taxes." He took a drink of his cider, and turned serious again. "But we will, we won't let them rest till they turn tail towards England."

Mouse looked up at him, then at me before he started out stuttering. "Wh . . . what . . . what about Mr. Adams' taxes?"

Burns looked at him in surprise, then gave a short laugh. "You see, Nicholas? I can't get down two swallows without having to answer a question."

After Adams had gotten the circular letter written up and passed by the General Court and sent to all the colonies last year—he had waited to take the vote until the country men who were against it had left for home at the end of the session—and the Governor stopped the General Court from meeting, some felt Adams had gone too far. He'd failed as a tax collector just as he had as a brewer, although he'd still drawn his pay from the town. All of the Tories and a few Whigs thought he shouldn't be allowed to go ahead when he had seven thousand pounds uncollected and the other collectors were almost current. Burns was one of those who helped him get an extension to pay what he hadn't collected. After Town Meeting had spent a whole day arguing, Adams had won out and gotten another six months to come closer to even. It worked even better for Adams when two of the selectmen who always fought him resigned in protest.

I waited a moment before asking Burns, "Well, it's a good enough question. Do you have an answer?"

Burns shook his head. He might have left Mouse with a joke but knew he couldn't get around me. "Some were paid in the fall, but it seems people have forgotten the rest for the moment, what with troops invading us."

Mouse had started it, but I couldn't let it go. "Who paid? It couldn't have been Adams. All he sees is the bottom of his purse when he opens it, and he's been too busy with his quill and his meetings to go out collecting."

Burns gave a small smile. "He has friends that help."

I waited but he volunteered no more. I couldn't help but shake my head. "He costs a lot, doesn't he?"

His eyes glinted now, and I could see he was ready to hoist a flag from the Liberty Pole and make a speech for the crowd, though it was only me and Mouse who listened. "What price do you put on freedom?"

"Do you mean my own or the word I keep seeing printed in the papers and flung about? My own is very dear, upwards of twenty pounds last time," I said, thinking of the invented debt which put me in gaol. I stopped a moment as Burns took a drink of his cider. "But giving Adams freedom to make trouble is a bit more expensive, and the price will keep going up. And the cost isn't just in pounds." Burns put a question in his look to me before I went on to explain. "Do you think the Tories will give up ordering us about like a scullery maid, take back the troops because we've behaved so well, pay a sum to make up for what we've lost in trade, then give us a gentle pat on the back? Maybe they'll thank us all for giving Samuel Adams the freedom to point out their mistakes. We'll pay the costs one way or another."

Burns shrugged, like it was a question of no moment. "You were talking about costs in sterling before. Hancock treated you as a friend once, and he didn't even know you. Don't you suppose he'd help a true friend like Adams now?"

"If those two are true friends, I'm a lord and master. They make as odd a pair as any I've seen—there's Adams in his worn homespun and preacher's look shuffling along beside Hancock in his bright satin suits like the cock of the walk. It's like putting a dull raven beside a parrot, but it's the raven that's taught the parrot to talk. The Tories say Hancock's just a milk cow for Adams bucket." I could see Mouse with a small smile now, turning to Burns to see what might come.

Burns took it all at ease. "They meet in the middle when the time's right. Adams would have us all pure, poor, and pious—he'd have good Americans making Labradore tea from our own bushes and eating gruel served in wooden dishes, then sitting straight and proud in our pews. Hancock? He wants to be free to spend as much money as the Tories on parties and Madeira and buy enough plate to break the sideboard." He took a short drink to wet his tongue. "But Adams needs his purse to make some things easy—feasts on the holidays, ink for the paper, loans for the merchants, jobs for the shipwrights. The crowds stay loyal enough when they owe a favor. And if Hancock hadn't decided to take Adams hand, the crowd might have torn down the Hancock mansion before they got to Hutchinson's. He dresses like a Tory, eats like one, and has the finest coach on the streets." He paused a moment in thought. "I don't know he wouldn't go back when the time and money's right."

I was surprised Burns was so plain with us, but he knew I wouldn't be spouting his words to a room full of dockhands and it was sure Mouse wasn't making speeches. Mouse went back to his paper after a bit, his finger like a twig moving across the page.

Finally Burns turned back to me after staring a moment at the smoky picture of the sunrise that hung over the hearth. "We'd still welcome you, Nicholas. I know which way you lean, no matter what words you say. You're as plain to read as the grasshopper on the Town House vane." When I didn't answer, he went on. "You'd be surprised how much we can help a friend."

I quickly shook my head. "But then I'd owe, wouldn't I, just like I'd borrowed fifty pounds? I don't have much, Burns, but at least I can go my own way when I choose."

"Did you explain that well enough to Grendel when he was here last?"

I clenched my jaw at that and bit off my next words. "That's none of your concern, yours or the Sons or Maggie or anyone else. I'll watch what's mine and you'd do well to watch yours."

It sounded good when I said it, and Mouse looked pleased after Burns left, but it wasn't two nights until Grendel proved me wrong.

WE KEPT the back door to the Sword locked most times, but someone had left it open and he came through it as we were just about to close. There were only two jacks left, drunk and arguing a bit and staring into the coals as the fire burned down. I'd heard the back door and assumed it was Mouse or Gillam who'd come in and didn't want to be seen at the front. When I looked up, I saw it was Grendel filling the door enough to block it off. Right away I moved back from him and called for Maggie to find Julius who'd gone out a bit earlier.

Grendel looked like he was out for a walk, breathing through his mouth like always, but nothing important on his mind. "You'll want to send them away," he motioned with his head toward the sailors, "we've got some business to discuss." They'd hardly noticed Grendel enter. I wasn't keen on talking with Grendel alone though I knew they'd be no help. If I could keep him for a minute, Julius might come or some other regular customer might happen in who would at least stand behind me.

"It's not closing time and I'd hate to hurry them through a fine drink they've paid for." They'd looked up now and saw Grendel in the back.

"You tars should walk out now or you won't be able to later," rasped Grendel loudly, and they took him at his word. Now it was just me facing him and I started to gauge how I might move to get my blade out and get in a slice before he could take it from me.

I talked now to give me more time. "What's your business, walking in a back door like it was your own? I see your size but I've seen plenty like you carved into fish bait."

He looked at me for a moment and turned his back like he had no worries. "There's someone out back who wants to see you."

Mouse lay in a heap on the muddy ground, his right arm folded into his chest, his breath short and forced. Behind him stood two men, one I'd never seen before wearing a cloth cap and holding a cocked pistol before him, and the other a curly-haired fighter who traveled at the back of some of the Liberty crowds. He held a staff beside him fitted with a harpoon's point. The back door was left part open so there was just a sliver of light into the black night.

I went to Mouse quickly and knelt by his side. He opened his eyes but he wasn't seeing much but the pain. I bent down to him.

"My arm . . . it's broken in two," he breathed out, then closed his eyes again. I moved around him a bit, turning away from where they stood.

Grendel's voice was rough in the night. "You should choose them stronger than that if they're going to be any help to you, Gray. It was no more than snapping a twig." I could feel the blood rushing up and I took a sharp breath in. "You didn't seem to take me seriously," offered Grendel, "but I'll wager you will now."

He moved closer so I could feel his threat and lowered his voice. "I wanted to start with you, but damage to you might have held things up more. This way you'll be able to start collecting what you owe right away." He paused and I could feel his eyes on my back. He shuffled up within an arm's length. "But next time it will be you, Gray, I'll break you up so everyone here knows what they did in London—pay me or suffer."

The knife came out as easily as ever and I got a backhand swing from one knee that caught the side of his thigh before he could move its great girth. He shouted out as the blade parted the cloth and sliced into muscle. Both his hands went to grab his leg and I began to get up but the harpoon point caught my shirt, just missing my shoulder, knocking me back. I grabbed at the staff with both hands, dropping the knife and getting a hold enough to drag Grendel's mate ahead and toward me. We tripped over Mouse who screamed as we fell in a tangle. I'd just rolled over on top and had a hand full of the man's curly hair when his other mate kicked me just beneath the arm and I could feel my ribs break up as the pain shot down my side.

I heard Grendel shouting and the two I was tangled with stopped suddenly as I struggled against the pain and turned over from my stomach. I could just see Julius behind him, Grendel on a knee and both hands on his thigh, Julius pulling his hair back to lay open his neck for the blade in his hand. Grendel's mouth was open and spittle dripped in a line toward the ground. The other two looked at me, eager to put me under, but their advantage wasn't great enough and they thought it better to stop than to watch Grendel's blood spill into a pool.

"Move on," said Julius, motioning with his head down the alley, "I'll let him stumble after you when you're gone."

"Go," said Grendel just loud enough to hear, "just far enough to watch what happens. You can train the pistol on either one and I expect you to shoot if they do me harm."

They both backed up slowly, far enough to be out of range of a knife or the harpoon staff, but close enough we wouldn't risk their shot. "Up now, you ox, or I'll slaughter you for market." Grendel struggled to get up, a hand still on his leg where his breeches were soaked with blood. Julius backed away, watching him closely and picked up the staff with his free hand.

As Grendel neared the other two, the pistol came up on Julius, but Grendel put out a hand to push it away. He said nothing and his jaw stayed tense, his mouth open just enough for him breathe. But he turned and pointed at Julius, then at me, slowly bringing his giant hand into a fist and then opening it as if he'd squeezed the life from a sparrow and then dropped it in the mud.

Seventeen

AT FIRST, I STRUGGLED with each breath because of the pain in my ribs. It lessened after a week, but I still felt a knife blade in my side with each bend and twist and not long after that, a cough took me. Maggie tied the wrappings as tight as she could, but each cough set me clutching at the pain in my side. When it lifted, I prayed it wouldn't return.

Julius and Gillam had found a ship's doctor that night to come and look us over, even though he was mostly drunk and ready to be plucked at a bawd's house on King St. He prodded about my ribs until I screamed, then built a straight arm for Mouse with sticks and wrapping. Maggie tended us both, Mouse laid out on a straw pallet in the hall beneath the back stairs, then bringing up food for me where I sat in my bed stewing and boiling like a pot hung over the fire.

At first, she worried over us and kindly gave us what she could. But once it was clear we'd mend, she began to grumble and act cross. When I lay in bed and heard her coming up the stair, I longed for the easy days of our early time, and a part of me regretted ever seeing Lilly. But before Maggie was done with the stew and the blankets, she'd usually spoken sharply enough that I wondered why she'd come at all.

After a few days, Mouse went back to his old ways, sleeping in a corner of an empty warehouse up Lynn St. or at the back of a nunnery around a corner from where his doxie lived. He would come in to the

Sword after we'd served dinner and prop his arm on the table in front, often studying his fingers and moving them about. When Gillam came to fish about for a card game, he'd tease Mouse. "What, Mouse, are you going to take up picking locks? Or maybe pockets? Or you could try Paul Revere. Maybe he would hire you to engrave punchbowls." Mouse was never good at easy talk, but didn't take offense, either. He would continue looking at his arm and then ruffle at the wrapping. When it smelled too bad, Maggie changed it so she wouldn't have to order him out the door.

It was clear that we'd had a go round with someone, but I kept it tight from Burns and the others who'd flap about it all around the docks. Someone made up a story about a drunken tar we'd put out front and I was glad to let them repeat it.

Mouse still managed to hear everything along the water, some from listening, but most from passing words with the others who lived in the corners and shadows like he did. They were small and quiet, able to disappear when they needed, vanishing somehow between the planks on the docks or the gaps between cobblestones. If they were caught at the wrong time, on a day some constable banged a toe on a hearthstone, they'd be ordered to the workhouse, but they were out soon enough. Some earned a few pennies from a scavenger for loading a stinking pile of garbage onto the wagon, or a liveryman for washing a carriage, or a rich man's housemaid for scrubbing the steps before a special supper. They might even stand in for a day of ropewalking when a regular slept through with a head full of rum. Their eyes and ears were always open and Mouse reported that Grendel was slow moving now, and his leg seemed stiff beneath him.

When she wasn't vexed, Maggie was at me to make a try with Draper again, although I was still weak from too many days and nights where my only thoughts were avoiding another stab in the side from turning or breathing. "It can't hurt you, Nicholas. I'll go along, even talk for you if you want. If you can get Draper to call Grendel off, we'd all breathe a little easier." I must have looked pained because she'd softened for a moment when she thought of what she'd said. "I'm sorry, Nicholas, I know you're troubled when you breathe. I meant we'd rest easier."

I was angry still, but didn't have the muscle to resist. "I'll go Maggie, if you'll talk. But I can't promise I'll leave Grendel to strut about without making him pay one way or the other. And I won't grovel for Draper either," I said with some force, but even strong words made me wince at the pain in my side.

Draper had been moving up gradually, now a leading member of the tricked-up "body" of merchants, the Boston Society for Encouraging Trade and Commerce, which approved Adams' nonimportation ideas. Of course, they let everyone vote as a merchant, as long as they shouted for whatever the Sons proposed. It was like town meeting where only property holders were supposed to vote, but the Sons got around it by declaring that every man who followed them *might* own property some day. Adams would have let Mouse vote on nonimport if he knew the right time to raise his voice. Draper was especially welcome because he was an actual merchant and new to their cause.

At the same time, he drank coffee with the Tories and found his way to some of their entertainments and suppers, explaining to the Sons that it was all in business and he needed terms to help him through, even if he was against the Townshend duties. He was good with a smile as long as he didn't have to keep it too long, and he had a hound's nose for the scent of money.

We tried at his store one day, but were told that he didn't come in every day because his wife was suffering from a nervous complaint. Maggie convinced me we should go to his front door since it would seem rude for a middling Whig like himself to send us away.

He lived in the South End now, not far from Rowe's new house, and since it was before noon and a warm day in late spring with a blue sky, we decided to walk down the mall on the Common. The people in Boston claimed it was the finest in America, though most had no way of knowing. The elm trees on either side did make a fine promenade, and they were mixed in with some apple and cherry trees showing late blossoms. If my ribs didn't make me consider where each step landed, it would have been easy to forget all of it—the duties, the docks, the brawling sailors, and the scheming men hard after me. For a moment, my thoughts went back to a rare spring day in Oxford near the river, when a fog had been burned away by the sun and I could smell the damp earth and the air was sweet and fresh with scents of lilacs and orange dogwood.

Maggie must have sensed my wandering mind, and for a moment she took my arm, as if all was well and our differences forgotten. I felt light for a moment until my breath caught again and I had to stop.

"You'll be whole again soon, Nicholas, if you keep from scuffling."

After I caught my breath, we started out again. "You say so, and I believe it, but it doesn't make it any easier to sleep. I've tried every direction."

We took a few more steps before she stopped to gaze at an apple tree as if she'd never seen one before. She spoke low and I didn't hear a threat in her voice. "What about your Lilly? Can't she make it go away?"

I turned to her quickly, then away as my face colored. I'd just seen Lilly two nights before and she'd stroked me with her hand, and me in turn for her, when I couldn't move about to get in her. Maggie held my arm tight as I began to turn away.

I spoke with some heat. "Here we are on to Draper's and you'd upset it all like that? I don't know why I've come anyway."

Maggie was silent but held me firmly while she gazed at the pink blossoms which would fall in a few days. "What's to upset you Nicholas? Are you surprised I'd know? Just because you don't speak up doesn't mean that others aren't." She waited but I could say nothing and couldn't look at her either. "Besides, we've been plain about it. I laughed at marrying and you at moving away, so what's to keep us? Especially when there's pretty young whores who'll part their legs when you want."

I turned toward her now but still couldn't find a word. If she was asking a question, I didn't have an answer.

"We said it was just business, Nicholas, and you've made certain of it now. You tend to what you need and I will as well. If I take a man, it'll be none of your affair." She stared at me and she could see my face working up to some words. "And don't complain either. It's your doing as much as mine. You've eaten your cake. It's boys that want to keep it, too."

I wanted to turn back, leave her and her words until I could sort them out. My face was flushed and hot, but she took my arm again and we walked the rest of the way in silence. As we came near Draper's door, she turned to me, and her face had turned bright enough that she might have just come upon a guinea in the gutter. "We're here to offer him a bit of sugar, Nicholas, try to remember that. He's trying to be a gentleman now, and it won't do to make a threat."

It was a fine brick house, two stories with a white fence around it and its own pump out back and a small garden, but you could fit it into Hancock's coach house with a bit to spare. A Negro serving woman came to the door.

"We're here to see Mister Draper about a special order from his store. We've already gone by and since it was such a fine day we decided to walk up to visit. This is Nicholas Gray and I'm Maggie McGowan." The door shut and we waited several minutes before she came back to show us up the stairs. The walls near the front door were covered with printed wallpaper, a silver pattern of diamonds on a light blue backing, as fine as any I'd seen, but it stopped after the parlor door. I imagined Draper getting some in an exchange or off a new shipment before anyone else knew it was there, but he didn't have quite enough to finish out the walls in the central hall.

Draper sat in an upstairs room used as an office. A pile of papers covered the small desk in front of him which was set at an angle to the fireplace, and a lamp burned so he could see to write. He gave us seats across from the desk and shut the door behind us after greeting us kindly and sending the woman downstairs. But his eye was harsh when he turned and there was little warmth left in his voice. His face still proved smooth and handsome, but his eyes seemed even more restive now, like a pet squirrel watching out for a hound.

"And to what do I owe a visit from the owners of a disreputable tavern like the Sword and Scabbard? Maybe you would like to borrow money? Sorry, I've forgotten. You already owe me and don't pay."

I shifted in my chair to make my chest a bit more comfortable before Maggie began. "First we thought we'd offer congratulations to you. It seems the Whigs have made you a friend. We hear your name sometimes when one or the other of the Sons starts talking about merchants."

You could tell it pleased him for Maggie to speak kindly, and he couldn't help a little flutter of his hand to show himself humble to praise. "I've listened to the sides and it seems the merchants here should get the same chance as those in London. There's money to be made in America and I don't think Charles Townshend should collect it all." He smiled at Maggie as he might over dinner to another merchant's wife.

"It seems you're prospering then, what with your windows full and your clerk doing most of the business there," Maggie offered.

He smiled again at her, always charming if it came to a lady. "I've made headway, yes, I won't deny it. If the port troubles could be worked out, we'd all be better off." He fiddled with a quill on his desk for a moment before turning again to us. "But I don't need to convince you. I'm sure that's all you hear from the rabble you serve." He gave a smile still, but there was a knife blade hidden in it.

I was ready to break in but Maggie looked hard at me before turning to Draper again. "We might discuss politics a bit more some other time and I'm sure you and Nicholas would agree on most points, but we're here on personal business." She waited a moment before moving on. "There's always been a question about what Nicholas owes you, and there's none to say surely he owes you at all."

Draper sat forward now staring at Maggie as if I wasn't there. "I know when someone's stolen from me and he's never denied getting swag from Brand." He turned to me now. "I saw it in his eyes and he left me before with a threat."

Again Maggie came with the hard look at me. "I can't speak to what his eyes tell you, but it doesn't seem you need it right now. If we can make an arrangement, we could pay a bit at the beginning of winter or the end of the year when it's all summed up. It's only a few months and you could have your man tend to more important business."

He was silent a moment, considering. "That would seem reasonable to some in the merchant business." He paused. "But you see, Mr. Greendale is in a different business, one all his own. He prospered in London and it won't be long until he has control here." He took another pause to see the effect on us. "I've given him authority to collect as he sees fit and he gets his percentage. He might be upset if I cancelled the contract when he's already invested time and energy." Now, he showed a small smile. "Do you have a cough coming on, Gray? You seem to be having some difficulty breathing."

I made to stand up quickly but I moved the wrong way and hunched over before I could get upright, grabbing under my arm. Draper laughed out right. "You're not so bold now are you? That's just what Grendel said—a little pain might change your attitude."

He stopped, enjoying the moment. I made to get up by turning to the side. "Have him stay, Widow, he needs to hear what I have to say." Maggie put an arm out and I waited, not sure whether my ribs or my pride hurt me worse. "I have a better proposition for you, my dear. You're a fine widow, even with your face as it is, and you're smart enough to run the tavern on your own. You could find anyone to hoist your barrels and put the ragged sailors in the street. Why not cut yourself loose from your anchor," his head nodded slightly in my direction, "and let someone with prospects help you?"

I shifted in my seat and tried to lean forward but I found no comfort in Draper's fancy arm chair. I sank back as Maggie responded. "What is it you're proposing, Mr. Draper?"

"It would be easy enough, Widow, I've plenty to offer. Turn Gray out and let him curl up in some whorehouse until Grendel finds him. They can dance any way they want and it wouldn't hurt you. I'd offer a man to help you, give you some money and goods to make your little fox den a place of respect—more barrels, more punch and Madeira, some plate for the tables, pipes and tobacco, maybe even coffee, whatever could draw a better crowd." He slowed a minute to let her think. "There are plenty that have the coin—not those on the docks, but the others I see on exchange and strolling on Sunday. We'd make little of politics and let them play at cards and dice. You might even find a girl or two who could serve in a room upstairs." He stared at Maggie, his eyes fiery now that he was talking money. "I might even buy the building so you wouldn't worry about the lease, and the license would come without trouble, too." He paused once more and licked his lips once over. "You'd find that I'm quite generous with those who are generous with me."

Maggie was taken back, I could see it, and no words came to her.

"You don't have to answer me now, I have time to wait—but not too much. If you want, I can draw numbers for what we'd need and how we'd split. I've always wanted into a tavern, and it would solve your problems, too." His voice lowered just a bit. "If I were you, I would hate to think of Grendel coming about to make a mess of my room or laying hands on me." He leaned forward one last time, all invitation and flattery. "If you knew me a bit better, you'd step right now. If you want, I could order some flattering skirts and such, caracos with material right off the ship. You'd get the best so you could welcome our new men at the door, they'd love to take your hand, and there'd be someone else to tend the kitchen and bar."

Maggie stood up suddenly, as if coming back from a dream. "I've heard your offer, Mister Draper, but it's nothing I've thought about. I've been proud to have the tavern on my own. We came to speak of an old debt which might be dropped or lowered."

Draper shook his head and his eyes turned sharp even though the smile stayed. "The debt will always be there if you let this dog in your door. You should know by now that he'll steal from under your nose and bring nothing back." He shifted his gaze back to me. "It doesn't take much to bring him up short, either. He's boasted to me but now he's caved in, like a straw man. The Sons might use him for Paxton's effigy."

I rose at that but held my ribs with one hand. I started to spit out some threat, but Maggie stopped me. "We're finished here Mr. Draper. We'll be on our way."

We moved toward the door and he called out after us. "But I notice you didn't say 'No' did you, Widow Magowan? I'll wait to hear, and I wager you'll see it, if you're bold enough to look—it's the best offer you'll get."

Eighteen

WE WALKED BACK in silence, slowly enough for my ribs, but my mind was running about like a cannon ball on the deck. When we got to the Sword, Maggie went to get her apron for serving while I sat out front. When she came back in, wiping a cup to put behind the bar, she looked at me sadly.

"You didn't say 'No,' did you Maggie?"

"You heard the same as Draper."

"So, should I go on now or wait till you add some figures and then send me off?"

She shook her head and moved towards the table. "What would you have me do, Nicholas? Tip his wig? Laugh in his face?" She advanced right across to me now and stood staring. "What if you took a notion to hie out to New York one night with your doll and your purse? It's all business, isn't it Nicholas? That's what we said as we walked to his house. You might find better business somewhere else." She began to walk toward the kitchen but turned back and came near. "I've got no protection, Nicholas. I could lose the license or the lease or the money for new barrels and I'd go under without a ripple."

"But Draper?"

"What difference does it make who it is? Why should I care where the money comes from? Do you think your thieving is that much better than his?"

I felt her words like a fist in the stomach, but I answered back anyway. "It's greed, Maggie, greed and gambling. He's got enough now to live easy in the middle, but he's got to have more, and he'd love to step on us if we're in the way." Maggie gave a puzzled look and a shrug, like what I'd said made little sense and carried no weight. "What about Mouse, then? He'll be lucky to be whole again, and Draper had a hand in that."

"I don't like that part, but I don't like any of the other parts, either. It's all a bad business, but it's still business. I've been a whore, Nicholas, I've taken money from all kinds of men and let them do their work. Some belonged in the garbage in the street, except they got hold of a bag of coins one way or another. Do you think yourself better?"

I wanted to thrust back at her, but I felt too tired, too sore, too weak. She searched at my face with her eyes, half a challenge and half sorry. Her voice was lower now. "You're here and I've done what I could for you, even when you've gone hunting like a tomcat. Sometimes I don't know why, I think I must be ready for Bedlam, but I've stood behind you when I could have turned away. If you'd have me prove something by upbraiding Draper, you've never taken a look through my eyes."

She rubbed the cup harder and the challenge came again, but it quickly faded and some of the color left her face. "You could think of reasons all day, just like Burns, and spin them out in fine words, and if I was foolish, I'd listen and consider. But it would be like standing on the gallows–when the trap door drops, the noose comes up."

I didn't speak and started to turn to get up, thinking I might find an empty dock where I could sit.

"I'm not ready to sell you, Nicholas, or send you for your trunk. If it was truly only business, I'd have jumped as soon as Draper brought it up. He was true when he said I wouldn't get a better offer." She paused and stared at me hard, but her eyes softened after a moment. "If you'd take a moment to think instead of flaming up, you'd see it's better that I said nothing. I have no love of Draper and I'd look in every direction before I took what he offered. I can let him wait for now and I wager Grendel won't come while I'm still thinking. It gives you a bit of time."

She paused, shook her head slightly and turned to go. "I pray you're true in our business," she said, turning back to look at me, "because your heart is a riddle." She took one more step and then turned to look one more time. "Sometimes I think you're like a loose cannon on the deck in a storm, and no one knows which direction you'll point, or when you'll fire, or who will get hurt. Not even you."

I sat for a long time after Maggie went back to the kitchen. I could hear Julius chopping his blade hard into the block in the corner, cutting up the two chickens he'd plucked clean after bringing them from the market that morning. Jezebel came to sit near on the bench but didn't venture onto my lap like she did with Maggie. I stared at the cold fireplace and its blackened bricks, but I didn't really see them.

There was nothing to keep me from leaving Maggie and the Sword. I could catch one of the coasters moving goods to New York and I'd be there in a few days without anyone the wiser. But it was a thought with no substance. I wasn't suited for hiding out like some. I thought Gillam could spend every day in a closet as long as he could play cards by a candle at night. I couldn't show my face to the Navy, but when I thought of leaving Boston quick and quiet, I saw a hare running for a hole with a hound at its neck.

I felt sad, and a little scared, when I thought of leaving Julius, and I realized that I welcomed the sight of Mouse like I might a young brother. Gillam was different—I knew his skill and trusted what he did, but there still seemed a trick up his sleeve, one that would stay as hidden as his picklocks. Maggie was right when she said my heart was a riddle, but the thought of leaving her and Julius and Mouse and the Sword made it jump like a frog. If I found a new town, I would never see Grendel again and be free of my worries that the Sheriff or Tobin or Hardy would get a hand on my throat. But I knew I couldn't leave

Maggie behind, not unless she sent me herself. Even though our words said that it was only business, I felt I belonged behind the bar at the Sword with Maggie at the tables and the others close by. It was the only picture I could see.

I'm not sure how long I sat, but sometime later I heard a sound and looked up to see Julius sitting down across from me. "You're not asleep, but you act like it," he offered. "I might have been a peg leg tromping up from behind and you wouldn't have known."

"I feel I'm in a cage, Julius, with bars you can't see."

"Who's got you, then? Grendel?"

"He's one."

Julius looked away and said softly, "If I'd cut him that night, he'd be no more trouble. I might have let him get up and come for me, and when he fell, we would have been rid of him forever. If it was the two of you, two white men, they would have called it a fair fight." He stopped and was silent for a long time, so much that I heard Bel rubbing against the loggerheads where they stood by the hearth. "Will you kill him now?"

I shook my head slowly, "No, Julius, I can't, not lying in wait. If he came for me, then . . ."

"You might kill him or he might kill you," Julius finished my sentence for me. "But it would take more than a walking stick to close his eyes." He paused a minute. "It's like baiting a bear, except he's off his chain. Most would bet on the bear."

"I can't think of anything else, Julius, nothing else seems right. I'll just have to take my chances."

Julius often wore a red kerchief, around his neck and beneath his shirt when he was walking about, and tied it around his head just across his forehead when he cooked, the tails hanging down to his shirt in the back. It crimped his hair, which curled out a half knuckle from his head like many in Jamaica, but longer than any slave or freed man I'd seen here. Sometimes when he cooked, he turned from the hearth and I could see the sweat standing out above the scarlet band. Now, he pulled it from his head and let it dangle in his hand. His eyes closed for long enough that he might have been asleep, until finally, he turned to speak. "There's always another way, Nicholas. We just need to think what it is."

It took us a few days to think of it and a fortnight to get it ready, but it seemed to suit our purposes. The only thorn was that it would put me in debt to Burns. But everything has its cost, and it was the debt that seemed the smallest, and one that I'd be able to pay.

No matter how many words flew out of the Town House or the Governor's Council, no matter what the state of importation or taxes or natural rights, even with troops stacked like cordwood all over Boston, commencement at Harvard would be a frolic like no other. Pope's Day was for the lower sort and offered them a chance to brawl and mock their betters, but the celebration at Harvard brought everyone to Cambridge, top to bottom, to enjoy everything the sour churchmen didn't want them to. There were only a few, like Samuel Adams, who refused to go. He thought it showed Americans to be too much like the weak lords in Britain whose only purpose was eating and drinking and dancing. Their actions proved they had no moral standing.

If a son was graduating, it gave the uppers a chance to show off their money by competing for the greatest feast served to the most people. They hired every servant and maid they could find and bought wagons of meat and fish from the markets and food straight from the ships and farms. They put up table after table, joining them end to end, and covered them all with cloths so they might sit three hundred at once. The carpenters had to be sure the tables were sturdy enough to hold a whole pig, a side of beef, venison, turtles, lobsters, partridge, turkey, and every other animal and fruit that might be found within twenty miles. The cakes covered tables by themselves and they served enough punch to float a dory. Everyone drank what they could and for several mornings the housemaids and butlers worked hard for their little money by cleaning up the gentlemen and ladies to look as good as they did the night before.

Although the servants and the rabble could only gawk at the tables and food and drink, they didn't want for merriment either. Every type of tent and entertainment came to set up on the common and it was a fair for all. Jugglers threw clubs and swords higher than their heads and another group balanced themselves one on top of the other until they could pluck birds out of the trees. There was all manner of drink and food for sale, bread and sweets and stew, and barrels of punch set up under every tree. There were card games and music makers to keep things lively, and some danced all night.

The Boston ministers and the Harvard elders had done everything to try to keep things more quiet and stately, including threatening the students and changing the date, but they'd failed completely and given up. The roads were filled with carriages and horses and carts and walkers, some going north to Charlestown by ferry and then west to Cambridge, others streaming out the Neck and around past Dorchester and Roxbury Hill. On a Wednesday morning every July, a party began in Cambridge and didn't stop until Sunday.

We were sure that Grendel would be there and we weren't wrong. Julius and Mouse and I saw him on the second day from a spot we'd chosen beneath a tree and slightly above the green. He was easy to keep track of because he was almost a head taller than the rest and the crowd usually parted about him when he walked. He stopped to stare at the hand tricks of a shabby man who made shillings appear and disappear, then moved off towards some wagons where another man stood in the back offering caged birds for sale.

We all stayed back, because Grendel knew us by sight. We didn't intend a fight, and it was best if he didn't see us at all. He'd never seen Gillam—few did if Gillam didn't want them to—but we knew he was in the crowd near Grendel somewhere. So was the man Burns had provided, a certain Mr. Armstrong who Burns said had no fear and would face off a pistol without a thought. He was a brazier with a small shop on Ann St. where he turned out fittings and hinges and fancy tops for andirons. He looked thin under a jacket that was too large and collar with too much to spare, but his hands were all sinew.

Two hours later, we drank a cup with Gillam in the Crow's Nest near the college and he warmed to the tale, his dark eyes bright with victory. "It was easy enough for me. Grendel's the type who doesn't feel much in the way of bumps and brushes, though the person he bumps might have to pick himself up. The crowd was around him and he walked enough to make it easy. I won't do it as a habit, because if something goes wrong there's too many near who might hold you down. But I'm good enough to pick a pocket when I need to." He smiled now and drank, proud and preening a bit, one hand brushing back his black, drooping mustache at the sides, the narrow fingers of his other holding his cup delicately. "But I've never done this one before. It's not picking pockets, is it, when you leave it heavier than when you started? I got it in his pocket easy enough and he took no more notice of me than he did anyone else."

"I moved off a little but stayed to watch. Armstrong played his part like an actor from a troupe. He wasn't minding his way when he bumped straight into Grendel. He was full surprised and raised his voice enough that all the others around could hear. 'Why don't you watch your way, you big ox? You almost broke my shoulder.' Grendel looked amazed when he spoke up. I'm sure most don't say a word to him even if he steps on their foot. Armstrong didn't even give it up then, making sure everyone saw. 'You're too big to be running about without a harness. You should be hitched in the road.' He held his arm tight and moved his shoulder around to see that it moved enough. Grendel finally found his tongue and growled at him to move away, he'd done nothing wrong. Armstrong acted as if he might consider saying more, but thought better of it and walked away muttering. The crowd talked a little but mostly went back to what they were doing."

"I followed Armstrong to see how he did it. He only walked ten paces when he made a show of stopping to search his pockets. He searched them all and then his waistcoat pocket a second time. He looked alarmed and started looking about and calling for a constable at the top of his lungs. Eventually he got to one of the watch who was standing under a tree at the side where we'd seen him before. I stayed too far away to hear, but Armstrong made all the motions with his hands and showing his empty pocket and measuring how tall Grendel stood. When Armstrong pointed out his head above the crowd a ways off, the watchman took Armstrong to the constable on the other edge of the common, trying to keep Grendel in sight. All three pushed through the crowd and came up on him from behind."

"'That's him,' shouted out Armstrong, 'that's the dog that took my snuff box' and Grendel turned to face them. The constable was a little slow at speaking but finally found his voice. 'This man says you knocked into him a few minutes ago and stole his snuff box at the same time. What do you have to say?' Grendel was quiet a moment, faced with the two constables and a crowd around them. His fists opened and closed a few times as he scanned about and finally said, 'He bumped into me, he wasn't watching where he walked.' Armstrong nearly shouted out and turned to the constable, 'Do you think I could miss seeing something like him? I'd have to be blind' and the crowd laughed.

"Grendel looked angry now but held himself tight. 'What do you say to the snuff box?' they asked him. 'I've no need of it and if I wanted it I'd bargain straight with him. He might sell it to me, but I'm no light-fingered thief. My hand wouldn't even fit in his pocket.' This bit put off the constable for a minute, but Armstrong stayed after him. 'Search his pockets then, and if there's nothing. I'll take my loss, though I wager he took it and passed it on.'

"The constable wasn't keen on searching Grendel, but the crowd was behind him, urging him on just to see the game. Finally, Grendel agreed as long as they left him alone when they were done, but the snuff box turned up just where I'd left it in the right-side pocket of his coat. You could see the lamp lit when he realized what was happening and I thought he might throw them all over and bolt, but he thought better, what with one constable armed with a pistol and the crowd following ready to help. Of course he threatened Armstrong when they led him away, but the constable warned him that threatening could be a crime too and he'd spend more time if it kept up."

Mouse had his arm unwrapped now but still spent time staring at his fingers and bending them about to be sure they worked. "That . . . that'll be the end of him then."

"It should be," I said. "They've got him cold for a pickpocket. He'll stay in gaol here until they decide what to do. Burns thinks they'll send him off, back to England or one of the other colonies. It would be a good trade, since they keep sending such a bad lot here instead of to Newgate." I drained the cup. "And if what happened today isn't enough, we can fix him solid by putting some goods at his room on Charter St. He could swing for that, though they'd have to use an anchor rope to do it."

We drank up then and I spent the next few days hoping I was right.

Section III

Nineteen

I EXPECTED to feel easier once Grendel was put away, but I knew better than to count a chicken before it hatches. I waited a few days for Burns to let me know what happened in the court in Cambridge and I didn't like the look of him when he came in one evening. He seemed a bit too jolly, clapping one of the mechanics on the back like he might have been his brother and telling some little joke which made the table of them laugh. He finally sat down by himself in the corner away from the hearth and faced the street, removing his drab green coat and three-corner hat and laying them on the bench next to him. I brought him rum and sat across the table. The windows were open to the street but I wasn't sure whether more heat came in or went out. At least the brick front wall stayed cooler than a wooden one.

"And how are you this evening, Mr. Gray?"

"About the same as this morning. No one has tried to steal my purse yet, but I'll watch it why'll you're here."

"Why so sour? Has your moll put you out at night?"

"If she has, it's no concern of yours, unless you're wanting a hand in, too."

He stared at me for a moment. "You're determined to be hard, are you? Can you never see the good in the cause?"

"Sure, I can, at least as much as those poor sisters with a shop down on Water St. I'm told they had to be given hard words before they decided to sign the nonimport papers last winter, and then your committee comes back last week and makes them give up some chests of tea and a whole tray of combs and women's baubles because the committee decided they'd arrived too late."

Burns raised his fair eyebrows a bit, as if to ask why it was important. "They'll be stored safely enough. We're using one of Molineux's warehouses until the agreement ends." His tone turned then, and a bit of anger crept in. "Anyone can see that if we don't enforce the agreement, all those signatures are just paper—and we'd have to pay a tax to Townshend on that, too." He paused and turned his cup in his hands. "It's kind of you to keep track of our committees for us. I'm surprised you have time to take the bung out of a rum barrel, you've got so much to do."

"It's not me keeping track, Peter Burns, but there are plenty of others that are, and they love to talk about it. They seem to think that it's only the small ones the committee visits while the rich ones get whatever they want. I've heard that John Mein, that narrow Scotsman, is looking at all the manifests and intends to print them in his paper."

Burns turned dark for a minute. "Mein is a beggar for trouble, and I wager he'll get his hat full soon enough." He motioned with his head at the table of mechanics. "But they'll have others things to talk about in a few days." He waited to see if I'd ask, but I knew he'd go on whether I did or not. "Governor Bernard may need to hire a merchant ship just for himself after the next *Gazette* is printed. If he stays here, he'll roast like a goose on a spit." He drank down the rest of his cup, and his blue eyes showed more pleasure than I'd seen since the troops had come. "We've got some of his letters, and some from General Gage and the Customs, too. We'll print them, a bit at a time to keep the interest up, and everyone will see that they plotted against our government. Bernard proposed appointing a council and taking away our elections." Now his eyes lit with anger, the same I'd seen when he first talked of his father's treatment by the Tory lenders. "We'll twist him until he begs to resign."

"You'll lack a target for some of your arrows if he leaves too soon. I've heard he's waiting for a pouch with orders for a new position in England."

Burns took up with excitement again. "Maybe he can go with one of the troop ships. They're going to send the Irish regiments to Castle Island and then maybe to Halifax or London after a bit." He motioned at his cup. "Get me another if you would, Nicholas, I'd like to make a toast to our success."

When I came back, he was ready to turn about and raise his cup to the table of mechanics behind him, but I stopped him before he began. "It's only half that we'll be rid of. There are still enough muskets to take the Town House if they wanted."

Burns looked dark again. "They'd be sorry if they tried. We've got plenty in town who would stand up and more in the country than they imagine." He dropped his voice a bit then. "I sometimes wish they'd go ahead, try what they intend, right now, so we can get it done and stop all the talk and dancing about."

I could feel my eyes narrow a bit and my jaw get tight. I shook my head. "Don't wish for it, unless you're in the market to sell shot and bandages and bury the dead." I suddenly smelled the smoke of gunpowder and cannon shot and the stench of blood spilled on a deck and cooked in the sun. I looked away to clear my head. "But I want to know about Grendel more than anything. He's my concern, not your speeches for a crowd."

Burns was silent for a few moments and I could hear one of the mechanics behind him talking bitterly. "There he stood, the redcoat bastard, right beside me, and said he'd carry timbers for the day for a shilling ten instead of two shillings like the Americans and the ship captain took him just like that and left me standing like a scarecrow. I don't know whose head I should crack first—the lobster or the bastard that hired him." The others at the table joined him in a round of oaths.

Burns finally spoke softly. "Why don't you get a cup for yourself, Nicholas, and sit comfortable so we can talk. I have some things to explain." His words made me uneasy while I turned the spigot beneath the bar, and after I returned, he took a long drink before starting in. "I'm sure you won't like swallowing it, but there's no harm to it and you're getting what you want." He held up a hand so I wouldn't interrupt. "I left the court today with Grendel. He's a free man but he won't bother you or Maggie or any of your crew again. He'll do as I say."

I started to speak, pushing back my bench, but Burns continued to talk before I could begin. "He'll be of great use to us on the streets—a man his size and fearsome to look at. There are times we need a man who can persuade someone that he's made a mistake or even break a head or two. What good is it for him to be locked down or sent away as long as he stays away from you?"

I just stared at him, my eyes narrowed now as I tried to see how many rings he'd try to spin so that I'd be puzzled enough to agree, but he plunged ahead. "I arranged a deal for him—Grendel said he'd found the box on the ground and Armstrong agreed he might have lost it when they bumped and was satisfied with getting it back. Grendel knows what he would have faced if we wanted to pin him—I even let him know that it could have gotten worse than just the snuff box—so it was simple to get him to agree to stay away from you and do us a turn when we need it in exchange for walking free."

"And you trust that's what he'll do?" I asked, and Burns nodded. "But then you've never had him staring you down, have you? I'd wager you'd have thought differently if it was your shoulder he threatened to pull out." I stood up now to stretch my legs and move far enough that I wouldn't be tempted to turn over the table at him. "Where does it stand now, Mr. Liberty, do I still owe a debt now that you've told some lies and changed your end?"

Burns' face was blank, and he showed no anger one way or the other. "It's the same for you either way—you don't have to worry about Grendel, and if he causes any trouble, we'll make him sorry, either in court or on a corner. You get what you want because we helped you."

"He paid nothing for breaking Mouse's arm."

"That's all one anyway, Nicholas. If he paid in court by getting his thumb branded or standing in the stocks or getting sent off, what difference would it make to you? Or your friend?"

"We'd know that he paid," I managed through tight lips.

"You'll walk about just the same. Save your spite for another time or use it against someone more deserving, like the Governor or Paxton."

"And why should I pay you if he's gone free?"

"You're out from under Grendel's weight." He stopped to see how I might react, then broke into a small smile. "And besides, you're a Liberty Son beneath your cloak. We won't ask till the time's right, but when we do, you won't turn us down. You owe us a turn." And with that he returned to a contented smile, happy with the way it had worked.

I backed away then, a little too quickly, because I knocked the bench behind me into the next one and the mechanics turned to see who was moving so quickly. But I held my voice down so that it was only Burns hearing. "You're no different are you? You'd like to think so because you take the side of liberty and use it like a cloak. You've even got the ministers preaching for you. But underneath, you're the same as the toughs in Covent Garden—you do as you like unless there's someone to stop you."

I walked away then, and stood behind the bar. Burns didn't stay much longer, stopping on his way out to say a bit more to the mechanics, talking of the Governor's treachery and how they could read it all soon enough. He told the story of John Hancock's ship in Rhode Island, too.

Customs had finally taken the *Liberty* and renamed it *Gaspee* and used it as a cutter along the coast, trying to seize ships before the Navy could get them. But the crowd to the south had taken exception and burned it like so much firewood. Burns and the rest raised a cup for a toast and Burns left without a look back.

Twenty

WE CLOSED UP like regular, collecting all the cups from the evening and the trenchers from dinner so Maggie could wash the ones that showed bits of food or stains from flip or punch. She would stand over the pot near the kitchen fireplace while I swept the tables and benches and all the dirt and mud that collected every day out the front door. Maggie disappeared up the stairs and Julius was already asleep on the bed he folded down from the wall in the kitchen. But I was as mad as a hornet and didn't relish lying in bed, or even in my hammock out the back door, thinking in the dark about Burns and Grendel and how we'd come up short when Burns did the counting.

When I went out the back and around the corner to the front on Fleet Street, the air was damp and heavy as a wool blanket, and though nearly all the people were silent in their beds, the crickets and frogs kept up a chorus to match Samuel Adams and his church choir. When I got near the docks, their song was replaced with the creaking and sawing of the ships at anchor, the rigging ropes rattling against the masts and yardarms, and the scurry of rats as they searched out every bit of garbage and the fish heads and juicy oyster shells that kept them as fat as a lord at his table. Some thought the smell of the docks was rank, and a few days of calm could cook it into a foul stew, but most days and nights I breathed it deep, the harsh salt cutting away at the smells of tar and wet lines and whale oil.

At first my stride was quick and bothered, but the night slowly loosened the string, and my thoughts drifted away until I suddenly found myself at Lilly's window at the back of Widow Marden's shop. I tapped twice at the glass and I heard her rustle from the sheets and come to the back to let me in.

We were quiet, like always, though I'm sure none of the other girls in the two rooms down the hall missed what was going on, and probably not the Widow in the front either. When we finished, I lay atop her, still joined, her legs in a circle behind me, until she made a slight move and I rolled away beside her. I was drowsy, near sleep, and my ribs were healed enough to forget them unless I took a hard knock there. But I felt her fingernail tap my chest and she spoke in a low voice, near a whisper. "Stay awake, Nicholas, I have some questions for you."

She must have felt me tense at the idea and she rubbed the flat of her hand on my chest. "Don't worry, it's nothing you'll need your knife for, I'm not after your purse." I didn't know she'd noticed it, flat on my hip in a leather sheath, just inside my breeches, but I realized her hands were more familiar with me than anyone else in the past months and she would be the first to know. "Who is it that puts a knife on your hip? The one who broke your ribs?"

I gave just the slightest nod. "Him and some others with him." I had no interest in bringing Grendel into my mind again, and I rubbed my hand down her shoulder until I could just cup her breast.

She sighed a bit but then moved my hand and pulled away. "No, Mr. Gray, I have something for you, but it's not what you're grabbing at." She pulled herself up a bit so she could sit and look towards me. "It's a business proposition."

I moved so I could sit as well. I could just see her in the dark, sharp in profile against the lighter square of the window, her nose with a slight hook down at the end, black hair tucked beneath her cap. There was no candle or lamp to help, but a half moon reflected off the building at the back and my eyes were good in the dark. She turned to me but I couldn't see her eyes.

"I think we should open a house together," she spoke in a near whisper. "You could see to the door and the rooms and collect the money and I could find the girls and keep them at their work."

I cocked my head a bit in surprise, but then shook it slightly side to side, without any thought. She reached out with her hand on my cheek. "Think about it for a moment, Nicholas, before you say no. You owe me that much, since I've never charged you a penny." She waited a moment before going on. "I know my worth. I'm young and I give as good as you can find. There's gentlemen here who'll pay two pounds or more for what we just did." I nodded, knowing she was right. "Think of the houses in London, Nicholas, with the girls on parade through St. James Park or dressed in silk at night for the theatre. They put the royal ladies to shame. Everyone knew Dennis O'Kelley and Charlotte Hayes, they got rich enough to buy horses and race them at the downs. They gave their girls new shifts each week and made them drink milk and let a doctor check them for the pox. There's no reason we couldn't do it here."

I realized then that I'd given little thought to Lilly. I came to her a beggar and she gave me a feast, taking me inside her and drinking my juice like it would give her new life. When I left her bed, I was sated, my hollow spaces filled, and thought that because she seemed to enjoy herself, that her thoughts were like mine—I took our pleasure as a dream in the night which had no connection to my life in the day.

There were a few times when we lay tangled in her bed, spent and slack, when she talked and I listened. She told of the men who paid her, one pound here and two there, but how little came back after the Widow took her share. She was mostly in debt, just like in London, after the Widow subtracted money for her clothes and food and room and it was the Widow who set the prices and kept the book. The middling men who came paid middle prices as well, although Lilly might have drawn more in a better house.

The Widow kept up her business in the front and actually expected her molls to work at sewing when they weren't working in bed, so there were no suppers and frolics like a few houses in Boston and the ones in London in a row down King's Place or off St. James. She wasn't a slave, but from what she said, our times at night were the only minutes when she did as she pleased.

At eighteen, she got her passage across from a captain who'd regularly enjoyed her bed at a house in London, and he hid her in his cabin so the bawd and her door guard wouldn't find her to take her back or collect her debt. He'd given her a gown and some jewelry when she'd stepped onto the boards of Long Wharf, but he was only back every few months and then spent most of his time with his wife.

She'd come from London with big eyes, hoping to be one of those she'd heard about who had come to the colonies and married up. Lilly hoped to catch a gentleman to keep her, but it hadn't happened yet, especially since most of the class who came to the Widow's didn't have enough to keep a mistress in her own rooms or at a country house. The Widow sometimes even took her to task for seeing me, as if any of the better men who paid for her might know what happened on the wharves after midnight.

"This isn't London, Lilly, they won't stand for it here."

"Why not, Nicholas? There's just as many here that pay for their pleasure."

"That may be, but they can't do it in the open. You'll never see a guide here, all printed up with the houses and girls and prices, like in Covent Garden. There are preachers here who will take a rest from attacking the crown and the Tories by turning on the girls and the pleasure houses."

"That's no different, Nicholas, there were churchmen in London who'd send all the whores to hell on Sunday and then pay their price on Monday."

"This is different, Lilly. Most of the Puritans actually listen in church. If their man in a black robe points a finger, they follow where it leads. They've closed down some houses here when they got too bold, and put the girls in the street or in the pillory."

She sat back then, her back against the cool plaster wall, and looked towards the window. Her voice had a bit of anger beneath it now. "We could do it, Nicholas, you know we could. You could figure who to pay and when so the doors could stay open. It wouldn't be much different than what you do now."

I was silent then, because she was probably right. But the truth was that I had no interest in selling girls like baubles from a case, with men picking them over to see which glitter caught their eye or which price matched their purse. I'd seen the high and low of it in London when I'd landed there at twelve, and I'd found protection in a house for a time by running errands and sweeping the hearth. For every rich madam like Charlotte Hayes or Jane Goadby, there were hundreds of girls in the streets and alleys that fell to the pox or fevers or from birthing a child or hiring a nurse in Ludgate to shrink her belly. There were some who went mad, others who'd trade themselves for a cup of wine or a spoon of laudanum, and more who took the dark look of a cripple in the street, knowing their end is coming soon enough and that the time in between will be rough and mean. I knew Maggie as the rare one, who'd come out with her health and her mind.

Lilly leaned over then and stroked down my chest and belly until I stirred beneath her hand. She murmured then, low and warm, almost a cat's purr, "Think of it, Nicholas. You could have me every night, and a full purse every day."

We slept a bit after that and I left quietly before dawn like always. I didn't go back for nearly a fortnight, but I found myself distracted at odd times of the day, hearing her voice and feeling her hand as it traced down my chest. It was a sweet song I heard, like a voice in a dream, but I felt danger there, too, although on its face I couldn't find what it was.

Running a house of molls was less dangerous than most of the thieving we'd done, since they never hanged a pimp, and the money was a good deal more certain. Once the men began coming and the word spread, my job would be simple: stand on the few who made trouble. Most wouldn't be the equal of the tars I'd thrown through the door at the Sword, and none as fearsome as Grendel or cunning enough to get me in debtor's gaol like Tobin. Of course, doormen were expected to use a hard hand to teach the rules to any of the girls when they strayed, too, something I had little stomach for.

When the first of August came, a calm fell on the harbor for three days. Although the heat was like a baker's oven and the garbage heaps for the scavengers and the gutters in the center of the street cooked and stewed until some took to pressing a handkerchief to their face when they passed, most of the town celebrated like it was one holiday after another. Governor Bernard had finally been given leave to return to England, but his ship was now stuck in the calm within sight of the docks. Church bells rang throughout the day to make the occasion holy and everyone with a musket took it to the end of Long Wharf and fired off a blast so he would know how happy they were at his leaving.

On the third day, the coasting captains had come for their regular dinner and ate four meat pies Julius had made with pork and onions and seasoned with part of the bundle of sage he'd gotten from the market the previous day. He always made a special punch for them as well, since they were willing to pay, flavoring the rum and water with lemons, sugar, some brandy, and nutmeg chopped and then crushed with the flat of his broad knife until it was as fine as sand.

It was usually quiet after they left, but since it was like a holiday, six mechanics walked in, already flush from another rum barrel and toasting their insults to Bernard with every new cup. I paid them no mind and sat near to Mouse who was following words with his fingers back and forth across the front page of a new copy of John Mein's *Chronicle*. My mind drifted back to Lilly and her words and hands until Burns came in and slapped a palm down on the table beside me.

"What's wrong with you, Gray? You might as well be out to sea rather than tending to business. Why aren't you raising a toast with the rest? We've chased Bernard like a fox and it's a pleasure to let him know it."

It took a moment to swim back from my thoughts and answer Burns' words. "You've had the luck on this one, and every bell must make Bernard feel like you've spit on his shoes, especially since it's not the gentlemen that bested him, it's rabble like you." Burns showed a wide grin then and gave a small bow, happy to be among those below Bernard's feet but strong enough to tip him in the mud. "But what's changed? It's Governor Hutchinson now, or it will be soon enough, and he doesn't quiver at the sight of a crowd like Bernard, even after they tore his house apart during the Stamps."

Burns still showed a smile, though not as wide now. "At least he knows we can bring a force together if we need."

I shook my head a bit and didn't answer. For once, Burns didn't try to make me a gull. The Sons and Adams and the upright Whigs always claimed that the damage a crowd did was like a fire from lightning, a natural occurrence that wasn't planned and couldn't be prevented. Most believed their words as much as those of Paxton when he claimed his only interest was in upholding Parliament's right to regulate trade while the money piled up around his feet.

It was quiet at our table a moment. Mouse looked up at me and then began to read off letters though he struggled to get his mouth to say the first one, "M . . . A . . . N . . . I . . . F . . ."

"Manifest," I said, "it's the . . ."

Mouse held up his hand to stop me and I could see he still held the fingers on that hand with a curve, like it was too much work to make them straight. "I . . . I . . . know about manifests. They're the lists they take in at Customs and match them to the goods."

Burns had been watching the table of mechanics for a bit but now turned back, staring at the *Chronicle* which lay on the table in its frame. "Why do you bring that refuse in here? It belongs in the gutter with the shit from your chamber pots."

John Mein had turned out to be a Scotsman with a very hard head. Since the Sons and the body of merchants had begun nonimportation, Customs had been giving Mein the manifests of merchant ships entering the harbor. He had taken to printing them in the *Boston Chronicle* and even wrote a special pamphlet on it as well. The manifests proved what many whispered: the large merchants, like Hancock and Rowe, were importing banned goods and then claiming they'd been in storage all along, while the small merchants had their goods seized for storage. Mein got regular threats at his shop and on the street, but he kept printing the lists that made Adams and Hancock squirm.

Mouse turned to Burns now but didn't say anything. "Is it lies he's printing?" I asked.

"It makes no difference. He'd have us kissing Bernard's feet and bowing down to Paxton when he walks by."

"If he's printing the truth, it's a step up from the *Journal* you print, with redcoats attacking every man and woman within reach," I shot back. He turned to me quickly, his eyes blazing now, and I saw I'd pricked him where it hurt. But he turned away and said nothing and Mouse began searching out words in the newspaper again.

I went back behind the bar for a few minutes and refilled the mugs of the mechanics who got louder with each round. Burns turned to me then and motioned for me to sit. His lips were a thin line now, with no smile behind them.

"It's odd that you would start talking about Mein today, Gray. He's the reason I've come in."

"Well, I only know his paper, and I've seen him about. I don't admire his printing for Customs, but they say his skin is as thick as any of the Scots."

"He knows the people are against him, but he goes on anyway. We need to send him a stronger message, and I think you're the one to carry it." Burns put it straight out to me then and I was almost glad, since it seemed an easy way to square with him for his help with Grendel. If it was much more, I might have argued with him about what was owed since he had changed the bargain. But I was tired of wondering what he might ask, and it was simple enough to make a plan to satisfy him.

We waited three days for a cloudy night, just in case the watch proved awake and unfriendly. The four of us—Julius to prevent trouble, Gillam to get in the door, and Mouse to listen—set off an hour after we closed the Sword at ten and walked to Mein's shop on Marlborough St.

We were in the door in a flash—Gillam almost laughed when he saw the lock—and we set about our work. I took the note Burns had written and pinned it to a table with a small knife Burns had provided. Gillam took some of the paper ready for the press and burned a few pieces in the fireplace, using a flint he carried and shielding it with his body so the light wouldn't show out beneath the door. He took the paper that was half burned and laid some pieces out next to the note. I looked through the racks of type with my lantern shielded until I found the largest ones he used for headlines, the rack near the top.

I went to lift the case out, and nearly fell flat. I muttered a bit to myself and called to Gillam. When he took his side, he whispered softly, "If Mein lifts these all day, he's a stronger man than me. Can't we just put a hammer to it here instead of taking it all the way to the dock?" I shook my head silently and we carried it out to the cart. Gillam locked up behind us and we dragged and pushed the cart all the way down Summer St. past Faneuil Hall. The case of type was so heavy it hardly made a splash when we dropped it into the sea by Bull's Wharf, going down like a cannonball off the deck.

Mein let our work and the threats that went with it roll off his back like water from a duck. About a week later, he printed another edition, although the headline was a size smaller than the type we'd carried off. But the words were just as pointed, accusing the Sons of enforcing a plot to run the small merchants out of business so the large could make even bigger profits. When Burns came in a few days later, he seemed dispirited at first. "You'd think threatening to destroy his building and do him personal harm would persuade him," he said, "but he must have a bull's temper about him, the way he goes after Adams."

"Is that what you'd do? Turn tail if you're outnumbered?" He shrugged like the question meant nothing and stayed silent. "If you did, you wouldn't be poking the soldiers every chance you get," I went on.

"It's hard enough holding the merchants together without someone like Mein slandering us."

"Is it still slander if the words are true?"

He shook his head then. "Now you've turned lawyer. I'll tell James Otis to hire you for his office, since he has a hard time keeping things straight. Like usual, you've missed what's important, and that's getting our rights."

"There's talk that Parliament may take back some of the duties."

"It's no matter, it's all or nothing now. They can say they'll take off all the duties but tea, but part is no better. They're still insisting their right to take our shillings with no recourse."

"It's easy for you to say part is no better, but for most of the merchants, it would be a far sight better. They could make their fair share on glass and colors and paper and pay out a bit on tea."

Burns just stared at me, the same look he'd given me before when we talked of ideas in the air. Finally he started again. "You have no idea of liberty, do you Gray? It's not like a loaf that you can slice a bit off the end and then have the rest." He thought for a moment struggling to think how he might explain to someone as thick as me. "It's more a living thing, like a fish—if you cut its tail off and throw it back, it dies."

I couldn't help a short laugh. "If you were hungry, Burns, you'd rather keep part of the loaf and most of the fish. I know I would."

Mouse laughed and I thought I might get one from Burns as well, but he said nothing before finishing his cup and walking out the door.

Twenty-One

I AWOKE a few days later and took bread from the shelves in the cold room and cut cheese to go with it and took it into the tavern room to eat along with a mug of hard cider. The ocean air cooled us more than those further in, but the heat still fell on us like middle summer instead of September and it was Tuesday, the day Julius baked bread for the week. The heat from the oven built next to the kitchen hearth could have boiled a stew across the room and Julius worked with his sleeves rolled to his shoulders, the muscles in his arms bunching like a knot in a bowline as he worked the dough.

Maggie came to sit a few minutes later and I wondered at how she always managed to look fresh in the morning, red-brown hair gathered under her cap, eyes clear as the waters off Jamaica, skin glowing as if she'd just scrubbed it with soap, though I knew she wouldn't dare wash every day. She sat across the table and took a long look at me. We hadn't talked much since our meeting with Draper, but sometimes we exchanged a few words in the mornings, though it always left me unsettled afterwards.

"What is it Nicholas? You've got the same hound's face and hawk's eye you've had for more than a week. Even Mouse wonders if you're about to disappear somewhere."

I shrugged my shoulders. "It's nothing, Maggie, certainly nothing that's concerns anyone but me."

She held my eyes for long enough that I finally looked away. "Come to the market with me, Nicholas. Julius needs a cone of sugar along the way, and we might even choose some vegetables to bring home. There are wagons full this time of year and some are near to giving them away."

I considered for a moment before answering. "Sure, Maggie, I'll come, if you promise to let me walk in peace."

We didn't talk at all as we made our way down to the market. Maggie bought a two pound cone of sugar at the largest of Rowe's three stores, where they sold everything from square nails to delicate china, and she carried it in the woven basket on her arm. When we got to the market, she took to picking up apples and peaches and green squash and inspecting them like she might a piece of jewelry. "Let's buy some new apples, Nicholas, we can keep them in the closet and eat them ourselves when we have a feeling for one."

I nodded and held the basket while she picked the ones that showed no worms and were firm beneath her fingers. I kept carrying it after we paid and she steered us down Ann Street, past Wentworth's Wharf where Lilly stayed. I kept my face wooden but Maggie must have felt the struggle.

She kept walking and looking ahead, but said, "It must be your girl that's got you twisted up so tight." When I didn't answer right off, she kept on. "It's always been a puzzle to me. Someone like Grendel might be next to breaking your neck, but it's a little bird that makes men like you forget where they are." We walked a bit more and she took us to the foot of Clark's Wharf where someone had placed an old bench to sit and watch when the ships unloaded.

We sat quietly and when she put a hand on my arm, I could feel my breath come quicker and my face flush a bit. When I turned toward her, she said, "You might as well tell me, Nicholas, because if you don't, you're likely to charge down a path and then forget how you got there."

I started to pull my arm away, but she held it instead, and I let her. Still, there was some heat when I answered back. "And you've got a map that sets it all straight?"

She still held my arm, but loosened her grip until she just touched me lightly. "You've seen plenty, Nicholas, I know that, and you've got a fair level head for ideas. But I think your heart can twist you in a knot."

At first I thought I'd argue with her, ask why she presumed she could read a book by looking at its cover, but instead I found myself picking an apple from the basket and using my hidden knife to cut it into slices while I began to talk. "She wants to open a house and put me at the door." I gave Maggie a slice and when she didn't answer, I went on. "There's money there, I know that, and it would probably be safer than picking up goods when a store is locked."

She bit a piece from the apple slice and I watched her lips purse at its sharp taste. "So what's keeping you?"

"I'm not sure, Maggie. It's not a business I've wanted." I took another slice of apple for myself. "When I was younger, I slept in the kitchen at a house on Piccadilly. It was better than the alleys around and I didn't work nearly as hard as I did when I was apprenticed in Oxford."

Maggie was quiet a moment. "And why were you there at all?"

It took a moment for me to answer and I realized no one had asked me that since I'd grown large enough to attract the press gang at sixteen. It was a simple enough answer but I found it hard to say. "My mother was always ill and the consumption took her before I was ten. When my father fell dead on the library steps, the men who paid him were bothered that they had to hire another man, but that was the last they thought of it. I never saw the inside of the library again, especially after I was put with a gunsmith and his wife who had me stoking the fires before the sun rose." Even now, there were times at night that I still felt the chill of waking in their house, damp cold that never seemed to leave. "I thought nothing could be worse, so I ran off when I was twelve. It was London or nothing."

The sun bathed my face in warmth but I could feel that it was already weaker than in high summer. "So I swept the hearths and cleaned the floors and emptied the pots. Some of the girls treated me like a little brother and some thought they could kick me like the dog."

"And why don't you go back to it? I know there are enough easy girls and easy coins to keep you busy."

I thought for a moment, since it was another question no one had asked. "I don't know, Maggie, it seems like nothing's there for me. I guess I could grow into a pimp. None of the mothers can seem to keep a doorman for long." My own story was easy enough to tell, but Maggie's questions always made me restless, like I was hunting for a grain of sand I'd never find. "What about you Maggie? Why aren't you in the trade? You could run a house yourself and it would be a lot less work than keeping up the Sword."

She was silent and stared at me hard. My eyes found the flat of her cheekbones and the scar trailing down her cheek, white now against her skin which stayed the color of the shells of Spanish almonds. She reached out for another piece of apple and turned away as she took a bite. "I have to say, Nicholas, there were times when it seemed we were royalty ourselves. There were lords who came who would bow down if I told them. We even came to Oxford one year when they have the parade..."

"The Encaenia?"

"Something like that, when they all dressed in their robes and costumes and took all morning to parade down the street. The young lords would get their parchment in hand and then drink toasts and howl at the moon like dogs. They went on for days."

I shook my head slightly. "You came yourself? I might have seen you there, if I hadn't run off. When the whores came to parade, it was more interesting than watching the men from the colleges, all puffed up. The boys would gather and we'd watch with our mouths open, though it wasn't much different for the men."

Maggie smiled a bit. "Like I said, Nicholas, there were times we were royalty. It was enough to turn my head. Sometimes it seemed easy work, at least when you saw the maids with dirty skirts and red hands walking home to a tiny room and thin soup after scrubbing all day." She stopped then and was silent a moment. "But it didn't last, it never did. If we didn't have the madam and her house, we didn't have anything. My price was high enough that I saved some aside, but most of the others spent the little they got before it hit the bottom of their purse. They charged us twice what they should for clothes and food, but what was the good of leaving to try business alone?"

I offered up an answer, although not a good one. "That's the way with sailors, too, Maggie, and even the store clerks. It's the ones that own the ship or the store or the house who decide the pay and subtract the charges, and you can be sure it's their chests that get filled, not some work horse that's easily replaced." I sliced the last two pieces of apple and gave one to Maggie. "If you owned the house, you could make your own rules."

She turned to me then, a hint of color in her face, but not from anger. "It wasn't the money, Nicholas, it was the life. I couldn't abide seeing the young ones come in, girls that still had a flush in their cheeks, that might have found a place somewhere or married a small tradesman and raised a family. But they couldn't see it, and Madam would show them the finest they'd get and they'd dream of lying on a down bed and being fed cream and berries. And before they were twenty, they looked twice their age, and got turned out into the street or sent to the ward for pox or got into Newgate."

"But look at you, Maggie, you came away on your own and you're none the worse."

She stared at me hard. "I've got my scars, Nicholas, you should know that, some on my stomach and one on my face, and the rest inside. It's just that I don't show them." I listened for a tremor in her voice, but it held steady as a cornerstone. "You'd never succeed at running a house, Nicholas, your heart's too soft. You'd let the girls owe you and you'd never drag the young ones in." I must have looked surprised, since I don't think anyone had ever accused me of being too soft before. "It's not the men and what they pay or don't pay that would give you trouble, I've seen you handle what comes. But you'd treat the girls like you do Mouse, like you're some sort of big brother, instead of a captain who makes sure the ship keeps sailing even if it kills the crew."

I was silent then, thinking a moment, then taking the apple core and flinging it as far as I could down the dock, where a gull might get it if a rat wasn't too quick. "Let's go, Maggie, I've had enough thinking for the day and maybe for the week. I vowed to walk in quiet, but you'd think we were a pair of magpies chattering away. I think you'd make King George answer questions if you got him alone."

"And you'd claim you don't like to talk. But some days, a hangman's noose wouldn't stop your tongue." She smiled then and took my arm as we turned back toward the Sword.

WE KEPT ON like usual the next few days, although I felt a bit uneasy sometimes when I'd catch sight of Maggie across the room at the Sword. She still looked a rare flower to me, standing in a garden of weeds, and I couldn't keep a faint longing from touching me. We'd built a low wall between us so we weren't always tripping and grasping at every step, but my heart had lifted some, and I wasn't sure if I played in her thoughts like she did in mine. She'd give me a smile sometimes, or flare up at me when I went around the bend just so I could make some fine point with Burns, but I didn't know what to make of her actions. She didn't explain and I wasn't about to ask since I had nothing simple to say. I wondered again if love was more a puzzle than a gem, and thought that a good love poem would have to be longer than any book.

A few nights later, Lilly opened the door to her room for me and we fell to it like usual, thrashing about on her bed until we were covered in sweat and breathing like a pair of stage horses at a gallop. It was rare that a moll enjoyed her work, and I don't know what she did with anyone else, but she acted the part with me and I found myself full lost in the tangle between her legs, like there was no other world and no other sounds save the slapping of our flesh and the wolf's growl in our throats.

We were still warm and twisted together, and my thoughts were far away when she spoke low in the dark. "Have you thought what's ahead, Nicholas?"

I shifted quick then, and pulled back a bit. "Do you change that sudden, Lilly, from hot to cold and back again?"

"You can take your time, Nicholas, but it's the question I want to know."

I waited then, wishing I could go back where my mind was quiet, but I knew it wouldn't work. Finally I answered. "I'm not made for it, Lilly, I just can't see myself guarding the door and watching the men come and go like drooling dogs. But I think if you could find someone else, you'd run as good a house as any here."

I could feel the breath go out of her and we lay quiet for a long time. After a few minutes, her voice was thick when she spoke. "I have another question then. Would you take me in if you had the money?"

Her words changed the air in the room and suddenly I noticed the outline of the window and the back wall of the iron goods shop which faced the other side of the wharf. "What do you mean, take you in?"

"Keep me in a room or share it with me. Buy me pins and hats and a bottle of Madeira. Dance with me at an entertainment party and introduce me to your mates." She moved away a bit now, untangling her legs and turning towards my face. "Make me a woman instead of a nun down the alley."

I closed my eyes to think for a moment but saw no answer. "I don't know, Lilly, it's all a dream you're talking, and I see better when I'm awake."

Her voice was low and deep in her throat when she spoke again. "Sure it's a dream, Nicholas, but I haven't anything else. The Widow's good enough to me, but I'll soon be too old or get pox scars or get a child in my stomach. If you'd tell me you'd keep me, I can think of it when a cold wind bites through my cloak."

I stayed silent, my lips pressed together. I wanted to ease her mind a bit, but I couldn't see what she dreamed, it was too far from the streets I walked. Even when I managed to see myself in a proper waistcoat, I didn't find her beside me. The silence stretched out between us, almost long enough to imagine she'd gone to sleep.

"I knew better, Nicholas, I knew it wasn't true and you'd never say it just to please me." She moved away enough that we barely touched, then turned her back towards me. After a minute, she said softly, "You can go now, Mr. Gray, I won't keep you and I won't ask you any more questions. Go back to your tavern and your night crew where you don't mind telling a lie."

I didn't want to leave without a word. It didn't seem she'd said the whole truth but I couldn't find words to start out either. I sat up and laid a hand on her flank. "My tongue is tied up, Lilly, I don't know what you want me to say." She stayed silent and didn't stir and before I knew it I was talking more to fill the silence. "How would you like to go to a room and dance, Lilly? There's a place I know that has fiddlers and cold meat pies and punch for an evening." She said nothing, but was quiet, listening. "It's not like the British lords, and they keep it quiet enough that the church and the middling crowd don't know. They pay the constables a bit to stay on another street." She turned her head slightly to the side, but still said nothing.

I went on, filling the silence. "I hear it's a bit rough sometimes, since anyone with two shillings can get in and it's mostly slaves that play the music. But it's a lively time. You could wear your new ribbons and no one would know who you are. It would be a lark for a day, with no harm to anyone. I can find enough to get in the door and buy our meals and some punch and we'd act like it was a summer night with green trees on the Common instead of bloodyback regulars."

She turned on her back now with the blanket to her chin and I thought I saw tears on her cheeks. She spoke so low I could barely hear her. "Talk some more, Nicholas, tell me about a day with no worries."

Twenty-Two

IT WAS JUST A WEEK LATER that Lilly and I walked past the burying place, Hancock's grand house, and Beacon Hill with its watch tower until we came close upon the slope the British called Mount Whoredom. The Black Bull was one of several taverns on George St. near its base which offered girls along with a mug of ale. At the door, I paid Mathew Hart for two suppers. I'd seen him about and spoken to him once or twice about the tavern business. The Bull mostly served the dock crowd and those from Boston, but occasionally a soldier or two, as long as Hart could keep them apart.

He gave me a bit of a look when Lilly and I came in, probably because he knew about my work with Maggie, but I didn't stay to explain. Lilly was dressed in her best and wore an embroidered shawl which proved that at least some of her time at the dress shop was actually spent with a needle and thread. Her dark eyes and hair shone against her pale white skin and she had earrings with stones that sparkled in the dim light. If I didn't know her any other way, I might think of a way to steal them.

It was Saturday evening and there were nearly forty inside, a mixture you'd be surprised to see in Boston if you didn't know where to look. First, there were men and women both. Most of the women were whores run by Hart or another house nearby, and most of the men bought them for the night. There were a few single men who walked with some extra bluster and powder on their wigs, but more had a lean and haggard look, like a smile would be a waste of effort. One group of whores with bright red cheeks sat off in a corner where their mother guarded them. She seemed content for the moment, sure they would bring a better price later in the evening.

There were tables at one side with hams and pudding and bread and Hart had slave girls bring more food when it was low. A place was cleared along the other wall with a stool and two chairs and there were fiddles hanging on the wall. We ate our fill, with Lilly putting away more than was ladylike, but she ate with abandon, like she moved her hips in the dark of her room, and she'd caught the eye of most of the men before we'd finished our meal.

Most of the plates were cleared by the time the fiddlers sat down. One was a dock hand I'd seen hoisting tea chests and nail casks onto carts. He was a rough plank with thick fingers and short arms and I'd never have guessed he could hold a fiddle without breaking it. But he sawed at it till it wailed and moaned, or hummed a comforting sound that made me think of creaking hammocks gently swaying below decks. He and a slave beside him fiddled for song after song and sang or called out directions to the dancers for all types of country steps I'd never seen before.

The dancing was new to Lilly as well, but she picked it up right away. I was more comfortable watching but I took Lilly out a few times and soon the penny macaronis were coming about to ask for her arm. She was flushed and excited, and she'd finished her punch in a couple of drinks and began another as soon as it was brought.

The room was smoky and hot and lit with lamps just enough to see, and it was easy to forget that ice and snow would come in a few weeks and that there was a brawl or worse waiting around every corner. At least it was for an hour or so until I heard the commotion at the door.

Hart stood near the front door as three officers came in, their redcoats and white vests bright in the dim light, and their buttons and sword hilts and boot tops glinting in the lamp light. Hart seemed to be suggesting they leave, and it wasn't long before their loud voices were heard above the fiddles and dancing feet on the plank floor.

Without thinking, I got up and moved around behind Hart. The lieutenant who stood at the front was small with a narrow face and sharp eyes that moved about the room quickly. His mouth was thin and pressed together when he wasn't speaking, like he had something better to say than what he was hearing but he was holding it back.

"Isn't this a public room, then?" he said, with a gesture around.

"Not tonight it isn't." said Hart. "Even so, we're full up already and the food is taken way."

"We're not interested in your food," said the lieutenant, "it's probably pig slop anyway." He stared at Hart, without a smile, but the two behind him couldn't help but grin at this wonderful joke. Their eyes were glassy enough to say they'd had grog for their supper. "I can see a table right there where we could sit. We'd just like to have a cup of rum and watch the country folk dance. It's bound to be entertaining."

Hart shook his head an inch to the right and left. "I apologize, sir, but I think it would serve us all better if you found the King's Arms or the Royal Stag tonight. I'm sure you'd find the company more enjoyable and there's plenty of rum and talk there as well."

The lieutenant took a step toward Hart and the two behind did as well. "Are you turning us away? I'm sure the constable wouldn't if we reported an illegal gathering here. Or I might come back later with a few others so we can decide if you have the right to keep us out. It might be crowded now, but we'd be glad to turn out some of the trash that's collected here so we could use the room." His eyes were glittering now, ready to bully the man in his own tavern and put on a show for the timid Americans.

Hart was silent and I found myself talking without thought from his side. "I'm sure you know a lot about what's legal and not, Lieutenant, since so many of your men stand in the dock. You might even end up there yourself. There's some here right now that would swear you've assaulted Mr. Hart when he simply explained that there were no tables left." The lieutenant turned towards me now, anger showing now that his sport had been interrupted. "Or you might find the way back here more dangerous than you thought. I've heard there are gangs about who love nothing better than knocking off a British hat and stealing a lieutenant's sword."

His hand went to rest on the hilt and his eyes roamed about quickly again before resting on me. "Who are you and what business is it of yours?" He moved towards me a half step but Hart moved in between, turning his back to the lieutenant and facing me.

He spoke softly enough that the redcoats couldn't hear. "It wouldn't pay to have a joust right here. There's time left for drinking and a crowd with ready lips. You can do your business somewhere else."

I glanced at Hart, then locked eyes with the lieutenant, like I've done before, often to my own harm. If I stood down now, I wanted him to know it wasn't because I feared him or his station. But the challenge in my eyes was usually too bald, the kind that couldn't be passed off by anyone but a coward.

I backed up a step and then turned to sit back with Lilly. I was surprised to see four or five others at my back, men I didn't know but who'd risen at the bait of redcoats in the door. They looked expectant and a little disappointed when I shook my head silently, but they opened a path and I sat down again without a word and the fiddles took up again before Lilly reached for my hand.

"Let's dance now, Nicholas, just you and me, like we're the only ones alive, like you'd never seen the men at the door or thought of the taxes or the blood to be spilled."

I puzzled at her meaning for a moment but there was something about her words that pulled me up with her. She was urgent, intent, maybe even desperate, and I followed her like a sheep.

It was another country song and I made the moves I thought the fiddlers wanted, but it made no difference. Lilly was caught then, flushed in her cheeks, moving like she might never dance again, and it seemed the whole room stopped to watch her, though there were plenty of others dancing at the same time.

When the fiddlers stopped, she closed her eyes for a moment, almost like she'd fallen asleep standing but then opened them again and looked at me. It was the same look she had sometimes after we'd danced in her bed, her eyes far away and empty, but complete, like something had changed inside her. I took her hand and we sat again, still quiet, while the noise and the crowd swirled about us.

We sat then for a few more songs without talking, watching people dance, both of us lost in thoughts that were far from the room, while the music filled every corner. I was ready to walk Lilly back to the Widow's dress shop when the room got silent. The redcoat lieutenant had gone to the fiddlers and whispered to them and gave them each a coin before turning and walking toward us.

He stopped a few feet away and the room was even more silent. "I'd like to lead this lady in an English dance so she can show her true beauty. These country dances are beneath her." He smiled at Lilly and gave a short bow and held his hand out.

I could feel the blood coming up in my head and I started to get up from the bench when Lilly put her hand out on my forearm. She shook her head slightly and rose, holding her hand out so he could take it.

My jaw was working hard now to stay shut and I grabbed the edge of the table to help me stay seated. Everyone in the room was watching and the lieutenant made the most of it. He'd paid the fiddlers to try something like a minuet and though Lilly didn't know the steps, she followed his lead. With all eyes on them, Lilly sparkled like a jewel, as if she belonged in the center and it was only natural that she was dancing on the arm of a lieutenant.

When they'd made a full circle, they stopped with the music and a few applauded from the side. Some urged the musicians for another round and some joined them to make the circle again, then stopped and bowed like they'd all been at a party for the King, far above the rough and rude dancing they'd been enjoying a few minutes before.

The British lieutenant tried to lead Lilly toward his table and the other two lobsters, but she shook her head and came towards me with the lieutenant at her arm. She gave him a final curtsy and sat down across from me.

"We might dance a bit more if you'd consent," he said earnestly, then glanced at me as well. "I'm Lieutenant Pearson of the 29th Regiment. You could find me easily if you'd ask—I have rooms not far from here." He paused and seemed ready to leave, but couldn't resist digging at me before he left. "You deserve better than this American dog to follow you about."

Again Lilly put her hand on my arm to keep me from rising. Hart appeared from one side where he must have been watching and stepped in between. Pearson turned and walked toward the door with only a nod at the other two to bring them along.

The music started up again before they were out the door and everyone seemed to relax once the door closed behind them. I stared a long moment at Lilly who didn't look back at me, her eyes on the country dancers now, one finger tapping rhythm with the fiddle.

After a few more songs, I told Lilly it was time to leave and once we were ready, she took a final look at the room, still warm and smoky. Her look was far away and sad, like a passenger might look back at shore as they set off across the Atlantic. When I touched her elbow, she turned quickly through the door. We didn't say a word on the way to her room and once we were inside, I stood and didn't take off my cloak.

"Why did you do it, Lilly?" I asked finally.

"Do what Nicholas? Have an evening of frolic? You're the one who invited me."

"He's a snake Lilly, I know one when I see one, and not just because of his uniform."

"What difference does it make Nicholas? Like you said, we took a night for a lark. He stands better than most in that room, and you won't keep me through a winter or feed me in the spring. I danced because he asked—and it seemed he enjoyed it, too."

I was ready to turn and go, but I couldn't help the words coming out. "He was there for a show, Lilly, he wanted to parade before the Americans so they could see how high he is in his bloody red coat and how low we are that he can take anything he likes—even our women." She didn't say anything and I turned to go. "But it's lost on you Lilly, you're too young to know."

The walk back to the Sword was colder than I expected and I couldn't keep from shivering when the fall wind blew off the water.

I DIDN'T VISIT LILLY again for a bit, almost two weeks, but when I did, she was gone. Her room at the back was dark and I knew it was empty.

I came to visit the Widow the next day, looking at the partially completed dresses hung on a wall while the Widow kept an eye on two comely girls stitching at hems.

"What could I help you with, sir?" she said as she got up and walked toward me. She looked to be just in her thirties and moved delicately on her feet. Her face might have been pretty once, but now the skin was tight across her cheeks, and she looked drawn and tired. Her eyes had a hard sheen in them and she worked her hands together like her fingers needed help in bending. "Does your mistress need a new gown?"

I shook my head. "No, madam, I wanted to inquire about one of your girls."

She was close now and spoke low, as if the girls shouldn't hear. "I knew that as soon as you came in. I can read men's thoughts without a word." She twisted her hands a bit more. "Is there one you fancy more than the other?" She darted her eyes over her shoulder where the two were now looking at me direct, with smiles and hungry eyes like I was a partridge on a plate.

"No, I'm sorry, I didn't make myself plain. I wanted to ask about Lilly."

She moved towards a front corner away from the girls and I followed. Her eyes went hard now, and she still spoke quietly, but her anger was clear. "You're the one aren't you? I should have known when you came in the door. You're the one who put ideas in her head. You should pay me a sum for what you've done." She stopped for a moment, almost talking to herself. "It's always a good bet they'll be gone when they start sharing themselves around for free."

"I've done nothing other than treat her like she wanted to be treated. She wasn't your slave to own. This isn't Covent Garden."

The Widow answered quickly. "With all I've given her here, and just two girls left, she should have stayed till I could replace her. She owes at least that." Her hands were working themselves now, the fingers of one hand squeezing and turning the knuckles on the other. "And she thinks she's got prospects with that officer." Her short laugh was scornful. "She'll be in the street soon enough and I won't take her back. She'll be like some of the others by the docks, wearing rags and inviting the sea dogs to have her standing in the alley. Mark my words."

As angry as I was at Lilly for leaving without a good-bye, I didn't want the Widow to be right. I'd seen too many without protection and her delicate face wouldn't stand up to a heavy blow on the cheek or a month of gruel or the French pox. "So she went with an officer?"

Again her tone was hard and angry, like she'd been robbed of a precious necklace. "He came in high and mighty with a couple of others following and took her right away. I watched what she took—she wasn't going to take any of the clothes I gave her, I let him know that—and walked right out the front door."

I'd found what I came for and readied to leave.

"Are you sure you wouldn't like to take tea with Patricia? She has the best manners you'll find and you can see that she's come to a full woman in just the last year. She's a maiden still and you'd be her first."

I stared at her hard, hearing the lie I'd heard many times before, but I left without a word, turning down toward the docks to find a place to sit out of the wind.

Section IV

Twenty-Three

NOVEMBER CAN BE A HARD MONTH in Boston. The fiery leaves are gone by the end of October and the cold wind and rain begin to rattle the branches like dice made from bones. But we went about our normal business, like everyone else, even though the snow and ice and frozen ground hovered like a pale specter around the corner. Julius cooked stews which made the kitchen smell rich and brought workers off the street, Maggie tended the business of rent and supplies and bills and keeping up the license and serving the tables, while I drew off the rum and served up the flip and punch and cider and kept an eye on the door.

I often thought of Lilly, but it was a path that ended in a thicket of thorns. She had made her choice and I could have sought her out—Mouse said she was in some rented rooms with Lt. Pearson off School St. for a bit, though he wasn't sure now—but there was nothing for me to say. I had turned down her proposal and offered little in return, just a few bright moments when our bodies locked together and everything else was forgotten.

I missed her at night, but not so much that I took to looking at other maids. I found myself at odd times staring at Maggie when she wasn't looking, but most often she would feel my gaze and turn to see me. She would simply stare as well, like I was a person with a familiar face but one who put a wrinkle in her forehead rather than a laugh in her eyes.

For all of us, the trouble in town was like a lion in the streets—you couldn't ignore it and you turned your back at your own peril. The soldiers had stomped their boots on our ground and bullied us about for more than a year now, though two regiments had been sent off to Halifax and two left behind. Nonimport had cut down the dock traffic and the off-duty soldiers took most of the lowest work in ropewalks and cargo holds at a shilling six a day instead of two, leaving the American dock crowd to drink and swear revenge.

At first, the scuffles had been like those the gangs fought a few years back on Pope's Day, plenty of noise and a lump on the head and three pints to tell the tale. But now the anger had turned hard and the blows were meant to break bones and spill blood. There were just enough redcoats to keep everyone in a rage but not enough to keep them afraid. They still had their muskets, but everyone knew they weren't allowed to fire without a direct order. It was like two brothers fighting, with the small one getting closer each time to pulling the big one down.

When I walked in the morning, it seemed the town echoed with the violent sounds of the last few months—insults and shouts, windows breaking, the rattle of muskets and clubs. At the docks in the South End, a miller named Robert Pierpont and a crowd of about twenty had battled the soldiers at the guardhouse on the Neck. He complained that the lobsters regularly stole firewood from the houses nearby and he'd fought with one he'd caught red-handed. When Pierpont took a constable back the next day, the soldiers laughed at the idea of giving over Ensign Ness.

So the crowd surrounded the guard house and began pelting it with stones. The soldiers came out with bayonets fixed and some with halberds and the crowd brought out their cudgels. As they traded blows, with a broken wrist here and a pierced shoulder there, a musket went off and hit a blacksmith shop across the way. It sent both sides home, but the guilty soldier was hauled into court the next day. Justice Dana followed the others judges in Boston and informed him he was in Boston illegally and therefore had no rights and no defense. He ended up paying a fine of four shillings, every penny in his purse.

When I passed the British Coffee House on King Street, where the Tories and British officers were served on fine plate and discussed the need to hang Adams and Hancock, I couldn't forget James Otis, the great lawyer for the Sons who could speak for hours at a time. He had been a puzzle in the last year, with ideas that spun about like the grasshopper vane on Faneuil Hall. First his words ran hot against all the Tory abuses heaped on Boston, then he spoke for royal privilege and Parliament's rights. Sometimes he rambled so far he seemed a patient for Bedlam, but some claimed it was just the effects of too many years with a Tory wife who would squeeze blood from a stone if it offended her.

When the Customs Commissioner John Robinson paid John Mein to print a pamphlet against Otis and some others, Otis couldn't swallow the insult. Armed with a heavy new walking stick, he found Robinson in the lion's den, at a table in the Coffee House with some friends, and when the words became threats, they swung their canes and Otis took the worst. He was been beaten silent, his skull dented like a squash, blood pouring down his face, and he hadn't spoken a good sentence since. The crowd that waited outside for Robinson didn't think it a fair fight, but Robinson escaped after hiding in the Coffee House overnight and took the next ship for London, never to be seen again.

When I walked halfway to Fort Hill and the South Battery, near Hutchinson Street, I saw the shops of the Governor's sons and thought of the broken windows and the rain of shit from the gutters regularly splashed on their walls. They had finally decided to sign the nonimportation agreement and their doors stayed clean afterwards.

Near Griffin's Wharf, I remembered the calls of the crowd when they fell on an informer named George Geyer. They bound his hands, stripped him, painted him with boiling hot tar, added chicken feathers on the top, and hung a heavy sign around his neck identifying him as a coward and an informer. A thousand friends carted him about town, stopping in front of Tory houses and shops so they could whoop like Mohawks and call out threats and break windows in houses that refused to light a candle for them. There were enough that they didn't mind threatening to kill the guard at the Custom House. They finally dumped Geyer out at the Neck after he promised never to return to Boston.

One morning, I found some street boys standing against the buildings across from the guard house straight up from Long Wharf at the end of King Street, in sight of the Custom House. Mostly I paid no attention to them, but that day they seemed especially alert. As I walked up to them, one ragged boy of about ten offered, "He won't get out while we're here."

"Who's that?"

"Why, John Mein, didn't you hear?" When I shook my head, he went on. "They almost had him, it was the captains themselves, Davis and Dashwood and Ingraham, and the coward ran in there." John Mein and his paper had continued poking at the merchants and ship captains and nonimportation, even after we had dumped his type and every other threat had been made. He'd kept up with the ship manifests, too, and finally some swore they'd stop him.

"They were ready, they were, they had some tools they'd brought along and I thought Dashwood would split him in two when he swung the shovel. They had him on his knees before he got his pistol out but they kept swinging and he dropped it." He stopped a minute and turned sly. "If you wanted to buy it, I might know where it is." I just shook my head again. "Well, we'll stay here as long as it takes. We know his looks and he won't get across the street before we call up the crowd again."

"Do you stay for the sport or does someone pay you?" I asked innocently.

A second boy, skinny as a yardarm, spoke up in a loud voice. "Oh, we'll stay for a bit of fun and wager who can knock off that guard's tall hat with a rock. I'm the best there is and if I don't get his hat, I get his head." He was puffed up now like a little rooster in the hen house. "But three pennies keeps me standing guard all day. Sometimes they feed us a bowl of stew by the fire at the Grapes instead. They say we're more important than any of the lobsters."

I turned to go and the first one asked, "You might know someone else who would pay for John Mein's pistol. You could send them back, right here, and ask for William. Mein won't be needing it anymore once they get their hands on him."

A week later, they guessed Mein had escaped by dressing as a soldier and marching off with the guard before getting a boat to Castle William. The sheriff was too scared to arrest Dashwood or any of the others, even though the new Governor Hutchinson ordered it, and within a week Hancock was in court with a case against Mein for debt, hoping to take away his precious press and shop now that he was gone.

When I walked by the Common, I felt like I was jabbed with a sharp stick. The soldiers weren't quartered there anymore, but instead of quiet grass and great trees, the grounds were littered with command tents, horses hobbled and grazing, officers shouting and drums beating as units drilled, and groups of redcoats gambling with dice and cards in full view. Every few days they made a great show of discipline, announcing floggings and executions so the crowds could gather and cheer.

It was slack time one afternoon and I'd already read the papers for the week, so I took a walk and found a crowd near the Common. They were preparing to whip a boy who had thought of trying to desert, turned in by a friend who earned a guinea in the bargain. They started in earnest and the blood drained from his back in streams. He fainted once, but they were kind enough to wait until the doctor woke him before they started again. I've never been sure why they chose the black drummers to swing the cat, maybe because they thought they looked fearsome, or maybe because they'd lose no friends since their only friends stood beside them in line to take the whip. The boy survived although it would be weeks before his back healed. Pains shot across my shoulders each time I remembered the crack and bite of the whip, and the rough skin there chafed against my shirt. It was a wonder my wounds had healed over without festering.

I was at the edge of the crowd and turned to go when I caught sight of Lilly. She had the arm of a lean man whose ruddy face came straight from Ireland. I approached around the side and finally found myself beside her as the crowd strained to see the poor boy's skin taken bit by bit.

"A pretty sight, eh?" I said, as if to no one in particular. Lilly glanced over at me, then grasped his arm tighter at her surprise. When she turned, I saw the grey-green color along her jaw from a bruise just ending.

"You could certainly call him a bloody back now," the man mused and looked over at me. The pox marked his face on both sides, but his nose was straight and his eyes were keen, reddish hair pulled back at his neck and a three-corner hat set straight across his head. His grey coat had been expensive once but now was frayed at a sleeve.

I looked at him straight. "You're not the one who marked her face, are you?"

He turned full on me then, his eyes hot. "Follow me, if you've more to say." He walked to the edge of the crowd then turned abruptly. "It's no business of yours, whoever you are."

"You'd be right most times, but I am acquainted with Lilly."

"I'm sure you're not the only one."

"My father taught me it was a coward's way to beat a woman. If that's you, you may as well admit it. It's not something you can hide."

He moved a step towards me, but wary, a fist curled up since he had no stick. I could see he'd had some experience in a scrape, not the fool gentlemen who'd puff up and fall down swinging.

But Lilly jumped between us, facing me with her arms out to block him. "Stop, there's no argument here. It wasn't him, it was Pearson, the officer." She spat out his name like it was poison. "Mr. Windham was kind enough to give me a place."

I kept my eyes on him, but relaxed a bit. "So this is the kind Mr. Windham?" Lilly nodded. "If you're telling the truth, I'll apologize."

Lilly nodded again and turned toward him with a soothing voice. "It's nothing now, Jacob, Mr. Gray has a high temper which gets away sometimes." She put a hand on each of his shoulders. "He's taken his words back and we can go about our business."

Windham seemed reluctant and kept his eyes straight at me. "It's good enough now, Gray, but if we cross again, I'll remember." He turned and walked back toward the crowd with Lilly quick behind him. She turned for one look at me and I couldn't tell if there was more anger or pity in her eyes.

I must have had my eyes down, thinking about Lilly, as I walked back to the Sword because suddenly the crowd before me thinned and I looked up to see Grendel standing between the next hitching post and the door to the Orange Tree tavern at the head of Hanover Street. All before me had veered into the street to avoid him. I stopped a few feet short of where he stood. I had Burns' assurance that I had no worry from Grendel, but he was a man that might turn about at any moment, and my breath caught before I could speak.

"Greetings, Nicholas Gray," he said in a voice that sounded like a metal file on an iron bar, "I see you're well-healed now."

"Well enough."

"I am, too, although my leg is still a bit stiff before it rains."

We stood looking at each other as others passed by into the street. "I won't walk around you, Grendel, for no cause. What's your purpose?"

"None right now, but that could change soon enough."

"You've no bone with me, at least that's what the Sons tell me. I understood you were their dog now, just like the big black hound Adams keeps that's always after redcoats and Tories but wags its tail at everyone else."

Grendel breathed heavily through his mouth. "You're mean enough when you're quiet, Gray, but it's your words that bring you trouble. You've always got just enough to light the fuse."

"Have you slipped the leash then? If you're a stray, you might end up back at gaol where they got you."

"I'm done wasting my breath with you, Gray, since you only understand a blow to the head. But I'm no one's dog and you're still likely to get hurt."

IT HAD BEEN SOME MONTHS since I had any special worries from Grendel, but facing up to him again gave me pause. A few afternoons later, Burns came in and bought a pint. Instead of his usual easy manner, with words pouring out like milk from a pitcher, he seemed to be muttering to himself. Gillam sat at a corner table playing cards with a carpenter who would probably wager his hammer and saw if he needed to and one of the coasting captains who came regularly for dinner. Mouse watched, his eyes darting from one to the other and the cards they played.

I sat down across from Burns. "You've no one to talk to for the moment, so you'll talk to yourself?" He looked at me sourly and didn't speak. "It's not so bad as long as you don't answer back."

"Why are you so lighthearted, Gray? Have you stolen the Governor's plate?"

"No, I have nothing to celebrate, although seeing you vexed brings a smile."

He stared at me for a moment, his eyes turning almost gray now, like the winter sea. "It's got no teeth, Nicholas, the agreement isn't hurting London enough because too many get around it." He leaned back from the table and put both hands on his mug. "There's only a few who still haven't signed, but it's the ones who signed and are getting goods just the same that hurt our cause."

I shook my head. "You must have known that when you started, and we've had words about it ourselves. Some will always take a handful if it's there. Just because some of your bigger merchants are a class above doesn't mean they won't cheat and steal. They're just better at it than the ones below."

Burns paused, his eyes with more light now that he warmed to the talk. "Never pass a chance to slander your betters, do you Gray? Of course there are a few, but we have to stop it there. We need to make more of them afraid to go against it."

"What would you have the little ones do? Go out of business? Then they can enjoy their liberty in the alms house and work in manufacture for Master Molineux." He didn't take the bait, so I went on. "Mein's paper said New York already quit the game. You know that any of the merchants with a big enough purse can have goods dropped in Portsmouth or Rhode Island and hauled in by wagon." He looked at me and handled his cup, but didn't answer. "Isn't the agreement due to run out at the end of the year anyway? It's only a month away."

"That's only what's on paper, Gray. We intend to keep it up as long as we need to."

I stayed silent, knowing the direction they traveled. Adams mocked those who spoke of their own rights to carry on business. Should they have the right to set fire to their own house, even if it burned down the whole neighborhood? Adams and Molineux were still pointing the angry men toward a shop or an importer's house to make clear their threats.

Burns kept going. "We need more information so the committee can make more inspections and lock down more goods." His eyes burned now, like a bonfire lit on a Tory lawn. "And we can't help what the crowds do if some merchant won't listen."

I looked across the room and watched Gillam lay down a card and lose a few shillings, like he always did near the beginning. "I would have thought you could get all your information from Mein's paper, but now you've run him out, too."

"Don't joke about him, Gray, I'd kill him myself if I could find him." His face was dead straight then, no glimmer in his eye. "It wouldn't be hard for you to help us, since you probably know the information anyway. If you helped us now, we could help you later on." My face must have turned sour, because his tone changed, now all business. "You'd be surprised how we can help if you get in a pinch."

"You want me to become an informer? Skulk about and peek in windows so I can sell what I see?"

"That's not it, Gray, it's just a step from what you know already."

"But it's no different is it? Ebenezer Richardson has made a tidy sum doing the same for Customs and he doesn't dare walk about without a hatchet beneath his coat. And they nearly killed Geyer." I turned to see Mouse glancing over at us, probably hearing every word though we weren't loud, and I could feel my face start to get warm. "I don't think so, Mr. Burns. If I wanted to inform, I could make a pretty penny from Paxton and the rest. It's no different doing it for you, just less money."

Burns gripped his cup tightly now and leaned forward. "Of course it's different. You're for liberty as much as anyone. We're at war, Gray, at least the beginning of one, and wars aren't won by being righteous." He leaned back and studied me. "Think it over once I'm gone and you stop grinding your teeth. I know you've paid back for the way we helped you, but you might even get on the other side of the book." He stopped and his look turned sly. "You might get back at some you think deserve it."

I took my time, shaking my head back and forth, before answering. "It seems Grendel might be thinking the same."

Burns looked at me sharply, then looked away. "He's been a bit more trouble than I hoped." I waited and simply looked at him till he continued. "He's been a great help on the streets and he does his job with vigor. We put him with the strongest men, but even some of them are afraid that he might mistake them for an enemy and break a limb before they know it." He took a moment before going on. "But now he's barking for pay. He thinks our play at Harvard has run its time and doubts we have the sand to lock him up some other way." He looked away then and didn't meet my eyes.

"And he's probably right, isn't he?"

"I don't know, Nicholas, he's done us good service and we have more important business than arranging to lock up a good soldier."

"All for the cause then?" I could feel the slow flush to my face begin again. "Where does that leave me? Or Mouse?"

"You needn't worry, Nicholas. We'll keep him busy, and probably pay him a little, too. You're still a small fish."

I was just able to stay seated, thinking how Burns would use his words to build up any idea or tear it down, depending on which side suited his purposes. My voice turned cold when I answered. "It's easy for you to say since he's not looking at you. If the chance comes, I'm sure he'll be happy to return the trouble we gave him."

I kept a sharp eye out after that, hoping to stay away from Grendel, avoid conversations with Burns, and steer clear of Hardy, the Customs man. I knew that words with any of them might lead down the wrong path. I'd cleared my way from most of the trouble I'd stirred up since coming to Boston, and there was no reason to open the doors again. I thought that if I was careful, I could keep walking the streets and breathing the air for some years to come. But for me, it seems the years gone by are never dead. I didn't guess that a shade from my past would strike before any recent ones had a chance.

Twenty-Four

MY WORLD TURNED UPSIDE DOWN the day I came out of the kitchen at the Sword and saw the Spider sitting at a table across the room, talking with Maggie. He wasn't remarkable to look at, a middling age, dark hair tied back at the top of his neck, dressed like a common clerk in breeches, shirt, and a gray woolen vest and coat, and slender hands that looked like he spent the day counting shillings in a port office, except that his skin was browned like a sailor's. He had a long face with a sharp nose and the pox had left only a few marks on his cheeks.

But his eyes gave him away. He had a piercing glance and though he didn't move his head quickly, he saw everything around him. His eyes shifted so rapidly that I thought of the lizards in Jamaica, too quick to catch, gone before your hand could close. His real name was Partridge but we named him Spider in Kingston because he could move in total silence and stayed in the shadows, unseen except for a hint of movement out of the corner of your eye.

His business there was trading information, and if he found out too much, he'd catch you in a web and sell your freedom. He wasn't large or especially strong, but I knew his hands and feet were quick as a snake's tongue and he never stepped outside unarmed.

I was just coming out of the kitchen and partially blocked from sight when I first saw him. My heart skipped and I backed up enough so that

I could just see him around the corner. Maggie kept serving as I waited out of sight, trying to figure what I might do.

Finally, Maggie came looking for me and was ready with a strong word till she saw my face. "What is it Nicholas? You look like you've seen a ghost."

"There's a man out there I'd rather not see. If you stand a bit in the way, I'll go out the back." She started to ask something, but I stopped her quick. "It's nothing for you to know, and I'll be back after he leaves. If he asks about me, give him a story."

She shook her head a bit, but turned to go back and I made my way to the back door without showing my face in the front room.

I watched the front from an alley two doors down and saw him leave, turning right up Fleet St. and walking with just a hint of a limp. After we finished up that night, and Maggie set the bolt on the door, she was quick to ask again. I held up my palm, flat towards her. "It's nothing to speak of, Maggie, just a bit of old business."

"It is something to speak of when your old business comes in my front door and I have to act the dunce."

"Oh, it's your door now, is it?"

She shook her head in frustration. "Don't go off on another path, Nicholas. It's the same door as before, but I want to know why you're hiding out. It's not like you."

"It's mine to handle, Maggie, and that's the end of it," I said as turned and left by the back for the second time that night. I sat huddled in my cloak by Hunt's Wharf for more than an hour and I only slept in fits later that night. The old dreams came back, foul air choking me, and the smells of iron shackles and mealworms and cold gruel filling my throat.

I had never thought of seeing him again, but I carried my days in the Navy and Jamaica with me everywhere. They were like a bit of lead from a musket ball lodged under a bump of thick skin, too deep to cut out without bleeding me dry. I didn't think it an accident he happened in the Sword, and if he came once, he would definitely come again.

A few days later at dinner, he was already in the door and waiting at the bar when I came out of the kitchen. I carried bowls of stew for a table of tars just in from Portsmouth with news and a load of lumber for merchant John Rowe. He took a long look at me and smiled a bit and nodded his head.

When I came back, I tried to keep my heart down and asked him like anyone else, "What's your pleasure today, sir?"

"I'll have a cup of rum and a word with you."

I picked up the tray of bowls and nodded, "I'm serving now, and our cook is sick, so maybe another day . . . ?"

He stood his ground and waited till I came back. "We'll need to sit and I know you'll find it important. You call yourself Gray now, is that it?" He nodded his head a bit, like he was agreeing with himself.

I had no choice. "After they finish up, we'll sit where it's quiet."

He busied himself with the *Gazette* which was hung on the wall until all had finished their dinners and left.

I sat down across from him, my heart in my throat, but I kept my tone as even as I could, hoping a bluff might help. "What so important that you'll wait this long for a man you don't know."

"I know you, just like you know me."

"You've made a mistake then. I've never laid eyes on you."

"You may as well give up the show, it's wasted on me."

"You can explain if you want, but if it's no more than mistaking me for someone else, I've other work to do."

"It's a common trick, you know, using a new name that starts with the same letters as the old."

I stayed silent now, knowing what was coming.

"You're Nathan Graves, wanted by the Royal Navy for murder—and a deserter as well."

I kept my voice calm though I could feel my heart pounding. "There are hundreds of deserters about, plenty of them walking the streets of Boston. The Navy is too busy to go looking under rocks, especially when there are so few who remember." I paused for a moment before going on. "Besides, I've heard that the *Dover* went down in a storm just after it passed Barbadoes."

He smiled as he answered back, but it was as false as a copper guinea. "I imagine you thought that lucky for you, though it wasn't for the ones who went to the bottom. It's only a man like who could hear of a hundred drowned and see a cause to celebrate." He peered at me hard then, his dark eyes lit with the treasure he lived for—an advantage to make someone do his will. "You may have heard some news, but you didn't hear enough. Two officers survived and were picked up by another ship when the storm blew past. I'm sure you remember Lt. Hanson."

I couldn't keep my face still and he enjoyed himself again. "It just so happens he's on the *Swan* in the harbor now. If I remind him of the story of Nathan Graves and the other lieutenant on the street, I'm sure he'll remember. I imagine he'd remember your face, too." Partridge couldn't keep from smiling now. "And once he did, he'd order up the guards and the shackles."

I could feel Julius come from the kitchen then as much as I could see him. The Spider was taken back a bit but he moved one hand to the heavy walking stick he carried and his other pulled back his waistcoat to show a small pistol tucked into a belt around his waist. "And don't think I can be scared off easily. I learned my lessons well enough in the islands."

I brought my open hand up a bit and Julius saw the sign and went back to the kitchen. "What is it you want? You must want something or you wouldn't have come here to talk."

"You're right, Mr. Graves or Gray or whatever it is. The reward for you wouldn't be enough for a good shoe buckle, though I wouldn't turn it down. But Paxton and the others pay handsomely if they can get their hands on a smuggling ship." My face must have given him a signal though I kept my lips tight shut. "You'll do it, I'm sure you will. Think of it as buying your freedom. Imagine that you're in debtor's prison or Newgate and need to buy your way out. If it came to that, you'd do most anything."

He looked satisfied now that he'd spelled it all out. I wanted to strike him now and send him crawling away, but it wouldn't help unless I sent him to the graveyard. I spoke with as much scorn as I could put in words. "Do they still call you the Spider? I always thought you were more like a crow or a gull, feeding on dead rats and fish guts, picking at what others wouldn't touch. Are you still selling out anyone if the price is right?"

He smiled slightly though his eyes continued to shift quickly about the room. "Names are nothing to me, unless they're like yours—worth some sterling when they're mentioned in the right place." He stood, ready to leave, but his tone turned angry then. "But you should be the last to judge someone else. I'd wager it was you that broke my leg in the dark at your hideaway by Kingston. The cutthroats you joined with would slaughter a child if it got in their way." His hand gripped his stick fiercely. "This is good enough for a club, but I'll probably walk with it forever. There's times at night I think my leg will never stop hurting."

I couldn't help jousting back. "If that's true, I'd wager you were somewhere you shouldn't have been and intended to steal what wasn't yours." His eyes narrowed a bit but he held his tongue. "Did you cross one friend too many and had to run out? I doubt you can hide here too long with all the traffic to the islands."

He laughed harshly. "I wouldn't come here just to follow you, the bounty is hardly worth a walk down the street. I didn't know where you'd gone, and didn't care much either. But Boston's a fine place for me now, with the soldiers in town and the Navy in the harbor and Customs with hardly enough time to count all their sterling. Information is treasure here and it's much easier to come by than gold from a chest." He got up then, ready to leave, his stick firm in his right hand. "I'll wait till you've got something that will bring a good sum. But I won't wait too long. They'd be glad to lock you up in the hold of a Navy ship if I point you out to Hanson." He turned to go. "Get word to me at the Royal Exchange tavern."

I wanted to shout something at him or at least answer back smartly, but I felt dumb, like the beggar I remembered who sat every day near London Bridge and could only bring pathetic moans and growls from his throat.

I still sat in the same spot, my eyes closed, my thoughts running in a circle inside my head, around and around like the horses at Newmarket, when I heard Julius step in from the kitchen.

He looked at me curiously when I opened my eyes. I had nothing to say and shook my head slightly.

"It's a miracle I've never seen," he said calmly, "you let him walk off without a word."

And I had no answer for Julius, either.

THAT NIGHT, after Maggie bolted the front door, I couldn't get up the stairs quickly enough. "Stop, Nicholas."

When I turned toward her, she said simply, "You're going to tell me, Nicholas, there's no way around it."

"What's that, Maggie?"

"Sit down and stop playing the fool. You haven't been the same since you hid from that man. You might as well be on a ship to Halifax for all the help you've been here."

I took a bench before answering. "I've been tending my business, Maggie, filling the cups and changing the barrels. It's best that you tend yours."

She flared up then, like I hadn't seen in a long time, her face flushed with color and her eyes throwing sparks. "If that's the end of it, then you might as well look for another place. We've been apart since you took up with that young whore, and we've agreed to go our own ways. And I'll admit there are times I've wished you'd stopped coming back." Her voice faltered a minute, but then she charged on. "But you're still here and we're still connected, I can't seem to change that and neither can you." She stopped a moment and her voice turned lower and more grave. "I'm not sure what we are, Nicholas, but I can't just break it in two like a broom straw. If you can . . . then leave now and keep your secrets to yourself. I'll make my way, like I always have."

I dropped my head, wanting to be anywhere but sitting across from Maggie right then. The pot was boiling already, and I'd learned that telling too many stories was a sure way to get burned. But I couldn't get myself to stand and walk out either because, in my heart, I felt just like she did: we were attached as surely as two sides of a coin. Finally I looked up and saw her eyes, strong and clear blue, and I felt something move deep inside me.

The whole story spilled out, beginning with my time as a sailor in the Royal Navy, pressed into service to fight the French, how I'd gotten at odds with Captain Carter and Lt. Halsey for the way they treated me and the rest and how I'd been flogged and chained below decks on the *Dover* in Kingston Harbor. When they finally unlocked me so I could work again, I'd kept my head down long enough to get ashore to help load supplies, and then disappeared down a street where I found a tavern to hide at, and later some men who took me on knowing I was wanted.

"They were a bad lot," I admitted to Maggie, "Red John Kimble at the head, with a Frenchman named George and a black Maroon called Goat. They would have been pirates if there weren't so many Navy ships about, but they handled everything that could be stolen from the Navy or any merchant brig. They let me stay where they kept their goods, at a building west along the coast toward Spanish Town. It was a prime spot to hide, since you could see anything coming over the water or along the road and the jungle was at your back. There weren't many white men who would step into those trees without a gun at their head."

My throat felt too dry, but I didn't want to stop. "But someone came one night when I was there by myself, the others were off in Kingston for a roll about, and they brought a wagon up the path. I didn't know if it was the Navy or someone else, but I surprised them in the dark and it must have been Spider, the man who was here, who went limping off moaning and holding his knee while the other held his shirt together where I'd slashed it open." Maggie just listened without a word, and I found myself gulping from a cup of rum as I remembered the fear that dogged me there.

"It took almost three months before I could figure my way out and it was during that time the lieutenant and two men fell on me in the street outside a tavern in Kingston. I fought them as hard as I've fought anyone, I never wanted to feel the shackles and go below decks again. It turns out that I'd killed him with a blow to the head and I put the others at a run besides."

I stood up from the table then, as it seemed I'd been sitting there for hours, and turned towards the fire that needed banking before we slept. "I stayed hidden until the *Dover* sailed off and I found my way as quick as I could below decks to Boston. I stayed quiet here, just a man to help at the Stag's Head. But it wasn't more than a few months when I heard the *Dover* went down."

The room was cooling now, but the shiver that ran through me was from my thoughts, not the air. "The storms there . . . typhoons . . . they come and go like lightning, and the wind will blow trees over so their roots are standing up. They can come so fast the captain barely has time to shout for reefing the sails. It's regular to lose a man from the rigging, when the wind comes up before he's got a proper grip . . ." I picked up the poker to dig at the fire, and watched as a few ashes glowed bright, then went dead gray and cold. "I still think of the men I knew, some good, some bad, and most in between, but they all went down . . . at least the water was warm there, they might have gotten some breaths and thought they might swim . . . But I wouldn't have, chained below or locked in a closet."

Sometimes the thought came to my dreams, and besides the shackles and choking air came seawater rising around me and I thrashed to keep my head up, but I stood no chance. I shook my head a little to erase the pictures and leave the memories for nightmares. When I turned back to Maggie, she sat in the same spot, but Jezebel had come to make a place in her skirts.

"It isn't easy to say when I think of a hundred men swallowing seawater . . . but I was lucky, not just to have gotten off the ship, but my troubles with the Navy went to the bottom as well." It was a piece of luck, but one that had never brought a smile. I felt my hands starting to work now, making fists when there was no threat. "At least that's what I thought, going on five years now."

I told her of Partridge, called the Spider, and his dealings in the islands. "Now, he's here with the redcoats and the Navy at his back, and claims that two officers survived from the *Dover*, and one's here in the harbor. He's ready to turn me in unless I give him a ship that Customs can seize. If it was just deserting, I wouldn't worry, there's too many for anyone to bother, but the other . . ."

Maggie listened throughout without speaking. When I was done, she stared at me for a long time, her eyes searching for anything I might have left out. "No more then, Nicholas?" When I shook my head, she took a sip of rum and spoke calmly, but her voice was warm now, a memory of our early days. "I'm not surprised. I've never seen you like that, even when you woke at night." She stared hard at me then. "It's bad, Nicholas, but why is it hard to figure? You can find what he wants and give it to him."

When she said it aloud, it seemed simple. But I'd be doing just what I'd scorned Burns for asking, and the thought made me twist around like a weathervane in the wind. "I've never helped Customs in my life, Maggie, and I've never sold what I know. The thought of Paxton and the like putting more coins in their purse makes me choke."

She gave a short laugh. "Better to choke on your thoughts than have the Navy do it with a rope." When I didn't answer, she went on, "I think the answer is plain. There's plenty who deserve some trouble, but why risk another enemy? You owe Draper some trouble. Find out when his next ship comes in and give it to the Spider."

Twenty-Five

I SPENT SOME TIME in the next days thinking how I might get around helping Customs and the Spider, but it was like trying to fire a musket with a short flint and wet powder. I couldn't think of anything other than giving him what he wanted—or killing him outright.

I set Mouse to looking and listening, and talked my way around the docks as well. There weren't many ships in at this time of year, but I knew that Draper was always climbing. A ship with cases and crates of brocade and satin, ladies' shawls and men's hats, would give him a leg up in the new year when the nonimport was due to end.

Expecting a greedy man to keep after the silver is usually a good bet, and I wasn't disappointed this time either. Mouse heard that wagons were needed to go south through Dorchester all the way to Quinsey's Creek, and I got an offer to help off load at Moon Island, just past Hangman's Island, near where the creek emptied out. After a bit more talk to Carleton, who worked Hancock's warehouse, it was clear that it was Draper trying to get in.

It was hard for me to swallow, like a bit of gristle stuck at the back of my throat, but I sent Mouse to contact Partridge and arrange to meet at dusk at the foot of Darby's Wharf, not too far from Adams' house and his empty brewery in the South End.

I stood with my back to a shop and watched the Spider approach to be sure no one was following him. There was just enough light to see his face, wary but eager still. "It's a good walk from the tavern to here, Graves. Did you need the exercise?" he asked as he drew near.

"Do you think I'd be seen in my end talking to the likes of you?"

He smiled. "And you're brave to come alone. I might have brought the guards."

"I watched but you didn't—and I might have brought a friend to break your neck." He couldn't help a glance over his shoulder but quickly caught himself. "But I won't waste my time being pleasant. Marcus Draper has a ship due in the next week, and there are arrangements to unload at Moon Island and bring the goods in by wagon. Your good friends from Customs could seize the whole lot, or get parts as they come in." I glared at him for a moment, but then looked down and away. I was angry at him, but as much at myself, for helping the soft Customs men get more plunder. They were pirates who didn't have to sail or swing a sword—they stole while they sat at a table and had their tea poured from a silver pot. He nodded but didn't respond. "This will be the last time I see you full in the face. If I do, you'll wish you'd never come so close."

I started past him but he put a hand out to stop me. "That's if your word is good and the bounty pays. If it doesn't, you're still on the hook to me."

MY MIND kept grinding away for the next few days. I hated the idea that I'd helped an informer sniff at the game so many worked to keep secret—everyone from the merchants at the top to the men on the street who pulled the ropes and hoisted the barrels. I tried to talk away what I'd done by telling myself that Draper was more Tory than Whig, and lied to both with a smile. After following the idea around the bush a few times, it seemed I could balance the books a bit by letting the Sons know that Draper was stealing their cheese as well.

Burns sat at a table in the Sword with the *Gazette* on the table in front of him a few days later. The first page included a list of seven merchants under the title "Enemies of Liberty." "There they are," he offered as I came to sit, "they're all listed. They won't last much longer. Either they'll see the light or lose too much in windows and business."

I laughed at him. "You think the likes of Nathaniel Rogers needs the sales from his store to keep bread on the table? He could eat for a year or two and wash it all down with Madeira before it would matter to him."

"That might be true, but do you think he wants the crowds after him? When the Mohawks make a visit, it's hard to forget."

I agreed with him but kept silent for a moment. "Do you want another to add to your list?"

He stopped reading and looked at me steadily. He took a careful tone and spoke like a lawyer when he answered. "We're always interested in information on those who undermine our fight for freedom."

It didn't come easy but I got it out. "I don't know about your fight or your freedom, but Marcus Draper isn't all he seems."

Burns looked at me and I looked away. "What do you know of Draper's business?" he asked.

"I know he's got new goods on his shelves, just like some listed in the newspaper–and there's more coming."

"You're keeping track, are you? That's the first time you've shown an interest." He tried a smile now. "Did his dog bite you?"

"I'm just wondering what it is that keeps some in the clear while others are listed as enemies," I said and motioned towards the paper.

He looked carefully at me then, his eyes troubled with thoughts turning round. "And you know of some plans even now?" I nodded without a word. "I'll check what we might do." He looked away then and spoke very quietly. "I know he's been a friend to the Sons. Hancock gives us most of what we need, but we can't take all his cream. There's Draper and a few others who pitch in a bit when we need some for printing or drinks or a meal for the men who fill the streets." He stood up and drained the last of his cider. "I'll let you know in a few days."

"Don't wait too long," I countered as I turned back to the bar. "You'll never lay hands on the goods if you do."

After he left, I wondered if it would be Customs or the Committee that got to Draper first, but I was sure it would be one or the other.

But once again, I was wrong.

It wasn't a week later that I spied Carleton unlocking Hancock's warehouse on a morning walk, taking the large key from where it hung on a leather around his neck.

"Maybe I'll follow you in," I called to his back, "I might find something that catches my eye."

He turned now with a half-smile, the lock undone but the wide plank door unopened. "That would be the end of me," he said calmly, "bringing in a thief to browse the wares."

"How would you know about thieving, Mr. Carleton, unless your thoughts ran the same?"

He came away from the door, still with a small smile and no worry attached. "How have you been sleeping, Gray? All quiet at night? Say, two nights ago? No fire to get up and ride a wagon over the roads?" I smiled as well and shook my head side to side. "You might have been there and taken home a guinea, if you had come around at the right time. No more than you've done a dozen times before."

I shrugged my shoulders like I had no interest, though I could feel the muscles in my forearms begin to tighten. "Smooth as the skin on m'lady's tit," he said, a bit of pride in his voice, then stopped as he looked at me. "Where are you off to so sudden? You'd think I told you your wife was keeping the reverend after tea. As if a wife would have you at all."

"No worry for me," I threw over my shoulder, "it's your wife I'd worry about."

I SENT MOUSE to find Burns, and he returned within a few hours. Like always, Mouse fidgeted some at first and struggled to get started. I'd noticed now that he'd flex his fingers as he struggled, staring at them when they were as slow to work as his voice. "He . . . he . . . he almost . . . didn't stop for me." I waited, not wanting to slow him down once the words started coming. "He walked out the door to Chase's distillery with his head in the air, just after some of the others, the ones they call the Loyal Nine. I had to follow after and call his name." I thought how hard this must have been for Mouse, calling out a name to a near gentlemen on the street, but he'd never been one to slink away either, not if he'd been given a job. "He said he was busy, there was so much to do, but he promised he'd come after I didn't step aside."

Burns came two days later, in the afternoon, when no one was about and I had just finished cleaning after dinner. He stood near the bar, but didn't sit. I looked at him without a word. "What is it Gray, now you'll send someone out to follow me?"

"Was it too disturbing for you, having Mouse call out your name?" He waved a hand to show his impatience. "What is it?"

"Either your watchdogs have been sleeping the last few days or you're taking up acting." When he didn't respond, I continued. "I've heard that Draper landed his ship and carried off the goods without a straw to trip him up."

Again, Burns waved his hand. "If I could watch every ship and every merchant, I'd be king of the docks, not a scribe in an office."

"So you don't care that he's brought in goods against your precious agreement?"

Burns could hardly stay still now, as agitated as I'd ever seen him. He turned a step to the door, but turned back, one hand raised. "Do you think it's me that doesn't care? If it was me, or Samuel Adams, for that matter, Draper would see his name in print, a sign outside his shop, and he'd lose his windows within a week if he didn't store what came in." His eyes were on fire now, and his slender hand pointed in my face, as if I was the one that needed a threat.

I looked at him hard then and he dropped his hand to take away the insult. "Who is it then, if it's not you or Adams?" I asked.

"The others—the Nine or some on the Committee, I'm not certain. But they decided he's given too much already and he'll keep on giving. He's signed on in public, and they think it's the ones who openly deny us that we need to break, like Rogers and some others . . ." He trailed off then and still saw the accusation in my face. "Do you think I like it this way, Nicholas Gray?" He stared for a moment, then looked off to the side and spoke softly and sadly. "There are times I wonder if anything we say has meaning, if a merchant with money can get around every principle."

He stopped then, and looked at the floor for a moment, as if he might read an answer there. When he finally looked up, his face was calm again, and his jaw set. "But we need to win, that's the most important thing. It's war, Nicholas, you must know what that means—there's no room for questions or cowards. It's fight or die, nothing else."

I stared at him a long moment and turned back to the bar. "Go on now, Mr. Burns, I'm sure you have plenty to do."

I wasn't surprised the next day when Partridge sent a boy to arrange to meet, and I thought I had no choice. We met at dusk again, this time just a few wharfs down from where we stood last time.

When he saw I was alone, he started right in. "The goods came just as you said, but I hope there was something else in it for you. It was worthless to me." I said nothing although I could feel the blood rising. "Draper has an arrangement with one of the commissioners. He pays a fee behind the door and everyone avoids the trouble of seizing a ship and protecting the goods."

My jaw was so tight I could barely speak. "You wanted information and I gave it to you. That's the end of it."

"If the information doesn't pay me, you've paid me nothing." He stepped back one step. "You can threaten me all you want, but if you don't come up with something better in the next month, it's the guards who'll take you away. And they'll be eager, too, since it's a murderer they'll catch."

I caught his coat before he could raise his walking stick and slammed my forearm across his throat. I dropped him in a heap, but I heard Julius' voice in my head before I beat him further. Partridge was like Grendel—if I didn't kill him, a beating only caused more trouble. Each blow would make him more eager to bring me down.

When I walked away, he called out after me, though his voice was a bit strangled, "One month, Graves, that's all you've got. And I'll be sure you taste the butt of a stick when they take you."

Twenty-Six

DRAPER'S MONEY bought what he needed both ways—the Sons took his money to pay some expenses and agreed to let him import some goods against the agreement, while Customs took his money to avoid duty and line their own pockets since it was easier than actually working the laws. It set me on edge thinking about it, but some of the Liberty leaders seemed to think the duties wouldn't matter much longer.

News came that Lord Hillsborough would take off all the duties except tea and many in Boston thought they had won a victory like the Stamps. They counted on the nonimport ending at the first of the year and the merchants were already putting in orders for a spring shipment. They were hoping for a quiet period, where both Whigs and Tories were free to spend their money.

But Adams and Molineux and those behind them wouldn't make peace—it was all or nothing for them. They kept up the commotion by sending crowds through the streets after a Town Meeting or a meeting of the merchants' "body," and praised the fighters who took stones and sticks to the redcoats. Some would come to the Sword, flushed with the fight and needing a cup, eager to tell of brave Samuel Gray, the rope walker, and Michael Johnson, the mullato near the size of Grendel, and the others who gave back better than they got. It seemed every tar carried a club.

But Spider Partridge still intended to reach back five years and put me in irons if I didn't give him what he wanted. In every idle moment, and some that weren't, I kept turning it over. One try at paying him with secrets was nearly more than I could bear. I'd given him an enemy of mine, but I couldn't see beginning to turn on people I had no business with. Customs had enough at that game already, and they were a hated lot, no better than the rats Jezebel ate with abandon.

Julius was cooking in the kitchen one morning when I came to watch. He swung his butcher's knife easily, carving the meat and breaking the beef bones for the marrow with blows that didn't miss by a fraction, and tending the stewpot like it was a wife.

After he'd heaped the meat and fat and broken bones all together and dumped them in the water, he turned to me. "Do you fancy becoming a cook now, too?"

"Not a chance, Julius, it's hard enough keeping the rum straight." But my heart wasn't in the jest and he could see it.

"You've still got worries then?"

I nodded, hoping that Julius could help me like he'd done before. There were times his eyes saw what mine couldn't. "There's a man around that will do me harm, maybe even bring me to the gallows."

He turned to the fire and dug at the logs to bring the heat up. He spoke with his back to me. "And you won't kill him?"

"No, Julius, I won't." I stopped, thinking how I might explain. "I just . . ."

Julius stopped me as he turned back but kept the iron in his hand. "I know, Mr. Gray, there's no need to explain. You'll wait to be attacked instead of striking the first blow, come better or worse." He shook his head a bit, like I was a puzzle to understand, then turned back to arrange the fire. "Well, you managed your way around Grendel when I thought he was better dead. Is he no threat now?"

"I don't know for sure, Julius, I don't think so, but that's a matter for another day."

"He was persuaded with the fear of gaol. Would this man see it the same?"

"No, he's too close with the Tories and Customs to worry. Even if we could get him in to start, he'd be sure that someone would get him out."

Julius put down the iron and used the long-handled spoon he used to turn the stew from the bottom. "Then it will have to be action that does it. You say he's close with the Tories? And Customs?"

"He's an informer, Julius, and a practiced one at that."

Julius turned then with a small smile. "Then he'd be a perfect target for the Sons."

I sent Mouse out early the next day to find Burns. I expected Burns to be uneasy after our last go round about Draper, so Mouse was to make sure he knew it was important. Mouse caught him this time just as he left his room on Hannover Street toward the Common. "He . . . he . . he looked vexed, like he wished he could brush by, but said you could come to the Green Dragon after dinner today if it was important, he'd be somewhere about."

The Dragon was just around a corner from where Burns slept, near the Mill Pond on Union St. Some claimed that most of the mischief connected to the stamps before and the nonimport now were planned in the Long Room upstairs, and a Tory wouldn't dare venture inside without a squad of redcoats alongside. Burns must have spent hours there, probably more there than in the law office where he worked, or the room where he slept. It was certainly a place he'd never hear an argument against the cause.

I took Julius with me, unsure that I'd be able to say what I needed on my own, and we sat in a corner away from the door. The room was similar to the Sword, except larger, with enough tables to sit nearly fifty at a time, mostly empty now. The girl who served us was all business and it might have been a counting house for the lack of excited voices or a hint of laughter. Most days, the Dragon was in the business of liberty.

They served Julius without notice and we only sat a few moments before the girl fetched Burns from above. He spoke immediately after he sat, though there was little warmth in his voice. I was glad since there would be little in mine either. "What can I do for you, Mr. Gray? It's not often you take a cup at another room."

"It's what you asked, so I've come." I took a long breath before beginning in earnest. "I know of an informer who's trouble for everyone in Boston."

There was a hint of a smile as he spoke back. "That's the kind of information a good patriot shares, Nicholas. We'll be glad to know and glad to squeeze him." He took a drink before continuing. "But I have to ask your interest. This is the second time you've offered information when you always held back before. Have you seen the light of Liberty?"

I was angry before I came in the door, but the mockery in his voice made it worse. "About the same as merchant Marcus Draper. Maybe we'll join him as true patriots and break some windows for you."

Burns turned his head quickly to see who might be near, but seeing the tables empty, he turned back with his eyes blazing. "Out with it, Gray, and be done. It's not your privilege to ask for my ear and then taunt me for no reason."

I paused before answering. "I thought it was every man's duty to point a finger at an informer."

Burns still glared and said nothing. Finally, Julius took my part and spoke quietly. "There's more. Mr. Gray needs the man to leave town and never come back."

Burns stayed quiet and looked back and forth between Julius and me before answering. "They say Geyer won't be back. Would you have him treated more roughly than that?"

Julius continued on. "Our interest is driving him away forever. It's yours to know how to do it—without killing him."

"I have a few that I think could do that well enough—you may even know one of them." I shook my head so he didn't go on. Finally he sat back from the table a bit, and moved the cup from in front of him. "We've traded some before, Gray, so you know that we'll come back for yours later on." After I nodded, he asked. "What's the name then?"

"Partridge," I replied, my throat dry and rough as bark on a tree. "He's at the Royal Exchange."

It was just before Christmas when Mouse came in, chilled and out of breath. The weather was warmer than it might have been, the sun melting snow on some days before it froze back into ice at night. I tended to a table of mechanics, but they left when they heard a commotion outside. Mouse followed, quick on their heels.

Nearly two hours later, Mouse returned, shivering like always beneath his thin cloak. He stood before the hearth so close I thought he might catch fire himself. He turned and started slowly, like always. "It was . . . a pretty sight, Nicholas. I watched it all."

I suspected what he meant but I wouldn't let on. "What's that now, Mouse, a doxy dancing for you?"

He shot me a glance and now his voice was stronger. "The informer they trooped around. You heard the noise yourself."

I had, but didn't want to see what passed by. The mechanics who Mouse had followed began to come back in now, loud and thirsty from their shouting.

Mouse plunged ahead now he'd gotten his start. "They said they took him on Ann St from behind. Two or three came from the front, and when he stopped to see what they were after, the others got his arms from behind before he could get out a pistol."

Another dockman came to stand next to Mouse before the fire. Robert Haley was thick through the arms with hands rough as barnacles from years hauling on ropes. Haley took up the story. "Yes, they had him alright, tight as a clam, with his arms tied up behind. But what was he going to do anyway, with that monster holding his arms?"

The others sat at a table now, listening and laughing as Mouse and Haley put on a little show. Mouse shot me a glance when Haley continued. "That man Grendel is big as a house, and fearsome, too. He looks a sight with his mouth open, breathing like a fish. But the others weren't small either."

"They . . . they had the pot ready for him down by Clark's Wharf," said Mouse, "tar enough to cover him, all boiling happy, and a brush to paint him."

"When they took his clothes, he looked a pitiful sight, like a chicken without feathers, but they fixed that quick enough." Haley got a laugh from the others. "He tried to beg off, claiming he could pay them, get more money than what they took from him, but no one cared. Grendel had to hit him on the ear to make him quiet down. Then they took turns pissing in a pot so he could have a proper drink of tea before they brushed him up." Haley made a show like dropping his breeches and pointing a stream at the fire and got another howl from the crowd. He moved over to Mouse and got Mouse to his knees to act the part. "It was plenty hot when they fed it to him, he screamed enough. I thought his neck might break the way Grendel yanked his head back." Mouse let out a strangled scream and kept wailing till I told him to stuff it up.

Haley kept playing to the crowd. "The tar was hot enough, too. They were determined this bloke wouldn't play the rat again, I knew that when I saw the rail. A cart ride was too good for him." He put Mouse on his side and played at tying him up. "We're never short of sailors when we need a good knot for a Customs dog."

The table of watchers agreed and offered that they were always glad to lend a hand when needed, before Haley went on. "It's a wonder he had any balls left at all, his feet and hands tied beneath like that, and the ride they gave him." Mouse and Haley took a little trip around the room, acting as if they held up a man on a rail between them, bouncing it up and down, and the crowd grabbing at their own balls and moaning each time they did. "It wasn't much of a parade though, just a stop by the Custom House and one at the British Coffee House. By the time they bounced him all the way down Orange St., he looked like a feathered doll for all the life he had left." Mouse played his part by collapsing on the floor, shuddering and moaning with each breath. "They had a wagon waiting for him near the Neck and a canvas to cover him." Haley acted like he'd cover Mouse with a blanket. "But Grendel had a final word for him. He put that horrible face right down to him and roared out loud enough for all to hear, 'If you ever come back, you won't live the day. And that's the same for your friends, too.'"

Mouse got up now, acting like one of the crowd for Haley's story. "It was a jolly march back, with everyone clapping Grendel on the shoulder and shouting out to all the Tory houses we passed." Haley and Mouse marched around the room a second time. Haley got back to the bar where I was standing quiet. "It's time to toast the Sons again, Mr. Gray. Can you fill their cups in the spirit of liberty?"

"If you have the shillings, I'll catch the spirit with the rest."

Haley looked at me hard for a moment. "For being a friend of the Sons, you're not one celebrate a victory, are you? You're as hard as a gravestone," he offered before going to collect some money from the table.

It was Mouse who came back with the money for the round of toasts. "Did Grendel see you in the crowd, Mouse?" I asked.

He shook his head quickly. "I . . . I don't think so." His hand shook as he put down the coins. "I'd sleep better if someone managed to get *him* out the Neck so he'd never come back."

Section V

Twenty-Seven

AT THE END OF A YEAR, with Twelfth Night coming on, some people are determined to celebrate, no matter what's gone before or what lies ahead. The situation in town didn't look that happy to me, but people shot off their muskets all day on Christmas and some ate a special meal. Even the dregs of the redcoats took the chance to let loose with a volley in the air, even though they were itching to fire at some jack on the street. There was a good group who spent all of their time tormenting the lobsters, knowing their guns were like pictures hung on the walls, decoration and no more. A Christmas shot in the air was about all the soldiers would get other than drills, since firing without orders would surely bring charges.

The thought of the Spider gone from the streets of Boston brought me some ease, although the way it happened wasn't as neat as I might have liked. I found myself with a smile now and again, and there were times I'd joke a bit with Maggie and she'd laugh or smile in return.

As the days of Christmas passed, my mind drifted back to Oxford and the few memories I had there. Some years, my mother lay sick in bed and we'd go for weeks when we searched our soup for a bit of beef from the bone or a wedge of turnip but my father always managed a gift for me and my mother on Twelfth Night. He said that if the Wise Men could travel that far and bring gifts, he could manage the same.

Once he'd brought us each a poem by John Donne. He'd copied them during the few minutes he stole each day from his hours cleaning at the library. Mine was about the sun rising, he explained, and how it shone on kings and poor men alike. Another year, he'd made a spinning top by carving away at a piece of kindling, smoothing it until it felt like it was made of stone.

I decided I'd give Maggie a gift, hoping that it might bring back her old smile, the one I thought she saved for me and gave so freely in our first months together.

When Gillam had brought home a few bits of jewelry from a Tory house more than a year ago, while Mouse and I watched outside, we were surprised to see a scrimshaw tooth on a plain leather string among the small pieces. The lady must have liked it because she kept it with her better jewelry, but she'd never wear it in public since it came from the rough hands of a whaler. Gillam actually got it by mistake since we wouldn't be able to sell it for much. Gillam told me to keep it if I liked, since he might as well pitch it in the ocean. I thought the tiny design was as pleasing as any I'd seen, with vines and leaves and flowers woven together all the way around the whale tooth so that you might turn it around and around and never find a beginning or an end.

WE'D DIDN'T OPEN for dinner on Twelfth Night since it was a holy day, and if there were some out on the streets later, and it struck us right, we might open in the evening. Julius would make a meat pie with pork and some nutmeg he kept in a corner of his shelf for special dishes and sweet yams with maple sugar. Gillam, who is lean as a whip, would eat till he looked like a fat pigeon on a branch and Mouse would match him, though he looked like no more than a stick man.

Mouse had come first and sat at the corner table, practicing with the cards we kept beneath the bar as Gillam had taught him. I laid out spoons and knives so we could all sit at once and Maggie came from the kitchen, with a smile. "Don't let the Governor in the door, Nicholas. I'm afraid if we do, he'll offer Julius a fortune to cook for him and you'll have to eat the dishes I cook."

Suddenly, I felt a warmth in my chest, and I thought I might lose the strength in my legs if I didn't sit. I wondered at the scene, and saw it as if in a dream, with the edges soft and the fire bright, safe from the weather, the doors bolted tight against the dangers outside, and a feast on its way.

"Sit here for a moment, Maggie." She looked a question at me. "I have something for you." I drew the scrimshaw from the hidden pocket where I usually kept my knife.

Maggie's eyes lit before she saw what I had, and then they turned quick to worry. "I don't know what you've got, Nicholas, but I have nothing for you. I can't . . ."

I cut her off with my hand. "Don't worry over it, Maggie, just take it, and you can fuss later on if you like." I put the scrimshaw in her hand, and she brought it before her face to see, and turned it round to take in all sides.

She looked at me then, her lips starting to move, but her eyes spoke better than her words, which never came out. Again, I felt the warmth in my chest, spreading now through my arms and down to my stomach. My eyes blurred and I saw what lay before me—Maggie, the fire, the familiar walls and scarred tables of the Sword, Julius coming from the kitchen with a steaming dish, Mouse close by—as in a dream, with no distinct sounds, just a friendly hum of voices in the background. My face relaxed into a smile, though no one else knew why.

But it lasted only a moment, then disappeared like a candle blown out.

We all heard the door at the same time and turned towards it. Someone was tapping there, not a strong fist, but they wouldn't stop either, keeping on three times with a few seconds in between.

"I'll see to it," said Maggie, "it's probably some beggar wanting a coin or a bite for the holiday."

She opened the door and stood for a moment with her back to me. I heard their voices but no words and I couldn't see past Maggie, though I wasn't looking hard, mostly staring at the fire again which we'd built bigger than usual. When she turned and called to me, it was as if the frozen air outside had come right through her voice. "It's for you to manage, Nicholas. It seems your doll has some trouble now, enough to come right to the front door. She says she won't leave until she speaks with you." Her eyes searched me over then, looking for something I didn't have. "I'll leave you," she said and walked off to the kitchen.

Lilly followed her in and shut the door, a relief to her since her cloak was a fine bright blue, but not heavy enough for Boston in January. She moved directly to the fire and stood there stiffly, her arms folded across her breast, trying to drink in the warmth without setting her cloak on fire.

I walked up to her side and looked at her. She gave a quick glance over at me, then turned back toward the fire. Tears had streaked her face like rain down a dirty window. The color of the bruise had gone away but I thought that side of her face still looked swollen. But most of all, she'd lost that air she'd worn like a crown, no matter what clothes she wore, knowing her beauty and her air, able to turn a man's head whenever she liked. She was sunken now, her shoulders forward.

"What would bring you here, Lilly?"

She unfolded her arms now and reached out a hand holding a small cloth bag. "Will you buy these, Nicholas? They're from London and they have good stones and silver."

I opened the bag and emptied the earrings into my hand, the handsome ones she'd worn to Hart's tavern. I looked at her more than the earrings. "What's happened, Lilly. Where's your Irishman?"

This time she cried outright before she caught herself. As she sobbed, I took her arm to sit at a table. She wouldn't look me full in the face. "He's gone, he just disappeared. He went out two nights back and never returned. Then the landlord came for the rent and threw me out." I looked away for a moment, hoping she'd stop her tears so I could think better. "I've nowhere to go, Nicholas, Widow Marden won't have me." Her anger helped her stop sobbing, though the tears still ran from her eyes. "She couldn't stop her smile once she found I was in the street."

"There's pawn shops will give you some if you really need it," I offered.

She shook her head quickly. "They might as well steal it from you outright."

"I don't know prices well, especially for jewelry. But I'll ask a friend later on . . ."

It was a surprise then when I looked to the front door and in walked Gillam just after I'd mentioned him. I'm sure Mouse was startled as well, hanging as he was on every word, though none were directed at him. But I didn't like the way Gillam's forehead wrinkled or the stormy look in his eyes.

I turned from Lilly and walked a step towards Gillam. "What's on?"

He motioned me over to where Mouse sat and stood with his back to Lilly. Gillam spoke low, but his voice was filled with anger. "We've been robbed." He went on quickly when I didn't reply. "It seems our watchman at the warehouse must have fallen asleep or gotten drunk or skipped a night. It's hard to tell because he's come with a few different stories already. He says he just noticed this morning that the lock had been broken."

I jumped in quickly. "But I checked just three days ago, I took a present from my corner of the chest . . ."

"I was just there." Gillam's shoulders moved just a bit in a slight shrug. "I go sometimes just to look . . ." He closed his eyes for a moment, before finishing. "They took it all."

My mind raced now, thinking of the jewelry and money we kept there. We hadn't added much since the summer, but we hadn't taken anything away either.

"The glitter and the coins?" I asked.

"All of it. What the four of us had together must have been worth near a hundred pounds."

I might have taken a bit longer to think but my legs were already driving me to grab my cloak from the peg on the wall and out the door. "I'll get a straight story from him one way or another. Maybe we can get it back."

Maggie called before I got out the door. "What about her?"

I looked back and realized that Lilly still stood by the fire, not looking much warmer than when she'd come in. "There's other things first. We can talk later on."

Twenty-Eight

THE MINDER was a short, round man named Sweet, with little hair on the top of his head. His eyes glowed red and he still smelled of rum from a long night. He must have seen the menace in my look because he started shaking like a leaf when I found him in his little room at the warehouse. I caught him by the collar and dragged him out into the warehouse, damp and cold as a tomb.

"Gillam is too pleasant most times, so you probably felt free to lie to him. But I'm not." I moved my hand to grab his shirt just below his throat and moved his back against the wall. "You'll need to tell it to me honest. Not part of it—all of it."

He started to moan and I tightened my grip. "Stop sputtering and start talking—just the way it was, or you'll lose more of your teeth."

In the dim light, I could just see the sweat on the crown of his head when he finally managed his voice. "I must have had a bit too much rum from the barrel here in the corner." His hand fluttered out toward the back wall. He tried a guilty smile. "It was stored by one of the captains but he hasn't been back since he left for Halifax. I had a moll in and . . . she agreed to trade for the rum. We stayed warm here until I fell asleep . . ."

"What night?"

"Two nights back. I was sleeping heavy and she was gone when I woke. I thought I heard something in the warehouse but I couldn't be sure, my head was pounding so. But I heard it a second time so I went out and he caught me from behind the door. Maybe she let him in."

"What's her name?"

He waited a minute before answering, as if he was ashamed to say, but I tightened my grip and he spit it out quick enough. "They call her Dirty Ann, or the Sweep, her skirt looks like she's been in a chimney. Mouse knows her."

"Go on."

His breathing was shallow now, fear leaking out with each breath. "He held a knife to my throat, said he'd gut me like a deer if I told anyone. He told me to go along like regular and tell you I didn't know what happened once you found out."

"Who was it?"

"I'd never seen him before."

"What were his looks?"

"It was dark . . . just a little light from the fire in my room . . ."

"Think hard. It would go better for you if we can get it back."

He was scared of the man who'd touched his neck with a knife, but now he was more scared of me because I had his throat. "Nothing special—lean not fat, a worn coat, pox on his cheeks. But I think he was Irish, he had that color, and way of talking."

BY THE TIME I GOT BACK and bolted the door behind me, Julius had set the meat pie on the table, but there were no pieces taken out. I was sure Gillam's anger made him forget his hunger, just like when he was dealing cards or rolling dice. Lilly sat at a table to the side with Maggie across from her. Mouse sat near Gillam while Julius stood in the kitchen door.

The blood was roaring in my ears but I tried to keep my voice calm. "He says a man robbed the warehouse two nights back and threatened to kill him if he told. He had a whore in who might have helped. You know Dirty Ann, Mouse?" He nodded. "We'll find her and ask, but I think Sweet was scared enough to tell the truth."

"It's not a story that gets him anything, other than a beating," said Gillam, the heat clear in his voice.

"We can think about him later." I turned towards Lilly and moved toward where she sat. "He described a man that might have been your Mr. Windham." Her face was still streaked but her eyes went wide now, and fear stopped her tears. "When did you say he left?"

Her voice was small now, barely loud enough to hear. "Two nights back." Gillam started to get up from the table but I motioned him down. "But I told him nothing, there was nothing for me to tell. I don't even know where your hideaway is!"

Still I tried to keep my voice calm. "Did he ever ask about me or any of the others?"

She gripped her hands together on the table in front of her. "Well, after that day you insulted him up by the Common, he asked about you. I explained that you helped run the Sword and you had a few other mates, but that's no more than everyone knows."

"Nothing else?"

She thought a minute. "He mentioned you a few nights later, said some others around suspected you for a thief but that you'd never gotten caught. He sounded like he was giving you a compliment."

"What was his business otherwise?" asked Gillam.

She turned towards him but then back to speak to me, since his face was still twisted in anger. "I wasn't sure, but he had enough to pay room and board. It seemed he was always finding things for some of the officers, like Pearson . . ." her eyes turned steely now, "things like extra blankets or a rundlet of brandy, other things they couldn't spot or the shops wouldn't sell them."

"What about the compliment? Was there any more after?" I asked.

"Oh, I just laughed a little and agreed with him. I told him if you were that good, you could probably fill up a warehouse."

Gillam was up this time, menace in his dark eyes as he moved towards her table. "I thought you didn't know our place."

"I didn't, I still don't . . . it was no more than an idle word." She cringed away now as he came nearer. "It was just what I said, 'a warehouse,' but nothing more. Nicholas never mentioned anything." She looked at me to help her.

Gillam moved to the table now and stood over her. "Why should I believe you? You give up your pelt to anyone who pays. Why wouldn't you give up our place if there was money in it?"

She cried now, full out. She went to put her head down on the table. Gillam started to reach out toward her, to stop her or grab her hair, but Maggie's hand was on his arm in an instant, just before mine.

She grabbed his wrist and stared him straight in the face, her color up and the scar on her cheek white against it. "You won't touch her here, Powell, or you'll answer. You can't watch your back every minute."

I took Gillam's shoulder and moved him away. "Sit down, Gillam. It won't do to fight among us."

He turned and glared. "She might be your whore, Nicholas, but if I find she sold what's ours, she'll pay."

"If she did, I agree, but I don't think she did. I know I never told her where we hid our goods, and she wouldn't be here selling her jewelry if she'd made something in the bargain." He didn't look satisfied, but he shrugged off my hand and sat down next to Mouse again.

"You were there today, Gillam, and when before? Some time to admire what we had?" I ventured.

"Are you accusing me?" This time the heat was even greater, the same tone that comes just before a knife appears.

"No, I'm not. I'm just trying to see what might have happened."

He glared for a moment more before answering. "Less than a fortnight. I'd won enough in a game that it seemed best to keep it there."

"Were you followed?"

"Not that I know."

"And you, Mouse?"

He was surprised when I asked, and shrugged as he began. "A . . . a . . . about a week ago." When everyone kept looking at him, he continued. "I just go to count it sometimes. I like counting the coins and seeing the silver."

"Did anyone follow you?" He shrugged and shook his head. I turned away from them a moment and walked toward the front door, then back. "We've been careless, that's all. I was there just three nights back to get the necklace." I was guilty and so were they. "I think our treasure is gone with Mr. Windham and we'll never see it again." I sat down now, tired in the legs. "If Windham was a good thief, he could ravel it out. Plenty know that we work together, and if he took enough care to follow without being seen, he'd find it. He probably didn't know what he'd find, but once he counted it up, a trip out of town was his best choice."

MOUSE AND I tracked down Dirty Ann at The Raven, up near the ferry to Charlestown, as dark a hole as you can find in Boston. The door didn't close proper and the smell of smoke and tallow lamps leaked out.

Mouse and I went to the bar where the tender stood. He was medium height and dark, with just one open eye. The other lid drooped down closed and his face on that side was all slack as well.

He nodded a greeting. "Mouse, what brings you here? Can I get you and your friend drinks?"

I shook my head. "We're looking for Dirty Ann."

He looked surprised. "I know she comes cheap, but you look like you could afford better." He looked at us through his one eye and tried a smile. "I could suggest the wench lives with me. She's a sight better looking and cleaner, too."

I looked at him hard now. "We don't need suggestions, we just need to find Ann." He stared at us, waiting. "And don't try to take a penny for it either or you're likely to be full blind for a few days."

He narrowed his good eye a bit and turned away. "She's in the back room."

Mouse was stunned, his eyes wide. "She ... she ... paid for a room?"

The tender turned back to us. "You don't think I'd let her stay free do you? She's come into some money, more than she's had before. She bought three bottles of rum at the same time."

We went to the back and I knocked on the door, hard. It swung open and we saw her huddled up in a corner of the bed, a rum bottle in one hand and an empty one on the floor. Her hair was matted and snarled without a cap and her dress filthy, but her eyes were surprisingly young and had a mad gleam to them.

"What, what do you want here?"

I wasn't ready at first and Mouse began to walk across the room toward her.

"Oh, it's some of this is it?" She reached down between her legs. "It's good enough for one or both, but it'll cost you more. I've got a room to pay for."

Mouse stopped and looked at me. "Who paid you to lay down with the watchman two nights back?" I asked.

She laughed, a drunken cackle, and nearly let the bottle roll from her hand till she made a fast grab. "Oh, that was pretty. I did the same as usual, but I got ten shillings extra. If he'd keep that up, I'd live in a room of my own." She laughed again and took a drink from her bottle.

"Who was it? Who paid you to let him in?"

"No one special, just an Irishman off the street, one that helped the officers."

"Windham?"

"Might have been. He didn't tell me, but I think someone called out to him."

I turned to go.

"You don't have to leave now, buy some rum and come back. I'm good for one or both and we'll drink the bottle dry."

I shut the door and walked quickly out the front, glad to find the air in my lungs. But clean as it felt, it didn't bring back a penny that we'd lost.

Twenty-Nine

THE EASE I felt in the days near Twelfth Night vanished with our swag. I felt like I'd stepped into an open hatch in the dark and dropped till I could go no more. The first few nights, the dreams came back, and I would wake in a sweat, fighting with my blanket as if it chained me to a ring. Even after I realized I was safe in my room at the Sword, the truth sank heavy on me: I had nothing and the distance to the gaol door for debt or otherwise was no more than a step, and a quick one at that. Maybe it wasn't a step at all, just a small stumble.

For some reason, Julius and Mouse seemed little changed, although Julius never gave away much with his face and less with his words. I saw a fire behind his eyes when it first happened, but now he was back to cooking and visiting Eve whenever he could, with no talk about what we'd lost.

Mouse never did act angry, although it might have been because our treasure was never real to him anyway. I knew what we had, though most was in jewelry and not coin, and I had begged Mouse sometimes to buy a new cloak or take a warm room for the winter. But he never answered other than "Maybe some time," and then did the same as the day before. I guessed that looking at what he had in the chest had been good enough for him, and if he spent it, it wouldn't be there to look at.

Gillam was dark and short-tempered, and I even saw him lose at dice and cards a few times when his eyes grew too big and he tried to take the pile all at once. Sometimes he would glare hard at Lilly, like it was her fault we'd been robbed.

After Lilly stayed the first night, I asked Maggie about where she would go. "Where should I send her, Nicholas? Out on the docks to sleep in the snow? To a new mother so every jack with two shillings can have her until she gets the French pox? She may as well stay here for now and help out."

"But . . . " I stumbled for a moment, trying to find some words that would work, "you bear no grudge because of . . . " I waved a hand in the air, but my words stopped before I'd said what I wanted.

Maggie was silent a moment, arranging her words. "She was a moll, Nicholas, trying to get a hold. She may have been soft for you–there's some that even think you handsome in a rough way–but it was more than you she wanted. It was over when you didn't take her offer." Then she turned to make certain she looked at me straight. "If there's anyone I should fault, it's you. It's a wonder you haven't gotten in more trouble, following your rod wherever it points."

Now my lips were firm stuck together, but she had no more words either, and turned away to go up the stairs.

At first Lilly slept on a straw tick on Maggie's floor, then moved downstairs to the hall that led out the back door. It was probably the coldest spot in the Sword, with no fireplace near and the wind that came down the hall through the cracks around the door, but she acted like it was a palace, and I noticed that Jezebel slept almost on top of her at times.

After a few days when I sank deeper with every step, Gillam called me over to the table in the corner on quiet afternoon. "We should look for coin, not goods," he said, "the goods take too long to sell and we'd need a new hideaway besides."

"True, but most people watch their coins more closely."

"Some of the redcoat officers don't. They throw hard money around like it was ashes. I've played in games where there's a pile this high on the table." He held his hand a few inches above the surface. Jezebel came mewing around Gillam's ankles, but he had no love of her and pushed her away.

"Do you have a plan, Gillam?"

"No, not a full one, but I thought it might interest you. You remember Lt. Pearson, the one who took Lilly?" He motioned with his head to where she was getting the ashes from the fireplace. "He likes to play and carries a pouch with him. We play every Monday at the Hare and Hound, it's a lively game, and Pearson leaves with more than anyone except me." He stopped a moment and a sly grin crossed his face. "I'd think it dangerous for a bloodyback officer to walk home in the dark with a full purse. I might even be able to help fill it up."

"It's a thought, Gillam, different than what we usually do, but then, who would have thought we'd be robbed of our own hard-earned goods?"

I turned it over in my mind for a few days. It would be a start, but a dangerous one at that, since there were always things that might go wrong in a scrape on the street. But it would be hard money, like Gillam said, something I had none of, and coins couldn't be traced like jewelry.

But it was Julius who lit a bigger fire a few days later. I had finished my hard cheese and bread in the morning and drained off my cider before bringing my dish into the kitchen. Julius was chopping beets already, some he'd bought last market day which had been stored in a root cellar and looked as fresh as if they had just been pulled up. The red juice stained his block and his fingers as well, light on the inside compared to his dark skin. He worked with his sleeves rolled almost to his shoulders and his forearms looked like twisted wrought iron. I watched in silence for a bit, and I noticed that Jezebel sat comfortably in a corner, waiting patiently for a scrap she knew would come.

He knew I was there but waited till he was done with what was on the block before he turned and spoke. "Do you remember when we spoke of visiting the Steuart's home some night?"

We'd talked one time of the Tory house where Eve worked for the Customs cashier. "Sure. Your lady spoke of a jewelry chest near full." It sounded interesting, but going into the house of a Customs officer was more danger than we wanted.

"Well, now she's offered me a job." I looked a question at him. "Not regular, just one time, some kitchen work for a party." He swept the beet tops off his block and threw them in the basket at the side so he would look through them later when he started soup. Jezebel looked disappointed that it wasn't meat and none was coming her way. "The Steuarts are ready to entertain and need some extra hands in the kitchen."

"They'll have in the commissioners and the like?"

"All the highest who will consent to attend."

I couldn't help a small smile. "Just the thing that Hancock would love, except Adams would have his head for mixing with the Tories."

He turned to begin with some hard squash, and I watched as his wide butcher's blade chopped down as regular as the pendulum in a tall case clock I'd seen in London. He watched his fingers, but not closely.

"I've seen the house and the kitchen in the back. There's a stair leading up." Now he gave just the slightest of smiles. "With all the confusion and people, it might be a time you could get into their rooms."

I liked the thought and started to nod. "But what about your lady . . ."

"Eve."

"Eve. Would she know? And if she did, could we trust her?"

"She has no love for the Steuarts. She's a free woman, and they brought her here, but they treat her like a slave. She'd never give us away.

I imagine she might get a small piece?" I nodded and he went on. "But there's another thing I'd like you to hear." When I questioned him with a look, he responded, "She'll be at market today, it's a time we can get a few words. I'll let her tell you herself. I'm not certain, but there might be some treasure there besides jewelry."

MARKET was held inside Faneuil Hall in the winter, on the lower floor, beneath the great room that was always filled for important speeches and meetings. Winter market was much smaller than the summer one, since nothing was growing, and even getting meat and fish over snowy roads was a gamble. But the sellers still took up most of the space along the walls and the air smelled as one great butcher house, even as cold and drafty as the room was.

Julius went ahead and I stayed near the north door when Eve came in the other end. I watched them greet each other carefully after he walked to her, but I could sense his joy from one end to the other, thirty yards at least. They made an unmatched pair–he was tall, muscular, and dark, she shorter than most women, delicate, and skin the color of cinnamon. Her white cap showed a red bow and sat precisely on her head. She carried her large basket with ease over one arm and walked as if each step was a dance.

They took their time walking down one side, stopping for a moment to look over four hams that had been smoked and stacked in a large cart by a man who looked to weigh as much as any of the pigs he slaughtered. When they came near, Julius brought her to where I stood with my back against the wall. It was as private as anywhere on the streets, what with the noise of people walking, chickens gabbling, and sellers shouting out at odd times.

"Eve, this is Nicholas Gray, the man I work for."

I nodded my head and didn't point out that he actually worked for Maggie, since it was her license. "Good day, Eve."

She made a slight curtsy but didn't bow her head. "Tell him about the book," prompted Julius.

Her eyes studied me so hard that another man might have taken offense and brushed her away or asked her if she thought herself a lady instead of a colored serving girl. But Julius had told me that she'd been born free in Jamaica and had served British governors and officials there ever since she could walk. Now she was a house servant for an upper Tory and had some airs that wouldn't serve as well in America. When she spoke, it was in the same English voice as Julius, learned carefully from years of listening to the lords and ladies talk.

"I was cleaning up in Mr. Steuart's office at home one day while he had a meeting with another Customs man, Mr. Geary. I understand he serves as comptroller while Mr. Steuart is cashier. Like always, they went ahead to talk as if I wasn't there. I was cleaning a bookshelf that holds a row of leather ledger books. I took one out to dust it and a smaller book, a thin one with a worn leather cover, dropped from where it was hidden inside the larger one. It made a noise and both Mr. Steuart and Mr. Geary looked up. I picked it up quickly and held it out to them to show the cause and hoped to apologize. 'This one just slipped out,' I said, and then went on, hoping I wouldn't draw anger, 'it doesn't seem to fit with the others. Might I place it somewhere else . . . ?'

"At first Mr. Steuart's eyes got large, as if he was shocked or afraid, then turned with a great laugh to Mr. Geary, mocking me. 'Put it somewhere else, she says, like it was of no value,' then they have another great laugh together. 'No, girl, put it right here on my desk.' Then he turns to Mr. Geary like I'm no longer there. 'If she only knew what she had in her hand. That little book is worth its weight in gold.'"

I cocked my head a little, trying to imagine what it held. "Did you see where he put it afterwards?"

"No, I didn't, but I would expect back in with the books. I don't think he'd keep it in his coin chest and I got the feeling it was his alone, not something for the Customs office."

I was lost in thought for a moment. "You might keep your eyes open for it and let Julius know if you see it again."

"That's easy enough, but I can't go searching. I'd never seen it before and I doubt I'll see it again."

I nodded to her with a bit of a smile before turning to Julius. "You were right, Julius, we might take time to look, as long as their plates are full."

I WAITED while Julius and Eve walked back along the other side of the market. They stopped so she could buy two chickens from a cage on a wagon and waited while the farmer twisted their necks. When Julius and I walked back toward the Sword, we were both silent, turning over thoughts of Steuart's house and the book, until we nearly walked into a shower of rocks and ice chunks aimed at Nathaniel Rogers' store on Ann St. Even though the agreement for nonimport had ended, Adams and the Sons kept crowds in the streets every Thursday market day. The merchants committee now numbered nearly two thousand, about twenty for every shop in Boston. Most of them wouldn't have known an account book from a school boy's primer, but they were sure they needed to attack any shop importing goods and paying the duty on tea.

Walking the streets on market days, you could usually find a straw effigy with a name on its chest hung from a tree near one of the Tory shops or one of the signs that looked like a giant hand and finger that pointed directly at a shop with the word "Importer" painted in bold letters, just in case you didn't know it's meaning. The previous night, some had given the door and walls of Rogers' shop a fresh coat of Hillsborough paint, straight from a latrine, and now there was a crowd cheering the boys as they threw their stones, trying to break a window.

But it was a long try from the far side of the street because Rogers had hired two redcoats to carry their muskets and face down any who came too close. We had to walk well to the back and I had to shout and push so they would move to let us pass.

Thirty

IT WAS NEARLY THREE WEEKS before the Steuart's party on Saturday, February 10, and I knew the time would crawl as we waited and planned. But I liked it better than going off like a pistol at half-cock. We needed a full plan to be able to visit the Steuarts, find what we needed and leave without alarm. It might be the biggest haul we'd ever taken, depending on what we found, and it was certainly the most dangerous.

Stealing from the house of a Customs official would mean a certain trip to the gallows if any of us were caught. We'd be locked away, our necks stretched, then buried without a mark as quick as any judge, Tory or Whig, could snap his fingers. I talked with everyone together—Julius, Gillam, and Mouse—on two mornings and it was Julius who made a clear picture on the second day. "Their private closet is just off the hall from the front stairs, and their bed is in the next room down," he told us. "His office is at the back, near the back stairs from the kitchen."

"The dinner will be served in the great room?" I asked

He nodded. "They're stretching out the regular table so they can cover it with cloth and sit everyone at once." He stopped a minute and looked about the table. "You'll be almost directly overhead."

I thought over our plan. It was bold, but sometimes that's best. People don't guard against something they can't imagine. "If we look like kitchen help and they're loud enough at dinner, it should work."

He shook his head. "There's too many to see you, even if you look like you belong in the kitchen. Someone might tell a tale afterwards. It's better if no one sees you." He stopped and made a wave with his large hand before holding a finger to his lips. "They'll be loud at dinner, but you'll need to be silent as a ghost."

My morning walks now steered away from the docks and toward the Steuart house, just off Marlborough Street on Winter Street, near the Common. I wanted to know every step I might take in the dark and where every path led if I needed to change course. I repeated the path from the end of Winter Street onto the Common toward the Work House several times and passed the other way, down Summer St. past Draper's house more than once as well.

I had just come back one day and was preparing the Sword to open. The coasting captains were due for dinner and I began to push two tables together so they could sit. Mouse stayed at a table in the corner with Jezebel on the bench beside him, trying to work the cards like Gillam was teaching him. His hands were no match for Gillam's who worked the cards like they were coated with whale oil, slipping one way and the other so fast you couldn't keep track.

I was surprised that the knock on the door didn't yield one of the captains coming early but instead, a clean cut young man in a tri-corner hat stood there smartly. When I asked his business, he replied, "I have a message here for Widow Magowan." When I waited, he added, "I'm to give it to her personally." After I let him in, he removed his hat quickly and reached inside the pocket of his soft wool coat to withdraw a flat purse for papers.

Maggie came from the kitchen just as I went to get her. "What's your pleasure, young master?"

The young man opened the purse and gingerly gave her a folded sheet with a wax seal, as if it was made of glass. He waited a moment and watched her. "Is there something more you need?" she asked.

"I was instructed by Mr. Tobin to read it for you if you had trouble."

Maggie colored slightly and gave him a hard look. "Mr. Tobin knows well enough that I can read and plenty of others here can as well. You can tell him he'll need more than that for an insult."

The young man was embarrassed a bit and cowed by Maggie's eyes. "Sorry, Madam, sorry, I was just doing as told." He fumbled with his hat and bumped the door as he backed up and left.

I watched Maggie break the seal and spread the paper on the table. She took her time reading and when she'd finished, she closed her eyes and dropped her head down a bit.

I sat opposite her and waited for her to open her eyes. "Is it that bad?" I asked.

This time I was sure that I saw a tear glistening in her eye, though not enough to roll down her cheek. She brushed at it and pushed the paper across to me. "It's the end of the Sword, Nicholas. When the lease is done, they'll open their own tavern or sell the building to someone else who will."

I looked over the letter with Tobin's signature at the bottom and Brown's below that.

I felt like a stone had dropped in my stomach, but I didn't show Maggie. "We have till the end of the lease, Maggie, a full month, till the end of February. We'll think of something . . . we made him sign that paper . . . we'll make a plan . . ."

I could see her working hard to keep her face straight, but the strain made her blink and squint. She shook her head just an inch, side to side. "We've managed before, Nicholas, and if it was just greedy men outside the law, I think we could—we could lay out a trap or you could use your hands or your stick to make them afraid. But this has gone too far already and the paper we hold over Tobin isn't enough. If it was, we wouldn't have gotten this at all." She was silent a moment before going on. "No, this is about money, and there's nothing to answer but the same." Her voice dropped so it was barely loud enough to hear. "It's how they win, Nicholas, it's how they'll always win."

I wanted to sputter something else or reach to take her hand, but the door opened then and two of the captains came blustering through. I glanced at Mouse and knew from his wide eyes that he'd heard our every word.

We served out the dinners and punch bowls and we all acted like it was none but a regular day. I wasn't jolly, but I acted the bartender, so my thoughts were of no interest to the drinkers. When the captains were gone and the Sword was quiet again, Maggie went straight away to her room, without a look or a word.

THE NEXT DAYS, my chest felt like someone had bound it tight with tow line, so tight I could barely breathe. My mind ran in circles and tangles, Maggie avoided me and offered no help, but I could think in only one direction—straight ahead where we'd planned. Once our job at the Steuart's was done, we'd know better where we stood.

On the third day, I was returning from a walk which had taken me in a circle around the Steuarts' house—up Pond St. and West St. to the Common then along the path and back down Winter St. onto Summer St. when I looked up and saw a familiar figure closing the gate behind her at Draper's house. It was Maggie, wrapped in her dark green cloak, and glancing about carefully. I pulled back enough that she didn't see me and followed her at a long distance all the way back to the Sword.

Even though the cold was biting me, I walked two more streets after she went in, down Ship St. before taking a turn to lead me north and back around to the Sword. I thought I had my mind settled, but I couldn't hide my look as soon as Maggie came in the tavern room from the kitchen. "What is it, Nicholas, you'd best spit it out before you choke."

"You've taken to walking some mornings as well, I see. It must be good for your humor." She stared at me, without a word. "Or maybe you have business we don't know about that takes you around town."

I could see the color start to fill her neck and cheeks, but she didn't drop her eyes for a moment. "You're still dancing about, Nicholas. Say what you will."

I put both hands flat on a table then and leaned towards her. "Did you make your deal with Draper today? Is he going to save you as long as you throw the lot of us out?"

I could see her eyes narrow, and the way her jaw set made the scar on her cheek quiver a little, but I couldn't stop. "You told me once that we were connected, that we couldn't be broken like a broom straw, and you act like you care about the Sword and all the rest . . . but the fog's gone now, I can see the land as it lays. . . ." My head nodded at the ugly sight I saw, and the words came out cold and hard. "It was all an act, just like when you laid with the rich pigeons in London. We're no more to you than dust you can sweep out the door. You want the money to keep you more than anything else. You said it's only money that will answer, and now you've got yours."

I'd said it now, and when she didn't answer, I started out past her, toward the back, but she caught my arm as I went, and spun me back like a top. I felt her hand as hot as a poker. She stood close now, well shorter than me, but her head was forward, like a dog at its leash.

"That's what you think, Nicholas? That I went to Draper to sell you?" She spoke with such heat that I backed away a bit, though she was truly no threat.

"What else would it be, Maggie, with your going off secret?"

"And when do you announce where you'll go and what you'll do, as if any of us have a claim?" she shot back.

I shrugged, unsure why I might ever tell my directions. "That's a different road, Maggie, it's nothing beside your selling us away."

Her eyes sprung up in tears then, the first I'd seen, but they didn't stop her tongue. "I might as well then, if that's what you think." She was close enough I could sense her breathing then, deep and slow, fighting to keep control. She turned quickly then, away toward the fireplace, and she shook her head side to side slowly, like she couldn't believe what she'd seen with her own eyes. "Draper's behind it, Nicholas, and I did all I could. I was trying to save what we have." She turned again, but made no move forward. "I begged him to give the money and let you stay on, promised we'd bring in all he hoped and more, guaranteed you'd work for his benefit. I did everything short of pulling up my skirts and spreading my legs, but he wouldn't have it."

She turned away to the fire again, this time her voice near a whisper. "I can make my way, Nicholas, I always have, and so can you. But I went there and bowed down so we could keep on together." Her breath caught then, but just for a moment and then her voice turned hard. "And you'd believe it was so I could take more for myself and give you the dirt." Her shoulders moved a bit as she tried to straighten up, still staring at the fire. "Well, I may consider it yet."

I reached out and laid my hand on her shoulder, but she shrugged it off. When she turned, I tried to speak. "I didn't know, Maggie . . . I didn't think . . ."

Her eyes were cold and I shivered when she spoke. "You can sputter all you like, Nicholas, and claim that you didn't think. But I've already heard what came first to your mind."

Thirty-One

THE TIME RACED BY during the next days, with thoughts of the silver stolen from us and Draper's move to take our lease snapping at me like mongrels. As much as I wanted to lash out and make them stop, there was little I could do to be free of them.

I made a few tries at mending the mooring rope I'd cut with my insulting words to Maggie. I hoped I could splice it together again, but she had little to say and less time to listen. One day as I made to explain again, she cut me off like the head from a fish. "Remember how you refused to think of the future with me? Well, the future will be here in just a few days and you're too late now." Her look was cold. "Look to yourself, Nicholas, like you've always done. I've made some plans without you, because I was always afraid this day would come." She turned away and I got nothing more.

It was still a week before we hoped to remove some jewelry from a box on the second floor of the house of a fine British gentleman while most of Customs and their wives and various other toads dined downstairs. Our crew had all met together, and I'd met with each one alone, going over what we'd planned and anything that might go wrong. Mouse was angry because he wouldn't be a part—there was no role for him and an extra man might only draw notice. I kept walking the streets near the house and so did Gillam. Julius spoke with Eve as often as possible and acted as any cook might in helping with a large meal—looking to the kitchen and the house, planning the pots and servers that were needed and making sure that all the supplies would be at hand at the right time.

But on the Monday night before, I stood alone and stone cold in a doorway outside the Hare and Hound on Back Street for a different purpose. It was a rough tavern which served anyone willing to enter, soldiers and Americans, a step up from the Raven where we'd found Dirty Ann, but not much. Gillam came for the card games where several pounds might change hands at a single round with as many as four British officers around the table, as well as Henry Richman, a Tory businessman who loaned money up and down the docks.

I waited in the shadows at one end of the block and kept telling myself that Lt. Pearson deserved to be robbed. I'd never worked at robbing on the street, I thought it too dangerous, and I generally didn't want to throw down someone I didn't know. Even if a man looked the dandy and walked like his purse was too heavy, I knew I could be wrong. His purse might be empty, or we might tangle up like I'd done in Jamaica and he might end up dead over a few coins.

But I knew Pearson and I thought over and over of the mark on Lilly's face when I saw her at the Common and his own smug look when he'd insulted me at the dance. He was the worst type of officer, like some I'd had in the Navy, and if I took his purse, it would be more justice than if he kept it. His coins wouldn't weigh me down, but it would be a start and give me enough to separate me from the scavengers and the gutter.

It was almost midnight when he came through the front door followed by another officer. Gillam followed and called out to Pearson, our signal that he would be a good target. "Lt. Pearson, my hat comes off to you as a fine officer of the British Army. You've taken most of the money from the table, even some of my own."

"You gave a little, but you took theirs as well," Pearson laughed, adjusting his coat and sword for the walk ahead. "They'll need to win some back to keep from selling their boots." He walked off, proud of himself. As I watched him, my heart turned hard and I could feel the anger fill my chest.

I knew that he would likely take Middle Street down to Union where he stayed, down a block past two alleys. I cut down Cross St. and through an alley to Union where I could wait for him. I'd hoped he'd be careless enough to walk close to the buildings so I could take him quickly from behind, but he walked farther toward the middle and the gutter. I came out just behind him and he turned quickly, hearing my steps. I was never as silent as Julius.

"Who's that? Show yourself."

I came straight on him and he drew out his sword, but it was no match for my oak cudgel, a perfect fit in both hands. He took a two-handed swing and cut a notch from it but his sword glanced off. I caught him on his shoulder and he dropped the sword and my next swing took his legs away when I connected with the side of his knee. I forced him down on his stomach, my knee in the center of his scarlet coat and the other on the frozen dirt, my stick hard on his neck. I took the purse from his belt and couldn't help myself from taking his sword as well.

I nearly spit out some words at him, wanting him to know who it was that held him down now and took his prizes. I would have done it without thought some years before, crowing in a moment of triumph. But now I heard Julius' voice warn me off, though he wasn't within a mile, reminding me that I gained nothing by naming myself. I knew what I'd done, and I had the bounty in hand, and that should be satisfaction enough. It had happened too fast and it was too dark for him to know me.

I stepped in the middle of his back to keep him there before I ran down Union Street to the next alley. Just as I was turning, I heard a watchman call out from down the street. "Stop, who's there?"

I kept going, careful to keep my hat low and face turned, with the sword down beside one leg, "It's naught, just another drunken redcoat, taking up the street," I offered.

I SLEPT with the purse and the sword in my bed that night and gave Gillam four pounds the next afternoon from the ten I'd counted out. He took them and tucked them in the purse at his belt before asking, "And you took his sword as well?"

I nodded.

"I thought you were after coin. If you're caught with the sword, you'll be shot on the Common like the deserters." He shook his head a bit. "And Pearson would cut you into little bits if he could. A proud cock like him, taking his sword is like cutting off his shaft."

I shrugged, but knew the words were true. "He cut a chip from my staff but he dropped it soon enough. It was there, so I took it." When I had no more to say, Gillam turned away and went downstairs to size up a table of tars for a card game.

It was only a few minutes later that I left the Sword by the back door. I carried the sword in my left hand so that the hilt was below my waist and the point high, near my armpit. I held a pinch of my cloak with my thumb and fingers so it would stay fully covered.

I went directly to the Green Dragon, since walking about with the sword in hand invited trouble with any soldier or Tory I might see, and I was careful to keep my cloak tight around me. When I entered the front door, I just waited, without going to a table, until the serving girl came to me. "I'd like to speak to Mr. Burns."

"Can I tell him who is calling?"

"Nicholas Gray."

"Why don't you sit, Mr. Gray, and I'll bring him along. Take off your cloak and I can bring you a cup if you'd like."

"No, I'll wait here till he comes." One table of drinkers sat with their cups and dice on the table and eyed me suspiciously as I stood with my cloak wrapped tight, but I didn't give them a thought.

Burns eyes were lively when he came towards me, but they were wary as well, not sure if we might have a friendly debate or angry charges, but his words were hopeful. "Have you come to help us, Nicholas Gray, seeing the service we've done? Or do you miss hearing my lovely voice near your fire?"

"Do you have a room where we can talk?"

"You don't have to worry about your words here, Gray, you could shout them at the top of your lungs, but no one would hear."

It seemed nothing came easy between us now. "Do you have a room?"

I followed him back past the fireplace down a hall where he opened a door on a room which held a table, a few chairs, and little else. As soon as the door was closed, I took out the sword and laid it on the table.

His eyes went wide at first, but quickly held a small smile. "Where did you come upon this?"

I shrugged a shoulder. "I found it. It doesn't matter where." I waited a moment before going on. "I thought you might know someone who'd like it."

"I might," he nodded, enjoying the thought.

"Some rich Whig who'd keep it at his home and show it around at dinners? Or you could make Molineux an officer. He could wave it about his head when he leads the crowd. Or even Hancock. I'm told he loves a fancy uniform."

"You owe us now, Gray, since we helped with Partridge. Would this be a payment?"

"You could see it that way, but it's worth more than I owe."

Burns turned sly then, a trader's look crossed his face and he shook his head.

"It would be worth ten pounds if it was straight money that was paid," I suggested. Burns rolled his eyes about, like he'd seen a circus clown. "If Hancock fancied it for himself, it would only be what collects in his corners like dust. It's a prize you won't find anywhere else."

Burns picked up the sword then and inspected it closely, first hefting it, then bringing it close to look at the ornamental scrolls engraved on the guard which protected his knuckles. "And think of the notice you'll gain once the Sons know it came from your hand." Burns tested the edge with his thumb. "I'll take five pounds and call our other debts even."

Burns laid the sword down again. "We'll have to see, Nicholas Gray. I'll let you know what it brings."

I breathed easier as I left the Dragon and headed back to the Sword. I might have been smart enough to keep from spouting my name to Pearson as he lay beneath me, but taking his sword was rash. They hung people for stealing pins, and they'd love to pay back the insult to a British officer with a snug collar and dancing feet. I'd have to keep my mind straighter in the next few days or I wouldn't live to see another year.

On Saturday evening, Gillam and I watched the Steuarts' back door in the dark from near the carriage house while the guests came in the front door. We'd come from the back side, down Rawson's Lane and across the open yards. The snow was hard and crusty and less than a foot deep and much of it had been trampled down by the children from a house on the lane and the dogs that ran forever back and forth. We managed to stay mostly in the footprints and the few tracks we made wouldn't be seen as a direct line to where we stood.

A few guests walked, but most came in carriages to the front and were helped down by a Negro driver—some slaves, some free—so they might walk with dignity down the path that had been scraped away to the front door. Sounds traveled quickly through the frozen air, and we could hear the horses and the drivers talking to them as if they were standing next to us. We even got a few snatches of the guests exclaiming as they were greeted at the front, so happy to be there, so honored to come. Although we couldn't see, we knew the women would have their wigs built high and swirled about and their best jewelry shining.

After we'd stood nearly an hour, Gillam said, "It shouldn't be long now," anxious to get on the way.

I spoke quietly without turning to him. "Julius said they're serving three courses. If we wait till the second, their tongues will be loose and they'll sound like a dog pen, yipping and barking away." We stood silent in the dark, huddled in the cold. "We need to wait like we planned. Julius will give the signal at the right time."

We began to hear voices from the inside and gradually they got louder. I could imagine the wine being poured from pitchers by the slaves and serving girls. Finally we saw Julius come to the back door and open it a crack. We went quickly and opened it further. Julius had his back to us, watching the front kitchen door to see if anyone came. Just as I took my first step up the stairs, I heard him walk toward the fireplace, speaking out in a loud voice, "It's not time to clear the plates, it's too soon, let them enjoy the last of their lamb. Pour more wine and we'll prepare the ham to serve and let the pudding cool."

We made our way up the stairs around the one turn in the middle as silently as we could. I'm not as light at Gillam or Julius, but this time I got up without a squeak or stumble, even though my heart felt like a hammer in my chest. The hall ran toward the front and we each stopped to light a small candle from the wall lamp burning low before we opened the first door on the right.

It was fixed as an office with a desk against the wall and a chair in the corner. The fireplace toward the center was cold and the room was completely dark. I motioned for Gillam to go to the next room, the Steuarts' bedroom according to Eve, where we expected Gillam to find the jewelry in a lock box.

There was a bit of moonlight from the window and with the candle shielded, I could just make out the room as Eve had described it. She had no more information on the small book she'd described, so I would have to search, hoping that her intuition was right and it remained somewhere in the office. If not, I would have to leave it, since we could only stay a short time.

There was no obvious cashbox or coffer which might hold coins or other valuables, and I checked in the corners and looked at the floor boards and found nothing. The papers on the desk were arranged neatly and I lifted them up carefully in a stack so I could use the candle on the floor to look. The first stack was nothing but letters received and the other held new ones ready to post.

The voices were loud from downstairs but the desk drawers hadn't been waxed recently and squeaked as I pulled them out. The last one stuck as I pushed it back in and let loose unexpectedly and closed with a bang. I froze and thought I heard the voices below stop as well, but the babble took up again right away and I took a moment to breathe and get my heart out of my throat.

That left the ledger books—three shelves of them, near four feet each, about twenty of the narrow books on each shelf. Our plan, the same one we used as often as we could, was to leave everything as we'd found it. There were many times a store or the mistress of a house didn't discover anything amiss for several days, even a week or more. If nothing was out of place, there were few who would notice what they'd lost till they had need of it again. It was rare for a person to check on their goods for no reason and when they realized what was missing, they wouldn't know when it had disappeared.

But I'd never have time to pull out each book gently and then replace it. I tried to imagine what Steuart might have decided. I pulled out the last in the bottom row, the one where Eve had found it first, but it held nothing but figures from some household in Jamaica. I chose the first one on the top shelf, and again found just figures, this time from more recent dates and what seemed to be expenses in Boston. I chose the last one on the top shelf, and opened it quickly to see if a smaller book was hidden inside. I chose the first and last on the middle shelf and the first on the bottom shelf. Still nothing.

I found myself getting anxious now, trying to imagine, where it might be. Would Steuart put it in a random place on the shelf, so he'd have to keep a note to remind him of which one? I started on the top row now, and found myself beginning to rush, pulling the books out quickly and shaking them out, then replacing them quickly. When I started on the second row, I pulled at the second book and two came out beside it, thumping on the floor. My fingers shook as I reached back and replaced them, straining to hear steps on the stairs or a shout below. I stayed there a moment when they were back in their places, my chest heaving and my breath ragged.

I just stared at the books, trying to find what was hidden. We didn't know what was in the book, but it was my aim coming in, and I didn't want to leave empty-handed. I was just about to reach for the next-to-last book in the middle row, taking my time, thinking I was drawn to it for some reason, when I felt a hand on my shoulder.

Luckily, my voice caught in my throat or I might have shouted out and jumped up quickly. Gillam stood behind me, motioning with his head towards the hall. It was time to go, and I trusted Gillam to know. As he turned, I went back to the next-to-last book and when I opened it, I felt the small book slide out in my hand from behind its back cover. I held it to my forehead for a moment, as if it was a cool stone that might quiet my racing thoughts, then tucked it down the back of my breeches and turned to follow Gillam.

We came down as silently as we went up and paused at the bottom, just out of sight and listened. When Julius looked back, I caught his eye and he nodded. He caused a bit of a commotion towards the front, something about stacking dishes, and we sneaked out the back.

Thirty-Two

WE DIDN'T RUN on our way back to the Sword, but we walked quickly, and I could barely catch my breath when we came through the back door. Maggie had been tending the bar and Lily serving the tables and I just caught Maggie's eye before Gillam and I went straight up to my room. We hadn't spoken a word on the way back; we were each too busy checking behind us and everywhere ahead and to the side.

Gillam began. "You first, Nicholas. Any coins in the office?"

"No, but that's not what we expected. I found the record book, but I don't know if there's any profit in it."

"I hoped you found something with all the noise you made there. They must have thought all that thumping was a gentleman's boot heel while his lady had her hand under the table."

I just shrugged. I could see from his face he was well-pleased with our night. "Show it off, Gillam. What did you get?"

He smiled and began to pull jewelry from secret pockets inside his coat. When he was done, the blanket on my bed glittered with silver and a bit of gold.

"They must have made a pretty penny in Jamaica or wherever they were. Of course, they'll have to start over now."

I looked at a gold ring, plain enough but heavy and thick. "Did you take it all?"

"There was some laid out in a box on the dressing table, but I found another box in a chest. It had its own lock but it only took a moment to open." His dark eyes were glittering now as well, almost as much as the jewelry, and his sharp face was eager. "I took everything from the box, and locked it again, but I left what was laid out. They probably won't notice what's missing for a while."

I admired him then. There aren't many who can look on expensive baubles and leave them behind to protect against a quick cry to the constable. It was one reason he was still free to roam about and why I trusted what he did, at least in night jobs. "How much do you think?"

"It depends on who is buying and where, but I'd say we'll gain upwards of a hundred pounds."

I looked at what he had spread out. We'd lifted just some of what they had, and we could only sell at a reduced price, but it was a sum most would never see in a lifetime. "I think you should go now, right away, like we planned." He looked at me for a moment to be sure. On other jobs, we'd keep it a bit before deciding. "We have nowhere to keep it now and when they find out it's gone, the Tories will have everyone but the Governor searching after it. The uppers aren't used to being robbed from their own houses."

He thought a minute. "It's true, the Sheriff has an eye for you."

"The sooner it's gone, the less we have to worry. How soon can you get to New York?"

He made each piece disappear in his coat. "I can be out by dawn, as long as the driver hasn't changed plans." It was all stowed now and no one would know he carried jewels and a set of picklocks. "But what if the price I'm offered is too low, Nicholas? You know that the coin isn't always there at the right time. Should I wait, or sell low?"

I thought for a minute. "Get the best you can, Gillam, but come back before the first of March. We'll need the coin to make arrangements when the lease is up and after that, you might have a hard time finding us all. You might even travel to Philadelphia if you think you have the time and you could get a better price. We'll be here waiting." I felt a small wave of fear when I realized I had no hold on him once he left the tavern with our treasure. I fixed him with a cold eye. "I know you'll be back."

After he left, I looked at the smooth, plain leather cover of the book I held, but I decided I'd wait till the next morning to study it. My heart had been charging so hard through the evening that now I could barely keep my eyes open. I slept sound that night, like a rock on the shore, almost like I'd rolled with Maggie and she'd taken all my thoughts inside her.

I WOKE with the dawn the next morning, the sun coming a bit earlier now, but I didn't go right down as was my custom. One part of me wanted only to stay near the back door with an eye to the front, wondering if somehow we'd been found out. But I was drawn to the book. It was the reason I had taken all the risk the night before, but I had no idea if it would pay. I went near to the window in back which looked out on the alley and sat on my sea chest to read it.

When I'd finished, I rose and laid it gently back on top of the chest, and took a deep breath. I felt the book was like a keg of gunpowder, and if I didn't place it just right, I'd go up in a blast. There were Tories who would break my bones to take the powder keg and make it harmless by throwing it in the ocean. The Sons would fight for it as well, except in their hands it would get a spark so they could see the lovely explosion. And neither would be particular if I happened to be sitting on top.

The book was smaller than normal ledgers and wasn't an official Customs record. Someone had begun to keep track of the secret business done by Customs starting around 1760. The first entries had to do with Benjamin Barons. He had been a favorite of the smugglers until he was run out when Parliament decided to get a real return on the trade in the colonies. Someone, maybe an earlier cashier, began to keep a record of the money he took by allowing ships in with no entry in the records or that declared only part of their value.

That list showed that the seeds that had grown into the fortunes of Hancock and Rowe and some other great merchants had come from ships full of molasses and European goods that were never entered in the royal books and paid no duty. That part of the record was interesting, but not really valuable since years had passed and the laws and the people had changed. Customs was no longer in the hands of a friendly man who helped the Americans avoid paying duty to the king while collecting a full chest for himself. Barons was long removed and the new commissioners were spitting in Boston's eye.

But the next section would make many of the Boston captains and merchants drool like a mastiff, as well as the Sons of Liberty and the Loyal Nine. At first I didn't know what the names and notations were, but once I saw Ebenezer Richardson's name, it was clear. It was a list of informers who sold information to Customs. Each notation included a last name, the date, and the amount paid out. Just before the troops came, Capt. Malcolm and a band of armed sailors had stood outside the Customs office and demanded to know these very names, and others had done the same before. Malcom's crowd had brought long swords, stout sticks, and heavy stones, but the commissioners had refused to give up the names. They endured threats in the street, angry crowds, and tar and feathers for their lower men to protect those who worked in the dark. It was just this secret list that I now held in my hand.

If the Sons got the informers' names, there would be a string of attacks more serious than any before. The dock crowd would howl with glee and all of the Whigs in Boston, from the black-robed ministers to the mildest bakers covered in flour, would applaud the punishments handed out to those who had brought Customs down on "honest" businessmen. The merchants and Customs were as close to a war as you could get without firing muskets, and if the informers were known,

Customs would lose any advantage they had and need to start over. I wondered at the power of the words on paper, just a few scratches with a quill, but these names carried the weight of an oak cudgel and the heat of boiling tar.

But the next section of the ledger went even further. I felt a small tremble of fear when I realized the book in my hand could turn Parliament on its ear and bring Customs to its knees. It was a record kept over many years, and I guessed that it was sold from one lower officer to the next, as a way to insure their kind treatment during their stay and after their return to England. Steuart must have purchased it and began keeping new records himself. The pages listed Tory merchant ships which had arrived and paid small duties, but paid extra beneath the table as well. Each was listed with a date and the amount paid for what were once called "indulgences." Most of the amounts weren't great, no more than fifty pounds, but there were pages filled with them, nearly a hundred in just one year before the duties and nonimport cut down the trade.

It added up to a tidy sum, and I was sure a large part made its way back to Paxton and the others. The book showed the high and mighty commissioners, the rulers of all the ports in America, with dirty hands. They stood with one palm out for Tory bribes while the other worked to strangle the Whigs and patriots, seizing entire ships and cargos for auction.

If Samuel Adams caught wind, he would get the news published in every American paper, have the colonies' agents in London bring the record before Parliament, and demand every Customs man be roasted over a slow fire. He was happy to "work the machine" by printing lies in the *Journal* and conjure demons and Catholics in speeches. But a bit of truth like this would set a fire in every colony. Everyone on both sides of the ocean suspected that the duties led to bribes and small fortunes, but no one had proof.

The Tories in London and Boston would never stop hearing about the sins of Customs and there would be little they could say in defense. Adams always painted the American cause as pure and righteous and the English government as corrupt and dissolute. The record in the ledger book would provide never-ending grist for the mill.

The one problem was that the book didn't mention any commissioners' names directly. If their names weren't written out, no one could prove that the money collected was other than just a bribe to some of the lower end like the searchers, inspectors, or even the solicitor. Any in the upper levels would deny they knew anything about the silver flowing from the secret payments. But if the book got to Parliament, it would embarrass the whole lot. The titles and pensions which waited for the commissioners when they returned, often worth hundreds of pounds a year, might vanish like the puddles on the docks when a hard wind blew.

Steuart had been right—the book was like gold itself—but only if I could keep it in my hands and find the right people to pay for it.

Thirty-Three

I CAME DOWN that morning to find Julius and Maggie sitting in silence with their bread and cheese. They both looked at me hard as I passed by, while Jezebel acted asleep beside Maggie on the bench, but none of us said a word. It was as if we were afraid any talk of last night would bring a constable storming through the door.

I sat with them in silence for a bit and Maggie decided she'd like some tea and came back to set the pot on the table. It was finally too quiet and I needed some words. "A quiet day so far," I mused.

"So far," said Maggie, "and we'll pray it stays that way." Julius just nodded and Maggie got up suddenly then and went back to the kitchen.

We spent that day and evening in much the same way, acting as if it was a day that none would notice or remember. But we were actually keeping a sharp eye on the door, and our ears were like a dog's which turns at every sound.

When we locked up that night, I somehow felt a great relief. Our visit to the Steuarts hadn't drawn any notice right away. I sat at a table with a cup of rum and caught Maggie before she went up the stairs. "One day done, and none the wiser," I said holding up my cup, hoping it might raise her spirits.

She looked at me but there was no smile to relieve her worried look. "I know you have hopes, Nicholas, and maybe you'll get some cash in hand before long. But it does little for me. We'll be out before you know it."

"Do you think they'll go through with it?"

"What else is there to think? They've gone to the trouble of writing up papers, and Draper seemed sure of himself. What's to change their mind?"

"I might be able to, Maggie, if the cards fall just right."

She shook her head, then, sad at my thin hope. "I've heard men say that before, Nicholas, but the cards they get are the ones that lose. It's not Gillam that's dealing them." She moved toward the stair, but stopped at the bottom. "If you have anything more than pretty dreams to keep us here, I'll listen, maybe even help out. But if you don't . . ."

"I'm working at it, Maggie, with all I've got. I just think it better not to spread the story around." Most would have thought that her look was blank before she went up the stairs, but it was one I knew as disappointment.

It was two days later when I sent Mouse to fetch Burns. Mouse had taken to sitting in the corner by himself ever since we'd finished our trip to the Steuarts. He'd had no part, though I'm sure he was somewhere near that night, but he couldn't tell us or share a story. He'd hesitated when I first asked him to go, as if he might be too busy, but I eventually got him to the front door. "And you can tell him there's a bit more to discuss than he thinks." He brightened a little then, always proud to speak up, even if it frayed at his nerves.

I clapped him on the back as I opened the door for him, just in time to see a commotion outside. There was Sheriff Greenleaf, who had always seemed keen on taking me in, and two redcoats backed against the front of the cooperage next door and a crowd of ten around them.

"I order you to go about your business," he shouted and waved his arms. "We're on lawful duty for the town."

The crowd jeered and kept close around them. Samuel Gray, from the ropewalk, another one with last name I'd chosen, stood at the front of a few others who had nothing better to do than roam about with a staff, hoping to bump into a redcoat. "You might be, Sheriff, but what of the two with you?" jeered Gray. "There's nothing lawful about them." The crowd hooted behind him.

"They've come because I asked them."

"Are you that afraid now Sheriff? You can't walk the streets alone?"

Greenleaf said nothing. He knew he had done too much to help the Tories and the troops to be left alone.

Gray continued to taunt them. "You don't think they're stout enough for us, do you, Sheriff? We'd break them in half."

One of the soldiers shoved his bayonet forward then, advancing a step towards Gray.

"Is that all it is, lobster? Come ahead if you dare." Gray hefted his stick with both hands. Greenleaf moved ahead and put a hand on the musket to turn it down. "You're lucky the Sheriff has more sense than you, lobster, or I'd break your head."

The soldier spit back at him. "We'll meet up soon enough and then we'll see whose blood runs."

"Come find me anytime. Ask on the street, or come to the ropewalk if you'd like to pay a visit." He twirled his club slowly at his side. "My name's Samuel Gray. Why don't you introduce yourself so I can invite you to a party?"

I could see the cords in the soldier's neck bulge and color. "I'm Kilroy and you'll be sorry you ever learned it."

Gray laughed at him, then turned to the others. "Let's walk a little further. I'm sure the Sheriff wouldn't want to see the end of this." They called out as they left, using colorful oaths usually only heard in the darkest corners or on a ship miles from shore.

When they'd gone down around the corner to Ship Street, Greenleaf turned and advanced toward me. "I have questions for you, Gray. Let's go inside."

"I won't have those two inside," I cautioned. Kilroy and the other one gripped their muskets a little tighter.

"You can stand watch out here," said Greenleaf, "I'm not afraid of him alone."

I raised my eyebrows to show he might be mistaken but I opened the door and we went inside. Greenleaf didn't waste time. "I'm looking for someone who's stolen jewelry, Gray. It might be you or someone you know." I made no sign to answer him. "There's a reward offered." I just shrugged my shoulders. "Should I tell you more?"

"It's no matter to me one way or the other. I haven't stolen anything and I don't know anyone who has. Your reward holds no interest for me."

"You might change if you need the money, so I'll tell you anyway. Someone stole a large amount of jewelry from the private room of Mrs. Steuart, the cashier's wife. They've hounded all the servants and haven't found it yet."

"When was this?"

"Sometime in the last two weeks. It was in a locked box and they didn't check it often."

I shrugged again. "There's no help here, Greenleaf, and I wager you'll find none in this end of town. It's best if you take your two dogs back where they've come from."

Greenleaf narrowed his eyes and clipped his words short. "You'll slip one day, Gray, and when you do, I'll step on your neck." Jezebel stood on the table next to the door, her fur raised at the back, and watched him go.

It was just a few minutes later that Burns came in, followed by Mouse. Burns began talking as soon as one foot hit the floor inside. "I was surprised to see Greenleaf walking down your street with his two redcoats, especially when Samuel Gray and some others waited just around a corner. I can't imagine what the Sheriff would want with any of the other shops on this street, can you Nicholas? Did you see him?"

I shrugged. "I saw him, but I imagine he goes where he wants. That's still his right isn't it, even if he does lick Tory boots?" The last person I wanted hearing a rumor about jewelry was Burns. "Have you had time to show what I left you?"

"A little, but I've been busy writing the *Journal* and watching the merchants' ships and their imports." I was amazed he could speak with such a straight face after the row we'd had over Draper and how he was allowed to bring in banned imports.

"We saw some of your work a while back at Rogers' store, with the shit on the door and the boys with rocks. Too bad they didn't have muskets so they could shoot out the windows instead of heaving stones." He just stared a minute before I went on. "I thought the nonimport ended at the new year."

"We've talked this out before, Gray, we can't give up now, they're still holding on to the tax on tea. You know they'll go back to squeezing us dry the next time it suits their fancy."

I felt a tight smile cross my face. "Which 'us' are you talking about—the merchants or the Mohawks in the street?"

Burns smiled easily then. "You know we're all in it together–we're one and the same." He stopped now, good-natured, like we'd shared a fine joke. "Always the magpie, aren't you Gray?"

I just shook my head and turned away. "I think we should do business now, and leave the speeches for later. What price did you get?"

He took a small bag of coins from the pocket of his worn coat and placed it on the table. "As much as you asked for–five pounds. The Nine have decided to keep it for their own. I'm sure they'll find just the right time to use it." I nodded at him and put the bag on the bench beside me.

"Is there more?" He asked and glanced at Mouse sitting at the far table now. "Your messenger spoke strongly about a matter for my interest."

I waited a moment and looked about, arranging my words and realizing there was no way to keep the discussion from Mouse, even if I sent him away. "What would you pay for some records which would shame Customs?"

He took a moment too, realizing we'd begun a grave subject. "It would depend on what they were, what they said, who they named. If they were as important as the letters of Bernard's we printed . . ." he waited a moment and gestured in the air, "if they made it certain to all that Customs are the criminals *we* know they are . . ." His eyes were hot now, and his delicate hand dropped to the table and drummed a beat. "Do you have them now? I could tell you more certain if I saw them."

"No," I lied, "but if I knew a price I might plan a next step. I'm told they might name informers, too."

Burns eyes went wide then, thinking he might lay hands on information that would set the docks on fire. "They'd be worth a lot, Gray, probably fifty pounds or more."

"I would think more than that, with all the risks involved."

Burns grew angry at that, and his words came quick. "You'd hold out for more money, Gray? That's a ransom for a dockwalker like you, enough to see you through a year or more. And that information is as dear to the cause as any." He looked at me but I didn't respond. "Sure, we point to the taxes and the imports, but we've been fighting Customs here ever since there's been a port. Turning them over would give us more liberty than anything else we could do, short of sending the troops away." His fingers beat the table again, more quickly now. "It would be a chance for you to do some good, show your true spirit."

He spoke well, strongly and with passion, but it was figures I saw, not ideas like "doing good" and "true spirit." Without money, I'd soon be casting about again and no help to anyone, the Sons or myself or Maggie. "I need a price to go ahead, Peter Burns. If I could get enough to cut the legs from Paxton and some of the others, I'd bargain for two hundred pounds." Burns eyes showed white with shock and he started to speak out again, but I put up a hand to stop him. "I'll wait two days to hear." I got up quickly then and walked back toward the kitchen, leaving him there with his words unspoken.

Thirty-Four

I WAITED three full days and part of another, before I gave up hope. With each hour, my thoughts twisted tighter, trying to find a way that gave me what I needed—a pile of coins big enough to protect me and the ones around me without sending their opinion of me, and me of myself, too far down the river.

I wanted to sell the book to Burns and let the Americans use it to shame the high Customs men because I hated the Tories like I hated the lords in London. It would be the easiest road as well—I could remain friends with Burns and his crowd and let the greedy gulls in Customs and their informers fall at their own hands. But without getting a good price, the Sons would be raising toasts by the fire with the book while I shivered outside in the cold.

On the other side, I told myself that if I sold to the Tories, I'd be no worse than Hancock or many of the others. Up till now, the liberty cause, dressed up as opposition to the Stamps and the Townshend duties, had brought the upper merchants bags of silver as well as making some of them heroes in the streets. If they didn't gain the gold, I imagined they might tip the other way. But I needed a good purse even more than they did.

I wondered if it was only those who had little to lose that would give all to the cause. You could number Adams and Burns among them, and certainly Mackintosh and the rest of the street crowd. They had no position to lose and they were right to expect the British government to deliver a blow to the head before a pat on the back. But there were others I didn't know, some who had a modest place but seemed willing to lose it, like Revere and the Loyal Nine and some of the Sons.

My sleep had been fitful and my best hopes had brought me nothing by Friday morning. I steeled myself and set off to see Pettingill, the Customs Solicitor. I'd decided he was close enough to the Commissioners that he could see their problem, but not feel the blood roaring up like Steuart, who had lost the book itself. Pettingill would be hard pressed to convince me he knew nothing of the payments or wouldn't suffer some if they became public.

He lived in a fine brick house on Long Lane, not far from Fort Hill. A comely maid, no more than sixteen, opened the back door and scowled at first. "What's your business here?" she tried.

"I'm here to see Mr. Pettingill." I smiled at her, sure to show I was a friend. "I know he'd pay to hear what I have to say." In the end, she smiled back.

Pettingill must have had unlikely visitors before, probably informers who'd stood on the same step asking admittance, because I didn't have to wait long. I was brought into the front parlor where he sat near a pigeon-hole desk set up for writing. The lace at his cuffs was fresh white and his face was heavy and red, with jowls like a bulldog. He removed the glasses perched on his nose and looked me over carefully. I could see the distaste in his eyes, even though he made a modest effort at keeping it from his face. "I don't know you, but I assume you have information for me." I moved towards him and handed him a scrap of paper.

He looked at it quickly, then up at me. "What is this supposed to mean?"

I felt surprisingly calm. "I'm sure you recognize the information. It's the name of one of the commissioners' favorite informers as well as a ship recently docked which didn't pay its full duties."

He narrowed his eyes. "Where did you get this?"

I stared back and I could feel a little heat building inside. "That's just the beginning. I have records which show all the informers and all that's been paid to let ships avoid duties."

"Let me see it," he demanded in a lord's voice, sure of obedience and ready to punish any who resisted.

I gave him a slight smile and shook my head. "It wouldn't be smart to carry it about town and let you get your hands on it before it's time. You might not pay what I'm asking."

He clasped his hands too tightly across his belly. He wanted to get up and stand over me, shout in my face till I cowered, but when he looked me over, he thought better of it. "So that's it—you want me to pay for it?"

"Just like others have been paying you." When he didn't respond, I continued. "But I don't expect you to pay all of it. You can take up a collection since the others will get a great benefit as well."

"Where did you get these records? And how do I know they are what you say?"

"It makes no difference where I got them, only that you need to buy them back. I'll send you a bit more information from them by note so you'll know their worth. But you'd use your time better getting the money together. When you pay me four hundred pounds, I'll give you the full record."

He sputtered then, something almost like a laugh. "You're mad. There's nothing you've got that could be worth that much."

"That's the price. Think of what you and your friends might lose if the information got back to London and Parliament. If Parliament refused just one pension, it would cost four hundred pounds in a year or two. And imagine your good name dragged in the mud. Paxton and Hallowell would probably think saving their honor is worth double the price." I started to turn. "I'll send you more tomorrow and then you can give word where I should come for the money." He was quiet now, filled with hate for me, but with nothing he could do to discharge it. "I know you'll come to the right choice," I added. "You've got until Monday to pay me or I'll sell it to Samuel Adams instead."

THE NEXT DAY, Saturday, I sent Mouse back with a note. I'd copied two more informers' names and added the dates and amounts paid by three more Tory ships. At the bottom, I added, "I have the full record for 3 years." I didn't know if I did, but I had enough.

I didn't venture outside the Sword except for a walk with Julius. I guessed that Pettingill didn't know who I was, but I didn't want to give anyone a free chance to grab me unawares. They might follow Mouse back after he carried the note, but he was good enough to either lose them along the way or send them sideways with a story about a stranger in the street who paid him to carry it. Even if they found he came from the Sword, they would still need to storm in the door, a risk when they didn't know what lay behind it, and surely noticed by some who would swear to their crime.

I'd instructed Mouse to wait for an answer and he told me that he had waited outside for more than two hours before he was given a note in return. It was short: "The back room of the Crown after dark Monday."

The hours crawled by until it came time. I tried to act as calm as if I had no cares in the world, just another bar keeper whose only purpose in life was to fill a cup and listen to every complaint, about wives and bawds, cold weather and slave's work for pennies, wrong numbers on the dice and salt in the stew. The only blessing was that Burns didn't show his face, so I was spared from explaining that he was too late.

When dusk finally came on Monday, I tucked the book securely inside my coat and met Julius downstairs. Mouse would follow at a distance and watch and listen while we made our way there and back. It wasn't too far–past the Town Dock and Custom House to School St.–but carrying what I was, it seemed a day's walk.

A huge grenadier without his coat, as tall as me but twice as wide, met us at the door and eyed us every way before showing us into the back hall at the Royal Crown. There was another who looked just the same seated near the fire in the back room, but he had no cup before him and his eyes didn't leave us. Hardy sat at the only table in the room. He'd gotten no further up in the Customs office since we'd dumped him in the ocean near Draper's ship, but he knew his way around now. Two others I didn't know stood behind him, their arms crossed, looking like they were anxious to start a scuffle. I knew that if Julius wasn't behind me, I'd be taken like a child.

Hardy and I looked each other over for a minute before I began. "Do you have the money?"

"I've got it. It's a bond."

I started to protest, but he shook his head. "You could hardly carry the pounds you're asking. Did you bring a wagon?"

I didn't want to admit I hadn't thought of it. "I'm ready to make arrangements."

"If you'd handled this much before, you'd know it's done this way. It's a bond guaranteed to pay whoever holds it from the Customs treasury. That way your name isn't written and once it's paid, it will be burned without a trace."

He laid down the bond and I saw the signatures on the bottom and the official seal at the top. But I didn't like the figure. "This is for only three hundred pounds."

"You're right, Gray. I'm glad to see you can read numbers."

"Four hundred was the price. I'll sell it to the Sons if it isn't."

"Don't be foolish, Gray. It's all that could be collected in a few days and it's a good price at that. You wouldn't get near that from Adams' Mohawks."

He was right. I didn't like to be bargained down, but I was near to picking up three hundred pounds, and I wasn't about to leave it behind. I took a minute before I gave a grudging nod and started to pick up the bond. But he laid his hand down on top of it.

"Now it's your turn."

I laid the ledger book on the table and he picked it up and looked at different pages.

"How do we know you haven't made a copy?"

"You don't, but I'll swear I haven't. There's more there than a clerk could copy in a day." It was true I hadn't made a copy, but I'd studied the informers enough to remember most of their names and many of the Tory merchants who'd avoided duties.

"It's done then. Take it and leave." But he couldn't resist a final word. "But you're known now, Gray, you and your Negro, there's no more hiding. You'll be as popular as Sam the Publican with the lawful government. And make no mistake—they'll put his head in a noose first chance. You won't be far behind."

I walked past Julius and out and then watched behind me to see him leave and shut the door. The bond seemed to burn in the pocket of my coat and I switched it quickly into the band at the back of my breeches. I stood with my back to the building and looked carefully down the street both ways before we started off.

We didn't say anything and I couldn't help but hurry, wanting to get back to the Sword as soon as I could where we could protect the bond better. But I might have hurried a little less and watched a bit closer.

We'd gotten past the Town House and were just on to Ann Street when I heard Mouse call out from across the gutter. I knew it was his voice and looked toward him though there was little light in the street.

"To your right," he called out, his voice strong and loud.

I turned just in time to see Grendel and two others come from the corner of an alley. One had a sword out at the ready.

I just got out my knife and took a slash at Grendel but he was watching for it this time and I only caught a bit of the skin on his forearm through a cloak he'd wrapped around it. He came down with a short stick on top of my shoulder and all the feeling went out of my left arm. I tried to breathe and move but he caught my shirt below my throat and lifted me up and threw me on the ground on my back.

He sat on me then, crushing the breath out of me, and what little I had left he stopped with his hand around my throat. I threw my head back and forth and just caught a glimpse of Julius dancing warily with the swordsmen while the other lay on the ground. My eyes started to go black and I thought I could feel Grendel's hot breath on my face, his mouth open and panting, as his hand searched in my coat pockets for the bond.

Just as I was ready to pass into a dream, I faintly heard voices and his hand eased a bit, though his weight didn't shift enough to get a full breath.

"Stop, stop, or you'll feel the point." His hand eased even more and I could just open my eyes. "Release his throat and you, put the sword at rest."

I could see their red coats now and the bayonet and musket aimed at Grendel's chest.

"What's this we have? Some of the Liberty boys brawling among themselves?" I could just make out a lieutenant and at least three others, two with muskets. "How do you have the time when you've got every soldier to fight with as well?"

One of the redcoats offered, "I've seen this one about, sir, the giant one with his nose mashed in. There's some of ours that would like to pay him back a knock or two."

"They've tried to rob us," offered Julius.

The officer laughed. "Rob you of what, your hat? If you're carrying anything more valuable, I'll kneel to the Pope." He looked at all of us for moment before going on. "You could kill each other for all I care, but some say we're here to keep the peace. You, put your sword away and you, you ugly beast, get up off him."

Grendel hesitated until the bayonet came a little closer. "I swear I'll run it in you, and your arm will never be the same," warned the soldier.

I rolled to the side as soon as he lifted off me and gagged in as much breath as I could take.

"Off now, to whatever hole you live in." I'd just got to my knees when the soldier caught me on the side of the head with the butt of his musket. "You're the lucky one today," the officer said looking down at me, "but don't think you'll be as lucky next time."

Thirty-Five

I KEPT THE BOND TIGHT to my chest all night and tucked it in my breeches again when I went downstairs. Julius had started the fires early as usual and was already stirring in the kitchen, checking the shelves and cold room to see what remained, just as if nothing had happened the night before. Lilly was cleaning up when Maggie came down.

"Good morning, Maggie." Before she got to the kitchen, I said. "I'd be pleased if you'd sit with me a moment."

She looked as if she hadn't slept well the night before and the skin was dark beneath her eyes. "I've got more than I can do to keep up things today and prepare for leaving next week," said Maggie, "I don't have time for a tea party."

I motioned her to the table. "Please, Maggie, it's important enough."

She sat down and stared hard, as if she was angry with me, though she didn't have immediate reason. "Get on with it then." But before I could begin she looked a bit closer. "What's the mark on your head? Have you been in a scuffle again?"

I stretched my hands flat on the table and took a deep breath. "I may not look well, but I'm happy enough." I swallowed hard before I went on. "I think I can buy the Sword."

She stared for a minute then shook her head. "It's no time for jokes, Nicholas."

"It's not a joke. I've got three hundred pounds."

She squinted her eyes a bit and waited, trying to see if I was true. Her eyes opened wider when she decided I was. "You're serious, aren't you? Where did it come from?" Jezebel had leaped on the bench with her and now sat in her lap while Maggie scratched her ears.

"It came from the job at Steuart's house, but not directly." She cocked here head a bit in question. "There was a record book there that turned out to be valuable. They took a collection at Customs to get it back."

"Three hundred pounds?" When I nodded, she went on. "I don't know what it could say that was worth that much."

"It would have put a black mark on them all, here and in London. Three hundred pounds is what Paxton or another commissioner might take from seizing just one ship, and they make twice that in salary. Then there's a pension to look forward to as well." I shook my head when I thought of it myself. "It's more than we can think of Maggie, but it's just another sum to them." Jezebel jumped up on the table then and I put out my hand out to her. "Not that they gave it willingly," I went on, "they even sent Grendel to try to get it back." I told her the story of the soldiers rescuing me from beneath him.

"You have it safely away?"

I patted my stomach. "It hasn't been out of my sight."

She stopped then and looked away at the sunrise picture over the hearth. "And you want to buy the Sword?"

"I think I could, Maggie, with this and a talk with Tobin."

"Why?"

I looked at her then, puzzled. "Why? What kind of question is that? Because we could stay here, Maggie, it's where we've lived." I shrugged a bit, since it seemed obvious to me.

"Not us, Nicholas. I've lived here and run the tavern and so have you, but we haven't always done it together." Again, I puzzled at her answer.

Finally I shrugged again, not sure what she wanted. "You've wandered all over town, Nicholas, and made your bed with Lilly for a time."

I could feel the blood starting to rise up a bit now. "What about Twelfth Night? Why do you think I gave you the scrimshaw?"

"It's beautiful, a fine present, Nicholas, but it's just a bauble that can be bought—or stolen." Her voice got quieter then. "It's not your heart." She waited, but no words would come. "With three hundred pounds, you might find a better room than the one you have here."

Now my words came easily, like they always did when I had some anger behind them. "What are you saying now, Maggie? If you don't want me, just say so. I'll find another place and you can take what you've saved and look to start over on your own. You've done it before, like you were happy to tell me."

"I'm not saying I don't want you, Nicholas. I just want to know what you're thinking."

"What more do you need to know? I've said I could buy the Sword and I would, if you wanted me to."

"But only then?"

I was stopped for a moment. "Yes, I think so. I never considered it, but I don't fancy owning it myself." I squirmed on the bench a little and leaned back, uncomfortable with the thought.

"Here's what I want to know: What do you see for you and me?"

Her look was so piercing then, her blue eyes so keen that I had to look away a moment. When I looked back at her, she still stared at me, but her eyes were softer then and I thought I saw hope in them. My voice came out a bit softer as well. "I thought we could keep on as we are, as long as we wanted to. You said you wanted to sleep knowing they couldn't take away what you had. Here's the chance." This time her eyes glistened with tears, the first I'd ever seen. "And I like it here—as well as any place I've been." Her eyes kept searching mine, like she there was more she'd find if she could only see into the dark places. "I want to be here—with you—and nowhere else."

She reached across then and took my hand from Jezebel's back. "Nicholas, I love you. And I think you love me, though you don't know how to say it, and you certainly don't show it sometimes." I wanted to draw my hand away from her but she held it tight in both of hers. "But we've come this far and I don't want to go back." She gave my hands a squeeze. "I don't want to go back to being alone."

My heart lifted up then, like a bird from a bush, and my tongue got too thick to speak. After a long time, I finally said, "I'll see to it then."

IT WAS ANOTHER MARKET DAY as I headed off towards Tobias Brown's office where Tobin worked. I was intent on getting there directly, with the bond in my breeches. But the shouting near Lillie's store drew me like a fly into a spider web. It was greater than just a crowd of ten or so, and I could hear the anger from a street away. When I turned a corner, there was Ebenezer Richardson flying past at a dead run with a pistol in his hand and a crowd running after him not more than ten paces back. I had to step back to let them all pass and then followed near the tail.

"What's on?" I asked a dark brawler who lagged behind.

"He tried to take down the effigy. He's a dirty dog of an informer and this time he'll pay."

Some of the boys in the crowd now stopped to throw rocks. Richardson had escaped across the gutter in the middle of the street and into his house, and you could hear him throw down a heavy bar across it. The boys came close then, and broke out the windows downstairs and some of the country men began to pound on the door, shouting out to kill him. Richardson opened a window upstairs and leaned out shouting and waving the pistol. The boys kept up with their stones, thumping against the boards of the house, then turned their mark to Richardson, right up until he aimed and fired.

I was lucky to be at the edge, because he hit in the middle of the pack. Three went down and one didn't get back up. He was a slip of a boy, skinny and ragged, a thin coat soaking up his blood and the rest leaking out his chest onto the ground around him. Some knelt down to help him, but there was little they could do. Six or eight men howled curses at Richardson, and finally one led the others to the door and attacked the house, battering at the door with their feet and shoulders and sticks, but it was a boy who finally got in through a window and opened the bar. They rushed upstairs and seized Richardson and dragged him down, apparently too slow to fire again or realizing that one shot wouldn't stop all eight. I think they might have beaten him to death in front of his own door if Molineux hadn't appeared to take him by the collar and swear no one would harm him before they found the sheriff.

I'd seen enough blood spilled, but the boy lying in the mud and snow in the street was enough to make me grind my teeth. I wanted to turn back to the Sword or find Burns and make him look at the end of his work. But in the end, my errand meant more to me than the boy's blood.

I was angry when I arrived, though I couldn't say at who, and I had to take a moment to remember my purpose before going in. The office of Tobias Brown was near enough to the British Coffee House on King St. that he could probably smell the coffee beans when they were ground up on a summer's day, a smell that could conquer the salt from the docks and the garbage at the street corners. There were some who took the dark brew instead of tea and claimed it medicinal for all ailments.

Brown's business was money, but you might not know it from stepping in his office door. It was an open room in the front with long, smooth pine slabs laid out on each side of a central walk with stools beneath so they could be used for copying documents. There was only one young boy at it when I came in, hunched so close down that he seemed to be writing with his nose rather than a quill. He didn't even look up at the bell which rang with the door when I came in.

But Tobin did, seated at a large desk in the corner with papers in stacks all around him. His eyes went wide when he saw me for the first time in almost four years and the memories were enough to send him scrambling to his feet. My blows in the back alley and my stay in debtor's prison came back to us in an instant, since I'm sure we had both spent time brooding on them.

Sometimes I had regretted that blow in the alley and my scornful words, since they had brought me an extra measure of trouble. But now I depended on a bit of fear remaining in Tobin's mind so I could get what I wanted.

He started to sputter some words, but I got near his desk in two strides and put a hand on him to keep him seated. "We've got some business and we might as well do it here." I left my hand heavy on his shoulder. "But you should send your boy away. He might hear a tale that would shock him."

Tobin looked again at me, and I could see the fear. When I lifted my hand, he stood up, found some papers on his desk and walked them over to the boy with a few words and came back once he'd left. Tobin was even rounder now than the last time I saw him so that he waddled more than walked, and his face was more red and pinched than before.

He'd recovered a bit from his first shock and his words were stronger now. "I'm sure we have no business, but you might as well say what's on your mind."

"Is Mr. Brown in? I might need to see him myself if things don't go well with us."

Tobin looked toward the back, but shook his head rapidly, clear that it wasn't something he wanted. "No, he won't be in before dinner. He takes it at the Coffee House and then only comes by on occasion."

"You bragged before how you could do as you pleased with the lease for the Sword, so I'm sure you can do the same with a sale."

"I need his signature, but he signs as I see fit." Tobin puffed up a little then with his power. "But there's no sale for your building, just a change in the lease. Mr. Draper has offered us a small sum for the change and a higher rent at that." He motioned with his palm up. "It's a bargain anyone would make."

"I'm glad to know you're such a sharp trader, Mr. Tobin, because I have an offer that will make everyone happy." I waited a moment before going on. "Especially you, since you won't have to see me again once it's done."

Tobin sputtered a little, and began to shake his head. "There can't be a change, we've promised Mr. Draper . . ."

"Here's what it is: I will buy the building from Mr. Brown for three hundred pounds outright and you can help Mr. Draper find another tavern to lease."

Tobin laughed out loud, but stopped when he saw the look in my eye. "It would be a fair price, but you don't have that much specie and there's no one who would sign behind you. And besides, I couldn't disappoint Mr. Draper." He shook his head a bit and his eyes lit now that I'd shown how foolish I really was.

I pulled the bond from beneath my shirt, and smoothed it a bit as I unfolded it and laid it on his desk. He reached a hand out but I kept mine on top as he leaned forward to inspect it. He took his time, running his fingertips over the heavy paper and the seal to be sure it was a true document. His eyes were wide again when he looked up. "It appears real enough, but I couldn't . . ."

"Yes, Mr. Tobin, you could, and you will. It's a good enough price to explain to anyone, but there's an extra reward that you don't have to mention. I'll return the note you signed admitting your interest in Widow Magowan, and the buttons from your waistcoat, too. I've got them here, and Mr. Brown and your wife and the minister will be never be the wiser." I watched his eyes as he began to calculate. "No one will hear how much extra you've collected for the tavern licenses, either." This time, I laid my hand on his shoulder again, even heavier than before. "But best of all, you can walk about without worrying that I might come out of the dark some day, wanting to settle a score."

Thirty-Six

I WAS ON MY WAY BACK to the Sword before dark, a legal deed in my coat pocket that I didn't have to hide. All the signatures were in order and the transfer recorded with the town register. Soon, I'd be liable for taxes and ready to complain like all the others.

Tobin had seen it my way in the end and drew up the transfer as we sat. He took it across to Mr. Brown at the Coffee House for him to sign, and though I don't know the story he gave, it took no more than a few minutes. I followed a few paces behind Tobin as we went to the Custom House, and waited in sight of the front door for him to come out. I had no desire to be seen anywhere near the bond, though there must have been several in Customs who already knew my name and what had happened. I kept my distance from the two lobsters standing at either side of the entrance and waited for Tobin to return. Later, we found the register before a pint after dinner at the Hunter's Hart rather than his law office. He accepted the paper Tobin had prepared and looked only at the signatures without a glance toward me.

I served out the drinks that night without a word to anyone, not quite sure of the truth. I'd never owned anything before beyond what fit in a seaman's chest or could be hidden in a secret corner, and I didn't know what it meant. I slept in fits that night and when I opened my eyes, I felt something amiss, like I'd forgotten to hide a pile of swag or I'd bet everything on a card game and lost. But soon enough I realized it was my name on the deed for the Sword which made me skittish.

The sun was well up by the time I made my way downstairs and found Julius and Maggie sitting at the table near the fire, their eyes fixed on me the whole way. I walked across the room like I was still asleep and laid the deed on the table before them. Maggie looked at it first then passed it across to Julius who saw the look on Maggie's face and saw the stamp in the corner before the smallest of smiles lifted his lips at the corners. He couldn't read, but he knew what lay on the table.

Maggie jumped up then and threw her arms around my neck, but I stood still and stiff, and looked over her shoulder as Jezebel stretched by the fire. Maggie stepped back then and took my shoulders in her hands. "You've done it, Nicholas Gray, you're lord of the house. They're your bricks now, and your boards."

"But won't they come for us now, try something to take it back?" I asked with some fear.

Maggie laughed at that. "They might. Like you said long ago, they can steal anything with the law and a judge, but you've got a legal deed in hand. They say there's little better in an English court, or an American one either."

My eyes cleared a little after that and I saw Julius again with a smile in his eyes, but none on his face, as he spoke. "I don't doubt we'll still have to fight, Nicholas, but now we'll stand on solid ground."

I could feel the strain come out of my shoulders then and my hands and fingers stretch out from where they curled into fists. I looked around me at the bricks in the fireplace, the wide boards with their beads along the edges which took every kick and bump along the walls, the battered bar with the portcullis pulled down from its hook on the ceiling, the tables and benches that were stained dark from the smoke and the drinks and stews that had been spilled there, the pine floor which only buckled in a few places. They were mine now, whether I liked it or not, solid pieces that might offer some safety, but would demand attention as well.

It was a new world I stood in.

GRADUALLY, the idea of being an owner was finding a place in my mind, though it wasn't news I gave out to anyone we served in the tavern. I was still a deserter with a false name, and a suspect in the death of a Royal Navy officer, but there were only a handful who knew that and less that could prove it. Those worries were more distant now and it seemed they might become like the land of Jamaica for me—a long distance away with only bits to remember.

I stood in the kitchen with Julius one morning after breakfast while he chopped onions from the cold room for a stew, their smell filling the air. "I have a question for you, Julius, if you have time to answer."

He turned and nodded to me. "You're always a man with questions," he said with a slight smile.

"How is it with Eve?" His look held another question so I went on. "At the Steuarts, I mean. Is she held in suspicion?"

He shook his head. "She says they can't put a finger on anyone, although they questioned all the servants, asking about the Steuart's chamber and the jewelry. They don't know when the goods were lifted, so the help at the dinner party didn't get special attention. And no one has mentioned the book out loud, since it seems Mr. Steuart didn't want anyone to know it existed." He looked at me gravely then. "If Customs knows it was you who ended with the book, why haven't they looked at you for the jewelry, too?"

"They sent Greenleaf one day, but there's nothing here to find, and the silver won't turn up in town. They have nowhere to step. I don't think Stuart or Pettingill mentioned the book to anyone other than the Customs men who would lose their standing from it. If there was anything more than the jewelry, the Sheriff and everyone else could only guess at it." I shrugged a bit, and held up crossed fingers. "Unless there's a typhoon hiding somewhere, I think we'll have clear sailing."

He nodded and turned back to the stew, giving it a swirl with his long-handled spoon.

"But that wasn't the only question I had." He continued at the stew but he nodded enough to tell me to go on. "I went ahead with the bond and the deed without thinking, there was the lease ending . . ." Again he nodded. "But it all came from the job we did together. The gain might be part yours and Gillam's, as much as mine."

He turned then and gave a smile, but it wasn't all warmth. "I've thought that, and you know if Gillam were here, he'd mind all the numbers." He replaced the spoon where it hung on a swinging iron mounted on the face of the bricks and moved to the block at the other side where he gathered the dry onion skins that covered it. I realized his size then and his strength as he moved in front of me, easy to forget when he became regular as the furniture. "But I've thought it out and it seems best as it is—that is, as long as Eve gets a piece like we said and Gillam comes back with a fair price."

I nodded, and waited for him to continue. "None of us could have made the book into money. Gillam wouldn't know who to bargain with or how to begin, and if I tried . . . they wouldn't have thought twice about wrapping me in chains and making me a runaway." He stopped a moment, the thought a sober one. "So it was only valuable if you took it to manage. And you were lucky to keep the bond from Grendel as it was." He paused a moment as more thoughts came. "I don't think any of us, not even you, could have walked in the door of the Custom House and come away with the treasure. They wouldn't let it happen. You had to go through Tobin."

He dropped the pile of onion skins in the basket, and bent to pick up one that strayed. "In the end, it's probably best as it is . . . I wouldn't want to own the Sword or even part of it. And Gillam wouldn't either, no matter what he'll say."

Our talk had arrived at the spot I had hoped. "I can promise you'll always have a place here if you need, as long as I have it, not just working, but a place where you're welcome, you can stay as long as you choose . . ."

"A home? Where you couldn't turn me away?" He gave a small smile then, and turned back to the fire. "I can't trade it for silver, but it's not cheap, either."

A FEW DAYS LATER Marcus Draper came through the front door on a quiet afternoon, and I started to smile until I saw that Grendel followed him in.

I stood up then, my heart beating hard, and I looked to the fireplace to see if the loggerhead was in reach. But they both kept near the door and didn't move forward.

"I just wanted to see what I'd been cheated out of," began Draper, his eyes quick around the room. His suit looked near to new, and a brocade waistcoat showed dark red against the white of his shirt and the deep blue of his coat and breeches. His shoe buckles flashed silver and he wore a large gold ring on his right hand. Behind him, Grendel stood fearsome and broad as an oak tree, all browns and grays, and I could hear each breath as he drew it through his gaping mouth.

I felt Julius come from the kitchen and I assumed he stood in the door as Grendel stared there without a flicker. But as I gazed at Draper, I realized I had little to worry about. I had a legal deed and Draper had no claim. When I looked at Grendel, he showed little interest and it seemed he came because Draper paid him and no other reason. "I could offer you a cup of rum, though you might find the price I charge too high. That's a fine thing about being an owner—I can charge what I like and turn away any trash I choose."

I could see Draper's eyes blaze up, but I saw no reason to stop. "And for someone so keen on bargains, I'm surprised you brought this bull with you. You must have paid a pretty price. Did you outbid the Sons of Liberty today? Or was it some Tory merchant? Maybe someone from Customs?" I looked at Grendel straight then, and said, "But his price must be dropping. From what I've heard, he's let some fish slip through his fingers.

I was surprised when Grendel didn't flame up at what I said, but instead showed a small smile and nodded his head just an inch, though it was nothing that Draper could see. Draper spoke back with scorn. "It could only be luck that let you have it at all, you and the Widow. You'll probably keep it as poor as it is now and let the same rabble drink for pennies. I'm better off without it." He turned so quickly he nearly ran into Grendel, but threw his words back over his shoulder like a grenade waiting to explode, "You're up now, Gray, you and the dregs around you, but you'll come down soon and I'll laugh watching it. I might even see to it myself."

I had nothing to say after he left and Julius kept his face like a stone.

As THE DAYS WENT ON, there was noise everywhere in Boston. They'd had the funeral for the boy Richardson had killed, more than a thousand marching down King St., and other than his poor mother, not more than a handful had known him. But they came to show their anger at Customs and a known informer who dared to walk the streets. In the meetings and newspapers, there was no word spared to condemn the Tories, the troops, or Hutchinson. The Sword was full with the crowd who were unable to walk ten yards without the help of a stout stick or the balance of a sword. It seemed that there were blows struck every day and the soldiers and the fighters passed threats back and forth like a plate of sweets—here's one for you, and I know you'll give one back as well. The fighters were bold now that they'd seen the redcoats for so long and there were only two regiments left.

But Maggie was still dancing lightly on the floorboards since no one would come to claim them from beneath her feet and her face lit when she proposed that we celebrate. I finally agreed and we planned to stay closed on a Sunday so we could eat and drink and laugh together. We would have a party and act as if we didn't have a care in the world.

Thirty-Seven

GILLAM HADN'T RETURNED by March 1, the day we'd set when he left, and hadn't appeared the next day either. I'd begun to worry a week before, fighting with the dark thoughts of betrayal and imagining all the other missteps that might have happened. He was a man known by a few to carry swag for sale to New York and he'd have to travel some very dark streets to make the bargain and return with the bounty. At the same time, I knew his thirst for a wager, and how he'd be sure he could double what he had, as long as he could handle the cards. He might have met a game as tilted as his own, or faced some angry players who knew that he was cheating.

It was a Friday in the afternoon, usually quiet enough, but the door burst open and Samuel Gray came in, followed by four others. They regularly looked as rough as any you could find, with their thick hands, matted hair, and worn work clothes stained with tar, but they looked even worse today. Gray had a welt down the side of his neck, a fresh one, angry red, with a small cut at the end, and his eyes looked nearly the same color. He appeared ready to swing at anyone who ventured a word.

I went to the bar and helped Maggie fill cups of rum once, then again as they drank them off like small beer. The second time, Gray held up his cup and made a toast I couldn't help but hear. "To dead lobsters," he said, "there'll be plenty tomorrow." They all joined in, loud enough, but fierce rather than gay.

I resisted for a bit, but finally walked to the table next to them and sat. "So you're after them again?'

Gray looked at me, his eyes filled with rage. "They're going to pay this time. We've got enough to see their blood run and we'll use their muskets for kindling." He drank off the end of his cup and motioned for Maggie to bring more to the table.

"Tell him what happened today, Samuel," said one at the table. I noticed he had some dried blood on his right hand.

Though I didn't ask, Gray started in. "One came by the ropewalk this morning. We were working away, walking the strands back and forth and twisting them just so, when a bloody back comes by. He stares in from the open side and Green here asks if he wants a job." They all laughed behind him now and Gray warmed up some. "'Sure,' he says, 'I do.' So Green says, 'Good, I've just the job for you. Go clean my shithouse.' That didn't sit well with him and he walked in to argue the insult, and before he was done, he struck a blow or two, but Ferriter beat him down and got a blade from him at the same time."

His voice dropped down a bit as he continued. "We were happy enough about it but he came back after noon with six or eight more. They brought their sticks and swords and even so, we gave them a fight." His hand went up to the welt on his neck. "But we had to give way finally, fighting with just our bare hands and some of the walk's wouldering sticks we use to twist the rope." He drank a swallow before he went on darkly. "We should have laid our clubs at the posts, so we'd be ready, but they've never come right in before." His eyes narrowed now and his next words held all the malice he could breed. "The bastard Kilroy was there, he'd come ready with a sword and club, but all he could do was make a nick here before I rattled his brains."

I got up from my seat, tired of the story. "Well, you're all here and ready for more. Seems like the same as last week."

But Gray caught at my arm as I was ready to pass and I had all I could do not to strike by instinct. "No, you're wrong, Nicholas Gray. We've had enough at their hands. It's time we run them out. If we all stood together, town and country, they wouldn't have a chance, we've got five or ten for every uniform, they'd have to turn tail and run." I removed his hand from my arm, but he went on anyway. "Now's the time, you'll see. It's more than just us at a table in the Sword. You can watch with the women and children if you don't have the guts to fight."

I wanted to spill him from his chair, but there was no good in it. I went off into the kitchen until it quieted out front and I knew they'd traveled on.

That evening, Burns came in and sat by himself at a table. I hadn't seen him in near two weeks, since I'd made an offer of information on Customs. I didn't relish seeing him at all, unsure of how the wind blew with the Sons and what he might know or suspect. But I decided it best to take the bung from the barrel and see what poured out.

He appeared pleased with himself as I sat across from him and brought him a cup of rum. He immediately held up his cup for a toast.

"What's your interest, Burns? Did the Governor stub his toe?"

His eyes sparkled. "It's a toast to you, Gray. Who would have thought that through hard work and perseverance, you could save enough to buy your own tavern?" I looked a bit sour at him before he went on. "Now, you'll have to make some honest money so you can pay the taxes." I didn't answer him and wasn't interested in announcing that I'd bought the Sword, at least not now. "I won't ask how you did it, but word is that it had something to do with Customs." He took a drink and set his cup down before him and his look turned hard. "I hope it wasn't the information we spoke of." I just stared back. "If it was, you'd be little better than an informer."

His voice was too loud for my comfort and his words could never be a joke in a tavern like ours, even if there was just one table filled. "I might tell you a few things sometime Burns, and you and the Sons might even gain something when the time is right, but I won't sit here to have you worry at my legs, like some hound at a deer." I grabbed my cup and got up to leave.

"Wait, wait, Nicholas, I'm just asking a question, making a joke. Sit down here and I won't speak of it anymore. We'll talk of something simple, maybe politics or the weather, enjoy a cup together." He motioned for me to sit across from him again and I did, though I took my time doing it.

He was still bubbling over like a forgotten stew pot. "I think we should make a wager. I say the bloody backs will be gone within the month." When I didn't respond right away, he leaned towards me and spoke a little more softly. "It's getting close, you know."

"What's that, Burns, another funeral? After you and your friends made that skinny German boy a saint at his, I thought you might want to wait awhile for another." I looked away a moment. "I watched him die on the ground."

"The funeral was what he deserved, Gray. He was shot down, innocent, by a man everyone knows is below a dog. There are brave men and boys everywhere, ready to fight for our freedom."

"That's a pretty picture, Burns, but all I saw was a boy throwing rocks."

Burns' glare grew fierce now. "We have to get them out, Gray, one way or another. They can keep their army in Britain and let us live as we choose." His words were short now as he spoke, like he had no time to linger on one or the other. "Ask Samuel Gray or the others on the street. They can barely move about without a soldier threatening."

He was right, but I knew the soldiers might say the same thing of the Liberty crowd. "I agree with you, they shouldn't be here, but what's the end of it? If they hadn't come or left on their own, would you let well enough alone?" When he didn't answer, I went on. "I don't think so. I don't think you'll stop as long as Parliament makes our laws and takes our money."

Burns had calmed now and looked confident. "We'll have some satisfaction, Gray. Soon. Very soon."

ON THE NEXT DAY, Saturday, there were letters passed from hand to hand in the Sword and all the taverns and a few hung on trees and posts. They looked real enough and were signed by soldiers of the 29th and the 14th, but if they were true, the signers were more ready for Bedlam than for war. The soldiers announced that they had a plan to strike the people of Boston like an army should, instead of scuffling like a dog with no teeth. A few shots and some dead bodies in the street would prove that Boston couldn't stand the smell of gunpowder. Now was their time to strike, they were ready to drop the rogues who had bullied them so long. It would be a bloody day soon, and they looked forward to it.

The letters said what many of the rough crowd believed already. After months of seeing redcoats with muskets at every turn, clogging the road off the Neck, standing at sentry boxes, drilling on the Common, shooting and flogging deserters, parading through the streets, and brawling with any brave enough to stand up, it was easy to think an attack would come. The soldiers wouldn't be restrained any more, and the Irish toughs of the 29th would be more than willing to shoot down anyone who caused a problem, whether it was one of the Sons of Liberty or not. Samuel Gray and his crowd from the ropewalk probably believed the letters with all their heart, but I thought it more likely that Adams and Burns and the Loyal Nine had labored to write them so the fear and anger would come to a boil.

The crowd in our door that day was restless, everyone talking of the fight at Gray's ropewalk on Friday and another that day where the giant mulatto they called Johnson cracked the skull of a redcoat and broke his arm in the bargain. Some said it was in the South End near the Neck, others said at the ropewalk, and a few thought closer to us, near the Custom House.

But no matter where it was, they knew there were more blows to be struck and they were ready, vowing revenge for every slight they'd suffered. The more they talked, the louder they got. There were some who were brave enough, and the constant talk made the others think they were, too. I was glad to get them out that night and know that we'd only have ourselves at the tables the next day.

MAGGIE had gone with Julius on the last market day and before they'd left, she'd jingled the fancy purse she used to carry coins, to show me she'd taken extra from her cache behind the beam upstairs. It was made from a fine, smooth cotton and stitched with a design of a bright bird on a limb. I laughed a bit when I realized I had accepted it from Draper some years ago along with some other goods when he didn't have coins for two trays of garter buckles and gold points that he fancied.

Maggie and Julius each carried a full basket when they returned, and delicious smells filled the Sword from the time I awoke on Sunday. By the time Mouse arrived, the smell of the meat pies Julius had stuffed with pork, apples, onions, and sage filled the kitchen and the tavern room. Eve came to the front door about noon, very proper in her cap trimmed with ruffles. The bright kerchief round her shoulders and the blinding white apron down her front made the snow lingering between the trees and at the edges of the streets even more gray and bleak.

Lilly had cleaned in the morning but found a way to dress as fine as she could, her shoulders more square now and she'd found black for her eyebrows. She'd kept her earrings, since we had nothing to buy them with when she'd tried to sell them, and they glittered from her ears. She gave me a small nod as she helped to prepare the table, different than the blank look she'd given me since Maggie had taken her in. She seemed a person again, with a bit of spirit in her face, rather than a pale maid with little more life than her broom.

The punch Julius had made with rum and sugar and a cup of tea and some other secrets was so full with pieces of orange and lemon and lime that when we passed the bowl, they bumped our noses one after another. Finally Julius brought a cloth from the kitchen and we passed it behind the bowl, wiping our lips with a laugh each time.

When we'd finished two bowls of punch, the meat pies didn't last long, nor did the sweet pudding from the bag. We sat for a moment after, filled up, and remembering the tastes like we might from a holiday feast. We managed to save just enough food for the fiddler I'd seen at Hart's tavern. I'd offered him a large meal if he'd play for us and he came just before dusk. Julius left with Eve to walk back to the Steuart's but was back again just as the fiddler took up his bow.

Once he started, we were all quiet to listen. He began with soft music, and when I closed my eyes I was in a rowboat on a stream, the sun warm on my face and the trees in flower. Of course, the punch we'd been drinking and the rum that followed might have kept my face warm on its own.

We'd been drinking from the good rum barrel we kept for ourselves, and before I knew it, we came to the bottom. Since we mostly sipped a cup here and there, I hadn't thought to check how it stood. But I was sure I could get another and I headed off without a thought, pushing the small cart we kept at the back door. The fiddler was just warming up and I knew he could play tunes that would make a cripple get up and dance. I didn't want to listen with an empty cup and David Wesley's warehouse wasn't more than a few hundred yards away. He kept a supply of Barbadoes rum that didn't pay duty in the corner of his warehouse and I was sure I'd find him in his room next door, since he never seemed to go anywhere else.

The rum had made me jolly and I was humming a tune the fiddler had played when I turned the corner on to Ship St. and saw a figure standing in the walk, his back to me. "Hello," I called out and when he turned toward me there was something familiar about the way he moved his head, quick as a lizard, and I recognized the outline of the Spider's face just as I felt the blow land behind my ear.

Thirty-Eight

EVERYTHING WAS DARK for a while, and when I first awoke I had the sense I'd been bundled about, maybe even carried in my own cart. My head throbbed down the right side from the crown through my neck and shoulder, and if I wanted to put up a hand to touch what must have been a lump there, I couldn't. My wrists were held by shackles with a short chain between and they were fastened around a post which stretched floor to ceiling in the center of a small, dark room, my arms in a circle around it.

The floor was rough planks and as my eyes gradually adjusted to the light, I could see that I was held in a small cold room meant for vegetables and cheese and the like, except the shelves were bare. I guessed that the back and one side of it were the outside walls of the building and were probably stacked high with firewood. The other wall was probably the last length along a hallway that ran out a back door. I could see the door to the kitchen or front room before me, but I couldn't reach it because of the shackles and I assumed there was a strong latch from the outside.

It wasn't long after I awoke that I heard voices from the front and heavy feet on the floor just before the door opened. A soldier I guessed to be a grenadier because of his size stood in the doorway, big enough to block it himself. He advanced just two steps to stand in front of me where I knelt down. He used a key to unlock my left wrist but held the chain that connected them. I made a quick move to bull past him, but I was slow and cramped with my head still ringing and he jerked the chain down so it nearly broke my wrist. I was on the floor again and this time he dragged me forward into the front room like a bag of bones, and I couldn't help but shout out with the pain as the shackle chewed deep into my skin. He fastened the other shackle as I lay on the floor and then rested the butt of a musket in the middle of my back.

I finally looked up to see the Spider seated quietly in a corner, a tight smile on his face. He nodded to the man who stood over me and the gun butt moved so I could rise up enough to get on my knees. "Surprised?" he asked. "You must have been since you were so easy to take on the street." There was another redcoat standing in the opposite corner, and I saw his smile as he remembered taking me down.

There was nothing for me to say, and I just stared at him as I struggled to my feet and glanced around the room. It was a front parlor room, with the hearth along a wall and the kitchen behind it to share the chimney. But there was only a single table and two chairs. He took in my glance and continued on. "It's good enough for the men I hire, and there are only a few who know about it. The barracks is on the next corner if I ever need extra. You won't find me walking alone again."

I hadn't spoken since I'd been hit, and my voice came out ragged. "Why bother with me?"

His eyes darted about then and I could see his lips purse together before he spoke. "I owe you a turn, Graves, some from back in Jamaica, and I'm sure your hand was behind the tar barrel as well. There aren't many who know me here and even less who'd turn me over." His eyes were hot for a moment, and his lips pursed again before going on. "But that's only a part. There's too little profit in turning you in for a crime so long ago."

His eyes lit a little then and he leaned forward in his chair. "They've wanted Samuel Adams for years now, he's a devil in their eyes, and never gives them a moment's rest. They tried to prove he was a traitor once before, but the man telling the tales had lied too many times, and even the Tory judge wouldn't listen. Of course that was before the Army stood behind him." He leaned forward in his chair, excitement in his face. "I was still picking the feathers off in Newport when I realized that you're just the one to deliver him. I'm sure you've heard him speak treason in that little den of yours." He waited to see how I would react and when I shook my head just a bit, he went on. "You'll get some time to think on it. You know what you'd face if I brought you to Lt. Hanson in the harbor. He knew you on the *Dover* and I'm sure he would remember your disgraceful stay in the Navy. If you want to stay stubborn, I'll help them get just the right size for your necklace so it fits snug under your chin." He got up from his chair then and moved toward me, limping even more now than before. "I thought you'd like to hear the bargain."

"If there's any bargain, I won't take it from you. Your word isn't worth a brass penny," I managed, although my voice was still weak. If there was any hope of escape, the longer I stayed near the docks and out of a barracks or ship's hold, the better. And if I could make him angry, he might slip a bit without thinking.

But he gave a small smile instead. "You'll have all night to think of it and you can discuss the fine points with Major Griggs if you like." He motioned to the soldier behind me who grabbed me by the back of the collar. "As stupid as you are, Graves, I think you'll see your only way out."

I was spun around before I knew it and marched out and my wrists locked around the post again, the door shut, and I heard the bolt slide.

IT WAS COLD that night, not just because it was still March and closer to winter than spring, or because I could just manage to get my cloak from where it lay on the floor and get it around my shoulders by stretching and tipping this way and that. It was cold because I was scared.

It seemed the Spider had learned his lessons well. He was intent on either delivering me up to the one man who could put me in a noose for the lieutenant's death in Jamaica or letting me trade for my freedom by condemning Samuel Adams. I had no doubt that the Spider would make sure I was hanged if I refused to swear against Adams. He might even get a small reward, and the Army and Navy were eager to show their discipline against any who deserted or brought harm to an officer. I'm sure he would feel easier doing his own business after I swung in the breeze.

I thought back to the one time Adams had been reckless with his words, when I'd heard him at the table in the Sword calling for arms and an attack on the British troops when they landed more than a year ago. If I chose, I wouldn't have to lie about hearing him utter seditious words or how he encouraged treason. If I just repeated what he said, and they could get him back to London, he'd be the one who was certain to be hanged. He chose the words he wrote and spoke very carefully in public, and he'd only strayed when he thought he was among friends.

But what would be left for me if I did turn him over? I could never stay in Boston and probably not anywhere in the colonies. I'd have to return to the warren of streets in London where a person's history goes no further than a night or two before.

As cold as it was, I found myself sweating as I thought of all that might topple on me no matter which way I turned. I kept coming back to visions of Adams as he spoke, his hand trembling, his reddish coat faded and worn, but his eyes burning hot. He would face up to any of the Tories and he spent every hour working against them. It was only in church, they said, when he seemed to forget the soldiers for a moment while his voice led the choir, and he sometimes closed his eyes in delight.

I knew his ways—he had spoken and printed lies and near lies for years, anything to keep the people of Boston angry and the troops and government vexed, and made friends with Hancock and others so the

Sons could use their money and their standing. He'd stood behind the crowds and the tar barrels and encouraged the rocks for every Tory window. I imagined he would have danced a jig if they'd caught John Mein one day and beat him bloody and senseless or shot him on the spot.

But regardless of what he'd done or how he'd done it, it wasn't for his own gain. His purse was empty and it would probably remain that way for years to come. It was something different that carried him on, something he could see bright in front of him while the rest caught only a passing glance.

As I drifted in and out of sleep, the worst of my dreams came back, and I could barely breathe when I awoke. But that night, it wasn't a room at the Sword I saw when my head cleared, and the shackles on my wrists were real enough. Struggling against their iron only brought more blood.

The light came slowly through the cracks in the walls and I heard someone kindling the fire. It wasn't much later I heard voices in the parlor room and the door opened. The same grenadier came in with the key and he warned me before he used it. "I was gentle yesterday. Today, I'll break your arm."

I saw the Spider standing in a corner and a British major sitting in the chair by the table. His face was soft and clear from pox and his coat was bright, as if it had been brushed that morning. He looked like he spent little time outside, his skin near white, and I thought he must give most of his orders from beside the fire. But his eyes were hard, pinning me with as little interest as one might show for a bug. I stood in front of him, one grenadier behind and the other near the hearth.

"I'm told you might give us Sam Adams. Mr. Partridge here says you run a tavern?" I nodded. "And Adams frequents it?"

"He's been in on occasion, but it's not his favorite."

"He's not one to stay silent. You must have heard him spout treason like he does at every stop?"

"I've heard him speak, but I couldn't vouch for treason."

He squinted his eyes at me then, as if to make sure what he'd heard, then turned towards the Spider. "Why am I here if this scarecrow can't say what he's heard?"

I broke in then. "How could I ever admit to what you say? I'd be chopped down and dropped over the dock before I got near my door."

The major looked calculating then, sure to offer just what was needed. "Oh, you'd be taken care of. You'd sign a statement under guard and we'd get you off to a ship in the harbor before anyone knew. You'd get passage across and probably be loose on the docks in London well before Adams got there." He stopped to consider his words before continuing. "Of course, there would be some pay as well, once you stood up in court."

The Spider came out of the corner then and stood by the major's side. "That's a fine plan for you, Graves, especially when you think of where you'll be otherwise."

But the major waved him away. "I don't care what's gone before, I only need to know if you'll give us what the King wants—Adams' head on a plate."

I shook my head as if I was confused. "I need time to think. How do I know . . ."

The major got up abruptly then and stood right before me, shorter than me by several inches, but his face came close to mine. "I'll wait till noon. After that, Partridge can do as he pleases. There are too many troubles with the gangs to keep dancing with you." He turned quickly and went out the front door. I stared after him, trying to figure what street the house was located on. But the Spider stood before me. "You can't decide?" His laugh was one of scorn. "Major Griggs gave you a few more hours. Maybe you'll come to your senses."

Thirty-Nine

I SPENT THE NEXT HOURS looking for any possible way to escape. Since I could only spin around a few feet one way or the other, moving as if I was dancing with the post, I didn't get far. The boards which covered the outside walls between the supports weren't any stronger than most, but I was sure they had firewood stacked against them, and the other wall looked strong and secure. I couldn't reach any of the walls without getting at least one shackle off, and I'd made no headway there, either. The skin on my wrists was so bruised and swollen and cut that I couldn't work them anymore. I'd have to be like some wolf that gnawed off an entire foot to escape a trap, but I didn't think I had the stomach or the teeth for it.

I looked at the round post in front of my eyes in every way. It seemed newer than the other boards in the room, since its color was lighter. The bark had been removed roughly and it was no more than five inches through. I guessed it might have been added to support the roof on the small room when it sagged beneath the heavy winter snow. But it went right through the floor to the ground below and was attached at the top with a peg through the notch which fit the rafter, and in turn held the roof. I wondered if I might tear it out, but the roof was just higher than my hands and I could get no purchase to pull hard with the chain between my wrists.

I decided my only hope was to wait until they took a shackle off and brought me to the front room again where I might make some desperate move, maybe swing the free shackle around to strike someone and hope the confusion could get me out the front door. It wasn't a real plan, but it was the only one I had.

But it turned out to be no plan at all. When I heard the voices and movement in the front room and the door opened, Major Griggs advanced on me as I stood facing him, both hands still locked around the post. I could see Partridge behind him and the grenadier just to the side.

"What will it be, Mr. Graves? I'll have your answer now, and I warn you, if you don't speak as you promise, you'll never see daylight again." I trusted what he said, and I was certain I didn't want to get in the hands of the British regulars any too soon. I'd escaped in Jamaica, but now . . . I couldn't think of it without feeling a heavy stone in my stomach.

Yet I had decided I couldn't sell Adams. He had done nothing for me directly, but nothing against me either. I had given away Draper, who was an enemy, and sold the Customs book to the Tories to save myself and the Sword, but somehow, Adams was different. I knew that if I chose to repeat his words and managed to keep my life, it would hold no joy, eating me from the inside like the worms from rotten food.

I tried to stand straight as I spoke, though my shoulders and arms felt like they were made from lead. "No, Major, you'll have to buy someone else. I've never heard Samuel Adams speak a word which didn't honor the King and praise the royal government."

As dark as it was, I could see his eyes shoot arrows for a moment but he turned on his heel quickly and strode toward the front. "Don't waste my time any more, Partridge, when all you've got is a chicken instead of a hawk."

The Spider stood in the doorway for a moment, staring in disbelief. Finally he spoke with a small laugh. "Well, you've chosen what you wanted, Graves. My reward will be a tenth of what it might have been, but it will still be worth my time, especially to see you act proud now, and begging at the end." He stopped just short of slamming the door shut, but when he threw the bolt, it sounded like a musket shot.

I EXPECTED to get marched off at any moment, and as the day dragged on I wondered at the wait. There were several times I heard shouting from the street at the front, as if there was a crowd about, and other times I heard the clatter of muskets as regulars moved through the streets. I remembered Samuel Gray and his crowd, the letters handed around, and Burns with his low assurance that there would be satisfaction soon.

As day turned to evening, I tried to imagine what might be happening. For some reason, Partridge hadn't brought the two from out front and one or two more to drag me down to a longboat that would take me into the harbor and away from any help I might have. Then I heard noise on the other side of the door, boots scraping, the chairs moving and I stood as ready as I might be, facing the door, my mind screaming for a chance to fight. If I didn't get a good chance, I'd take a bad one, just to know I'd struggled.

But I heard a woman's voice from the front, then a laugh and another woman's voice and more laughter. I prayed that it might be someone to help, but it was hard to make out any words or hear one voice rather than another.

It wasn't long before the voices and giggles quieted some, followed by a heavy thump when a body hit the floor. There was a panic then, a female shout, the front door opening and quick steps across the room. I heard the bolt pulled and Julius stood in the door. I could see Maggie to the back, standing beside the soldier who lay face down, with Lilly to the other side.

Julius took in the shackles. "Where is the key?"

"Try the one on the floor, he's had it before."

Maggie knelt over his back now, checking for a string around his neck, in the pockets on his coat, and all around his waist where he might have kept a purse. He moaned and moved one arm slowly, but was still dead to the world around him. She turned and just shook her head, empty hands in the air. She'd found nothing.

"The Spider or the other one must have kept it. Where are they?" I tried to keep my voice down but there was too much pressure behind it.

"They left some time ago, up toward the barracks." Julius' eyes roved about now trying to figure a way to get me loose.

"Can you pull this down?" I shook the chain against the pole. "The top would be the only way."

Julius looked at the top closely for a moment before going into the other room and returning with the soldier's musket. "Get down as low as you can," he said, before taking a grip on the musket so the butt stood forward, his right hand grasping the barrel, his left near the trigger.

I crouched near the floor and I could hear his breath explode as he made a great arc to catch the top of the post with the butt. It didn't give way but the blow rattled the walls and the shelves and a wooden scoop which must have been left behind clattered to the floor.

He swung the butt again, then again, and the last time I heard wood break and splinter. He dropped the musket and grasped the top with both hands and pulled with all his strength, his hands near to circling the post and his eyes wide with effort. When the peg broke through the mortise, he pulled the post's top down and the bottom gave way as well, moving to one side so the top was free.

I stood and slipped the shackles and chain over the top. I started for the door, but Julius stopped me and draped my cloak over my shoulders and I held it closed with the tips of my fingers.

The noise we'd made must have been enough to raise the dead, and just as we neared the front door, it was flung open by the grenadier who had yanked me about before. When he saw Julius, he fumbled for his sword, but Julius was on top of him before he knew it. I saw Julius swing his forearm and catch the side of his face, and he fell in a tangle at his feet. "Go," Julius shouted, and I stepped around and over the fallen soldier through the door. Julius came a moment later, followed by Maggie and Lilly.

I recognized the street as Cornhill by the sign for The Sun tavern which hung a few buildings down across the street. I took a moment trying to decide which direction to go and Mouse rushed up from where he'd been across the street. "Take them," I shouted to Mouse and motioning with my head, "down the alley there, it meets with the square by the Town Dock." He hesitated a moment and I shouted at him again. "Go, they won't follow, you're not who they want." Maggie threw a worried glance over her shoulder as she went along with Mouse and Lilly, then she was gone in the dark.

I was ready to head down Cornhill, towards the Old Meeting House, away from Murray's Barracks where most of the 29th stayed. I took a few steps in that direction with Julius behind until I looked up the street to see the Spider limping towards us as fast as he could go, a pistol waving from one hand.

We had no choice but to go the opposite way and I feared running in the streets when we might meet a gang of soldiers at any turn, searching for a fight. I was slow as it was, my hands bound together and my cloak held close to conceal the shackles. And just as I feared, when we neared the area of the barracks down from Brattle Street, the street was filled with redcoats, holding swords and sticks high in the air. I could see three or four on the far side threatening two citizens who retreated in the other direction, one holding his head as if he'd taken a blow.

Julius and I stopped short and backed into a doorway. We considered going back to try to catch another cross street, but when I looked back, I could just make out Spider with his two hired soldiers behind him, though Spider was slow and the soldiers moved slowly as well, as if waking from a dream and unsure what had happened. We decided to try to get around a corner into an alley before the group in front saw us and hope that the Spider and his two couldn't catch up.

We got around the corner safe enough but in just a few yards faced a crowd advancing on us from the other direction, filling the dark, covered alley side-to-side. The soldiers had been making so much noise themselves that we hadn't heard this crew of Liberty fighters raging towards us, the sounds roaring in the narrow space and echoing off the walls and what served as a roof. There must have been thirty or more, all shouting at the top of their lungs and banging their sticks and fists on the walls of the buildings as they came, a fearsome noise as they came nearer, and there was no room to pass on the side. We backed to the buildings as flat as we could. It was Johnson at the front, the mulatto as tall as Julius and wider through the arms and shoulders, a huge club in one hand that he waved to us as he approached. "Come with us," he shouted, "we're out catching lobsters."

I looked to Julius and he nodded at the same thought I had. We let ourselves join the crowd as it swept up the narrow alley. It came out on Cornhill and turned towards where the soldiers were a moment before, but they were retreating now, back towards the barracks, and I glanced back at where the Spider and the others followed us. I just caught sight of them in the shadows at a corner.

The crowd was nearly running now, and shouting louder than ever, and when it reached the barracks where the last of the redcoats had disappeared, they went right to the door and hammered on it with their sticks, while others banged on the shutters at the side.

I thought Julius and I might slip off then, knowing that Spider and his hired soldiers wouldn't dare wade into this crowd to get at us and we might get a good start on a route they wouldn't know. But suddenly, the Meeting House bell began ringing down toward the Custom House, the signal for fire. And before long we heard another from nearer on Brattle

St. and another from toward the South End. Johnson stood at the front then and roared out, "Now's our time!" and led them at a near run back towards where we'd come. I wasn't ready to step out of their safety yet, hurrying and tripping along with my hands in front, and I managed to stay in the middle of the crowd with Julius at one side.

As we neared King St. and the Custom House, someone started up the shout, "Turn out, turn out, town born turn out" while banging on every door, and others shouted out "Fire!" since that was usually the reason for the bells. When we got to the open square in front of the Custom House, men seemed to be arriving from every direction, most shouting and waving sticks in the air. With the bells ringing, it was confusion all around, but soon the crowd began turning towards the front, near the Custom House. Julius and I had gotten far to the east, closest to the docks furthest from the soldiers, but there were still shouts all around us as people jumped and jostled to get towards the action at the front.

I felt Julius put his hand on my arm and his head cocked off to the side where we might proceed along the docks to the Sword, but my eyes were drawn back to the front of the crowd, and because of my height, I could see over most of them. The moon was only a quarter, but it reflected off the snow and the buildings to show the square packed with people on all sides.

The crowd in front of us was pressing forward, waving sticks and some swords in the air, and shouting at the top of their lungs. The noise was deafening, what with the shouting from all sides, bells ringing, and men at the edges rapping their sticks against the building fronts and walkways. Some looked like they'd been fighting already and couldn't wait to start again, while others kept joining from the edges, from all directions. They filled the square, at least two hundred crowded together.

I looked over and saw a man I thought was Burns on the north side in a new red cloak, a white wig, and three-cornered hat. The light wasn't good, but I could sense the fever in his actions, shouting with the rest, encouraging those just in front of him, challenging them to show what they were made of.

At the front, backed up against the Custom House steps and the sentry box were seven or eight redcoats. They had their muskets with bayonets out, the stocks at their waist with the bayonets tipped up to chest level, trying to keep the crowd back. Chunks of ice and stones and oyster shells sailed from the back of the crowd every few moments and some found their mark, catching a soldier on the shoulder or hands. Their Captain stood nearby, sword out but down, shouting for the people to stop, to move back, but his voice was swallowed up in the shouts all around.

Johnson was at the front, first waving his club above his head, then bringing it down to point it back at the soldiers as if it had a bayonet attached. Samuel Gray was there as well, and the others across the front jeered and spit at the soldiers, while those at the back shouted and pushed the front line forward, some climbing on a friend's back so they could see what was happening.

I wondered if the muskets were loaded with powder and ball, and what the Captain might do. So far, their muskets remained down, not at their shoulders, while the crowd shouted and taunted them.

"You'll never fire here. Put it down so we can have a real fight."

"If you fire, you'll swing for murder."

"Fire then, I dare you."

I heard Johnson in front roaring out, "I'll have a lobster for dinner." He swung his club enough to knock on a bayonet. Others along the front did the same and you could hear the rattle of sticks and bayonets, while others at the sides banged their sticks on the walls or posts.

A club flew from the back and caught one of the soldiers on the shoulder and he fell. The crowd howled and shouted and he scrambled back up with his musket at his shoulder. The crowd sang out:

"Fire."

"Fire and you'll hang."

"Fire, you dogs, fire if you dare."

And suddenly they did.

I heard one shot first, then several soon after and the explosions echoed off the buildings around. There was a moment of quiet before more shouting began, this time more like cries of pain than anger. As the smoke began to clear, I saw Kilroy standing near Samuel Gray's body, his bayonet bloody, Gray's head collapsed and pouring out blood, and the others hurrying to reload.

Johnson lay with his head in the gutter and I could just see several others down and bleeding, a few from the crowd kneeling beside them. The soldiers now presented their weapons again, aiming down the barrels but their officer got in front and ordered them down. Some in the crowd shouted out, "To arms, to arms," but most in the crowd retreated, fading back and away, their clubs and stones now useless. A few stayed to tend to the bodies, blood staining the snow and stones all around like someone had smashed the top of a barrel of claret and dumped it all through the square. I looked up to find Burns, but he was nowhere in sight.

I stood still, as if fixed to the spot when Julius pulled at my arm. "Let's go Nicholas, there's nothing good can come of staying here."

Forty

I<small>T</small> <small>WASN'T</small> <small>LONG</small> before we were back at the Sword and Julius spoke through the back door to get Maggie to open it. Lilly and Mouse stood in the center of the room and Maggie followed us back in.

"It's done now," was all I could find to say, "it's done. I just need to get these off." I began to think of ways I might get the shackles off, wondering if we could chop through a link with an axe on a block or figure a way to heat the iron without cooking my arms. But Maggie stepped toward me and fished in a pocket beneath her skirt to come out with a key.

"It was the second one that had it," she said, "and he wasn't awake after Julius knocked his head."

"I wanted to go," Lilly burst out, "but she kneeled down just the same and came up with it." When Maggie released the irons, I could barely raise my hands, but I felt the warmth of blood come into them, and curled them a few times to feel them move.

We checked the door locks then and I slept with my back to the front door that night and Julius the same way at the back. My head was filled with more than it would hold, from the fear I'd felt at the Spider's threats to the bodies strewn about like dead fish before the Custom House. But as much as might be going on in the streets right then, with the door hard behind my back, when I closed my eyes, I slept in silence with no dreams. I felt like a swaddled baby, silent and warm, with no more worries than what my belly might demand in the morning.

We kept the doors locked the next day, and I heard the story of my rescue–how Mouse had found me by asking a doxie who worked out of a tavern near the barracks and then watching the doors on Cornhill to see who came and went; how Maggie and Lilly had acted the tarts to get in the front door and how Maggie had swung the lead weights to bring the soldier down so Julius might come in.

Mouse convinced us he should be out to see how things worked and he returned by early in the afternoon, happy to give a full report. It seems that as soon as the soldiers fired, the Sons of Liberty started the business of ridding Boston of the army. Near to the middle of the night, they fetched Governor Hutchinson to see the bodies and stains in the snow and he had the officer, Capt. Preston, and the soldiers from the square arrested right then.

By early the next morning, there was a crowd of several thousand at Faneuil Hall with more streaming in from the country every hour, nearly all carrying muskets, their faces grim and angry. The story that Adams and Molineux told traveled through the crowd like lightning: it wasn't only the soldiers who fired without cause, but others had fired on the crowd from the windows in the Custom House. It was a planned attack on the people of Boston.

The selectman met at the Hall and chose Adams to lead them back to the Town House where they could make demands of Hutchinson. The crowd was restless, and most stayed in the streets, speaking loud threats and thumping their musket butts into the ground, all mixing into an ominous rumble that couldn't be ignored. But those who crowded inside listened in near silence as Adams gathered his thoughts. He had an open field for attack, the council hard at his back.

Mouse made a good representation of Adams, a bit feeble with his palsied hand, but his words were keen and sliced straight away, like he'd been sharpening them for years. After describing the horrors of the night before, Adams demanded the troops be withdrawn. Hutchinson answered boldly, he had no authority to order the troops out, that only the military commanders could do that and they had no orders from London. Adams responded that if they stayed, he couldn't guarantee that the people of the town and country wouldn't use their own muskets to get revenge against the 29th, even if the troops were confined to their barracks.

Hutchinson wavered then. He had the king, the army, and all of Britain behind him, but they were weeks away, across the ocean. He saw the hall flooded with angry men and heard the thousands who were now crowding the streets, knowing they had finally traded their stones and sticks for powder and ball. If they attacked immediately, the ragged and untrained men would slaughter the few hundred redcoats who remained. After a short break, he swallowed hard and offered to send the 29th off to keep the peace.

Mouse puffed up then, like a player on the stage, ready for his big part. I'm sure it was the same for those who were there to see it, since it's a rare moment when a penniless brewer in a worn coat gets to make demands on a royal governor in his robes and wig. Mouse kept his shaking hand at his side then and held out his other, an accusing finger pointed directly at the Governor. "If you have the authority to order the 29th away, you have the same authority for the rest. The people of Boston will stand for no less." Hutchinson knew he was beaten then, and it wasn't long before he gave the order.

The Commissioners and their families got on boats for the Castle or left for the country even before the meetings were done. Later, Mouse saw Spider Partridge taking a small bundle with him as he joined a few others favored by Customs on a long boat toward the Castle. Within a few days, we heard he purchased a spot on the first royal ship out, the same one Commissioner Robinson boarded with the reports of the bloody riot for the British government. Without troops to protect him, the Spider had no more safety on Boston's streets than Ebenezer Richardson before him. With Customs cowering in the countryside or at the Castle, he'd have no one to pay him his informer's portion anyway.

That day and in the ones that followed, Molineux and some others stood guard while the crowd mocked the troops when they marched out to their ships. It took more than a week but they were finally all gone. The officers were embarrassed and the soldiers didn't like the crowds taunting them, but I'm sure the soldiers were as glad to leave as the people of Boston were to see them go. The only sorry ones were the hardest of the Tories and anyone connected with the royal government or Customs.

While the Tories called it a riot, the Sons took to calling it the Bloody Massacre. It was, right enough, what with five dead and six more wounded, and no guns fired from the crowd. They got Paul Revere to make an engraving from a drawing which showed a British officer ordering his men to fire into an unarmed crowd. It added a gun firing out a window in the Custom House, too, which bore the name "Butcher's Hall." It wasn't close to what happened, but it was what Adams wanted people to know.

Adams and Molineux did their best to keep their story alive, getting a boy to claim he saw a musket fire from the window, the same as Molineux saw. Eventually, both were proved to be lying, but there were plenty who remembered it the way they'd seen it in the picture. The engraving was printed and sent to all the colonies, and they couldn't write enough in broadsides and newspapers about how the brave men of Boston had been slaughtered by the brutal redcoats in a planned attack.

Burns didn't come in for more than a week. I'm sure he was working with the Sons and the Loyal Nine day and night to make sure the Massacre stood as proof of a plot to murder brave Americans. The funeral was even greater than the one for the boy Richardson had killed. Some said there were ten thousand who marched and watched. Every carriage in town followed, and they circled the Liberty Tree with drums beating. They buried them all together in the burying ground, even Johnson, who they had decided was actually a runaway slave named Crispus Attucks. Some said he was part Indian, others part Negro, and a few decided he was both. Speakers praised them all as brave men fighting for freedom. The ministers prayed over them like they were saints, though they would have refused Attucks or Gray or Maverick or Caldwell entry at the church door if they had come while they were still alive. None could afford a pew and they would have frightened the members who came to sit among equals. They buried the Irishman, Carr, in the same spot a few days later, though he was Roman Catholic and had no one to say words for him.

I sat with Burns when he did come in and he looked like the cat who'd eaten the bird. He toasted me, "To the departure of the British Army. We waited long enough and we'll suffer no more." He took one drink and offered, "Just as I said."

I drank with him before I asked, "Were you there that night?"

He shrugged, "Most patriots were."

"I thought I saw you in a new red cape. Do you save it for special occasions?"

Again he shrugged. "Someone loaned it to me that night. They thought I'd stand out if any needed to find me."

"Find you? For what? I wouldn't think you'd want to be found." He sat silently, and I kept on. "Was it a plan then, with the bells and all?" It was easy to think the Sons had kept pushing it all to a point where the troops would have to fire. Even a slow man could see that if they did, and everyone heard the right story, the troops would be held at fault and the government would be forced to remove them.

Burns just shook his head, not to deny what I'd said, but to tell me he'd say no more. After a moment, I asked, "So you think that's the end of it?"

He smiled. "First, we'll get the soldiers hung like they should be."

He was too sure for my taste. "Do you really think London will let the people in Boston hang an officer and his men?"

"They have no choice, Gray. They're our courts and our judges, we can use them as we like. They can't be taken to London since the murders happened here and there's no tie to the Admiralty Court." He took a long drink and licked his lips in satisfaction. "It will be a day to remember Gray, the day they're hung. I wager we'll celebrate as much as the day they took back the Stamps."

"So you've won a victory, then, you and the Sons?" I waited a moment as he tried to puzzle my meaning. "They killed five and you're hoping to hang eight."

"I don't know what you'd want, Gray," he fired back, "to live like a dumb ox under the yoke? It's a war, a clear one since they sent their troops. They should know that a standing army can't win, if the people don't want them. A musket bore can make men toe a line, but it will never change their minds. It only makes them angrier."

He was right, but it didn't mean that the British government wouldn't keep trying. It was sword and musket which put them at the top to start and it was the same they would use to stay there. "But what's on now, Burns? Will we get to live in peace for a bit, go about our business?"

Burns shrugged, then turned a smile at me. "What about your business, Gray? Will you go back to collecting what's not nailed down?" I narrowed my eyes at him, but he went ahead anyway. "Or will you climb up to middling and grow a round belly from your dinners? Will you count your pennies and hide them from the taxmen so you can buy a silk waistcoat?"

I put up a hand for him to stop. "I don't know what's ahead, Burns. Maybe you do, but I don't think so. Just because the troops are gone doesn't mean they won't be back. But I'm sure of one thing—if it's up to you and Adams and the rest of the crowd at the Grapes, you'll keep at the Tories and Hutchinson and the whole government until they fight or leave. And you'll drag the rest of us with you if you can."

He didn't answer for a moment, then just smiled and held up his cup for a toast.

THE AIR turned warm for a few days at the end of the month and the snow melted away and birds sang in the mornings. It was market day and Julius had gone off alone while Maggie and I walked up toward the Common. You could see the heavy buds on the elm trees that line the Mall and the apple and cherry trees couldn't wait much longer either.

Maggie took my arm then, and we walked and looked, with the sun warm and the ground soft beneath our feet. "It's a beautiful spot, isn't it, Nicholas?"

"It is, Maggie, especially with the troops gone. It was a long time when we only saw their horses and drills and floggings."

She was silent for a bit and stopped to look at the beech tree a few yards off where we'd watched the young deserter shot, its bark still ragged with wounds from the musket balls that went through him. "What do you think will happen now, Nicholas?"

"I don't know Maggie. At least we won't have to listen to the brave brawlers for awhile, telling their tales of bloodied redcoats."

Maggie smiled but only for a moment. "What about Partridge?"

"I don't know for sure, but I don't think he'll be back. He needs too much protection. He needed the lieutenant from the *Dover* to make me a deserter or a murderer, but now he's gone with the troop ships. He was the only link, and who knows where the Navy will send him now.

If I was the Spider, I'd never set foot in Boston again. But that's what I thought before, and he still came back."

"And Gillam?"

I narrowed my eyes and I could feel the worry and anger cross my face. "I don't know, Maggie. We'd counted on what he brought back to pay Julius and Eve, but now . . . I don't know. I don't fancy going to New York to find out, but I may have to."

She let me walk a bit so the anger could drain away, then put a hand on my arm. "What will it be for us?"

I shook my head a bit, fighting with a question that was too hard to answer. "I don't know that either, Maggie. We still can't marry, even if we wanted, not and keep the license for the Sword." She stopped us and turned towards me. "You've still got the license as a widow and I own the building. We're a business, if nothing else."

Maggie turned to me then and put a hand on each arm. "Does that make it easier, Nicholas, thinking it's business keeps us apart?"

I shook my head at her. My heart was leaping about in my chest and I felt my breath shorter than I wanted. Her blue eyes caught the sunlight and they looked like a candle burned behind them. "I don't think anything makes it easier, Maggie. It seems we're always one step closer, then one step back. It's like we're dancing some minuet and the music never stops."

She looked at me and then stepped back and whirled around once before facing me again. Her voice was light and she smiled as wide as I'd ever seen. "Then we'll just have to keep dancing along, won't we Nicholas?" We were a bit off the path now and when she reached up to give me a kiss on the cheek, I could feel my heart pounding again, and I got both arms around her for a hug. It lasted for just a moment before she broke away and looked around us. "You're a property owner now, Nicholas, you can't be doing improper things in public."

Her eyes sparked then, like I remembered. "But there's some you might try in private." She walked away then, with just a quick look over her shoulder, and I followed like a sheep.

About The Author

Allen Woods is a freelance writer living in Greenfield, Massachusetts. He has written everything from magazine features to readers for primary grades. The spark for *The Sword and Scabbard* came in the midst of research for an American history text. He plans a series which will follow Nicholas and Maggie through the Tea Party, Lexington and Concord, the War itself, and the early years under the Articles of Confederation and the Constitution. He welcomes e-mail at the book web site www.theswordandscabbard.com.